BELIEVE NO ONE

A. D. GARRETT

Constable & Robinson Ltd
55–56 Russell Square
London WC1B 4HP
www.constablerobinson.com

First published in the UK by C&R Crime,
an imprint of Constable & Robinson Ltd, 2014

A copy of the British Library Cataloguing in
Publication data is available from the British Library

ISBN 978-1-78033-980-1 (hardback)
IBSN 978-1-47211-393-1 (ebook)

This book is dedicated to the investigators and volunteers around the world who strive to find missing children and bring them to safety.

The Investigators

Missouri
St Louis Method Exchange Team
Detective Greg Dunlap (East St Louis PD)
Detective John Ellis (St Louis PD)
Detective Valance (St Louis PD)
Special Agent Dr Detmeyer (FBI)
Detective Chief Inspector Kate Simms (Greater Manchester
  Police, UK)
CSI Roper (St Louis PD)

Oklahoma
Williams County Sheriff's Office
Deputy Sheriff Abigail Hicks
Sheriff Launer
Professor Nick Fennimore (UK-based forensic scientist)
Dr Janine Quint (Forensic Medical Examiner)

Aberdeen, Scotland
Josh Brown (doctoral student)

Acknowledgements

A lot of people helped to make this book. In Oklahoma, Mike Nance, co-founder of the International Association of Cold Case Investigators (check out their Facebook page), was guide, facilitator, host, historian and wise counsellor. His gracious presence gave access to a host of professionals in Oklahoma law enforcement. Thanks is due to the many departments and agencies who gave a warm welcome, interrupting their frenetic daily schedules to explain procedures and protocols, tolerating often bizarre questions, answering them patiently and with great good humour. Particular thanks to District Attorneys Pamela Hammers and Brian Keuster, ADA Nullonney, Judge Tom Gillert, CSI Margaret Loveall, OSBI Special Agent Vicky Lyons, and Forensic Anthropologist Angela Berg. The detectives in the Homicide Department of Tulsa PD provided two important elements: context and character. The stories you told could make a book in themselves – would that there had been more time to sit and listen.

In St Louis, Bill Baker, Executive Director of the St Louis Major Case Squad, and Joe Burgoon, Godfather of Homicide, and now Investigator at St Louis County PD's Cold Case Unit, gave valuable insights into homicide investigation, as well as the work of NCMEC and Team Adam which have informed and enriched this novel. Their rambunctious tales were tempered by stories of dedication, quiet humility and deep compassion that will resonate in this and future novels. For information, Dominic's on the Hill is a real restaurant, and they really do serve the best Italian food in St Louis. Sincere thanks for advice given by St Louis Chief Medical Examiner, Dr Mary Case, in the USA, and Police Forensic Pathologist,

Dr James Grieve, in the UK, which steered the storyline away from a couple of unlikely scenarios. Crush asphyxia was definitely the right way to go.

A Hawick Word Book, by Douglas Scott, was extremely helpful in researching Borders Scottish. An illuminating email discussion (in multicoloured fonts) with Dr Caroline Logan on the psychopathology of serial killers was crucial in the creation of two very bad men; particularly useful was the exchange on haemochromatosis, which made sense of a number of disparate ideas.

'Hard-bitten' is an expression often used to describe those tasked with bringing killers to justice. But it was a constant surprise and joy to meet men and women whose compassion for the victims and their families was profound and affecting.

Preface

If there's one thing an Oklahoma farmer values, it's water.

Lance Guffey's grandfather had lived through Black Sunday, 14 April 1935. It was the day Lance's father was born; it was also the day America came face to face with the great Dust Bowl. A hundred million acres of good topsoil stripped from farms in the West fell like volcano dust in towns and cities east of the Great Plains, clear to the Atlantic Ocean, a distance of 15,000 miles, blackening the skies over the nation's capital.

Oklahoma learned its lesson the hard way, but learned it well, creating more lakes, post-Dust Bowl, than any other state. In that one year alone, Lance's grandfather dug two ponds for irrigation and by the time Lance himself was ten years old, they had five, each one up to an acre across. His father told Lance that for weeks, digging those ponds, his skin was the same rust red as the clay, from his fingertips all the way up to his elbows, and the iron in the clay smelled of blood, so you carried the stink of death with you.

Just now the land smelled of sweet grass and sunshine; soon they would be taking the first cut of hay. They'd had some good spring rain, but nothing for two weeks past and with temperatures already in the eighties at the beginning of May, they would need every drop of water in those ponds. It was one of the smaller ponds he was headed to right now; a windstorm the night before had brought down an old cottonwood. It lay half across the shallow incline; his cattle used to get in there and wallow when it got real hot, and a cow could break a leg stumbling over branches hidden in the mud.

Lance Guffey looked at the big old tree. The storm had ripped it out of the soil; it lay crushed and splintered over a hundred feet of grazing, its shimmering leaves already losing their shine. The roots were upturned, ten feet off the ground, a wide, flat disk – blood red, like an afterbirth – leaving a hole in the ground twenty feet in diameter. He scratched his head and walked left and then right in a semicircle, decided which limbs he needed to trim first and how many sections he would have to cut the trunk into to make it manageable. Finally, he reached in the cab of his tractor for his chainsaw. Three hours later, his small herd of black Angus cattle looking on, he had the accessible sections sawn into logs and was ready to drag what remained onto dry land.

The woman had settled in the soft mud of the pond over winter. Wind-rock shifted the cottonwood in the October storm, sending drifts of fine silt and mud from the bank of the pond, protecting her from the attentions of predators, cocooning her in mud. Five months she had waited, which was not long in the great scheme of things, in the long years of for ever. Not long enough to ripen the first crop of wheat, nor even to carry a child to full term. The woman was a child herself when she bore a son; the boy with her at the end would have celebrated his tenth birthday in June, but he had seen too much and could not be allowed to live. He was gone, as she was gone, the woman hoping in her final moments of pain and fear and confusion that she was going to a gentler place than this earth had been for her.

The jangle of chains and grappling hooks disturbed the mud, stirring up thin threads of red clay that rose like dark plumes of fresh blood. The red wisps reached the barrier between water and air, and spread and billowed like smoke under glass. A grappling hook snagged in the elbow of a branch and the massive trunk of the cottonwood, and the submerged brush of twigs and arrow-shaped leaves raked deep in the mud, ploughing up what had been planted where it could not grow.

Lance Guffey smelled the sulphurous reek of rotting leaves and the blood-iron tang of the clay, and at last the smell of death rolled up and penetrated his farmer's sensibilities. He looked around him in alarm, counted his cows as he killed the engine and climbed down from the cab, anxious to know if one of his heifers had already run foul of the reaching, grabbing branches of the downed tree. But the herd was accounted for, every one; they watched him still, thoughtfully regurgitating and chewing the tough prairie grass, waiting till he was done so they could cool off in the pond.

He took a step closer, covering his mouth and nose with his shirt tail, and saw a glimpse of flesh, camouflaged in the tangle of branches. The body seemed clothed in leaves and waterweed, like a nymph in the old-time fairy tales he read to his daughters. Sunshine dazzled off the water that clung to the cottonwood's waxy leaves, half blinding him, but he saw enough to be certain this was no water nymph.

1

Insanity: doing the same thing over and over and expecting different results.

EINSTEIN

Aberdeen, Scotland

Nick Fennimore stared at the new mail in his inbox and his mouth dried. The subject line: 'Is this your daughter?'

His hand jerked involuntarily. He slowed his breathing, forcing himself to look closely at the email, to think like a scientist and not a father. There was an attachment. He'd had messages like this before – usually from sick, sadistic men for whom causing others pain was a release. Those messages had been posted on the Facebook page he'd created in his daughter's name, but this was the first he'd had direct to his academic account. The sender was 'anon67912' – a Hotmail account.

Fennimore ran the email and its attachment through his virus checker: no Trojans, spyware or viruses. He clicked to open the message envelope. There was no message – just the subject header and the attachment. He wiped cold sweat from his upper lip and double-clicked to view the attachment.

It was a girl. Just a girl. She was slim, serious-looking; she walked alongside a man. He seemed older – mid-thirties, at a guess. Suited, stocky. Dark hair, full lips, otherwise unexceptional. His eye was drawn again to the girl. Could this be Suzie?

He loaded an image file he had created: his daughter, aged up from ten to fifteen. It was already out of date – soon, Suzie would be sixteen years old. If she lived. The statistics said not: the statistics said that Suzie died five years ago, shortly before or after her mother was murdered, but on this matter, Fennimore had never been able to think like a scientist, only as a father.

He looked again at the email, his fingers hovering over the keys. *This is madness*, he thought. *It's probably just another crazy*. But he clicked the 'reply' icon anyway and typed in a few words. 'Please, call me.' He added his office and mobile-phone numbers and hit 'send'.

He resized his photoshopped image of his daughter and slid it next to the email attachment on the screen. His impression of Suzie at fifteen showed a face that brimmed with good health, a mouth that was always ready to smile. The girl in the attachment was sombre; she gazed ahead as though thinking of something else. Fennimore wondered what the man was saying to her. She looked about the same age as Suzie; she had dark hair and brown eyes – like Suzie's. But she wore a knee-length dress in burnt orange and brown, cinched at the waist, a tiny clutch bag emphasizing her slim form, and she strode out in high heels. Fennimore shook his head absently – hard to imagine his tomboy daughter in this graceful young woman.

A two-tone audio notification interrupted his scrutiny of the photograph. A new message in his inbox. Eagerly, Fennimore maximized the Outlook screen. But it was a bounce-back: anon67912 no longer existed.

He called up the original email and a few mouse clicks later he was scrolling through the email's 'properties'; it would surely have been routed through an anonymous server – only an amateur would send an email like that from a naked IP – but he had to try. Astonishingly, the IP address *was* there, in amongst the jumble of letters and numbers. The IP could give him a physical location. Excitement building, he traced the IP number using WHOIS, and found the service provider.

He cursed, softly: it was blocked as private. The service provider *could* give him the sender's location, but wouldn't – not without a warrant. He thought of Kate Simms, stationed for the next few months half a world away in the United States. But even she wouldn't be able to obtain a warrant on such slim grounds.

He looked at the picture again. Just a teenage girl walking along a sunny street with an older man. They walked about a foot apart, the girl to the right, next to a sheer wall. No windows that he could see. The man's left hand was raised to waist height as if he was gesturing to emphasize a point; the girl seemed distracted. Nothing wrong in that; nothing sinister. So why did he find himself searching her young face for signs of distress? And even if it was there, couldn't there be an innocent explanation – an exam to take, a dreaded dental appointment?

That being the case, why did somebody watch those two and photograph them and send you the image? And whoever sent the image had taken the trouble to find out Fennimore's academic address; this was personal.

He stared at the image for so long that when he glanced away he could see the silhouette of the girl and the man ghosted on the grey sky outside his office window. He blinked to clear the after-image and took a fresh look at the photograph. A hard line of shadow ran between the man and the girl so that they might almost be walking on different pavements at different times of day.

Later he would compare ratios for the girl's face: distance between the eyes; position of the ears relative to the eyeline; size and shape and position of the nose and mouth. It would only ever be an approximation – he wouldn't be able to use facial-recognition software, not with the already approximated aged-up image of Suzie he had constructed. For an accurate comparison he would need to know the distance from which the photograph had been taken, and the angle. It seemed to be from slightly above – a bridge, maybe? He looked for a clue, and found a small circular segment of something, tight to the wall. He opened the image in Photoshop and zoomed in on that section of the photograph. It looked like a metal dome attached to a bracket – a street lamp, maybe – in racing green. A bridge, then – or maybe the street sloped uphill while the pathway continued on the flat. In the distance, behind the two figures, the number plate obscured by a section of wall, the back of a white box van with a squiggle of black spray paint at the top of the roller door.

His eyes were drawn again to the girl's face. Suzie, or a perfect stranger? Impossible to say. The dress, the well-styled hair were hard to reconcile with Suzie zipping around on a skateboard. He felt a sharp spike of excitement – the accident: Suzie had fallen trying a new stunt on her board and cut her head badly. The scar – a small diamond-shaped patch of red on her left temple – had just begun to heal when she disappeared. Would it remain, after all these years? He snatched up the mouse and zoomed in on the girl's face. At high magnification he could see that portion of the image was slightly blurred – camera shake, or perhaps a breeze had ruffled her hair at the moment the photographer pressed the shutter. The girl's hair was feathered over her forehead and combed right to left. Was that deliberate – to hide the scar? The shadow cast by the strands of hair, together with the blurring, made it difficult to tell if they were hiding anything. Fennimore brightened the image and played with the contrast. It took an hour, but at last he thought he saw it – a small diamond-shaped imperfection. He needed to trace the email back to source. He checked his watch; it was 7 p.m. The IT team would be long gone; his inquiry would have to wait until morning. The heating had clicked off a couple of hours since and the temperature in the life sciences building plummeted – early May in Aberdeen could feel like February.

He should go back to his flat and relax for the evening, but rest was impossible.

Coffee, he thought. Then he would get to work on those ratios.

2

East St Louis, Illinois

Detective Chief Inspector Kate Simms stared out of an SUV onto mile after mile of burned-out houses, boarded-up apartment buildings, empty factory units and vacant lots, crowded with saplings and trees, competing for space. Rubble was strewn across the vacant lots. Rubbish littered the streets and piled up in ragged heaps against chain-link fences and corrugated-iron hoardings. This was East St Louis, Illinois – a city in its own right – though it was only a two-minute drive across the Mississippi River from St Louis, Missouri.

Simms was on a three-month method exchange with St Louis PD; her assignment, to undertake case reviews and share UK investigation protocols, processes and skills. The UK's Association of Chief Police Officers was funding her and a CSI, as well as paying consultant fees to Professor Varley, a forensic psychologist she had worked with the previous year. The American contingent of the Method Exchange Team included, from St Louis PD: Detective Ellis, a granite-faced man with a buzz cut and a blunt manner; a soft-featured young detective named Valance; and Roper, a tall, hyperactive CSI. FBI Special Agent Dr Detmeyer, on loan from the Bureau's Behavioral Analysis Unit, would give the American psychological perspective. The last member of the team was Detective Dunlap, a grey-haired African American in his early fifties, on assignment from East St Louis Homicide. As he put it, 'The Two State area shares crime freely, so we figured why can't the good guys share resources, too?'

Simms gazed through the windscreen at the scene of apparent devastation. They were looking into a cold case and were en route to the scene of the murder in East St Louis. Everyone wore body armour, including Simms and the CSIs. Detective Greg Dunlap, the East St Louis detective, drove one of the SUVs. Dunlap was soft-spoken and sad-faced, but when he walked into a room, people paid attention.

'I checked the address on Google Maps before we left the station,' she said. 'I did wonder why I couldn't find street-view data.'

Detective Dunlap nodded. 'I know I wouldn't chance expensive camera equipment on these mean streets,' he said. 'Most folks blast through here at seventy miles per hour – you can get a bit of camera shake at those speeds. There were twenty-eight murders here in East St Louis in the last year alone, in a population of just twenty-seven thousand.'

'That's a hell of a statistic,' Simms said.

He nodded. 'What East St Louis lacks in size it makes up for in grim determination. It's right up there with Baltimore in the murder stats.'

They drove on in silence for a while and Simms gazed about her, finding it hard to square this ravaged landscape with the thriving community on the west side of the river. 'What happened, Greg?' she asked, thinking, *Riots, tornadoes. War zone.*

'Manufacturers went bust, or moved on to states with better tax breaks or easier access to the raw materials they needed. There used to be a saying, "If you can't find a job in East St Louis, you can't find a job anywhere." That was a long time ago. Now, the kids who need to pay for themselves

7

to go through college have to travel out to the strip malls in Fairview Heights to find a job. The public schools are failing, and most kids leave school illiterate, unemployable and mad as hell.' He shook his head. 'The only way boys in that situation can prove themselves is with violence and criminality.'

He paused, nodded thoughtfully, his expression almost wistful. 'Wasn't always this way. Steamboat Willie was born here, and Miles Davis was raised here; Barbara Ann Teer grew up a few blocks from where we are now – she founded the National Black Theatre in Harlem. There's a long and honourable roll-call of eminent African Americans with East St Louis connections.'

'You were brought up here?' Simms asked.

He dipped his head to get a better view of a Youth Correctional Facility as they drove by, a large Victorian complex surrounded by chain-link and razor wire. 'That used to be the high school.' He nodded towards the car park. 'Under that parking lot is the football field where I got scouted for a scholarship to St Louis University.'

They passed a boarded-up house, a message painted on the board: 'I am black, like you. I am poor, like you. But you broke in here and took everything I had.'

Half a mile on, they turned off into one of the public housing projects. Block after block of two- and three-storey tenements stood derelict or in such a sorry state that they might as well be pulled down.

A group of men and boys sat on sagging chairs and rat-eaten sofas in the centre of a demolition site. The men watched them drive by, an East St Louis police vehicle and two unmarked SUVs. The men's heads turned slowly, eyeless behind wrap-around sunglasses.

As if at a predetermined signal, the boys leapt up and ran, disappearing around corners, into buildings, sending up a chorus of shouts and whistles.

The convoy drew to a halt outside a three-storey tenement. Simms knew from her background reading that it had been tagged for demolition in 2010, but the city had run out of money even to pull down the obsolete housing that attracted squatters, drug manufacturers and their customers.

'You stay close to me, okay, Chief?' Dunlap said.

It felt odd being called 'Chief', but Simms had quickly learned that the Americans were punctilious about the use of professional titles, so Simms said, 'Okay, Detective.'

He waited until the East St Louis PD officers got out of their patrol car before climbing down from the SUV. There were five patrolmen, headed up by a sergeant in uniform. He and Dunlap shook hands.

'You go on ahead,' the sergeant told them. 'We'll take care of the vehicles.'

'Surely they wouldn't mess with police cars?' Simms said.

'A couple years back, some guys stole the radio out of the Chief of Police's car right in front of City Hall,' Dunlap said, with a small smile. 'Which was embarrassing. Now, we take no chances.'

The sergeant lifted his chin to Dunlap. 'You be all right in there?'

'We'll be fine,' Dunlap said, looking past him. 'You should watch your own backs.'

A small crowd had already begun to congregate on the derelict land.

Elleesha Tate was seventeen when she died. For a time, her pimp was in the frame for the murder, but he had an alibi, and his DNA was not found on her. To date, nobody had been held to account for her murder.

On the face of it, Elleesha Tate's murder didn't look a good bet. The protocols for selecting which cold cases to review were very similar both sides of the Pond. Both worked from checklists, and although the questions on the checklists were slightly different, investigators in the US and the UK preferred cases where there was a good chance that the offender was still alive. In Detective Ellis's words: 'We like to put the bad guys away, and you can't try a dead man.'

But the final decision to select or reject a case rested on its solvability, and as they'd sat around the conference table a couple of days earlier, presenting the arguments for and against, Detective Ellis had laid out the reasons why Elleesha Tate's murder would probably remain unsolved.

'She was a crystal-meth addict; she fed her habit through prostitution. She had a lot of male callers the day she died – and not the kind of men who would stand in line to give evidence, either.' He paused to tuck a starched white expanse of shirt fabric into the waistband of his trousers. 'She was stabbed thirty times, but East St Louis PD got no trace evidence, no blood – except hers, there was plenty of that. The semen in her was mixed, and unusable.'

Simms ran down the checklist in front of her. He was right: Elleesha's was not a good review case.

'Anyway, your guys *had* the perp,' Ellis said, nodding towards Dunlap, the East St Louis detective. 'You just couldn't break his alibi.'

'I remember that case,' Detective Dunlap said. 'I never thought the pimp was a good suspect.'

The FBI behaviourist stirred, spoke like a man coming out of a dream. 'I would agree. Pimps are more inclined to use cruelty and fear as a means of control; it's far more likely that Elleesha was murdered by a client.' Dr Detmeyer was on assignment from the BAU's Unit 4 – the unit responsible for the Violent Criminal Apprehension Programme, ViCAP, so he would know.

'Chief Simms, what's your take?' Dunlap asked.

'I'll go with the consensus,' Simms said. But—' The word was out of her mouth before she could stop it.

'Go ahead,' Dunlap said. The American team seemed

curiously non-hierarchical to her British sensibilities, but Dunlap often assumed the role of the designated spokesperson.

'You know how it is – the place tells a story, gives you the context.' Simms heard herself paraphrasing Nick Fennimore, and she told herself to stop – she didn't need Fennimore in her head just now. 'Okay, Elleesha doesn't fit half the criteria, but that building might be pulled down before anyone gets another chance to revisit it. Even if no new evidence comes out of it, at the very least we'd have an opportunity to compare crime-scene procedures.'

'So you guys can show us how to "do it right"?' Detective Ellis raked air quotes with his first and middle fingers, the clean white linen of his shirt cracking like a sail in a crisp wind.

'Hey, come on, now, Ellis.' This was Detective Valance – young, boyish and blue-eyed. He wore his fair hair cropped tight to his head, Simms suspected, to make him look tougher, but it only emphasized the softness of his features.

'It's okay,' Simms said. 'Now is as good a time as any to set the record straight.' She looked around the table, making eye contact with everyone present. 'UK police forces have lost over seven thousand front-line officers and twelve thousand back-office staff in cutbacks. We need to learn how to work more efficiently – and you guys work a higher volume of murders than we do. We're here to share expertise, and pick up a few tips on the way.'

Ellis looked a little abashed, but made no apology.

'So, how about it,' Dunlap said, his voice warm, and rich, and reasonable. 'Fresh eyes?'

Valance nodded, enthusiastic. Roper said, 'I'm in.' Detmeyer watched them all.

'What have we got to lose,' Simms said. 'A few hours?'

'You could lose a lot more than *time*, heading into East St Louis,' Ellis grumbled.

11

Soft laughter around the table elicited a scowl – Ellis did not play the room for laughs. 'I'm serious.' He jerked his chin to Dunlap. 'Dunlap, *you* know.'

'Yes,' Dunlap said, 'I do.' He thought about it for a few seconds. 'And I say it's worth a shot.'

The stairwell smelled of mould and burning plastic.

'Meth,' Dunlap said.

Methamphetamine had been the curse of inner-city and rural communities alike over the last twenty years. According to the RAND stats, meth addiction was costing the United States up to $50 billion a year.

Looking up the centre of the stairwell, his hand on his pistol, Dunlap added, 'They probably scooted when they got word Five-O was paying a visit, but let's be careful.'

They cleared each floor as they came to it, and when they reached the third landing where Elleesha had lived, Detective Ellis stood guard on the door while the rest of them went inside.

There was no light or power, and the boards on the windows put the apartment in gloom, but the CSIs set up three battery-powered LED spots in under a minute.

'Wallpaper's been stripped,' Simms said, comparing the scene photos with the dove-grey washed walls.

'They detailed the apartment after the CSIs had finished in here,' Dunlap said. 'Stripped the walls and repainted, glossed the doors.'

'The crime-scene report said the attack began on the bed,' Simms said.

'Bed was under the window.' This was Paul Roper, the St Louis CSI. He was tall and wiry, a spare man who seemed to hum with nervous energy. 'She bled out in the corner, between the bed and the window.'

'Defensive wounds to her arms suggest she fought,' Simms said. 'Maybe she rolled off the bed to get away from him.'

Roper moved to the wall, a blow-up of a crime scene photograph in hand. 'There was a lot of arterial spray and cast-off,' he said.

Simms looked at the picture. Arcs of arterial spray on the wall, window and sill; scattered amongst them a few drops that didn't seem to belong – cast-off from the knife as the killer drew his arm back to strike again.

'But this one looks off,' the CSI said. He circled a single drop on the photograph with the tip of his right pinkie finger.

'Off, how?' Ellis demanded from the doorway. It was hot in there; his shirt had lost its starched freshness and clung damply to him; he looked out of sorts with himself and the world at large.

'You've got a lot of blood spatter radiating out from where she lay.' Roper indicated some teardrop-shaped blood drops on the image. 'As the perp pulled the knife out and back, droplets would move in the direction of his hand.' He passed the photograph around while he mimed the movement of the blood spatter from the knife to the wall. 'Some droplets look like they got flicked back, some up, which is what you'd expect.' He plucked the image from Valance's fingers. 'But this looks like it impacted from the vertical.' He indicated a single drop that looked like an inverted exclamation point.

'So, it went up, then fell, hitting the wall on the downward trajectory,' Dunlap suggested.

The CSI looked doubtful. 'This is more of a blob than a streak, which means low velocity.' He darted forward to lay a photograph of the bed where it would have been at the crime scene. 'The foot of the bed was about . . . here,' he said, sketching a line with the blade of his hand and taking a step back. 'Elleesha's body was in the corner at the bedhead.'

The photographs showed the densest concentration of arcs and blood spatter under the window and in the corner, as Elleesha pushed and kicked and squirmed backwards, trying to escape the blade. The blood drop Roper was interested in had been on the wall a couple of feet away from the foot of the bed.

'This drop of blood is at least *nine feet* away from where the main assault occurred. Why?'

'Because plunging a knife through flesh and muscle thirty times is tiring work.' These were the first words the FBI behaviourist had said since they walked inside the building.

They turned to look at him.

FBI Special Agent Dr Detmeyer rarely spoke, yet Simms got the impression he was in constant dialogue with himself. He was a slim man in his early fifties, medium height, with an intense gaze and quick, precise movements. He paced to the corner in three steps and hunched over, mimed a few strikes. 'Elleesha stops struggling as she bleeds out, he stands back to take a breath, maybe he staggers a little.'

'Or his foot gets caught in the bedclothes,' Valance said, his young face eager.

The FBI psychologist regarded him calmly and he flushed, apologizing.

'No need,' Dr Detmeyer said. 'It's a good suggestion. So, he staggers – or stumbles – holding the knife point down, and tries to recover his balance.' He jerked both hands in a typical startle reaction to an anticipated backward tumble. 'A drop of blood rolls to the tip of the blade and falls, making contact with the wall on the vertical at low velocity. A blitz attack, the victim fighting back as Elleesha did, the blood gets everywhere,' the psychologist went on. 'Blood is slippery stuff – you'll often see cuts on an attacker's hand where it slipped down the knife onto the blade.'

Simms felt a tingle of excitement. 'So, we could be looking at the offender's blood.'

'A *picture* of it,' Ellis said over his shoulder. 'This area wasn't sampled. Wallpaper's gone. There's nothing left *to* sample.'

Simms stared at the photograph under the arc lights. A thin, brownish-red trickle of blood tracked down the wall from the drop singled out by the CSI. She crouched, photograph in hand, comparing the position of the window, estimating the length of the bed, trying to approximate where the blood had traced down the wallpaper.

There was a hint of shadow at the crucial point along the skirting. 'Could we get a light in here?' she said.

One of the LED arc lights was repositioned. They all saw it: a tiny gap between the wall and the skirting board. One by one they straightened up, crowding around the image of the drop of blood, looking from the image to the wall, each doing their own mental calculations.

Simms moved in and pressed her cheek flat against the wall. Someone handed her a flashlight and she shone it down into the crack. 'I think I see a brownish stain,' she said. 'Could be blood.'

'Only one way to find out,' CSI Roper said, grinning, as he headed for the door. 'I'll go fetch the power saw from the SUV.'

3

It is estimated that forty-two per cent of marriages in England and Wales end in divorce.

OFFICE FOR NATIONAL STATISTICS, 2012

St Louis, Missouri

The publicist was smiling. She took each copy of *Crapshoots and Bad Stats* and turned it efficiently to the title page, using the dust-jacket flap as a page marker, ready for Fennimore to sign.

As the final cluster of fans made their way to the door, she said, 'You have a really interesting demographic, Professor. It's unusual to have young males of . . . uh . . . an academic turn of mind, attending the same event as, well as—' She lifted her chin towards the blushing group of young women who turned to wave him goodbye.

'You mean you wouldn't expect a popular-science text to interest geeks *and* fan-girls,' he said.

She straightened with a frown of disapproval, and he realized he'd offended her, which puzzled him. He didn't think 'geek' was offensive – after all, *he* was a geek. And fan-girls? A lot of regular book eventers would write their name on a slip of paper to be sure the author got their name right when they personalized their signed copies, but only a fan-girl would add her phone number to the slip. And Fennimore had half a dozen of those tucked in his jacket pocket.

He knew he wasn't good at the niceties of social diplomacy he couldn't think of anything to say that would improve the situation, so he said nothing, and she busied herself stacking and counting the remaining books.

The bookseller, pleased with the sales he'd made already, sidled over to ask if he would mind signing the rest for stock, and thankfully the publicist's smile returned.

He scanned the bookshop in the fading hope that he might see Kate Simms, a sardonic look on her face, leaning against one of the bookshelves. He had emailed to say he was in St Louis and asked would she like to meet. She hadn't replied. Since the previous case closed, she had been avoiding his phone calls, was slow in answering his emails and was very businesslike in her responses. He'd tried texting her, but without success. Finally, he'd contacted the head of the St Louis Major Case Squad and asked him to pass on a message. Kate replied to his earlier email with a vague apology – she'd been incredibly busy; hopefully they would find time for coffee before he went home. A coffee. Hopefully, no less. Well, at least she hadn't come right out and told him to sod off and leave her alone. So he'd sent her a ticket for the book signing.

Fennimore was due to speak at the International Homicide Investigators' Association annual symposium in St Louis in a couple of weeks, and his American publisher asked if he might squeeze in a few signings and public lectures. The university's summer vacation was under way, and he was owed time; it made sense to travel to the States early, do the tour at a more leisurely pace. The university's IT department hadn't been able to trace the anonymous email. He'd posted a message on Suzie's Facebook page, asking anon67912 to contact him, but heard nothing. The picture might yield something, but he would need Kate Simms's help, so he'd arranged for Josh Brown, a postgraduate student, to deliver his summer-school classes and swapped the bitter cold of the

Granite City for the soft humidity of St Louis, Missouri. He'd even wangled an invitation to deliver a couple of lectures to St Louis PD. But his best efforts had come to nothing; Kate was avoiding him.

In the taxi heading back to his hotel, he got a text. Kate: 'Sorry – couldn't get away. I hope it went well.'

He dialled her number straight away, and – minor miracle – she actually picked up.

'You're forgiven,' he said. 'If you have dinner with me.'

'I can't.'

'Of course you can.' It was so good to hear the sound of her voice – even telling him no, it lifted his spirits, her warm tones washing over him, giving him a jolt of energy. 'Come on, Kate – my treat – Dominic's on the Hill. Best Italian food in St Louis. Let me know where you are; I'll pick you up.'

She didn't speak, and he thought he had her, but then she said, 'Nick, you know that wouldn't be a good idea.'

'What? It's a meal – everybody's got to eat.'

'You're not listening.'

'Is this Kieran?' Her jealous prick of a husband. 'Because—'

'No,' she interrupted. 'Don't bring Kieran into it. This is me – *I* am saying no.'

For a moment he was stunned; when he found his voice, he said, 'Kate, I need your help.'

A pause, then: 'Suzie?'

'Yes,' he said. 'I think . . . Yes.'

The silence that followed said that she was still hurting from the disastrous consequences the last time he'd asked her for help: when his wife's body turned up, six months after she and Suzie disappeared, Simms, then a detective sergeant, had given him access to information and even evidence that he should never have been near. Between them, they had burned through thousands of pounds worth of Crime Faculty resources without sanction and had potentially compromised the investigation. Kate was kicked off the Faculty, and her career had stalled for four years as a result, but she had always said she didn't regret her actions. And with a ruthless, shameless, single-minded focus on what he needed from her, he hoped that she was sincere in what she said.

'Okay,' she said, at last. 'I'll meet you there.'

Dominic's on the Hill was a favourite with the St Louis PD, and a crowd of cops were living it up at a twelve-seater table in the centre of the room. Fennimore had worked with two of them in the past, and he'd met others after one of his lectures. They invited him to join them, but Fennimore declined, waiting instead in a booth at the back of the restaurant, nervously watching the door.

Ten minutes later, Kate Simms walked in, and he had to grip the table to quell the urge to surge to his feet. With cops, a look could be cause for speculation, and gossip could quickly turn to outright scandal; Kate had come all the way to the United States to avoid exactly that, so he kept his seat and waved her over, trying to look insouciant. They looked anyway – how could they not? She was tanned and fit, dressed in a plain white blouse and navy cotton chinos. The last time they spoke, her brown hair was cut pixie-style, but she'd grown it out, and now it hung, straight and glossy, to her shoulders. One of the cops made eye contact and grinned. Fennimore frowned and made a point of shaking her hand and offering her a seat with ostentatious formality.

Kate played along. 'Cops?' she said softly as she sat opposite. 'How marvellous.'

'I'm sorry. I didn't think.'

The look she gave him said that was par for the course.

'How are things at home?' he said, breaking a pause that threatened to become a silence. 'Becky must be in the middle of her GCSEs.'

'Oh, Becky's *seething* with teenage hormones just now. Exams are *killing* her with stress. Or boredom. Or both, simultaneously.'

'Sounds grim,' he said.

'She'll be fine once the exams are over and she can escape back to London to see her old schoolfriends.' The family had relocated to the north of England after Simms's relationship with London Metropolitan Police soured.

'And Tim?' he asked cautiously. Fennimore had only found out about the five-year-old the previous year. Simms must have fallen pregnant just before he took flight to Scotland. But she had proved evasive on that interesting coincidence.

'Tim has Granny wrapped around his little finger,' Simms said, with an affectionate smile. 'Kieran's the only one who can do anything with him – he's a daddy's boy.'

'So Kieran's managing okay without you?'

'Well, Mum's there, of course, and Kieran . . .' A strange light came into her eyes, and he waited for her to say more, but after a moment she braced, forcing a smile. 'Kieran's having a blast in his new job.'

'That's good.' The peculiar light flashed in her eyes again and her left thumb found her wedding ring. She worried at it, the smile fading from her face, and he added, 'Isn't it?'

'Yeah,' she said. 'Great.'

Fennimore looked into the soft brown of her irises; when Kate Simms was angry or amused, amber light seemed to flash from the centres, but this was different; more complicated. He wished he was better at reading people, but as Simms often told him, he lacked the social skills for subtlety. Oh, he recognized evasion and bullshit easily enough; that was the scientist in him. Assume everyone lies, believe no one and question everything. But the subtler emotions and non-verbal cues often escaped him.

'"Great"?' he repeated. 'Am I missing something here?'

'I do hope so,' she said. 'Shall we order?'

'Okay. You don't want to launch straight in?'

'Will an hour or two make a difference?' she asked.

'No,' he said, sad to admit it.

'Then whatever you need to ask will wait. I'm homesick, and it's good to speak with an old friend.' He thought he saw her eyes begin to glisten, but she picked up her napkin and flicked it open, adding with a half-smile, 'And I may as well get a decent meal out of you, if I'm expected to sing for my supper.'

He showed her a printout of the photograph after they'd ordered coffee at the end of the meal. She gasped, seized the photograph and pored over it while he told her that it was sent by anonymous email, the account opened with the purpose of sending it and closed immediately after he'd received the attachment.

She set down the photograph carefully, looked into his face. 'Nick,' she said. 'You've had scores of just this type of thing over the years. If it was genuine – if the sender *believed* it was genuine – they would have sent contact details.'

'Not if by sending it they would implicate themselves in some way.'

'Then why send it at all?'

'I don't know. Guilt, or concern, or—'

'Cruelty?' she finished. 'What if this is just another sadist who wants to twist the knife?'

'It may be,' he agreed. 'But you have to admit, you thought it was Suzie.'

'Yes, I thought it looked like her – at first. But a thousand sixteen-year-old girls – a *hundred* thousand – will look like Suzie.'

'I know – I know that. But, Kate – do you remember Suzie had that nasty accident on her skateboard a few weeks before—' he faltered '—before she went missing?'

'Of course.' Suzie had been practising kerb drops on a board she'd borrowed from Kate's daughter, Becky.

Fennimore turned the photograph, located the exact position of the mark on the girl's temple and placed the image in front of Simms again. 'See?'

21

She looked at the picture, then up into his eyes, and he read compassion and weariness in hers. 'I see a shadow, Nick. A smudge on the screen.'

'That's why I need your help.'

'With *what*?' Now she just seemed exasperated.

'Digital enhancement,' he said. 'I have the software, but I don't have the expertise. If the image was enhanced, I could be sure.'

She shook her head.

'There might be contextual clues in the picture – things I've missed—'

'No,' she said. 'A hundred times, no.' She had raised her voice, and heads turned at the cop table on the other side of the room.

She flushed, lowered her voice. 'You need to stop torturing yourself. I thought you had a lead, something I could work with. I'm sorry, Nick, truly, I am.' She gathered her belongings and slid out of the booth. 'I wish I could help you. I—' She stopped, took a breath. 'Have a great trip,' she said, then she turned on her heel and left.

Alone in his hotel, Fennimore checked his daughter's Facebook page. His coded message to the anonymous emailer remained unanswered. He read the latest comments, deleting the hate and allowing the rest into the public domain, then checked the three email accounts he kept active. There was no sign of a reply from 'Anon'. He found an intriguing message on one of his private accounts – an address he gave out to delegates at conferences. It was from A. Hicks at Williams County Sheriff's Office. The only A. Hicks he knew was a deputy sheriff in Oklahoma.

Sheriff's Deputy Abigail Hicks. Fennimore had been in the US for an IHIA annual symposium the year before last, and accepted an invitation at short notice to host a seminar at the Christian Laurie Conference in Mountain

Home, Arkansas. The excellent fishing, low crime rate and cheap real estate made it a popular retirement destination for police officers. They took it personally when a young woman was murdered at a rest stop just off I-40, near the city. The retired police officers created a charity and raised funds to set up the conference named after the young murder victim. They ran the conference on a tight budget to keep it affordable to delegates, many of whom were self-funding: deputies, paralegals and CSIs from the rural counties who couldn't afford the cost of bigger venues. Deputy Hicks worked out of the sheriff's office in Creek County. She impressed Fennimore as sharp, astute and persistent.

Her email was formal, restrained, and the style didn't match up with his recollection of her forthright and friendly manner. She was investigating the murder of a young woman, she said, discovered by a farmer when he went to drag a fallen tree out of one of his ponds.

'The body was buried in mud when the bank of the pond collapsed. The landowner reports that the pond was frozen between November and March. In consideration of the climate and geographical factors, the Medical Examiner estimates that the body was probably put in the water in late October or early November, before the frosts set in. The body was well preserved because of a combination of cold and the mud protecting her from animal predation.'

It read like a report from one of his undergrad students, and he wondered if she was practising her skills on him. Deputy Hicks thought that the death of this victim might be linked to another murder, three years earlier.

She had included her mobile number. It was 11 p.m. and when she answered the call, he heard country music in the background, a clamour of voices.

'Professor!' she exclaimed, in her old friendly tone. 'How're you?' Not waiting for an answer she said, 'Hold on

– I'm gonna step outside.' A few seconds later, the music and background chatter cut off abruptly.

'You got my email,' she said. 'Thanks for getting back.' He could hear the grin in her voice. 'So, will you look at my case?' she asked, direct as always.

'That depends. What makes you think it's linked to the earlier murder?'

'Both those women were in water, both were found within a mile of I-44 and they both had duct-tape residue in their hair.'

'Well, water does wash off evidence, which is why it's such a popular medium for dumping bodies,' he teased. 'Interstate 44 is a very long road, if memory serves, and it's not unusual ` for killers to gag their victims.'

'Is that what they call British sarcasm?' she asked. 'I *do* know that water destroys evidence and murderers gag their victims, thank you, Professor. And I drove from Wichita Falls, Texas to St Louis, Missouri along I-44 more'n once, so I know how long it is.'

He was smiling, enjoying the fact that she would not take crap from him, even when she was asking a favour, but his scientific antennae twitched with what she said next.

'But here's the kicker: the glue was too high up on the head for a gag. I'm thinking it was more like a blindfold.'

'That *is* unusual.' Already he could feel himself being drawn in.

'Isn't it?' she said. 'Why blindfold a person if you know you're going to kill them? I mean, they're going to be *too dead* to identify you. And why'd the perpetrator cut it off when he dumped the body?'

He thought about this. 'Was the victim clothed, or unclothed?'

'She was naked – no jewellery, nothing.'

'So, he was removing anything distinctive.'

'Duct tape – "distinctive"?' she said.

'Come, now, Deputy,' Fennimore chided. 'I know you've had a beer, but you're not thinking. What if it was a new brand, or a specialist tape, or extra strength; there might be something unusual in the fabric weave or in the chemical composition of the glue.'

She said, 'Uh-huh,' and he got the feeling she was making notes.

Suddenly, he remembered something. 'You said the tape was *cut* off?'

'The ME's report said some of my victim's hair had been cut straight across, right where the glue was situated.'

'Of course, he'll have the glue analysed . . .'

'It's at the lab over in Tulsa now.'

'Then it's simple – all you need to do is talk to the Medical Examiner, ask him—'

'News flash – not all doctors're men,' she said. 'Dr Janine Quint was the FME.'

'Okay, ask *her* to compare the samples from the two victims. If the chemical composition is the same, it strengthens your case.'

'I can't do that – for one thing, we don't *have* a sample for comparison off of the first victim.'

'You just said there was duct-tape glue on both bodies.'

'Professor, do you know how county sheriff's departments operate in the United States?'

'I've watched *High Noon* a few times.'

'Well, some would say it hasn't changed a whole hell of a lot,' she said with a chuckle. 'Sheriff is elected, and him – usually it *is* him – and his office're funded through local taxes. Now, if you live in one of the poorest counties in the state, with household incomes forty per cent below the national average, the local law-enforcement budget is apt to get squeezed.'

She seemed to have wandered off the subject, but Fennimore didn't mind – he liked the way that Americans would begin an explanation by telling a story; most he'd met told a good tale, and country folk were the best storytellers of all. Stories gave context, and context was everything in his line of work.

'In the state of Oklahoma, a lot of counties will take you on as a deputy on a suck-it-and-see type of contract for six months,' Hicks went on. 'During that time, they can pay you minimum wage and they are not required by statute to provide professional training. After those six months are up, the county is obliged to pay to have those deputies CLEET trained – that's the Council on Law Enforcement Education and Training. When you're CLEET trained, you can take the oath and become a *certified* Law Enforcement Officer – with full entitlements *and* a hike in pay, too.'

'You're about to tell me that a lot of deputies don't make it past the suck-it-and-see,' Fennimore said.

'Spit out in the dirt like sour candy,' she said. 'No notice period, no severance pay. Some give up, go to work at the county jail, if they'll have 'em, Walmart if they won't.'

'And some move on to the next county?'

'Including me,' she said.

'Where are you up to now?' he asked.

'Williams County Sheriff's Office is my fifth in three years,' she said. 'In all that time, about the only law-enforcement training I got was the Mountain Home Conference, and I pay for that out of my own pocket.'

He grunted in acknowledgement. 'Which means that untrained police officers regularly go out to complex crime scenes and trample all over the evidence.'

'Yes, sir, they do.'

Ah, now they were getting to it. 'If I can hazard another guess, I'd say one of these untrained officers messed up your first victim's crime scene.'

'That untrained officer was me, Professor. It was my first murder; I compromised the scene, lost vital evidence, got in a shitload of trouble with the Medical Examiner's Office. I can't go to the ME with this because in this part of Oklahoma all forensic autopsies're carried out by the FME's office in Tulsa, and it happens that Dr Quint was the ME did the autopsy on the first victim.'

Fennimore paused. 'O-kay . . . I can see that would be awkward. But you could talk to your District Attorney.'

'DA's an asshole,' she said. 'The ADA's all right – I *would* take it to him – but I just don't got enough.'

'Which is why you've come to me. Is Dr Quint really so unforgiving? Maybe I could talk directly to her – she's best placed to do any supplementary tests or examinations.'

She sighed. 'Professor, I made a *big* mistake recovering that body.' For a second, all he could hear was the creak of katydids and crickets, then she puffed air into the mouthpiece. 'It just about kills me, telling you this, but here goes: I was a sheriff's deputy over in Creek County, a little bit south-west of here. Six weeks in and I was green. The victim was found in a creek by a fishing party. It had been raining for three days and nights. Whoever dumped her didn't weight her right and she floated, got carried to a bend, washed up on the shingle. When I got to the creek, the rain started coming down hard and she began to float again. Seeing her there, thinking that water was going to carry her away before too long, and those fishermen waiting on me to do something, I guess I panicked. Sheriff's office was out of range of my cell, and the patrol car was parked a mile up the track. I should've got those men to help me, anchored her to a boat, wrapped her in a tarp – done *some* damn thing to preserve the evidence. But I rushed right in, dragged her out.' She sighed. 'Stupid rookie mistake. I didn't even get pictures. All that rain, the river running full, me manhandling the body—' She stopped and again, he heard a long outrush of breath. 'That body was almost skeletalized; you know how it is – in that condition, they can pretty much fall apart on you if you don't treat 'em right. The current pulled me off balance, I stumbled . . .'

'You lost the hair, and with it the duct tape-residue.'

'Wouldn't be so bad if it was just that – I lost the hair, the jaw, some of the neck bones. I only kept a hold of the skull because – oh, well, you don't want to know.'

He could guess: Deputy Hicks fumbling in the water, snatching at anything that would give her a finger-hold – there are only so many things you can grab onto on a human skull.

'I lost the evidence, but that glue was there all right,' she said.

'I believe you,' he said. 'Have you run this past your sheriff?'

'Sheriff Launer isn't interested in other counties' homicides. Anyway, he thinks the answer to this crime is in the backwoods. We got a lot of families out here used to deal in home-made hooch; now they grow cannabis out in the woods, or cook up methamphetamine. The Sheriff is convinced our victim stumbled across one of those backwoods factories, or pissed off her supplier.'

'Was she a meth addict?'

'There were physical signs, but she had been through rehab, seemed to be getting her life together, before she died.'

'But your sheriff is resistant?'

'He's campaigning for re-election, drugs is a major problem out here. He doesn't want me messing with this, Professor: he wants me out there, proving to the voters that he is doing his job.'

'I don't see how I can help you, Abigail,' Fennimore said.

'Why don't you come on over, take a look for yourself?'

'It's a bit of a hike . . .'

'Three and a half hours max from St Louis to Tulsa.'

'How did you know I was Stateside?' he asked. 'Deputy Hicks, are you stalking me?'

She laughed. 'It's on your publisher's website.'

Fennimore's publicist would harry him every few months for an update, and he would send the less sensitive aspects of his schedule, but he'd never checked out the website and rarely even thought about what went up on it.

'According to your schedule, you did a book signing in St Louis tonight,' Hicks went on. 'You've a couple of lectures in Chicago and the IHIA symposium after that, but not for a couple of weeks – so I know you got the time. Unless you got some secret mission going on.'

In truth, Simms was his secret mission, and now that she was firmly out of the picture, he was stuck in St Louis with time on his hands, and he knew from experience that would lead to brooding.

'I know you like to fish,' she said, her tone coaxing. 'We got great fishing down here.'

'Fishing,' he said. 'What kind of fishing?'

'Bass and catfish, bluegill—'

'Trout?'

She clicked her tongue. 'Oklahoma is kinda warm for trout fishing,' she said. 'We got all kinds of bass, though.'

She must have sensed his disappointment, because she said, 'But if you're real sneaky and know where to go, you can fish for trout near Tahlequah, Cherokee County. There's a couple of ice-cold streams below Tenkiller Dam, about an hour's drive from where I'm situated.'

Three and a half hours' flying time, Fennimore thought. Far less time than it took to travel from Aberdeen to London by train. It was ninety-five degrees in St Louis, humidity in the mid-eighties. Country air, cold streams and fly-fishing were just too a tempting prospect – and he remembered the deputy as pert and pretty.

'All right,' he said. 'You got me. Meet me off the first flight into Tulsa tomorrow morning.'

4

Location: Scotland

The kill is strapped, naked, to a table. Her hair is mouse brown, her nose small; there is a hole for a nose stud in the crease of the right nostril. Her head is tilted back, her mouth slightly open, revealing a chipped front tooth. Her skin has the colour and translucence of skimmed milk. Her lips are almost blue. You can't see her eyes, because thcy are covered with tape. It is wrapped tightly around her head in a double layer.

A man stands over her. He is tall, dressed entirely in black, apart from the purple nitrile gloves he wears on his hands. His face is covered with a black ski mask. He hooks his gloved thumbs in the pockets of his pants and tilts his head on one side, thinking.

'The angle's off,' a voice says from behind him. 'Move the cam left a bit.'

The masked man turns obediently and makes an adjustment to a webcam attached above the screen of his laptop. 'Okay?'

'Better.'

Fergus sighs, settling back into his armchair to view the action. A wood fire crackles in the hearth, a cold north-easterly spatters his windows with sleety rain; winter has lingered in Scotland.

Over the years, he has received videotapes and, as the technology improved, DVD recordings, but he always watched the kill in real time first. The recordings were delivered to a drop-box a month or so later. Until Skype, the two men had used live-streaming to a private URL for the kill; it was relatively low risk, but there was always the chance that some Red Bull-swigging Nethead in continuous surf-mode would stumble onto their web address. The risk went off the scale of acceptability with the invention of automated web 'bots and crawlers. But Skype had its limitations, and the recording suffered from audio lag. So, the live Skype event had been disappointing. Thankfully, he'd had the foresight to insist on a backup digital recording – not just for the better image quality, but for the chance to replay the action. Fergus rationed his viewings because the law of diminishing returns applied; no matter how exciting a thing is to watch, if you see it too often, it ceases to be exciting. Even if it is the death of another human being.

He is watching now on a newly purchased fifty-five-inch, high-def widescreen TV with 9.2 surround sound and high-speed internet access; for future events he will be able to Skype direct to the big screen, which might even compensate for the less-than-perfect picture quality.

'Shift the spotlight,' he hears himself say, though he doesn't recognize his own voice, disguised as it is by voice-changer software. Coming out of the new speakers, it has the slightly echoey quality of cinema sound. Darth Vader issuing orders to a minion.

Obediently, the minion moves a lighting stand and directs the spot lamp to the woman's face, but she is unresponsive.

'Is she unconscious?'

'Watch this.' On-screen, the man takes hold of the kill's

foot and scrapes his thumbnail along the sole from heel to toe. Her toes flex.

He faces the webcam. 'She's fakin' it.' His accent is Midwestern United States, though some might say it is not entirely authentic.

He takes out a box cutter and presses the cold blade against the skin under her eye. 'Stop fooling,' he says, 'or I'll cut you.' He has a thing about blood.

He doesn't cut her, but the threat is enough and she squeals. There's a displeasing distortion, and Fergus makes a mental note that adjustments will need to be made to get the sound levels right next time. It would be useful to do a sound-check in advance, but he fears this is beyond the capabilities of his accomplice.

Exasperated by his own inability to relax and immerse himself in the moment, he rewinds to the point where the kill's toes flex, and lets the recording play on.

'I want you to bind her,' he says.

'Dude, she's already tied up.'

'I said "bind", you glaikit lubbert – *bind*.' The man in the ski mask looks into the webcam, uncertain of himself, and Fergus says, 'Use the food wrap. Take the roll and wrap it around her chest.'

This is new: he has read that you don't need to compress the chest hard to cause asphyxia; simply restricting the rise and fall of the ribcage can have the same effect.

'*Encircle* it. Yes. Now step away.' But the other is slow to comply. 'Get out of the frame,' he yells. 'I don't want to see you.' Control of the other is part of the thrill.

The new cinema system makes it feel as if she's in the room with him – that he is alone with the kill. Her breasts are mashed flat under yards of plastic food wrap. He turns up the volume, listens to the gasp of her breath.

More than once, he complains, 'I can't *hear* her,' frustrated by the limitations of the equipment and the distance between them. But now, listening to the recording again through his new speakers, he hears more than he ever did before. He hears his accomplice mutter a curse, the thrilling stutter and sigh of the woman's breath.

The wrap restricts her movement, takes her to a new level of fear – which is in itself exciting – but she's still breathing, still conscious.

'Fuck's *sake*, I said wrap it tightly. Can't you do *anything* right?'

'You want to come do this yourself?'

'No,' Fergus yells. 'I want you to act less like a moron and more like a thinking human being.'

The slump of other man's shoulders say he's hurt, and when he speaks, he sounds apologetic. 'It isn't my fault – this stuff is designed to stretch.'

'Can't you do *some*thing? Anything?'

He shrugs helplessly. 'That's as tight as it goes.' He stares down at the woman as though she's a DIY problem he hasn't the brains to solve.

Which, at the time, gave Fergus an idea. Right there and then, he dictated a shopping list; this kill just got a few hours' reprieve.

A rest is good for the kill, and it's fun to watch them come round, to see them struggle when they realize the nightmare isn't over. If they give up too easily, accept their fate, he will tell the other man to bring the child in. It's an empty threat – the children are always disposed of by this stage – but it gives them a jolt of energy, peps them up in a very useful way.

Fast-forward two hours.

He watches the man on-screen rig up the apparatus he has purchased at the Home Depot. It's beautiful. Elegant in its simplicity. On his command, the apparatus is brought into play. She passes out. He issues an order and she is revived, so the process can begin again. He hears himself say, 'Try this. Do that,' and all the time, he's thinking of ways to modify, to improve – to get the great lolloping brute right out of the frame.

The other man stands with his back to the camera, shoulders heaving, and Fergus knows he's trying hard to control his temper. Sweat soaks the cotton of his long-sleeved T-shirt, darkening it under the arms and around the collar. It's boiling hot under the lights inside the kill room; those two must be poaching like sardines in a tin. He tugs at the mask and Fergus knows he would love to tear it off, take a huge gulp of air, but that will not be tolerated. So the man works on, taking orders, puppet to the Master Puppeteer.

His senses are alive to every movement, every twitch and groan and whimper from the kill. This one responds to everything as if they had flayed her skin and applied electrodes to the raw nerves, and he is brought to the edge of his seat by her pain. She revives for the third time with a start, flails about, or tries to, and the new sound system relays the creak and tick of duct tape and food wrap as she strains against it. But she doesn't seem fully conscious – her responses are less acute, less exciting. They are nearing the endgame.

'Okay. It's time. Let me see her eyes.'

He sees the other man shudder; he can't stand to look into their eyes. But for Fergus, the months of careful preparation, the hours of play, all build to this final moment. He needs to see their eyes at the last.

5

Lambert Woods Mobile Home Park, Williams County, Oklahoma

Seven-fifteen in the morning and Jake Owen was singing 'Summer Jam' on Cougar-108. The red-headed boy cranked up the volume on his old Sony pocket radio and dreamed of the coming vacation. Momma's new boyfriend was home for a few days; they were making noises in her bedroom, and he cranked it up all the way so he could fix himself a peanut-butter and jelly sandwich at the kitchen counter without barfing. It was hot and getting hotter, but there was pop in the fridge and he knew a cool spot in the woods.

Their trailer was jacked up at one end on account of the slope, so he felt the vibrations of her footsteps through the floor seconds before his momma slammed the bedroom door open. The boy snagged a Coke and stuffed it in his schoolbag without turning around.

'Turn down the goddamn noise,' she yelled.

'I will if you will.'

'What in the *hell* do you mean by that?' She took a step into the kitchen. 'You're too damn young for that kind of talk.'

Experience had taught him that Momma was apt to

35

throw things when she was mad – and cracks in the grey plastic casing were witness to the fact his ancient pocket radio did not bounce well – so he swept that into the bag alongside his Coke and scooped up his sandwich with his free hand.

Then he turned, gave her the dead eye. 'Not too young to listen to you and him going at it, though, huh?'

She lunged, but the boyfriend appeared in the doorway and snapped her back like a dog on a chain. 'C'mon, honey,' he said, scratching his butt lazily, still holding onto her skinny wrist. 'Boy's got a point.'

The big redneck had a knack for making the boy feel he was in the wrong by saying he was right.

'"Boy's" going out,' he told his momma, imitating the man's voice. 'You and mullet-head can make all the noise you want.'

'You better show some goddamn respect,' she yelled. 'He's got a name.'

'They all do, Momma,' the boy said. 'They just never stay long enough for it to stick.' He tapped the side of his head.

'Oh, I don't mind.' Boyfriend number fifty-kazillion dropped Momma's hand and combed the fingers of both hands through the longer hair at his neck. 'I *am* a mullet-head: all business at the front and party at the back.'

His brow creased and the boy could see the dumb redneck's brain cogs working, going over what he'd just said.

'Going *out?*' he said. 'Now, son, you know it's a school day . . .'

'It is,' the boy said, thinking, *I ain't your goddamn son.* 'Which is why I'm headed out to the bus.'

'You know I will check on you?'

'I do.' *And who made you my truant officer?*

'Because your momma got a call from the school last time you didn't show up, and we do not need that kind of hassle.'

'I *know*,' he said, feeling hot behind the eyes.

'Well, that's just fine.' He smiled, relaxing. 'Did you eat

breakfast, Red?' Like he was his dad or something, like he even cared.

The boy held up the sandwich and headed out the door. The boyfriend whispered something, Momma giggled and they tumbled back into the bedroom before the boy even slammed the back door shut.

Red was nine years old; he could not remember living anywhere else in his life except trailer parks, nor his momma ever being without a man. 'Woman needs a man to look after her,' she would say. But looking after usually meant taking what they could get, and they always ended up using their fists on her and him both. The one good thing was they never stayed long. Except for this one – he broke two records in one, sticking around at a hair under six months without ever raising a finger to either of them. Momma liked him 'cos of that, and because a month ago, he moved them out of that shitty trailer they rented in Avant, Osage County, and found them this nice two-bedroom home in Williams County. He bought her things and they always had enough food – sometimes he even took them to the McDonald's in Hays, which maybe should have been enough to make the boy like him, too. The boy had his own room and a roof over him didn't leak when it rained, both of which he liked. As a bonus, the boyfriend was away a lot, so it was mostly peaceful. Red liked the country and the quiet, shady lot where the trailer was parked, but he did not like losing his old friends. Momma and her new man also made the boy go to school, which no one ever did before, and the boy did not like that one bit.

The kids in his new school were mostly from Durell, a suburb of Hays, which Momma said was 'up-and-coming'. They called him 'Trailer Trash' and 'Welfare': 'Hey, Trailer Trash, where d'you think you're goin'?' and 'You better sit up front by the door, Welfare, so you don't stink up the bus.' He'd got into more than one fist fight on the schoolyard, and mostly they left him alone now, but it was tiresome, and when the school called to say he'd skipped out, the boyfriend got good and mad.

The new man said, 'Call me Will,' which he never had. In turn, the boy got called 'Red', which he liked, and 'Son', which he did not. And that more or less summed up how he felt about Momma's mullet-headed boyfriend – kind of twisted up inside, so he didn't know how to feel.

Red stared into the solid green of the woods and wished he could go there, but the boyfriend was a man of his word – he would nag Momma to call the school to find out if he had made roll-call. So he shrugged and sighed, turning his back on the woods, and trod the twenty yards along the rutted track, feeling the sun on his head, where it shone through the leaves of the oaks. At the end of the track a concrete access road had been laid for the main park: fifty mobile homes on a cleared section of land that looked down all the way to the crappy two-lane blacktop into town. He should've taken the road, being the quickest way – he could see a few other kids waiting for the bus in the lay-by – but he liked to walk through the park, look at the people.

He passed the man with new modular-type home who most days sat in a rocking chair on his porch with a 92FS Beretta at his hip and a Smith and Wesson .38 revolver in his lap. A few yards in, a lady was hanging out washing. He smiled at her and she scowled, said, 'Move on.' He grinned wider, said a jaunty, 'Good morning!' just to piss her off. Two homes down the slope a fat man in a Metallica T-shirt sat drinking beer next to a Fat Boy Harley. The legs of his plastic chair splayed out like a whitetail fawn just finding its feet. The boy walked on, chewing on his sandwich, watching the guy out the corner of his eye – he had been known to pitch an empty can at the back of a person's head, and that man could throw like Steven Okert of the Sooners.

Off to his left, a trailer boomed out Chicano rap. The boy

could feel the bass rhythm in his chest. Over the racket he could hear the hard machine-gun rattle of voices: a man and woman arguing in Mexican. He turned his head to look, but whipped back, catching a movement to his right – a flash of brown and white rushed at him from under a trailer. He jumped back and the dog's claws got him in the side. It came up short on its chain, a mean-looking pit bull, slavering and drooling, its eyes wild with rage. He heard the fat man's laughter at his back. The boy lifted his T-shirt to check for damage: the claws had raked three red scratches across his bony ribcage. Suddenly he was furious.

Glaring at the dog, he scuffed a stone that stood proud of the mud by the side of the concrete pavement, digging heel and toe, working it out of the baked dry mud. He picked up the stone and took a bead on the dog, which by now was rattling the whole trailer, spit and froth flying out its mouth as it lunged and strained on its chain. Before he could let fly, the door opened and a bearded guy with a bald head stood watching him. He was six foot four and about three feet across. After a second or two, he squeezed sideways out the door and came down the steps and kicked the dog, which yelped and then lay down quiet.

'You sure you wanna do that, kid?' the man said.

'He went for me,' the boy said, his blood still up.

'He's on a chain.'

'He still got me.'

'I don't see blood.'

'So what if there's no blood – he fucking went for me.'

The bald man's eyes widened. 'Now don't you cuss me out, you ginger bag of bones. You don't have no call to walk through here – you should stay on the road. Now you can get going, or I can let this dog off his chain, see whicha you can run fastest.'

The boy's chest went up and down, up and down. He wanted to kill that goddamn piece of crap dog. His hand closed over the rock, and the man bent to the dog's collar.

The boy dropped the rock and spun, running, kicking up dust, flying past the trailers and beat-up cars, knocking over chairs, setting up a racket of shouting and barking in his wake. He heard – or imagined he could hear – the pit bull panting and growling, getting madder and madder and closer and closer as it tripped and dodged and worked its way around the obstacles. He kept running, made it to the park fence and climbed it, falling down the other side, praying the dog was not so agile he could follow after. Trembling and sweating and panting, holding onto a fence rail to keep from falling down, the boy stared wide-eyed as the pit bull, frustrated to have been outrun, went for a mastiff tied to a trailer nearby. It took the beast by the hindquarters while it screamed and howled, squirming right and left, trying to grab the pit bull by the neck.

Two Hispanic men piled out of the mastiff's trailer swinging baseball bats.

Blood, spit and fur flew and the other kids gathered round for the show. The pit bull finally let go, but the men kept whaling on it. The bald man lumbered slowly towards the two men, who kept on beating and kicking the pit bull. He grabbed the bat out of the hand of one of them, felled him with a headbutt, whacked the other one with the bat, catching him across the temple as he turned to see what had happened to his friend. He bent, lifting his dog by the collar, then hoisting him up in his arms. The animal's head lolled and the mastiff, still on its chain, made a feint towards them. The man bared his teeth and the dog backed off.

He shifted his weight, rearranging the unconscious pit bull's limbs and turned to the knot of kids at the fence. Red tried to worm his way to the back, but the other kids pressed forward.

Someone said, 'Oh-oh.'

The bald man stared hard at Red. Didn't say a word – didn't

need to – the look on his face said he knew exactly who to blame for his dog's injuries, and he was not the kind of man to forgive and forget.

6

Method Exchange Team Headquarters, St Louis, Missouri

The lab found a small amount of blood between the skirting board and the wall of Elleesha Tate's apartment. It gave them a full DNA profile of a drifter named Jordan Driver. It didn't take them long to track him down: he was in Cook County Jail, Chicago, awaiting trial on charges of sexual assault and battery on a seventeen-year-old girl.

Jordan Driver was five foot four, scrawny. 'Just smart enough to know better than to pick a fair fight with someone who can hit back,' Detective Keith Valance said. 'First words out of his mouth? "I did it". He chose death row in Missouri over fifteen to twenty in Cook County jail – how about that?'

Detective Ellis said, 'Can't say I blame him.'

Simms looked to Detective Dunlap for an explanation. 'Cook County has quite the reputation,' he said.

Valance would collate the evidence and compile the police report; for the rest, it was back to the selection process.

Simms had been working through case files since eight thirty that morning. She was in shirtsleeves, a tall pile of documents on her left, a smaller pile on her right, in the conference room at Brentwood Police Department. The building was a single storey on an industrial estate about eight miles from the centre of St Louis. The small, obscured-glass windows gave little natural light and the low hum of the air conditioning sounded like a child blowing over the open mouth of a milk bottle. Occasionally, someone would shuffle paperwork or she would hear the creak of upholstery as one of her colleagues adjusted their posture or reached for a new file. The glass-fronted room had been allocated to the Method Exchange Team by the department's police chief; it was theirs for the duration.

'Has anyone else picked up on Fallon Kestler?'

'Picked up on?' Detective Ellis said. 'I swear, you Brits talk a foreign language.'

'Does anyone else feel we should look into it further,' Simms said, with a twitch of her eyebrows.

They were looking at a selection of thirty cases – cold and recent. Working through the list that turned up Elleesha Tate, there had been a lot of negative comparisons between UK and US protocols, but now they were beginning to work as a team, trying to identify best practice with no regard for where it originated.

'Mother and child,' Simms said. 'Found dead three and a half years ago, in a marshy tract off I-44—'

'A *what* tract?' Ellis again.

Ellis could be very grumpy about English as spoken by the English.

'For simplicity, let's just call it a bog,' she said.

'I'll just call it a swamp, you don't mind.' Working as a team did not always mean complete harmony. Detective Ellis checked back through his notes. 'We're grading the cases same way as before, right?' he said.

'We are,' she said dryly.

'Okay, let's see . . . You got water, a long time from dump to discovery, unreliable witnesses . . .' He glanced up. 'This one's dead in the water.' From the look on his face he hadn't intended the pun.

'A child was murdered – surely that would make it a public-interest crime?' Simms argued.

'You're learning,' Ellis said. 'But it was investigated, and they got zip.' He ticked off a few more negatives on the fingers of one hand. 'We got no primary scene, no physical evidence, no suspects, no family looking for justice . . .'

'She was twenty-six years old,' Simms said. 'Her daughter was just nine – and *no one* cares that she was murdered?'

'Welcome to Cranksterville. They don't "do" quilting circles or clambakes. Their version of a yard sale is breaking into their neighbour's shitty dive and stealing whatever isn't nailed down.'

'Thank you for that illuminating cultural précis, Detective Ellis,' Simms said, flaring a little.

He bowed his head in mock chivalry. 'My pleasure, Princess Kate.'

She narrowed her eyes and saw the vaguest hint of humour in his face – nothing so extravagant as a smile, but something akin to sunshine behind a thin veil of cloud.

Dunlap spoke up: 'They were found in water, and you know what water does to DNA evidence. Without it, on a case like this, we're not gonna find the killer. Sorry, Chief, this one doesn't look good for a conviction.'

Dunlap, the voice of reason and authority. He was right, of course; they had nothing else to go on. Even so, Simms couldn't bring herself to set it aside. She read the autopsy report and sifted through the crime-scene pictures and thought about Rachel, Fennimore's wife, found on the Essex Marshes, months after she and Fennimore's daughter vanished.

7

Most serial killers have very defined geographic areas of operation.

SERIAL MURDER: MULTI-DISCIPLINARY PERSPECTIVES FOR INVESTIGATORS (FBI PUBLICATION)

Williams County, Oklahoma

Lance Guffey met Deputy Hicks and Professor Fennimore on the porch of his family home.

'Deputy Hicks.' He came down the steps with his hand outstretched.

Hicks introduced Fennimore as a forensic-science professor from the UK, and Guffey offered him a firm handshake and welcomed him to Oklahoma. He was six foot two and broad-shouldered, a thirty-something with a sun-lined face and calloused hands. He offered them refreshment, but Hicks said they should get to it. Guffey pulled an Oklahoma Farm Bureau baseball cap out of his pocket and fitted it to his scalp. His face was grim, and he said little as they drove to where he'd found the body, except to ask if they knew the name of the victim yet.

Hicks said, 'No, sir. But I'm working on it.'

'Well, the Good Lord doesn't need to be told,' Guffey said, 'but it would make it easier for us to pray for her if we at least had a name.'

After ten minutes of bumping over cropped turf, Hicks's

police SUV drew to a halt a short distance from the pond. Thirty yards wide at the nearest point, the pond stretched off for about a hundred yards to a slightly raised line of trees. The water reflected blue sky and a few high stratus clouds, the green and silver foliage of cottonwood trees around the rim of the pond adding contrast.

Fennimore gazed out across the water, smiling in wonder. 'Back in the UK, we'd call your "pond" a good-sized lake.'

Guffey scratched his chin and tried not to look too proud. 'You need to go a little further, Deputy,' he said. 'Just head around to the left.'

Past a bend in the lake, the water line curved inward like a kidney bowl. The ground still bore the scars of the fallen tree. A great tree stump lay some yards from the water's edge, its red plate of roots upturned and drying in the hot May sun. Beside it, Guffey had created a neat stack of logs and a less tidy mound of branches and twigs, the leaves already dried and turning to dust.

Hicks killed the engine and they got out and walked the last few yards, down a mud-churned incline to the pond. A small herd of black Angus cows were wallowing knee-deep in the muddy water.

'Reminds me of home,' Fennimore said, with a nod towards the beasts. 'Except for the warmth and sunshine.'

Guffey looked at him in question.

'I teach at a university in Aberdeen. It's on the north-east coast of Scotland,' he added, thinking there must be half a dozen Aberdeens in the United States.

'Those guys knew how to breed good stock,' Guffey said appreciatively.

The animals chewed the cud, watching the humans, indifferent to their admiration.

The pond water had receded for lack of rain, and the water lapped against a three-foot strip of cracked mud, leaving cattails and other marginal plants high and dry. The collapsed the section of bank under which the body had rested during winter was clear to see, as was the cause – two small, shrubby-looking trees, which had fallen landward. Diagonally opposite that, the kidney-shaped curve of the pond was missing a large oval chunk of clay, like a bite out of the rim, where the big cottonwood tree had been torn out by the roots.

'You found her in the mud under the collapsed bank?' Fennimore asked.

'That's where she started,' Guffey said. 'I didn't know she was there until I dragged her a ways.'

Fennimore tried to picture the scene. 'So the cottonwood fell from right to left, some of it on dry land and some in the mud.'

Guffey nodded. "Cept, this was mostly water here at the time. Level's gone down in the dry spell.'

'Do you know when those smaller trees came down?'

'Been puzzling on that,' Guffey said. 'We had a storm October twenty-nine, last year – probably the same wind that shook the cottonwood loose. Soon as we got the storm warning we rounded up the cattle from here and put them on the pasture near the house, so I know those trees were standing then. That was real a bad storm,' he reflected. 'Next morning, I drove over the farm to look for damage. Took me two days in all, fixing as I found, and I seem to remember seeing those two late on, so they must've come down between October twenty-ninth and November first.'

'That narrows down the dates,' Fennimore said. 'You didn't do anything about the damage?'

'The pond was full at the time, so I couldn't see the mud-fall on the edge, and those trees weren't in anyone's way. Didn't seem much point messin' with 'em, when there was fences to mend.'

Fennimore nodded. He turned full circle, noting the line of trees that ran along a slight ridge about thirty yards from where they were standing, taking in the short turf they had just traversed, the SUV's tyre tracks showing plainly the path they had taken to get to the pond.

They had driven down farm tracks, through two gates – both chained and padlocked – to get there.

'Whoever left the body in your pond could not have come via the farm, because you would have seen them, and even if you didn't, the locked gates would have stopped them.'

'So, he carried her, or dragged her, up here,' Hicks said.

'A body is heavy,' Fennimore said, doubtful.

Hicks raised her eyebrows.

'I know,' he said. 'Stating the bleeding obvious, but people often underestimate just how heavy and awkward dead weight really is. Even a fairly small female is about a hundred pounds, and – crucially – it's unevenly distributed weight – arms and legs flopping around . . .'

'They could've used a fireman's carry,' Guffey suggested.

'Maybe, but most people couldn't lift *or* drag a body for more than a few hundred yards, and I don't see a convenient roadway.' He squinted again at the line of trees on the ridge. 'Unless there's one up there along the treeline.'

Something bright flashed in Guffey's eye. 'Can't give you a road,' he said, 'but maybe something as good.'

He led the way to the ridge. They found more cottonweed, red cedar and a type of birch with an exceptionally flaky bark, the outer surface shining silver and the curled inner cinnamon red, like pencil shavings. In the treeless fields, the mating call of cicadas was an annoying whine, but up in the line of trees it was almost deafening. Hanging onto a branch for support, Fennimore looked six feet down to a stony track, rocky at the bottom, with a thin trickle of water oozing over the stones.

'Mud Creek,' Guffey said.

'Wide enough to accommodate an SUV,' Fennimore said. 'What about access?'

Guffey pointed downstream of the sluggish trickle towards a massive turkey oak. 'Beyond that oak, there's a bridge runs over the creek. Part of Wilson's Road; it's nothing much, just a dusty back road, but it crosses the highway a couple of miles west of here.'

Now here was a possibility. 'Who knows about this?' Fennimore asked.

'Most folks. Kids hereabouts use it as a shortcut to bike into town.'

'You said the pond was full after the storm last autumn. Was the creek, too?'

Guffey shook his head. 'That creek hasn't been full in sixty years.'

Fennimore walked along the ridge, head down, looking for a place that showed no signs of disturbance. He found a convenient spot and scrambled down the slope.

'Where're you going, Professor?' Hicks said.

'Mr Guffey, would you mind coming down here?' Guffey obliged. 'You're two or three inches taller than me,' Fennimore said. 'Can you see over the ridge to the pond?'

'No sir,' he said.

Fennimore headed downstream towards the massive oak and Hicks slid down the gulley after them. The bridge was just fifteen yards beyond the tree and, looking down from the road, he could see nothing of the pond.

'A man driving aimlessly, looking for a place to dump a body might have left it under the bridge, or in the dry creek, where it would have been perfectly well hidden, but he didn't. He drove or carried or dragged the body fifty yards further.' He pointed back the way they had come. 'You can't see the pond from here, but he knew there was water on the other side of the ridge.'

Hicks adjusted her hat. 'Local knowledge.'

'Or Google Earth,' Fennimore said. 'The point is, he planned this. Your killer is methodical, he plans ahead.' He turned his back on the bridge and looked across acres of unenclosed land, planted with wheat; so much empty space where the killer could have dumped the victim. He turned again and looked down onto the sad trickle of water which was all that remained of Mud Creek. 'He didn't chance upon your pond, Mr Guffey, he chose this place.'

8

Basically, I'm for anything that gets you through the night –
be it prayer, tranquilizers, or a bottle of Jack Daniel's.

FRANK SINATRA

'They're praying for her,' Fennimore said.

He and Deputy Hicks were headed back to Westfield. She was just as pretty as he remembered. Her hair, black with a rusty tinge, was straight and lustrous; just now, it was tied in a French knot under her hat. She had startling blue eyes with a darker rim, but her high cheekbones and the almond shape of her eyes suggested native lineage, and Fennimore was reminded that this north-eastern area of the state was part of the Cherokee Nation's Tribal Jurisdiction.

'The Guffeys are country folk, born and raised,' Hicks said. 'They believe in God and family and that every child is born in God's likeness. It surprises you, they pray for her?'

How could it surprise him, when thousands had done the same for him, and for Suzie and Rachel? He didn't believe in God, or an afterlife. Was it perverse to find it comforting that at least some of the people who prayed for him were like the Guffeys?

'You still haven't had anything from CODIS?' he asked to change the subject.

'I'm waiting on the call,' she said. 'But she would have

to've committed a felony crime for her DNA to be on there. You heard of NamUs?'

'The United States national missing persons database,' Fennimore said without hesitation.

'I put the victim's age and physical details on there,' Hicks said. 'You can also input reference DNA samples from the family. Soon as a new unnamed person's DNA goes on there, it's cross-checked with all the reference DNA on the system – if they reported her missing, we'll get a name.'

'*If* it goes on the system,' Fennimore said. NamUs was less than ten years old, and from what he remembered of the lecture he'd attended, the biggest difficulty they'd had was getting word of its existence out to front-line law-enforcement officers. 'As I understand it, filling out the forms is not mandatory. Plus, her family would have to know she's missing, *and* they would need to know about NamUs *and* they would have to give a damn.'

She looked downhearted and he realized he'd jumped on one of his hobby horses and ridden it too hard. But Fennimore found it hard to apologize; Kate Simms always said that it was his least appealing characteristic. By way of making amends, he said, 'What d'you need from me?'

She showed no emotion, but he noticed she did put her foot on the gas. 'Would you take a look at the files? They're in the centre console.' She patted the armrest.

The possibility that the two cases were linked was slight. But he was here because he had time to spare, and Abigail Hicks was a pleasant distraction from his own concerns. He lifted up the armrest and drew out two folders. One bore the six-point star of Creek County Sheriff's Department. He didn't ask how she'd got hold of a file from a county sheriff she no longer worked for, but he admired her resourcefulness.

They drove past sagging wooden shacks – a hairdresser's, two bait shops, one derelict – then on into the town proper. Westfield was a solid Midwest town; the architecture mainly early twentieth century, square-built red stone, except for the Court House, which gleamed white, set back from the road amongst lawns and trees and bright municipal flowerbeds. But every third shop on Main Street was closed down and, at 9.15 in the morning, it was empty of people.

The Creek County victim that Hicks had found and almost lost entirely, three years back, was Shayla Reed, twenty-two.

'Shayla was taken into foster care after her momma died of an overdose and her daddy walked out, leaving her and her baby sister in a two-room rental with a packet of Cheetos and a can of Tab each,' Hicks said. 'Shayla ended up in foster home after foster home, and drifted into addiction and occasional prostitution.'

Shayla's body had been found by Deputy Hicks's fishermen several months after she was dumped.

'We ID'd her through NamUs,' Hicks said. 'It happened that her sister checked out the website for the first time just after I put Shayla's details on there – you believe that? Shayla had been out of touch. At first, her not being around seemed like a good thing, 'cos all she ever wanted was a handout. But it wasn't like Shayla to miss birthdays and Thanksgiving. She wasn't at her last known address, so her sister did an online search, found NamUs, typed in her distinguishing features.

'There's a snapshot of Shayla with her sister's kids – it's in a buff envelope, near the back of the file.'

Fennimore rooted through and discovered an 8 x 5 glossy: Shayla, laughing, on her hands and knees with a toddler riding bronco on her back. He flipped the photo; the inscription read, 'Shayla on Bobbie's fourth birthday. Happy times.'

Shayla had been living on a trailer park just off Interstate 44 in Creek County. Fennimore skimmed the rest of the report, and his eye snagged on a detail that Hicks had chosen not to mention.

'There was a child,' he said.

'I told you that.'

'No,' he said, his chest tightening. 'You didn't.'

'Thought I did . . .' she said, lying badly, but covering fast. 'I talked to the trailer-park manager. He told me there was three sharing that trailer: a man, a woman and a girl of about ten. Now, I told you I made a mistake getting her momma out of the water. But we had volunteers up and down that creek for three days looking for that child – even dragged a pond upstream that'd overflowed in case her momma had floated out of there. With the rain and floods, a lot of creeks and ponds had broke their banks; that little girl coulda been carried a mile by the floodwaters.'

Fennimore felt a prickling at the back of his scalp. Could that have happened to Suzie? She was always there, his little girl, like a dull ache behind his eyes.

'You should've told me, Deputy,' he said.

'I know.' She gripped the wheel hard. 'But the young woman Mr Guffey found in his pond had a complete hysterectomy. The ME said internal scarring looked like a botched abortion. They probably had to do the surgery to save her life. She was no more than nineteen – doesn't seem likely she had a child, aside from the one she terminated. I thought if I told you that, then you'd say there was no link and you wouldn't look at the case, and I *really* need you to look at this case.'

He blinked, surprised. This wasn't about him – she wasn't trying to spare his feelings or draw parallels – this was purely about her case and her need for his help. Since last winter, he'd become so obsessed with Suzie that he saw the fingerprints of her abductor on every case involving a child. He couldn't help wondering, though, why Abigail Hicks moved from county to county the way she did, why she relied on jobs with low pay and no tenure. Could it be that, like the victims, she had no family support? Was that why she felt so strongly about Shayla Reed and this new victim?

Hicks's phone rang. 'DNA results are in,' she said, cupping her hand over the mic. 'Hold on, I'm going to pull over.'

She drove to the roadside. 'Go ahead,' she said. For several minutes she listened and made notes.

'Can you mail me a mugshot?' Hicks thanked the caller and hung up.

'The body in the Guffeys' pond is Ellen "Laney" Dawalt. We got lucky – she's on CODIS. She was charged with meth possession, which is a felony crime in the state of Oklahoma. She got a community sentence with supervision and treatment.'

Her phone buzzed. 'That'll be the mugshot.'

According to the height board behind her, Laney Dawalt was five foot three. In the photograph, her hair was bleached, but darker at the roots. Her right profile revealed a nose piercing.

'That's your victim, all right,' Fennimore said, checking the description against her file.

'Right down to the chipped front tooth,' Hicks said. 'She lived in a trailer park in up Stilwell, Adair County. Asshole dumped her over the county line, thinking we wouldn't bother to do a full search for her.'

Fennimore thought that if the local sheriff had his way, their killer would have been right. 'Can we go and talk to people out there?'

She grinned. 'You mean, you're in?'

He tilted his head, undecided.

'Okay, I'll talk fast. Adair Sheriff's Department doesn't want the case, but the Assistant District Attorney fixed it for me to go talk to the trailer-park manager with an Adair County deputy.' She glanced at him from under her lashes. 'Want to come?'

The manager of Country Roads Mobile Home Park in Adair County was a fat man of around forty, in motorcycle boots and jeans and a T-shirt with the arms ripped off. The modification revealed, not impressive biceps, but alarming underarm hair growth. He stood behind the reception counter under a cooling fan blowing at force ten, but he still sweated profusely. Against one wall a few shelves were stocked with sweets and snacks, and a large fridge held cold drinks.

No, he did not know Laney Dawalt personally, he told them, least, not to make small talk.

'You might pick something up in the trailer,' Fennimore said.

'I moved someone in there two days after she went off.'

'When?' Fennimore asked.

'Five months ago, maybe more.'

'And you didn't think to tell anyone that this woman was missing?' Hicks said.

The man laughed. 'You're joking, right?'

Deputy Hicks hitched her thumbs in her belt and gave him a hard stare.

The manager rolled his eyes. 'They lit out owing me two weeks' rent. People move on owing money, you don't need to ask the reason why – and you don't call the cops.'

'People?' Hicks said.

'Huh?' He looked at her like she'd said, *Aliens?*

'You said, "they" owed you. You said "people", which usually means more than one person.'

'Well, yeah,' he said, tucking his right hand under his left arm and tugging thoughtfully at a tuft of underarm hair. 'Her and her boyfriend, and the boy.'

'The "boy".' Hicks looked at Fennimore. There *was* a child. 'How old was this boy?'

'I don't know, your guess is as good as mine.'

'Really?' she said, scratching the back of her neck. 'I was hoping your guess would be *better* than mine.'

The manager frowned at the countertop. 'If I was pushed to it, I'd say he was nine or ten.'

'What about the man she was with?'

'What about him?'

'A name would be a good start.'

'I don't remember.'

'Well, what'd he look like?'

'Ordinary, I guess.' He saw the look on her face. 'Look, I only saw him close to the one time, okay?'

'Okay. Was he my height?' She jerked her head towards Fennimore. 'His?' Finally, she jabbed a thumb towards the Adair County deputy, who was midway in height between the two of them. 'Or his?'

'Taller than him,' he said, chin-pointing to Fennimore. 'Brown hair.'

'How old?'

He sighed like she was asking him to do mental calculus. 'Uh, younger'n him.'

It seemed that Fennimore had become the template for comparison.

'Was he the boy's daddy?'

'I don't know – I never saw them together, 'cept in the car,' he added quickly, before she could give him that look again.

'What kind of car?'

'Some midget European piece of shit,' he said with startling venom. 'Grey.'

She asked him if they had supplied proof of ID, but neither of them had. 'How'd they pay the rent?' she asked.

'Cash.'

'Did you use a rent book?'

'Uh, yeah.'

'You got it?'

He nodded. 'She left it behind at the trailer.'

'Good. We'll check it for fingerprints,' Hicks said.

He shrugged. 'Okay. But it'll only be hers and mine on there.'

'Receipts,' Fennimore said, glancing at the snacks on the shelves.

The manager fixed him with a beady eye. 'Mister, we sell

potato chips and Cola, mostly. I don't write receipts for those.'

Fennimore recalled a locked wire cage outside the office, stacked with propane gas bottles. 'Did he ever pay for cooking gas?'

'Uh . . .' He stared past Fennimore's shoulder and scratched his underarm hard enough to draw blood. 'Maybe one time . . .'

'We'd like to see the registration forms, too,' Hicks said.

For a second, he didn't move, but when the two deputies and Fennimore stared at him expectantly, he gave a little start, and said, 'Oh, you mean now?'

'That would be real helpful, sir,' Hicks said, without a trace of sarcasm.

While he searched out the relevant documents, they made their way to the edge of the park, to the trailer formerly occupied by Laney Dawalt.

'Where is that little boy?' Hicks said, half to herself.

'He could still be in the pond up on the Guffeys' land,' Fennimore said.

'Why wouldn't he come up when Laney did?'

'It's to do with their size, and Body Mass Index. Often children don't float to the surface in the same way adults do,' Fennimore said, blocking images of his wife from his mind.

She stopped at the top of the rise, and the local deputy came puffing up behind them. Hicks took out her phone and moments later she was telling Forensic Medical Examiner Dr Janine Quint that they had a potential second victim: a nine-year-old boy.

'Doctor,' she said, 'I'm sidestepping my boss, coming to you. Sheriff Launer will not like the extra cost this is going to mean.'

When she closed the phone, she gave him a brief smile.

'Good news?' Fennimore said.

'She said she would talk to Sheriff Launer, tell him we need to send in a dive team.'

The mobile home where Laney Dawalt had lived was a good size – more chalet than trailer. The new tenants had planted a small garden and built a low brick wall at the front of the property. The grass each side was cut short and neat and the place had an air of respectability.

Hicks took a photograph on her mobile phone, slipped that back in her pocket, took out her notebook and began sketching the position of the trailer in relation to the road, the fence and a couple of other homes further down the slope. Every window in the place stood open, and a radio inside was playing country music, the screech of the cicadas outside almost drowning it out.

A curtain twitched and suddenly the door flew open and a woman stood glaring at them. She was large and blonde, and wore a cotton housedress and rubber gloves. She held a kitchen sponge in one hand and her face glowed as if she had been scrubbing floors.

'What?' She looked from face to face with furious dislike.

'Nothing, ma'am,' Deputy Hicks said. 'We're just leaving.'

As they walked back down the hill, Fennimore said, 'Where are we going?'

'We need a warrant,' Hicks said.

'Why don't you just ask if we can take a look around?'

She looked at him with frank surprise. 'This is the United States of America, Professor – you need a good reason to search someone's private property. Protection against unreasonable searches and seizures is enshrined in the Fourth Amendment.'

'So why go up there in the first place?'

She handed him her notebook and fished her phone out again to take a picture of the sketched position of the mobile homes. 'Trailer parks are kind of fluid, and I would look pretty foolish if I gave the judge the wrong location. It would also make the search illegal and inadmissible.'

'Okay,' he said. 'I surrender – you need a warrant, and

you've got to get your facts straight. But Ms Oxy-Clean is obliterating evidence as we speak.'

Her blue eyes sparkled with humour. 'Being out in the backwoods and remote from the seat of justice, we are allowed a little leeway.' She handed her phone to the local deputy. 'Think you could speak to the on-call judge, see if you can get a telephone warrant?'

Fennimore grinned. 'Bloody genius.'

9

Lambert Woods Mobile Home Park, Williams County, Oklahoma

Red stayed clear of the north-east section of the park after what happened with the pit bull. The other kids said the bald man took to patrolling that section with a baseball bat in his hand and after a week he took the dog with him on a chain. They said the dog walked with a limp and had one dropped eye, and it was meaner than ever. If you could believe the older boys, the man kept asking where the skinny ginger kid was at.

Red told them he wasn't scared, but he took to wearing a baseball cap and walked along the western edge of the park where the woods came all the way down to the highway, only hopping over the fence when the bus pulled into the lay-by. On the return trip he would leave the bus early, walking a couple miles extra to get home safe. Today the big yellow bus pulled in to pick up the kids for school at seven thirty on the dot. Red was about to break cover when he saw the big bald man turn left out the main entrance. He stood ten yards from the kids with his dog on a thick plaited leash. He did not carry a baseball bat, but why would he need one with seventy pounds of pure muscle and canine aggression by his side?

One of the kids threw a scared look towards Red and he stepped back behind a trailer. Looked like school was out today. Not that he minded that so much – only that the big boys' talk was true. He worked his way up the gentle slope again, not daring to cross the gap between the woods and the trailers till he could be sure the man had not followed him and could not see where he was headed. He did not think that pit bulls were good trackers, but he sure did not want to put that to the test.

At the north-west corner of the clearing, the distance between the trailer homes and woods decreased, and this was where the boy was headed when he heard a voice behind him. For a second he froze, but the voice was too light to be the pit-bull man and the words too friendly: 'Miss the bus?'

He turned.

Mr Goodman, their nearest neighbour, was stretched out on a chaise longue by the open front door of his trailer. He was about the same age as Red's mom, his brown hair cut neat and short, and his beard was trimmed into a short goatee. A cooler box sat in arm's reach and he was sucking on a can of Sprite.

'What's it to you?' the boy said.

'Nothing at all.' He smiled like he thought it was a little bit funny. 'Lord knows I played hookey more'n once myself when I was your age.'

'Never said I was playing hookey.' Red checked around the corner of the trailer.

'Who cares?' The man took another chug of soda and squirmed his shoulders into the back of the chair. 'School learning's easy forgotten.'

'Uh-huh.' All Red cared about was the bus was gone and so was the big bald man and his ugly-assed dog.

'It's the lessons you learn from *life* you never forget – right?'

'I don't know,' the boy said. 'I only lived nine years, so far.'

'Nine, huh?' He didn't take it like the boy was sassing him, even seemed impressed. 'You're tall for your age – I'd of put you at ten at least.'

Red felt a small spark of pride. 'I will be, come September.'

Mr Goodman nodded, and Red took another peek down the slope to the highway.

'That bus is long gone,' Goodman said. 'You might as well relax, enjoy the day off.'

'I intend to.' Red shifted his backpack on his shoulder, getting ready to leave, but he lingered, staring at the can of cold Sprite sweating in the man's hand. The heat of the sun prickled on the back of his neck, and watching the man drinking down his soda gave the boy a powerful thirst. He couldn't go home and get one 'cos his momma was there and so was her boyfriend, back from his latest trip after two good days of peace and quiet.

Suddenly Goodman seemed to understand. 'I'm forgetting my manners,' he said. 'Here.' He lifted the lid off the cooler and tossed the boy a soda.

It felt cold and good in his hand. The boy reached for the ring pull.

'Wait,' the man said. 'Roll it against your neck.'

Red hesitated and Goodman said, 'Go on, give it a try – you might like it.'

Red pressed the cold metal against his skin and felt the pulse jump in his neck; it did feel good.

Goodman licked his lips and said suddenly, 'You like garter snakes?'

'They're all right, I guess.' It seemed like an odd question.

'Held one?'

'No.' Red cracked the can and drank deep, tilting his head back.

The man watched him. 'You got nothing to worry about – garters are not poisonous, not to humans.'

'I know that,' Red said, nettled that anyone would think him ignorant of what was basic woodsman's lore.

'I offended you,' Goodman said. 'I apologize – a lotta kids even older'n you wouldn't know.'

Red shrugged, secretly pleased. He took another long pull on the soda and wiped his mouth on his sleeve. He was ready to leave.

The man sat up, swinging his legs over the side of the lounger. 'I got five garter snakes – three common, two chequered. The male chequered's got ivory and lemon chequers and salmon-pink eyes – a genuine albino. Wanna see?'

'I don't know . . .'

'He's quite a sight,' the man said, as if to say, *It's up to you, but you really would be missing something.*

Red frowned, scuffing his shoe against the edge of the concrete driveway.

'The female common garter is bearing young. Later in the summer, I should have a whole mess of snakelets. I could maybe give you one.'

'Momma said snakes stink.'

'Naw,' Goodman said. 'Their *crap* stinks, but only till it dries, then you would hardly notice it. And I'd be sure and give you one that don't musk when you handle it.'

Red glanced up from his shoe point; Goodman did seem to know what he was talking about . . . He felt a little tug, like someone had taken hold of his sleeve and pulled him towards the door of that trailer.

'I'm not allowed no pets,' he said, still resisting.

'That's mommas for you – always out to spoil a boy's fun.'

The man grinned like he thought the boy should too. Red knew he should defend his momma, but in truth she *did* spoil his fun. If she went out to work, they would have money so he could have a garter snake and maybe even a dog he could take with him when he went out in the woods.

The man was watching him. 'Let me tell you a mystery of this world I wish someone had told me when I was your age:

64

what Momma don't know, Momma can't nag about. I mean, what you do in your own room is your own business – right? You *do* got your own room?' Red nodded and he said, 'Good. All you need is a glass tank – I could give you the loan of a spare. Sneak that into your room, under the bed, in a closet – hell, you're a smart kid, I don't need to tell you, do I?'

Red bit his lip and the man's face twisted up and straightened itself out fast, like he had gas.

'I should go,' the boy said.

'You don't you want to come see my garter snakes?'

Red glanced uncertainly at the door of the trailer, at the darkness within.

'What d'you say? Five minutes – I'll even let you hold the male.'

Red looked hard at the man. 'Depends . . .' he said, but he already made up his mind.

The man's eyes widened. 'On what?'

Red chin-pointed to the cooler. 'Got any beer in there?'

'Sure.' The man dipped in the cooler box and offered the boy a can of Coors, a slow smile spreading across his face.

Red snatched it and ran, vaulting lightly over the fence into the woods. Safe on the other side, he yelled 'Pervert!'

Goodman came after him, but Red pitched the half-full soda can at him, getting him square in the chest. The boy did not wait to see the result; he ran, kept running, dodging and weaving like a football player, leaping over fallen branches and logs, beer can in his hand, his backpack bouncing on his shoulder, pushing deeper into the woods than he had ever been before, on and on, till the hot wet air almost smothered him. Panting, he climbed a rocky slope, crushing the spotted green leaves of elk heart underfoot so that the stink of rotting carrion followed him and kept on running till he breathed fresh air again.

Finally, he stopped, laughing and out of breath. 'Goddamn pervert can hold his own "male",' he said out loud, then spat to get the ugliness of the words out of his mouth.

He looked about him at oak and hickory and moss and briar, the moss so thick on the rocks it looked prehistoric. He turned full circle and it was the same all round.

'Well, boy, you are lost,' he told himself. It seemed to quiet the fluttery panic rising in his gut, and he took a moment to get his breathing back to normal and just listen; if he could get to a roadway, he could find his way home. Over the high rasp of bugs he heard woodpeckers some way off. He saw a tree creeper going up a nearby oak in spirals, using its curved beak like a third foot. A wren gave a few short bursts of song close by then dashed across a deer trail ten or fifteen yards ahead, and on a whim Red decided that was where he would go. Ten feet along the trail, he was about to open his hard-won beer when he heard a low sound in the brush – almost like a shuffle. He glanced that way but moved on, heard it again, a minute later – a soft crunch of twigs and leaves and a single breath, somewhere between a sigh and a groan. The hairs on the back of his neck stood up; bears and mountain lions lived in the woods out here in Eastern Oklahoma. He had seen a black bear with his own eyes – the fat black rump working slowly through the underbrush not more than fifty yards from their trailer in early spring. He listened hard, but heard nothing more.

He took a few steps, heard again the movement of soft, careful footfalls.

If it was a bear, you were supposed to stand still and shout, 'Hey, bear!' at the top of your lungs, 'cos bears will attack if you surprise them or get between them and their cubs, but they will do most anything to avoid an encounter with a human if they know you are around. But Red did not think it was a bear. Red thought it was a mountain lion.

The woods had got real quiet, like every bird and critter was holding its breath same as he was – even the bugs stopped chirping. He could climb a tree, but so could a cougar, or he could run, but not as fast. For a long minute he just froze, not knowing what to do. Then it was like someone turned the sound back up: the bugs and the birds started first, then he saw a whitetail on the trail ahead of him. It turned and saw him, kicked up its hind legs and vanished before he could get a good look at it. Seeing that whitetail move seemed to give him a nudge and he started to walk – slow and cautious at first, then bolder as the trail got wider. On a tree he saw a 'No Trespassing' sign, but it looked old and lopsided and kind of friendly, like a kid would put up outside his den, so he didn't pay too much mind to it. He needed to find his way back, and the best way he knew was to find people, so more than anything he was encouraged by the sign.

At a clearing the trail disappeared. Grass and ferns grew tall in the first flush of spring green, and here and there he saw a butterfly flitter over the white and pink flowers down in the grass. He stashed his can of beer in his backpack, sat on his haunches and tracked left to right, looking for signs of a trail, and off to the south-west he saw it – a dip in the grass where it had been trampled. Remembering the soft footfall he had heard earlier and the stillness in the woods, Red stayed on the edge of the clearing, working his way around in the shade, using bushes and scrub for cover. He saw a pile of old chicken wire twisted up and dumped to the edge of the clearing. An empty plastic sack lay torn and empty under the wire, alongside a plastic gutter pipe. The path ran through a stand of oak and hickory. It widened to a kind of crossroads under the trees, and here the boy saw tyre tracks in the mud. He took a guess, turned right, but kept well off the track. A creek ran alongside the track a ways, but further on it diverted left into a biggish mosquito-infested pond. Someone had rigged a channel of plastic guttering from the pond. At intervals, black ribbed pipes led off from the channel into a stand of cut-down brush. He followed a section of pipe a few steps, tripped and fell headlong. Something swooshed a few feet over his head, swung back, thudded to a stop. He rolled and looked up. A rock the size of his head was embedded in the trunk of a sycamore just off the path. But as it stopped swinging, he saw that the 'rock' was a block of wood; six-inch wood spikes stuck out at every angle.

The boy looked down to the place where he had tripped and saw a thin strand of copper wire. *Booby trap.* 'Shit . . .'

Trembling, he stood up, ready to duck if something else came swooping out of the trees. That trap had been put there to protect something worth stealing, he reckoned. He followed the tube of ridged pipe, watching where he put his feet. A strong, heavy smell reached him. Snuffling, he followed his nose and the black ridge pipe through the piles of cut brush into a sunny clearing. It was just like the one he had come from about a half-mile away, only this one was packed with tomato vines. Rows and rows of them behind a chicken-wire fence. The vines were trained against sugar canes and were almost as tall as him already. Tiny yellow flowers hung in bunches on the stems.

Why in the world would someone plant tomatoes this deep in the woods, and protect them with booby traps? The tomato stench was intense in the heat of the sun, but there was something else in there too – something sweet and pungent at the same time, like fresh-mowed grass.

On the lookout for tripwires, he got over the fence. The first three rows were tomatoes all right, but after that every third plant was tall and jungly. He recognized the five leaflets and the smell of sweet and citrus with just a hint of skunk mixed in. Cannabis. He had stumbled on a pot grow.

Working quickly, Red took one leaf only from each plant, at different heights, some from inside and some on the outer edges, careful not to tear the stems, moving down the rows till he had thirty or more in his backpack. He would've like to take some buds, but maybe it was too early in the season, 'cos there was none that he could see.

In the distance he heard the high whine of a truck in low gear. Red crept out of the enclosure, finding cover in the cut brush. He kept his head down until the engine was shut off, a door slammed and he heard footsteps headed towards him. The vehicle was a Ford pickup with a tarp thrown loose over the back box; the driver seemed to be on his own, a small, heavyset man with a full black beard. He wore blue jeans and ankle boots and smoked a pipe to keep the bugs off, but he waved his hands and slapped his bare skin anyway, cursing and muttering the whole time.

He stayed a half-hour, turning on taps to flood the rows and checking his tomato vines and the tall cannabis plants, stopping every five minutes to relight his pipe. When he'd finished, he went around a second time and turned the taps off. The boy shadowed him, peeking through gaps in the piles of brush and praying the man would not see the sprung trap. But he only seemed interested in getting his crop watered and getting away from the skeeters that swarmed in a circle over his head, waiting for when his pipe would go out. By the time the man headed back to his truck, Red had climbed the tailgate and crawled under the tarp next to a set of weeding tools and a lockbox.

The suspension springs creaked a bit as the man got into the cab, still grumbling, but Red waited, hardly daring to draw breath until the engine was running and they were headed back down the trail. Then he sighed and reached in his backpack for the Coors. It was warm by now, but it tasted just fine.

10

Stilwell, Adair County, Oklahoma

Professor Fennimore had stayed over at Laney's trailer to supervise the CSIs, while Deputy Hicks sought out Mr Thomas Dawalt, father of Laney. Hicks stood at the gate outside his small clapboard house on the edge of Stilwell, Adair's county seat. Two feet away, a German shepherd dog half choked itself at the end of its chain, snapping and snarling. The steel ring it was attached to was rusted and the concrete it was set in looked like it had taken a lot of wear. She exchanged a look with the Adair sheriff's deputy. He had his hand on his sidearm and she did not doubt that if the dog broke loose he would shoot it dead.

The front door stood open, and Hicks could see all the way through the house and out the back door to a patch of green in the backyard. Hicks caught a movement in the shadows near the back door and raised her voice over the dog's frantic barking.

'Mr Dawalt – sir – we need to talk with you.'

The shadow lurched down the hallway and, a moment later, Thomas Dawalt appeared. A rangy man with a pronounced beer belly, he wore a grey T-shirt, stained under the arms, bile-coloured pants and a couple of days' beard growth. He looked like he hadn't washed in a month.

Dawalt slouched against the front door frame, a sardonic look on his face, a sweating beer bottle held loose in one hand.

'Help you, Officer?'

The animal worked itself into a frenzy at the sound of its master's voice. It leaped at Hicks, front paws outstretched, but its bark was choked off by the snap of the chain.

'It's Deputy,' she said. 'And yes, sir, you can call off your dog – that would be real helpful.'

Dawalt looked at the Adair County deputy; he hadn't moved or said a word, but his hand closed on the grip of his pistol and, after a moment, Dawalt shrugged, put the beer bottle to his lips and tipped his head back, swallowing the last of it. Then he straightened up and sent the empty bottle spinning through the air. It hit the dog square on the back of the skull. The dog yelped, tucked its tail between its legs and dropped flat on its belly.

'Well c'mon,' Dawalt said, 'he won't touch you.'

Hicks glanced at the deputy. He stuck his hands in his pockets, said, 'Hell, no.'

She opened the gate slowly, alert for any sign of movement from the dog, but it stayed down, nervously licking its lips and eyeing the newcomers. As Hicks walked past, her heart thundering, the animal threw an uncertain look over its shoulder at Dawalt.

The roof of the house sagged and the paint had long ago peeled off the boards. A car was parked nose-in under the window. One pane of glass had been smashed and was covered with cardboard. On the porch, a pile of broken wood panels and planking had been stacked.

Dawalt checked her badge and ID, then gave her a long look over. 'You lost, girly-girl?'

The feel of his mud-coloured eyes on her made her skin crawl, but she held his gaze. 'Like I said, it's Deputy. And I'm here with the Sheriff's permission, sir,' she said, trying to

71

be polite, even if he was an asshole, knowing that she was bringing him bad news.

Dawalt squinted past her to the Adair County deputy who had his right hand on his gun, his left hand holding the gate closed. 'I guess he's watching your back then, huh?'

The deputy looked away, and Dawalt laughed.

'What brings you all the way from Williams County, Deputy?' he said.

'Your daughter, Laney,' she said, and watched for his reaction.

'She don't live here no more,' he said, his eyes guarded.

'No, sir.'

He waited, but Hicks wasn't about to talk about his daughter's murder on his front stoop. She raised her chin and looked him in the eye, and, finally, she could see his brain begin to work through the afternoon beer fuzz.

He sighed and turned back into the house. 'You better come in.'

Hicks braced herself and walked into the dark house. The door to the front room was firmly shut; the bedroom, which she glanced into as they passed, a tumble of rancid bedclothes and black plastic bags. The house smelled of stale beer, takeouts, sweat and cat pee. Old food containers were stacked up in the kitchen – on the small yellow-top table, in the sink and in, on and all around the trashcan. There was no sign of a cat, but working at the hard end of rural policing for three years, Hicks knew the fishy reek of a methamphetamine addict – Dawalt must be sweating pure ammonia.

He kept on walking, out into the bright sunshine at the back of the house, where he lowered himself into an old camper chair in a tiny patch of shade and waved her to the lounger next to it. She set that to one side and rescued a plastic chair from the tumble of salvage and garbage on the lawn, placed it opposite him. He shrugged and reached into a cooler box next to his chair, took out two ice-cold bottles of Bud, offered one to her.

'I'm good,' she said.

'That may be.' His lips twitched. 'But are you thirsty?'

She was, and the sun beating down on the back of her neck only made it worse, but she had a job to do, and tiptoeing around Laney Dawalt's drunk, meth-addicted daddy was not getting it done.

'Sir,' she said, 'I have some bad news.'

He took a pull of beer and looked at her, his eyes muddy. 'She's dead, isn't she?'

'Yes, sir.'

A pause, while he swallowed more beer.

'You don't want to know how?' It was the first question most people asked.

'Drugs, or suicide – take your pick,' he said. 'She tried both.'

He sucked on his beer again and Hicks had to work real hard not to knock the damn bottle out of his hand.

'She didn't "pick" this one, Mr Dawalt,' Hicks said. 'Laney was murdered.'

The bottle clinked against his teeth and he spilled beer down his chin. He looked down at the new stain on his T-shirt, brushed at it as he said, 'That girl made some bad choices. Living the way she did, was only a matter of time.'

'Living the way she did . . .' Hicks looked around her and let the words hang.

He looked at her, his head loose on his neck, and she thought, *Don't piss him off – he'll just tell you to leave.* So she swallowed her anger and asked like she really wanted his opinion, 'What kind of choices, sir?'

His brows drew down and his face darkened. 'She run off.'

'When was this?'

He waved his hand. 'After the—' He seemed to check himself. 'I don't know. A few years back. DHS took her and the boy away after that.'

The Department of Human Services. 'Laney was in foster care?'

He looked at her as if to say, *So what?*

'Autopsy found she'd had a complete hysterectomy. The ME said internal scarring looked like she'd had a botched abortion.'

He shrugged.

'You said the first time she ran away *after* something. Did you mean after the abortion?'

'Yeah, it would be about then. Where'd you find her?'

'Up in Williams County, in a farm pond.'

He sucked his teeth and sat shaking his head and nodding now and then, as if he was having a conversation with himself.

'But before she went missing, Laney was living with a man on a trailer park just outside of Fairfield.'

Jerked out of his dark thoughts, he stared at her. Fairfield wasn't more than five miles from where he sat. 'I thought you said you found her in Williams County.'

'Yes, sir. But before she disappeared, she was living right here in Adair County.'

He snuffed, took a swallow of beer. 'Figures.'

'There was a boy with her, aged about nine years old.'

He nodded. 'My son, Billy.'

'She never made contact?'

'What d'*you* think?' he snarled.

Hicks leaned forward. 'I think it's odd that we've been talking five minutes and you didn't once ask about your son, Mr Dawalt,' she said softly.

He dropped his gaze and his chest heaved a couple of times, then he said, 'Well, are you gonna tell me, or have you just come to torment me?'

'We don't know what happened to him, sir.'

His eyes teared up suddenly and he tightened his grip on the beer bottle. After a few moments he wiped his nose with the heel of his hand and sat up in his chair, his eyes fixed on the bottle. She waited. Sometimes the best a law officer could do was just give a man time to talk.

'We were a real family, once,' he said. 'But after the cancer took my wife, I got sick – depressed. Billy was so like her, I couldn't bear to look at him, I just couldn't.'

It was the sort of sob story Hicks had heard many times: parents too doped up to give a damn, leaving older children to look after the younger ones.

'So Laney took care of Billy,' she said.

Dawalt raised his head, fixing his muddy eyes on her, suddenly angry and self-justifying.

'She was *fifteen* – old enough.'

Something in his words jarred, but Hicks was here to seek out clues to the boy's whereabouts, so she let it pass.

'Sir, I need to know about Laney – friends she might confide in, she might've told someone about the man she was seeing.'

He snorted. 'You think *I* would know?'

In truth, she didn't, but she had got nowhere talking to the residents up at the trailer park, and she was desperate. She tried a different angle.

'Is there a place Billy might go if he was scared, somewhere he might hide?'

'What're you *talking* about? It's *four years* since I saw that boy,' he said.

'Maybe some place you would take him fishing when he was little, or—'

He cut her off with a wave of the hand. 'I look like a fisherman to you?'

She wanted to say, *No sir, you look like a self-pitying doper*. But she didn't; she waited again, and hoped that he would say something that might help her to find his little boy. But it seemed Mr Dawalt was done talking. He jammed his empty bottle head down in the cooler and took out a fresh Bud, opening it with a bottle opener on his key ring.

He chugged down half the bottle before he came up for air.

'Sir,' she said. 'I'm just looking for leads.'

After another swallow of beer he seemed in a better frame of mind to talk.

'That girl poisoned Billy and got him took away from me, and when she was done with foster care she went and took him for herself.'

'And you haven't seen him since then?'

'Have you been *listening*?' He was suddenly angry and irritable again.

Hicks decided to ask her next question before his mood turned entirely against her. 'Do you have anything of Billy's in the house? Anything we might get DNA off of?'

His eyes teared up again. 'You think he's dead.'

'I don't know, sir – and I'm sorry to ask – but it would help us to find him if we had his DNA. There's a database for missing children; if I could get Billy's DNA on there—'

'I can't help you.'

For a second, Hicks was too shocked to say anything. 'Can't, or won't?'

'Can't. I sold what was worth selling, burned the rest.'

She stared at him.

'What else could I do with all that *stuff*?' he said, a hard, righteous look on his face. 'Wasn't like he was coming back.'

She covered her mouth with her hand because the words bubbling up at the back of her throat would not help to find Billy.

'Well, sir,' she said, when she had full control of herself, 'if I could get a DNA swab from you – you being Billy's daddy and all – it would be the second-best thing.'

His face closed; all expression left it – the offended self-pity, the righteousness, even the suspicion, all gone. He was still, his eyes dull and hooded. Hicks recognized it as the look of a criminal in self-preservation mode.

'Sir?' she said, hoping against all hope that she was wrong, that she had misread him. 'It would only take a swab of your mouth – you wouldn't feel a thing.'

'Oh, now, that would be an invasion of my privacy, Deputy,' he said.

'Mr Dawalt,' she said carefully, 'this would be what we call a Family Reference Sample; it will get compared to the Unidentified DNA on file and nothing else.'

'So *you* say.'

'Sir, I'm asking you to help find your son.'

'If he's alive, he can tell you himself. He's dead . . .' Dawalt shrugged. 'Well . . . it won't matter to him no more.'

She'd had all she could stomach. Deputy Hicks left Dawalt huddled in his chair in his festering backyard, sucking on a bottle of beer like it was a comforter.

The dog leapt to its feet as she walked out through the front door.

'Stay down,' she commanded, and it dropped to the hot concrete.

The Adair County deputy eyed her with new respect; he held the gate for her, grinning. 'That told him.'

The dog got to its feet and the deputy hastily closed the gate.

'That animal has been chained up in the hot sun without water,' Hicks said. 'Are you going to do something about it?'

'Really? You want me to write Dawalt up on a code violation?'

'Never mind,' she said. 'I'll call the Humane Society myself – after we've dropped by the Department of Human Services. I want to know why those kids were taken into foster care.'

He looked at the house and back to her. 'You need a social worker to tell you that?'

She flashed him a chilly smile. 'You know what they say – the devil is in the detail.'

11

**Method Exchange Team Headquarters,
St Louis, Missouri**

'Does this sound familiar?' Detective Dunlap said. 'Mother and child vanish from home; mother found in water, child gone.'

Simms looked up from the file she was reading. 'How old was the child?'

'Eight years,' Dunlap said. 'A boy.'

'It sounds a lot like our swamp victim, Fallon Kestler,' she said. 'Her little girl was nine.'

'But they found the kid in the water with Fallon,' Detective Ellis said. 'Like I said before, a body found in water means no DNA, added to which they had no primary scene, no witnesses, no suspects.' He spread his hands. 'And do I need to point out she was a *girl?*'

Simms didn't respond, unwilling to let this one go, so she held out her hand and Dunlap passed her the file. 'Just to satisfy my curiosity,' she said.

The murder victim was Kyra Pender. Her life had been short, her ending brutal. The ME recorded death by traumatic asphyxia. There were no signs of strangulation, but the ME noted petechiae on the inner surface of her lower eyelids.

The small, pinprick reddish marks resulted from minute haemorrhages of the capillary blood vessels, and were typical of strangulation or asphyxiation. Kyra also had two broken ribs.

The CSIs believed the body had been dropped from a bridge; tyre marks indicated a compact sedan had burned rubber leaving the scene. This was twelve months ago.

Simms read part of Kyra's life history aloud. 'Her mother was sixteen when Kyra was born. Mother and child moved from a low-rental apartment to a mobile home shortly after the birth. Kyra began stealing her mother's prescription meds at the age of twelve. By the time she was sixteen she was addicted to meth and crack cocaine, pregnant with her first and only child.'

'And so it goes,' Dunlap murmured. 'I want to say it's a cycle of nature, but nature cleans up its messes, and this drugs situation just keeps getting messier and dirtier.'

'Kyra's little boy was never found?' Simms asked.

Dunlap shook his head. 'He's gone.'

'There are some useful details: her body was dumped inside cargo netting. Local rocks were used to weight her. The net was stitched together with grey cord.'

Ellis shook his head. 'This case has already been under the microscope.'

'What makes you so sure?' Simms asked.

'Child case,' he said. 'It's a no-brainer.'

'You would think so, wouldn't you?' Dunlap rubbed a hand over his grey curls. 'But the fact is, Kyra Pender is not in ViCAP.'

'What?'

'I got no returns from NCIC, either.' This was the National Crime Information Centre, covering records both of crimes and missing persons.

Ellis gaped. '*What?*'

'Nothing,' Dunlap said. 'Zip.' He turned his laptop for Ellis to see. The page header bore the bold red, white and blue FBI insignia, fronted by the lion mascot of LEO, the Law Enforcement Online portal. 'See for yourself.'

While Ellis searched angrily through the databases Dunlap had already searched, Dunlap turned to Simms and explained: 'That little boy's details should've been on at least one of a half-dozen databases – Federal and independent. The fact he's not on either of the two main Federal databases is—'

'*Unbelievable* is what it is,' Ellis growled.

Dunlap glanced at him, but continued calmly, explaining the procedure to Simms. 'Kyra Pender's body is found; the local law enforcement agency might think it's no big deal, given her history. But her child is also missing – and that is *huge*. A missing child goes on *any* of the FBI databases, NCMEC is automatically notified. That's the National Centre for Missing and Exploited Children. When NCMEC is notified, they deploy a Team Adam consultant to the investigating agency. Those guys have all kinds of technical resources and funding and expertise, and their single mission is to find missing kids.'

'But Kyra's case details were never entered into any of the FBI databases, so NCMEC never got to know,' Simms said, pronouncing it 'Nec-Mec', as he did.

'Right,' Dunlap said. 'Which is *crazy*. Budgets being squeezed the way they are, you jump on whatever money is available.'

'Come on, Dunlap, you know what this is about.' Ellis again.

'Ellis . . .' Dunlap said.

'See, Chief, the FBI is only interested in serial killers,' Ellis said. 'Which is kind of a disincentive to anyone with a plain, old-fashioned murder to investigate.'

Simms knew that this was one of the many beefs that state investigation agencies across the US had with the FBI.

'Problem is,' he went on, 'unless you have *all* the cases,

how're you supposed to *know* which murders involve a serial killer?'

Special Agent Detmeyer didn't seem inclined to defend or criticize the Bureau's policies; he gazed calmly at Ellis, interested but in no way abashed.

Ellis eyed the FBI agent a moment longer, then reached for the case file, snatching it from under Simms's elbow. 'This happened in the Two State area,' he said, scanning the report. 'Jesus, she was dumped in Forest Park, practically under our *noses.*' He stared, aghast, at Dunlap.

'You know how it is,' Dunlap said, ever the diplomat. 'A case like this, where you don't even have any family waiting for news, you can get distracted. You mean to put the data on the system, but the next homicide comes in, you're following leads on other cases, you forget.'

'Would *you* forget?' Ellis demanded. 'With a kid involved?' He turned to Simms. 'Would *you*? I didn't think so. The lead investigator didn't do his job – this is a complete screw-up.'

Simms said, 'You know, in the UK, we have a dedicated team of analysts to do the data input—'

'Well, good for you,' Ellis interrupted, in a tone that meant, *Screw you.*

'I'm not trying to score points, Ellis,' Simms said. 'I'm saying that our national code of practice *requires* police forces to submit crimes that fit the criteria: the bulk of the work is done for them, and a sizeable percentage *still* don't send the case files in. There are weaknesses in any system – you have to accept that, and do the best you can.'

'Is that so?' Ellis said. ''Cos I get one hundred per cent of my cases on the system. I fucking *hate* filling those forms, worse than I hate filing my tax return, but I still do it. *That's* doing the best you can.'

12

Fennimore's hotel near Westfield, Williams County, Oklahoma

Deputy Abigail Hicks finally caught up with Fennimore around midnight. She had booked the professor into a family-run inn a couple of miles out of Westfield. The management described the place on their website as 'authentic Midwest architecture'; covered wooden walkways with kitsch horse rails were rigged up outside the ground-floor rooms, but a beat-up Ford Mustang was the closest they ever had to a horse nosing up to those rails.

Fennimore was sitting on a straight-back chair outside his room, the chair tilted back, his feet propped up on the rail. He held up a hand against the glare from the headlamps of her ten-year-old SUV, and she killed the lights and grabbed a paper sack from the passenger well before stepping down.

'You look nice.'

She had changed into jeans and a T-shirt, twisted her hair into a chignon to let the air at her neck – wanting him to see the woman beneath the badge.

'I went to the trailer park to give you a ride home,' she said. 'Found you gone.'

'I bummed a lift from the CSI.'

'And he obliged?'

'It's not that far over the county line,' Fennimore said. 'Why so surprised?'

'I talked to him before I came over. He said you were rude.'

He raised his shoulders, hands spread – a picture of injured innocence. 'What, because I said it would be a bad idea to splosh Luminol around indiscriminately? It happens to be biochemically destructive and often unhelpful at crime scenes.'

'Now if you'd said *that*, it wouldn't be so bad,' Hicks said. 'But you talked about magic tricks and pretty colours. He *said* you implied he was a street hustler—'

He thought a moment. 'With hindsight, I was rather rude, but evidently I won him over with my encyclopedic knowledge of forensic methodology.'

She smiled. 'I do like to hear you talk.'

'I'm gratified,' he said. 'There are some of lesser discernment who say I talk like a textbook.'

'Oh, you do, Professor,' she said.

The corners of his eyes crinkled, and she felt pleased; most of the time he looked so sad.

There was a second straight-back chair on the walkway and he extended a hand, offering it to her. She took it with a sigh, feeling the long hours she had worked in every muscle. 'So, did you find anything helpful over at Laney's place?' she asked.

'It's clean,' Fennimore said. 'Shiny clean – I mean *OCD* clean. The landlord even stripped out the carpets before the new tenant moved in.'

'The manager didn't seem "The Customer is King" type,' Hicks said.

'We aren't talking about the average customer here, Deputy.'

She had to agree. 'If the rugs went to landfill, we could maybe—'

'No such luck,' the professor interrupted. 'They were destroyed on the park's burn pile. On the plus side, if Ms Oxy-Clean is ever a victim of crime in her home, you'd have a pristine environment to pick up forensic clues.'

She chuckled.

'Seriously,' he said. 'I've seen dirtier DNA labs.'

'I wish I had better news,' she said. 'Laney signed the registration forms, and the only prints we got on the rent book were hers. On the upside, you were right – the guy with her did pay for propane gas.'

'I'm guessing cash,' Fennimore said.

'Yeah. We did get a partial palm print on one of the receipt carbons, but not enough to get a hit on AFIS.'

Fennimore nodded. 'Palm prints can be trickier than fingerprints.'

'We checked it against the manager, and Laney's police records. No match to either one of them.'

'So it *could* be the man Laney was living with.'

'Or the next person who came in to buy gas,' Hicks said. 'And even if it *is* Laney's guy, we don't know if he had anything to do with her murder.'

'He disappeared when she did,' Fennimore said. 'He has to be a strong suspect.'

She nodded. 'But we have no clue who he is—'

'And so we come full circle,' Fennimore sighed. 'Why don't you tell me about your visit with Laney's father?'

'All right. But I'm hungry and dog-tired, and pretty fair depressed with human nature, right now, so I'm going to need food and liquor inside me to tell that story.'

She opened the paper sack next to her chair and he perked up a bit.

'You brought food?'

'Pulled pork sandwiches and pickles. Didn't you eat?'

'Under the shadow of a magnificent bear rampant, modelled in plastic and polyester,' he said. 'But that seems years ago. And I declined the offer of booze, which I now regret.'

'I might have a few bottles of Sierra Nevada in the trunk of my car,' she said, but sounding vague, not wanting him to think she had come *too* well prepared.

He stood and held out his hand. 'Give me the keys and I'll fetch them.'

'Oklahoma liquor laws are real strict on drinking in public places,' she said.

He looked around him at the silent parking lot, empty except for a few cars. 'How public is public?'

She hesitated. 'We're going to have to take it indoors.'

'I promise I'll be the perfect gentleman,' he said, waving her inside.

The ale tasted of malt and caramel and new-cut grass, and it was good and strong, and blessedly cool. It took the edge off the anger that had been gnawing at Hicks all afternoon, so that she could tell Laney Dawalt's sad story without wanting to break something.

'The boy was her brother?' Fennimore said.

'Yup,' she said, noticing that he said 'was'. It seemed Professor Fennimore, like the ME, Dawalt and just about everybody else she had spoken to, believed that Billy was dead. 'Mr Dawalt said he was too "sick" to look after his son. Said Laney was "old enough".'

Fennimore said, 'Old enough for what, exactly?'

Hicks grunted. 'What I thought. He said he hadn't seen Laney or Billy since they went into foster care, so I paid a visit to the Department of Human Services in Adair to find out more. Laney got pregnant a few months after her mother died.'

'Oh,' Fennimore said.

'Mr Dawalt didn't have a single thing of Billy's that might give us his DNA. I respectfully requested a cheek swab so I could get a Family Reference Sample into CODIS. He declined. You would think a man would move mountains to bring his child home safe, but this asshole literally wouldn't spit to help find his son.'

'It's beginning to look like Mr Dawalt has something to hide,' Fennimore said.

'You bet. Dawalt admitted that the first time Laney ran away was after she'd had an abortion.'

'That tallies with the ME's autopsy report.'

She nodded. 'I confirmed it with county hospital. Laney got rushed into the ER when she was three months gone. She lost four pints of blood. The surgeon told me Laney was so messed up they had to perform a total hysterectomy. She was fifteen years old, Professor. *Fifteen years.*' She broke off, took a swallow from the bottle and ran her tongue around her teeth, tasting bitterness that did not come from the ale.

'You think Dawalt was the father,' Fennimore said.

She shrugged. 'Only reason *I* can think of why a man would take his underage daughter to a backyard abortionist. Hell, wouldn't surprise me if he took a wire coat hanger and scarred up her insides himself. Wasn't even Dawalt called the EMS – it was Laney's five-year-old brother did that for her. Her daddy just put her in the bathtub so she wouldn't mess up the couch.'

'Was he prosecuted?' Fennimore looked sick.

'Claimed he wasn't home. Laney wouldn't say what happened – I think she was scared of what Dawalt might do to her brother. The DHS put them in different foster homes, but on her sixteenth birthday, she went looking for Billy and they ran off together.'

He shook his head in disbelief. 'She got them both killed.'

Hicks felt suddenly hot and angry. 'How can you say that? Laney had lost her momma less than a year before. She was probably raped by her own father, who then forced her to abort her baby. Yet she still had the goodness and the strength of spirit to want to take care of her little brother.'

'He *was* being taken care of.'

She gave a bark of laughter. 'Excuse me, Professor, but you do not know what the hell you're talking about.'

He opened his mouth to speak, but a second later, she saw recognition flash at the back of his eyes. 'You're right,' he said. 'I'm sorry. I don't have the first idea.'

Hicks had never heard him apologize and mean it. He knew she was talking about herself. *Damnit*, she thought.

The last thing she wanted to talk about was her own messed-up childhood, so she said, 'A dive team from Tulsa PD is coming tomorrow to search Mr Guffey's pond, but I don't think Billy's in there. It could be his DNA is already in CODIS, and there's just nothing to match him to – and I need more than his sister's DNA to make a definite match.'

'The hospital might have Billy's heel-prick card,' Fennimore suggested. 'That's a blood sample hospitals take shortly after birth to check for congenital diseases.'

She nodded. 'We call it a Guthrie card. But Oklahoma Medical facilities destroy them after forty-two days.'

He gazed at her, a thoughtful look on his face.

'I looked it up,' she lied.

'How did the mother die?' he asked.

'Cancer,' Hicks said.

'All right, then the hospital might have tissue samples.'

'*Now* you're thinking, Professor,' she said and they chinked bottles. 'I'll talk to the surgeon operated on Laney, see if he can help.'

'Mum's and big sister's DNA will get you some way,' Fennimore said. 'But Mr Dawalt's would give you Billy's full profile. I suppose the Family Reference Sample has to be voluntary?'

She nodded. 'And to be in CODIS, he'd have to've committed a felony crime. Judging by his reluctance to donate a sample, he may well be in there as an unidentified crime-scene sample, but I have no probable cause to—' She jumped out of her seat. 'The dog!' she exclaimed.

'What dog?' Fennimore said.

He looked so puzzled, she laughed. *Oh, this was just too beautiful.*

'I can't believe I didn't think of it before. I witnessed Dawalt commit a felony crime with my own two eyes.' The sheer beautiful truth of it made her want to whoop. 'There was a dog chained up in Dawalt's front yard, without shade or shelter, or access to water in ninety-degree heat. He threw a glass bottle at that poor animal – hit it square on the back of the head. It's in the statute books, Professor – animal cruelty is a felony crime. I'm gonna get that DNA sample after all.'

'Well, that calls for a drink.' He offered her a fresh beer from the cooler. 'Are we allowed the rest of the evening off?,

She gave him a doubtful look. 'I did want to put some case notes on the FBI databases tonight, but the department's computer is on the fritz again. Won't get fixed till tomorrow afternoon at the earliest.'

'Doesn't Oklahoma have a State Bureau of Investigation?'

'The OSBI can only get involved in an investigation if they're invited.'

'So, invite them.'

'Not gonna happen.' She shook her head, feeling the beer swirl inside her brain.

'Why on earth not?' Fennimore said. 'They have experienced agents, don't they? Lab facilities, cash?'

'All of that,' Hicks said. 'But the local field agent ran against Sheriff Launer four years ago – almost won, too – and the Sheriff is not a man to let bygones be bygones.'

'Ah,' Fennimore said. 'So, you're stuffed.'

She looked at him over the rim of her beer bottle. 'Oh, I'm not ready for the taxidermist just yet. Have you heard of the National Centre for Missing and Exploited Children?'

'Of course,' he said. 'The UK's Child Exploitation website links to your "Missing Kids" website.'

He probably checked out the site about a million times looking for his little girl, she thought.

'As soon as NCMEC get word of Billy Dawalt, they will deploy a Team Adam consultant to advise,' she said, pushing on, pretty certain that he would not want her pity any more than she wanted his. 'Team Adam brings a *lot* of resources to the table.'

'And since Sheriff Launer has no axe to grind with NCMEC . . .'

'Those resources will come to me.' She gave him a sly look. 'To *us* – if you're still willing.'

'Oh, I'm having fun,' Fennimore said.

Fennimore's whole face lit up when he smiled, and boy, did she want to kiss him right then.

'So, you wouldn't mind letting me use your laptop for a little while?' she said.

'Is that what the sandwiches and booze were?' he asked. 'A bribe?'

'I would not have put it that baldly. But if your laptop is encrypted, I could get onto the Law Enforcement Online portal without even breaking any rules.'

He set down his beer and reached for his carryall. 'I've got to say, I'm disappointed,' he said, looking at her over the monitor of the computer while it booted up.

'How so?'

'I was hoping you were here to do some night fishing,' Fennimore said.

Hicks gave him a slow smile. 'It's still early, Professor.'

13

Lambert Woods Mobile Home Park, Williams County, Oklahoma

Red sat on an old chair cushion, his back against the broad grey trunk of an oak, and listened to Country Variety on his pocket radio, waiting for the baseball scores at the top of the hour. He had found a blue plastic sheet on the park dump and tacked it between the oak and a hackleberry bush for shade; it would double up to keep off the rain in case of thunderstorms. His den wasn't more than a fifteen-minute walk from home, but it was far enough that his momma wouldn't always be hollering for him. He sipped a beer and smoked the butt-end of a joint into which he'd mixed tobacco and some of the weed he stole from the marijuana patch in the woods.

The Ford pickup he hitched a ride off of a few days back had taken him by the back roads into Durell, seven miles from home. He could've jumped down a dozen times, the heavyset man having to slow up and even stop once or twice at crossings, but Red was curious and it wasn't like he had anything else to do with the day, so he rode the truck all the way into town and hopped off at the hardware store, intending to hitch a ride back. He thought he knew who the heavyset man was – the kids on the park said there was a family lived in the backwoods name of Tulk. They owned Lambert Woods Mobile Home Park, and the woods where he found the pot grow. The other kids said he was crazy going up in the woods – there was traps all over, and the Tulks did not take kindly to trespassers.

He paid for Sprite at the Family Dollar and stole a bag of Skittles, then waited across the lot for his ride, drinking his soda and popping candy into his mouth, chewing slow to make it last. But the driver trolled out of the hardware with a big flatbed cart stacked high. He loaded up the back of the truck with fertilizer and wood stakes and rolls of chicken wire until it was full, then he tied the tarp down real tight, and the boy knew he would have to walk home.

It took him two and a half hours to walk home that day. Since then he dried and flaked the weed and sold some of it to a kid in school. But the kid wanted his money back the next day, saying it was no good, being leaf, which didn't have enough THC in it for a good hit. They negotiated a deal which meant the kid paid for what he already smoked and gave back the rest. All Red made out of it was five dollars; enough to buy the beer he was drinking, and some cigarette papers. He thought maybe he would go look for the place again in July, see if the buds were ripe for picking. For now, he intended to enjoy the last of what he had.

He took another toke from his joint and closed his eyes. Mellowed out as he was by the weak leaf and a few sips of beer, a rustle in the low brush a distance away gave him no cause for concern; he opened his eyes but didn't see anything and closed them again, scratching his back lazily against the rough bark of the oak. He heard it again – a crunch of leaves and twigs – but could not be bothered to get up, so he waved one hand like he was greeting a friend and said, 'Hey, bear!' giggling as he settled back again.

For a half-minute there was silence, and he began to doze

off – till he heard a heavy pounding off to his right. The boy turned, but couldn't see for the plastic sheet. Something came out of the woods, a dark blue shadow, getting bigger and darker as it rushed him. He began to scramble out from his shelter, but he was slow, the beer and the weed having furred his mind, and it was on him before he could get clear.

A man, not a bear. He took Red by the collar, knocked his baseball cap sideways, grabbed the can.

The boy yelled, 'Hey!' swiping at the strong hand that held him.

He said, 'Hey yourself.' It was his momma's boyfriend. He shoved Red against the tree with one hand and held the can outside of the shelter to the light. 'Coors?' He took a chug from the can. 'Cool, too.' He handed it back and let go the boy's collar.

Red was so surprised, he slumped where he was, didn't even think of running. He picked up the joint from the ground where Red had dropped it and pinched it out, rubbing it between his palms to shred it, then holding his palms out flat so the air could carry off what was left, but he did not comment. He sat next to Red, his long legs sticking out of the shelter.

He dug in his shirt pocket and took out a pack of Dunhill lights and a Zippo lighter with a wolf etched on it, offered the boy a cigarette like it was the most natural thing in the world.

'Got a nice place here,' he said, when they had both lit up. Around them, food wrappers and crushed pop cans – the debris of two days playing hookey. 'Easy to spot, though, with all the garbage in your yard, and this tarp flapping about like the Stars and Stripes on Independence Day.' He squinted up at the plastic shelter and the boy looked away, feeling foolish.

'It's good to have a beer, maybe even a little weed, to wind down at the end of a hard day, but you make that what you're all about, you'll finish up with all those other welfare losers, sitting outside their trailers at eight in the morning scratching their balls and sinking beers.'

Red felt a band of hotness across his forehead and around his eyes.

'I understand it – really I do,' he said. 'You had it hard, your momma hitting the dope and the booze like she used to, stepping out with so many men.' Red shot him a burning look. 'I know, kid – I'm one of 'em. But I do try to do right by you and your momma.' He nodded and said half to himself, 'Truly, I do.'

'I know,' Red said.

He looked down, surprised, and Red felt his face heat up.

'Did you just pay me a compliment?'

'I sure hope not.' The boy held his face still for a few seconds, but he could not keep it up and he grinned.

Momma's mullet-headed boyfriend smiled, too, then he took off his cap and wiped his brow with his sleeve. 'Man, it's so hot, even the crickets are looking for shade.' He nudged Red with his elbow. 'Could you spare a swallow of that beer?'

Red handed him the can and he drank and handed it back, then he leaned back against the broad trunk of the oak and smoked his cigarette for a few minutes, staring out into the dense green of the woods.

'You are a smart kid,' he said, talking in that low, flat way he had. 'You'll get away with more than most 'cos you're quick in mind and body. But, Red, you do have a knack for pissing people off, so you got to stay sharp.' He slid his hand under the cushion the boy sat on. Red yelped and jumped to his feet.

He came up with a small plastic bag between his first and middle fingers. Red's stash: the dried remnants of cannabis leaf. 'You can't stay sharp when you're stoned, kid.'

This guy hadn't called Red 'kid' since he moved in with them. Red felt his disapproval, and that he'd earned it, too.

'I understand why you're mad at your momma – and me, too. But, Red, your momma's had enough troubles – she does not need the sheriff's office coming around, and she does not want to lose you to the system.'

'Did you say something to her?' the boy demanded, on guard again, ready to come out fists swinging. 'Did you tell her about this?'

The man sighed. 'For a smart kid, you sure can be dumb. If I'd a told her, she would be here right now, filled with righteous rage, and she would not be sharing no smokes with you, neither.'

'Oh,' Red said. 'Okay.'

The boyfriend laughed and Red scowled, asked him what it was he found so damn funny. But he just laughed harder and slapped him on the shoulder and said, 'That was as near as you ever got to saying you was sorry, son. '

Red shrugged. He guessed he *was* sorry. The big redneck could've come in and broke up his den, but he didn't.

'I'm about to head back,' he said, putting his baseball cap back on. 'You coming?'

'You go on,' the boy said. 'I need to pick up some trash.'

'Want some help?'

'No,' Red said, stooping to pick up a few scraps. 'It's my mess, I'll clean it up.'

'All right.' The man handed the slim bag of weed back to the boy, but did not let go right off. 'Think about what I said, okay, Red?'

'Uh-huh,' the boy said, but could not meet his eye.

'Good,' he said, ''Cos that really coulda been a black bear creeping up on you, and I do not want to come up here one day and find nothing but meat and entrails under that tarp o' yours.'

14

Method Exchange Team Headquarters, St Louis, Missouri

The Method Exchange team were working around the conference table at Brentwood PD in St Louis by 8 a.m. It could take weeks to track down and verify all they needed to complete a full ViCAP entry for Kyra Pender, but Valance had stayed late to input information on her eight-year-old son, John, into the National Centre for Missing and Exploited Children database.

They had a new discovery, Rita Gaigan, who seemed worth a look. Fallon Kestler, Rita Gaigan and Kyra Pender were all single parents, all former sex workers, each with one pre-pubescent child and a history of drug abuse. Fallon Kestler had disappeared three and a half years before. Rita Gaigan vanished from her trailer home a year later Kyra Pender a year and a half after that. Neither Rita's nor Kyra's sons had been found. Fallon and Rita had been cremated because their families couldn't pay for interment. Kyra was buried in a communal plot, so they might be able to recover her body if they needed it, but for the other two, they would rely entirely on autopsy photos and Medical Examiners' or coroners' reports.

The temperature outside was in the high eighties, humidity about the same, but the air conditioning kept the room at a steady 65 °F. For four hours, the team scoured the reports, each in their own idiosyncratic way: the CSIs and DCI Simms compiled lists of similarities and differences; Dunlap made summary notes for each woman on sheets of paper that he laid side by side, like playing cards; the FBI analyst used a bullet-point system, and he plotted each case onto a wall map using self-adhesive dots and Post-it notes; Valance seemed to be working with a computer program, while Ellis tore backwards and forwards through the case files like he had lost a hundred-dollar bill in amongst the sheets of paper.

By midday, they were ready to share. Simms went to one of the whiteboards.

'I'm having difficulty holding all of this in my head – d'you mind?' she said, picking up one of the marker pens.

'Go for it,' Dunlap said.

She quickly sketched a summary chart, entered the victims' names, last known addresses and where they were found, then invited the team to contribute while she acted as scribe.

Victims	Last known address	Body found	Cause of Death	Physical evidence
Fallon Kestler (26) & Mae-Beth (9), daughter, (found with mom).	Trailer Park near Rolla, Phelps County, MO.	Marsh off I-44, Nr St Roberts, Ft Leonard Woods, Pulaski County, MO.		
Rita Gaigan & Trey (10), son (still missing)	Trailer Park Near St James, Phelps County, MO.	Hwy 86 nr the Wildcat Glade, Newton County, MO, near border with OK.		

Victims	Last known address	Body found	Cause Of Death	Physical evidence
Kyra Pender & John (8), son (still missing).	Trailer park near Union, Franklin County, MO.	Pond, Forest Park, St Louis Metropolitan area, MO.		

'Kyra and Fallon both had broken ribs,' Valance said.

Simms entered the details into the chart.

'And all three victims had glue residue in their hair,' CSI Roper said. 'Fallon and Kyra's autopsies said it was on the skin of the upper face and adhering to the hair at the temples. Rita – we don't know. Cause of death recorded as asphyxia. She had petechiae on the inner surfaces of both upper eyelids, "bruising" to her lower ribcage and liver – no specifics.'

'Well, who's got the pictures?' Ellis said.

The CSI shook his head. 'We don't have autopsy photographs for Rita.'

'So we go back to the pathologist on that one,' Simms said over a huff of disgust from Ellis.

'Both Rita and Kyra had petechiae on their eyelids,' Dunlap said. 'Any clue what caused Kyra and Fallon's broken ribs?'

Roper shook his head. 'The ME couldn't identify the cause, but he was sure they *weren't* caused by blunt-force trauma.'

'Okay, so, similar pattern of injuries,' Dunlap said. 'Let's look at other similarities.'

'Obvious one – they all lived on trailer parks,' Simms said. 'And they'd all moved into a new area a few months before they disappeared.' She noted the number of weeks under 'Last known address' on the board.

The FBI psychologist had made no comment. Dr Detmeyer struck Simms as an observer rather than a leader, contributing when he felt he had something that might be useful, but remaining unselfconsciously silent if he had nothing to add.

Valance seemed to be working on a theory, puzzling

through something on his computer screen and jotting down numbers into a notebook at his side. He asked her to add an extra column saying when they were found, Simms obliged and they continued. When the physical evidence section was complete, she stood back and studied what they had.

Name	Last known address	Body found	Cause Of Death	Physical evidence	Date – before present
Fallon Kestler (26) & Mae-Beth (9), daughter (found with mom).	Trailer Park near Rolla, Phelps County, MO **Resident 12 weeks**.	Marsh (swamp) off I-44, Nr St Roberts, Ft Leonard Woods, Pulaski County, MO.	Unknown. Two broken ribs – not Blunt Force Trauma.	Cargo netting, bound with cord. Rocks to weight. Glue residue in hair at temples.	42 months.
Rita Gaigan & Trey (10), son (still missing).	Trailer Park Near St James, Phelps Count, MO **Resident 10 weeks**.	Hwy 86 nr the Wildcat Glade, Newton County, MO Near border with OK, in water.	Asphyxia? Petechiae, upper eyelids, bruising abdomen, liver.	Cargo netting, rocks to weight. Glue residue in hair. Position?? No photos in file. ?? cord.	30 months
Kyra Pender & John (8), son (still missing).	Trailer park near Union, Franklin County, MO **Resident 12 weeks**.	Pond, Forest Park, St Louis Metropolitan area, MO.	Traumatic asphyxia. Petechiae. No signs of strangulation, but two broken ribs – not BFT.	Cargo netting, bound w/ grey cord – red and blue flecks. Rocks to weight. Glue residue in hair at temples.	12 months

'There's a hell of a lot of similarities,' Ellis said.

The FBI psychologist considered the question. 'We went looking for single mothers with one child; sex workers with a history of drug use. All this tells us is that these victims fit our parameters.'

Ellis was offended. 'A simple "no" would be fine.'

'But it *is* significant that they moved out of the area – changed counties, even – with a school-age child.' Detmeyer said. 'Two of those children were Child Protective Services interventions.' He shifted his gaze from the board to Ellis. 'But when a family moves from one area to another, it can take a while for a social worker to be allocated, paperwork gets jammed up . . . It almost looks like the killer was trying to cover his tracks, delay the moment when alarm bells would start to ring.'

Valance was staring at Detmeyer with a studious look. Suddenly, he opened his laptop. 'I think you're right, Doctor,' he said.

Detmeyer raised an eyebrow, but Valance missed it, his attention fully on his computer screen. 'Okay . . . when you look at the number of months between the killings, it doesn't look much like a pattern. But when you look at the actual *dates* . . . Fallon went missing around Thanksgiving. Rita, the same time of year but twelve months later, and Kyra vanished around June of last year.' Valance looked around the room, his eyes bright with excitement. 'They all went missing just before a school vacation.'

Simms nodded slowly, excitement fizzing under her skin. 'Schools are often the first line of defence for children like these; if school's out, who else is going to take notice?'

Detmeyer was thoughtful and still.

'But if it is the same guy,' Valance said, looking a bit downhearted, 'why'd he change his kill cycle? Two around Thanksgiving – a year apart, but there's a big gap between Rita and Kyra – and nothing for the last year.'

'Could be he was in prison, or sick, or out of state,' Detmeyer said.

Dunlap was watching the FBI behaviourist. 'What do you say, Doc, are we on to something?'

Detmeyer tilted his head, doubtful. 'What we have is still a little sketchy,' he said.

Ellis rolled his eyes, but Dunlap said, 'What do we need to complete the picture?' He looked around the room, inviting suggestions.

'Rita Gaigan's autopsy photographs,' Simms said.

'We'll have to bring in the physical evidence, look at it again. Start fresh.' This was CSI Roper.

'I'd like to know more about the cord used to bind the cargo netting,' Dunlap said.

'There's a cordage institute in Maine,' Roper said. 'I'll talk to them.'

'We should interview witnesses and the families again,' Detmeyer added.

Simms checked back through her notes for family connections. 'Wait a minute – Rita Gaigan's son didn't go missing until *after* Rita's body was found. The day before she vanished, she put Trey onto a bus from St James in Phelps County to St Louis, to stay with his aunt. We need to know exactly when he went missing, and what was done to find him.'

'I'll see what's on ViCAP and NCIC,' Valance said. He swiftly shut down the program he had been using to collate his notes and opened the FBI's LEO portal. He was fast and confident when it came to computer systems, and Simms was reminded of Josh Brown, Fennimore's PhD student.

'Team Adam must have been involved in the search for Trey Gaigan,' Simms said. 'Would they be able to give us some background on the search for him?'

'We can ask,' Dunlap said. 'Be good to get an unbiased opinion of the investigation. But Rita's body was found across state, practically at the Oklahoma state line. We need more people to bring in all the evidence, get the job done. The Chief here in Brentwood is on the Major Case Squad's board of directors; I'll talk to him, see if they can help out.'

'Hey.' They glanced over at Valance. He was sitting with his hands frozen five inches above the keyboard, as if he was afraid what he was looking at might vanish if he touched anything.

'You okay, Valance?' Dunlap said.

Valance was wide-eyed. 'I didn't check the databases when I got in today – I mean, what's going to change overnight, right? But the entry for Kyra Pender was flagged. Possible link to the abduction–murder of a woman, disappearance of a child.'

Ellis looked up from his note-making. '*Another* one, here in Missouri?'

Valance shook his head. 'This one's in Oklahoma.'

15

Williams County Sheriff's Office, Oklahoma

Deputy Abigail Hicks smoothed her hands over her hair to check for loose strands. Sheriff Launer had called her into his office, and she figured it could not be good.

He sat behind his desk, looking like the realtor he was at heart. His uniform was crisp and fresh, his cheeks smooth-shaved. A box of flyers sat on his desk; a sample stuck to the side of the box showed his smiling face and listed his achievements, which included a reduction in drug crime by 30 per cent.

'Missed you at the debate last night,' Sheriff Launer said. He and his campaign rival had been in a head-to-head at the local Baptist church in town.

'Sorry about that, Sheriff. I was working late.'

He chuckled. 'So I heard.'

Her SUV parked up outside the only motel in town from midnight to 2 a.m.; the small-town gossips must've had the phone lines glowing white hot. *Smart move, Abigail.*

Defending herself would only make it worse, so she cleared her throat, said: 'The debate go well?'

'Never mind that,' he said, with a smile. Sheriff Launer had the slick good looks of a soap star and the smile of a shark.

'I don't recall seeing you at the office yesterday.'

'I had a day owing, sir.'

'You took a day owing, but were working late, *and* you took your police vehicle across the county line without permission.' His mouth set in a hard line. 'Explain that to me, Deputy.'

Crap. She took a breath and launched in. 'It was police business, sir. The girl found up at the Guffeys' farm? We got an ID – she was from Adair County—'

He waved a hand, cutting her off. 'Laney Dawalt, yes – I got the memo.'

'I went over there to—'

'You can put the details in your report,' he interrupted again. 'I thought I told you to do the paperwork on the body in the pond, Deputy.'

'Yes, sir. Paperwork's all up to date.'

He narrowed his eyes, scrutinizing her for signs of disrespect. Hicks stared at the nail on the wall behind him, where he hung his Peace Officer's certification, and after a few difficult moments, he said, 'Let me be clear on this: I do not like my deputies swanning off with Sheriff's Department ordnance without my permission.'

The Sheriff did like to call police vehicles and weaponry 'ordnance': it reminded people of his military background.

'Laney was murdered, sir,' she said. 'Her little brother was with her when she went missing, and he is still missing.'

He sat back in his chair, his hands on the desk in front of him, fingers loosely interweaved. 'Why didn't I know this?'

'I was going to put it in my report, sir.'

Anger flashed in her boss's eyes and Hicks stood rod straight. She was tired and a little hungover, but throwing Launer's words back at him was plain stupid. She focused on his Peace Officer's certificate again, waiting for the slapdown.

The first surprise was that it didn't come; the anger dissipated, leaving a look in his eye she couldn't quite read.

'Laney and the boy were from Adair County?'

'Yes, sir, they were living in Adair, but the killer brought her here, so—'

'So, technically, the abduction is Adair's case.'

'Technically,' she said, fearing that her plans to bring in Team Adam had fallen at the first hurdle, but willing to give it one more try. 'But, sir, Adair don't *want* it.'

He leaned forward, eyes gleaming. 'Good,' he said. 'That's good for us.'

'It is?'

'Best news I've had all week,' he said. 'Here's what you do: get everything you got onto the NCIC database. And the whatjamacallit – the Missing Kids website.'

'Yes, sir. I mean, I got case details up on NCIC and NCMEC last night, sir,' Hicks said.

He quirked his eyebrows. 'You *did* get a lot done with your day.'

'Like I said – working late.'

Sheriff Launer smiled his shark smile. 'All right, I'll give you that one, Deputy. You should hear from Team Adam today. When you do—'

'I already did, sir.'

'You did?'

'I got a call from NCMEC early this morning. They said they could send a Team Adam consultant from Tulsa just as soon as we want.'

'What did you tell them?' The skin around his mouth tightened, and she wondered if he was about to turn on her again.

'I said I would talk to you about it, check it was okay.'

'Well, get back to 'em, tell 'em to come on over, and welcome. We could sure use their kind of firepower. Those guys're goddamn heroes since Katrina.'

Now she understood Sheriff Launer's thinking: the whole nation had seen the TV coverage of tearful families reunited, kids swept up in the arms of moms and dads they had not seen in months since the hurricane, law officers standing in the background, all smiles. It was the last few weeks of Sheriff Launer's election campaign. Right now, he was picturing himself on TV screens in every household in Adair County with Team Adam. Those guys *were* heroes – righting wrongs, standing up for family and the sanctity of childhood innocence – and Launer was thinking some of that heroism was bound to reflect on him.

She had met two Team Adam consultants at the Mountain Home Conference last spring. Good men, both. Old school, modest, though they must've had thirty-five years' experience of homicide investigation apiece. They were proud of Team Adam, but their pride was in bringing lost and stolen children home; they didn't need the ego rub of personal recognition, and they did not have careers to build or maintain. Those two men were content to facilitate and mediate, and let someone else take the glory – which would leave the stage and the spotlight entirely to Sheriff Launer.

Hicks made the call to Team Adam from the desk she shared with two other deputies. A Post-it note on the desktop computer monitor read: 'Out of Order.'

The consultant allotted to the Dawalt case turned out to be one of the two she had met at the Mountain Home last April. Kent Whitmore was a big, soft-spoken man with a West Oklahoma drawl. They small-talked for a short while, then Hicks gave him the news that the Sheriff would like him to help with the investigation.

'I can be there in a couple hours,' he said. 'Is there anything you need right now?'

'Technology that works would be nice,' she said, flicking the yellow note on the computer screen.

105

'Computer problems?' he said.

'Only one in the department that works right now is in the Sheriff's private office, and we're not allowed to touch that.'

'Well, if your computer's fried, you won't have seen your email yet?'

'No, sir,' she said. 'But hold on . . .' She pulled up her sheriff's office email account on her cell phone. 'I got a message from a Detective Valance at St Louis PD.'

Always the gentleman, Whitmore said, 'I'll give you a moment.'

Her heart pounded as she read the email. 'Good Lord,' she murmured, scanning a list of common features the detective had included. 'This does look a lot like the Dawalt case, doesn't it?'

'Kyra Pender was flagged as a possible link to your victim on the NCIC database,' Whitmore said. 'You might want to talk to Detective Valance before I get there.'

'I will. And we got a partial palm print – I'll send him that, along with the files.' It was a slip of the tongue, and Whitmore was instantly on it.

'Files?' he said. 'Are we talking more than one case, Deputy Hicks?'

'I don't know, Mr Whitmore.' She glanced towards the open door of Sheriff Launer's office. She had already pissed him off, investigating a murder that could have happened in Adair; she didn't know how he'd take to her looking into a three-year-old murder in Creek County. 'Can we talk about that when you get here?'

'You bet.'

He said it without hesitation, and she remembered the watchful grey eyes of the ex-cop, and the wisdom and kindness in them, and was thankful for his tact.

She hung up and immediately dialled Professor Fennimore. 'Professor,' she said. 'We need to talk.'

16

Castle Point, St Louis Metropolitan District

Trey Gaigan's aunt had bounced from housing project to housing project around St Louis. They finally tracked her down to the dilapidated suburbs of Castle Point, about ten miles north of the metropolitan area. Dunlap and Ellis found her in a one-storey clapboard house. She showed them into her tiny living room and stared at the mess of toys and kids, clothes on the couch, as if she could will it away with the power of her mind. The sliding doors to the backyard stood open and the sound of children playing was carried in on the hot, damp air. The woman cringed at every shriek or burst of laughter. Presently, her eyes were drawn to the TV in the corner of the room, where Oprah was nodding in solemn agreement as a chiropodist talked about the importance of foot care to a general sense of wellbeing. Dunlap turned off the TV and cleared a space on the couch and she sat down, though it looked more like a slow collapse, her legs giving way under the burden of her cares. He took the chair opposite, but Ellis remained standing, his eyes tracking the room.

'I don't under*stand*,' she said. 'The police investigated when Trey went off. Those Team Adam guys came and—'

Her nasal whine was cut off by the sudden appearance of a boy, no more than three feet tall; he charged into the room, roaring, his fists raised, and his mother gave a little yelp of alarm. The boy tripped over Dunlap's long legs, but the detective caught him and set him on his feet. The boy stuck his thumb in his mouth and chewed it hungrily, struck dumb by the appearance of two large men in his house. Ellis glowered at the boy and he jumped, turning one-eighty degrees, and ran back the way he'd come, clearing the steps to the backyard at a leap.

The woman sighed as if she had been holding her breath and pressed her palm to her forehead. 'I forgot what I was saying.'

'You were telling us about Team Adam,' Dunlap said.

'Oh,' she said, 'yes. They gave us that TV.' She looked vaguely at the screen and her brow furrowed, as if she could not imagine why it was blank. 'But it's like I *told* them, Trey wasn't *missing*, he ran away. He was *always* running away. I can't say *how* many times he ran away from Rita. It's just something he *does*.'

'But he came back all the other times,' Dunlap said.

She stared at him, perplexed. 'Well, *yes*, but only because they caught him.'

Ellis shifted his weight and Dunlap sensed his impatience. 'Why don't you tell us what happened?' he said.

'Nothing *happened*. Rita sent him here – well, not *here*, exactly – we were up in Benton Park West right then. It was a small apartment – I mean *tiny*. The kids had to be out on the street – they just had to – I didn't have *time* to watch Trey as well. And she was supposed to wire me some money, but she never did.' Ellis *tsked*, and she blushed. 'Of course, I know *now* that Rita *couldn't* send that money because she was, you know . . .'

'Dead?' Ellis said.

Dunlap shot him a warning look, and Ellis shrugged and

wandered off to the doors to the back garden, his big frame blocking the light. The children must have felt the shadow of his presence, too, because the screaming stopped and a nervous silence fell.

'What made you think Trey ran away?' Dunlap asked.

'He *said* he would. Said he didn't have to stay with me. He *hated* living with us. He hated the baby keeping him awake nights. Hated *me*.' She shook her head at the impossibility of his dislike. 'He'd go out in the morning and wouldn't come back till suppertime. I *tried* to contact Rita, to tell her to take him back, but the park manager said she moved out.' She shook her head, remembering. 'I was so *mad* at her, leaving me with another mouth to feed. Then they found her . . .' She wiped her nose with a trembling hand. 'The apartment was so small. The kids had to play on the street – they just *had* to – I got three of my own, and Trey was getting big—'

'It's okay, ma'am.' Dunlap patted the air with his hands. 'Just tell me what happened.'

'The police came, told us ab—about Rita. Trey – he wouldn't talk to me, or the police. He just stopped talking – I mean altogether, like he was dumb or something. To be honest, it was a relief. Then, about, I don't know . . . *two* weeks later? I called the kids in for supper, like normal, but Trey was gone.' She reached out to touch his hand, but drew back before she made contact, put her fingers to her lips instead. 'But he was *fine*. I *knew* he was, 'cos of the postcard.'

'What postcard?' Dunlap said.

She blinked, her eyes wide. 'The one Trey sent.'

Dunlap relayed the rest of the story to the team an hour later, back at Brentwood PD. 'They put out an Amber Alert. They searched the local area for him; they went to Phelps County, where Rita had been living before she went missing, canvassed the trailer park and the wider area; Team Adam helped with state-wide news coverage.'

'They were thorough,' Detmeyer said.

Dunlap nodded. 'But they didn't find a single clue about that little boy's whereabouts. Then about a month later, his aunt got a postcard—'

'Wait a minute – *about* a month?' Valance said.

'When she got it, she left it on the TV stand,' Dunlap said. 'Didn't think she needed to tell anyone. It was only after one of the Team Adam consultants checked in on her they found out about it.'

'There must have been a date stamp on the card,' Simms said.

'It was mailed from St Louis three weeks after Trey disappeared,' Dunlap said. 'The message read, "I'M FINE. TREY". Trey's fingerprints were on it – the detectives running the investigation checked them against his stuff at his aunt's house.'

'Did Trey give the police a description of the man his mother was with?' Simms asked. Children's descriptions were often quirky, but even a vague idea of age, build and height would be better than nothing.

'He never got the chance,' Ellis said, his face hard. 'When Rita turned up dead, the boy stopped talking. I mean literally – he never said a word from that day to the day he disappeared.'

'So, we've got a probable abduction–murder in one county, body deposition in a second, disappearance of a child from a third,' Simms said. 'Where Trey ended up is anyone's guess. This bastard really knows how to cover his tracks, doesn't he?'

Ellis looked at her, startled. 'Did Princess Kate just curse?'

But Simms wasn't in the mood for jokes. 'The killer came back for Rita's boy,' she said. 'Took him right off the street because he knew Trey could identify him.'

'We don't know that,' Dunlap said.

'So where is he, Detective?'

'Maybe he really did run away,' Ellis said. 'The aunt didn't want him there; he couldn't stand her or her kids. And by the way, she's a real piece of work.'

'Then why didn't he tell his aunt where he was?' Simms said. 'Why send a card at all, if he hated his aunt so much?' Ellis shrugged, and she went on. 'Because the killer wanted the police off his back. He wrote the message, planted the boy's prints on the card and then he—' Her imagination refused to go further, because Simms really did not want to imagine what had happened to Trey Gaigan after that.

'The lead investigator on the case is coming over on his lunch break from Third District. He'll bring everything he's got, fill us in on anything that didn't go in the report,' Dunlap said.

'What's happening on the Oklahoma case?' Detmeyer asked.

'The Sheriff is territorial,' Valance said. 'He won't allow the Oklahoma State Bureau into the investigation.'

'He give a reason?' Dunlap asked.

'He was in a hurry – he was due on TV. He did say he was concerned that making this interstate might turn the investigation into a circus.'

Detmeyer said, 'TV – he's made a statement on the case?'

'No,' Valance said. 'It was local – cable TV. Sheriff Launer is on the campaign trail.'

Simms looked from Dunlap to Detmeyer and raised her eyebrows.

Valance said, 'What?'

'Just thinking that Sheriff Launer might not mind a circus if he gets to be ringmaster.'

'We got the green light from Major Case Squad,' Dunlap said. 'They'll fund an interstate investigation. Launer wants to arrange the initial meeting in Williams County, we'll move our guys over there.'

'Did you talk to the deputy who's investigating the case?' Simms asked Valance.

'Yeah,' Valance said. 'She thinks she might have another murder in Creek County, but doesn't have enough evidence to make a strong link.'

'Did you ask about cause of death?' CSI Roper asked. It hadn't been listed in the autopsy report of the Oklahoma murder on the NCIC database.

'Body was too far gone to tell,' Valance said. 'But the victim did have glue in her hair, and the victimology's the same – recovering addict, single parent – though the kid in question was her brother. Laney Dawalt went missing from a trailer park in Adair, Oklahoma, along with the kid. She was found over the county line in a farm pond in Williams County. No sign of the kid brother. Tulsa PD's diving team just finished searching the pond – the boy isn't there.'

17

There's no such thing as altruism.

Westfield, Williams County, Oklahoma

They held the first Task Force meeting in the town of Westfield, Williams County, Oklahoma. The inn where Nick Fennimore was staying was chosen as the venue: the proprietors were delighted to dust down their function room. Fennimore walked up a flight of stairs and opened the doors on to a buzz of conversation; the sharp, bitter-chocolate aroma of strong coffee was balanced by the sweet smell of warm cookies. Flyers bullet-pointing Sheriff Launer's successes during his term of office lay in three neat stacks on a table directly in front of the doors. Fennimore skimmed the list, intrigued by $60,000 dollars saved in 'creative sourcing of office ordnance'.

A portable projector screen was set up out of line of sight of the doors; chairs had been set out in rows facing the screen, and a laptop and digital-media projector on a stand in front of it. Four-foot-high posters of Sheriff Launer had been hung on the pine panelling around the room, one placed just right of the projector screen, with the American and Oklahoma State flags propped either side of his smiling image.

Sheriff Launer himself stood at the centre of a knot of deputies, beaming like a senatorial candidate, but keeping a sharp eye on the room, and Fennimore saw him notice his arrival. His gaze switched quickly to another part of the room, and Fennimore realized the Sheriff was watching Abigail Hicks walk towards him, clutching a neat black slipcase under her arm as if she was afraid to put it down.

She greeted him with a handshake.

'Is that a netbook?' he said.

'Brand new,' she said, beaming. 'Compliments of Team Adam.' It seemed they had taken her seriously when she said she could use a functioning computer. 'Best thing is, I get to keep it.'

'I'd get that in writing if I were you,' he said, thinking about Launer's election flyer and his 'creative sourcing'.

She leaned in close. 'Way ahead of you.' Her face betrayed nothing; they might have been exchanging information about the running order for the day.

Launer was working the room, shaking hands, playing the part of the good host.

'It's quite a turnout.' Fennimore had counted over thirty in the room.

'Yeah.' She scanned the room. 'We got people from St Louis Major Case Squad, NCMEC, Team Adam. The International Association of Cold Case Investigators is here, too. They want to develop a worldwide database of cold-case homicides – it's kinda new. One of the guys on their board of directors is also a Team Adam consultant – he hitched a ride out of Tulsa with the NCMEC team.'

Fennimore nodded, making a mental note to exchange details later. He scanned the rest of the room. The head of the Major Case Squad in St Louis had called him as soon as he'd learned that Fennimore was advising Williams County Sheriff's Department. Fennimore explained that he was there in an unofficial capacity, but was persuaded to attend the meeting. He recognized the detectives by the St Louis shields they wore on lanyards around their necks. A couple of CSIs with badges stitched on their polo shirts mingled with the rest. 'Who's the sombre-looking fellow in the suit?' he said.

'FBI Behaviourist,' she said. 'There's a British Chief of Police here with a CSI, too. She's here on a look-see with St Louis PD.'

His heart rate picked up a notch.

'Simpson, or Simmons,' Hicks said. 'I forget.'

'Kate Simms,' Fennimore supplied. Was she in the room right now? He searched the clusters of people, feeling that he should be able to sense her presence. 'She's a Chief Inspector, a bit lower down the chain of command than your Chief of Police – a Chief of Detectives, if you will.'

'If I will?' The corner of her mouth quirked into a smile. 'You do talk like a knight of olden times,' she said. 'Did you work with this Chief of Detectives?'

'A lifetime ago, at the National Crime Faculty in England.'

'But you knew it was her right away,' Hicks said.

Oh, she's sharp.

'We email occasionally,' he said, trying to sound casual. 'She might have mentioned that she was planning a research trip to St Louis.'

Hicks raised her eyebrows; the dark outer rim of her blue eyes giving her gaze an animal, almost wolf-like intensity.

He saw Kate Simms through the crowd. She was over by the coffee table, choosing something to eat with her morning coffee. She exchanged a few words with a young detective, smiling, and Fennimore had to stop himself from calling out her name. 'That's her,' he said. 'Let me introduce you.'

But one of the techs called Hicks over. They needed her USB 'flat', he said, so they could show the images of her victim and the location. She turned to Fennimore. 'You should go ahead,' she said. 'Say hello before we get started.'

Fennimore edged through the crowd until he was by Simms's side. She hadn't seen his approach, but as he reached past her for a plate and a cookie, she glanced over her shoulder. A light flared in her eyes, but was gone in an instant.

'Nick.' She smiled. 'Now, why am I not surprised?'

'Can I help it if we're fated to meet?'

'You're a scientist. You don't believe in fate.'

'I'm a statistician, I believe in probabilities.' He poured himself a coffee and filled another for Simms. 'Anyway, when you made it clear you were "too busy" to see me, I came five hundred miles *away* from St Louis to help with a case in a rural county, in a different state. A case which, until yesterday, had not been reliably linked to any other murder, anywhere else.'

'You've been in on the investigation from the off?'

He dipped his head, modestly.

'Is there a woman in the case?'

'Am I so transparent?' Fennimore said, his tone playful.

'As glass.'

'Half empty or half full?'

She shrugged. 'Either way, you can see right through it.'

'Have you never heard of altruism?' he said.

She gave him a sardonic look. 'Is that what they're calling it these days?'

A sudden clatter of crockery jarred him from a contemplation of Simms's eyes and Fennimore realized that Deputy Hicks, unobserved, had joined them at the table.

Kate Simms took a nibble of her cookie, eyebrows raised, looking from him to the deputy and back again. 'Glass,' she said, chuckling as she took another sip of coffee.

Her laughter sent a ripple of pleasure through his chest, which lodged at his heart and loosened something that had been growing tighter ever since she had stalked out of the restaurant in St Louis.

'Deputy Hicks,' Fennimore said. 'We were just talking stats.'

'Yes,' Simms said, her eyes dancing with laughter. 'Improbabilities.'

Fennimore made the introductions, and Kate wiped her hands on a paper napkin before offering her hand to the deputy. She smiled at Hicks. 'Outstanding job on the case,' she said.

'Professor Fennimore's been real helpful,' Hicks said.

'He can be.' For a brief moment Simms was serious. 'Just don't let him hustle you with his numbers lark.'

Maybe she was puzzled by what Simms had said, but whatever the reason, Hicks didn't answer, and after an awkward silence Simms excused herself and headed over to the St Louis team.

A second later, Sheriff Launer appeared at Hicks's side. His shirt looked like it was fresh out of the packaging and his hair was suspiciously brown for a man in his early fifties.

'You ready for the Show and Tell, Deputy?' He was affable, even smiling, but his smile had a ferocious quality, revealing too many teeth, and it was clear to Fennimore that he intended the 'Show and Tell' remark as a put-down.

He got no reaction from Deputy Hicks; she looked at her boss with her intense, hunting-wolf eyes and said, without rancour, 'Yes, sir, I'm ready.'

'I'll handle the introductions, then you can take the floor.'

'Talking of introductions, sir, this is—'

'Your pet professor.' Launer stuck out his hand, beaming, and, as Fennimore took it, the Sheriff gripped his arm with his free hand, just above the elbow. 'I hear she's been keeping you up at night.'

Fennimore let go of the handshake, but the Sheriff kept a grip on his upper arm, squeezing the muscle as if testing for bulk and tone.

'Nice meeting you, Professor,' Launer said, loosening his grip and finishing with a friendly pat to Fennimore's shoulder. 'Well, c'mon, Deputy Hicks,' he said, still beaming. 'It's your time to shine.'

Detective Dunlap spoke first. He began with a valediction

117

to Sheriff Launer, thanking him and the county for their hospitality, and praising Deputy Hicks's work in flagging up the link to the St Louis murders and finding the partial palm print on the invoice copy. Fennimore was impressed by the man's calm authority.

Sheriff Launer stood next. He beckoned to someone at the back of the room and, as people turned, the doors from the landing opened and a man carrying a camera and a woman with a notebook stepped inside.

'Come on up,' he said, positioning himself between the two flags. 'This is Merl and Shona from the *Westfield Examiner* – covers the entire county. Won't take but a minute, folks,' he said.

Glances were exchanged, but no one commented. The photographer had been well briefed. Merl snapped three of the Sheriff on his own, standing in front of his own image, striking the same pose, smiling the same smile, so that he looked like an infinity reflection in a mirror. Launer asked the FBI agent up. Detmeyer hesitated, but seemed to decide it could do no harm and submitted to a handshake, Launer grinning like a toothpaste ad, the FBI agent sombre and unsmiling. Finally, the Team Adam consultants were asked to join him for the photo op. As he shook their hands, Launer said, 'Here in Williams County, we care about family values.' He spoke slowly, glancing at Shona with her notepad, making sure she was getting it all down. 'Having discovered a connection to murder–abductions in Missouri, this sheriff's office has brought together the St Louis Major Case Squad, the Federal Bureau of Investigation and those wonderful guys from Team Adam to see if we can't solve this case.'

Fennimore glanced cautiously around the room. These were experienced law-enforcement officers; they didn't reveal anything in their faces, but he could feel the tension like the silence before a thunderclap.

'I cannot speak for the other agencies present,' Launer said, and someone coughed. 'But neither I, nor anyone on my team will rest until Laney Dawalt's killer is brought to justice, and little Billy Dawalt is home with his daddy.'

The press dispensed with, Sheriff Launer yielded the floor to Deputy Hicks. He stood to the side, but still in her line of sight, his arms folded, watching her avidly. She presented the evidence she had in a clear, unshowy way, tolerating interruptions and asides from Launer with good grace. Dunlap was the first to speak up when she invited questions from the floor.

He said, 'Our victims had recently moved counties – would you happen to know how long Laney Dawalt had been living at her last address?'

'She moved back to Adair nine weeks before she disappeared,' Hicks said, without hesitation. 'Before that, she was just outside of Chandler, Lincoln County.'

'Did you talk to anyone there?'

'Haven't had time yet,' she said. 'But if Sheriff Launer will—'

'Anything you need, Deputy Hicks,' he said smoothly, all white teeth and insincerity. 'We just want that boy home safe, don't we?' He spread his hands like a Baptist preacher inviting an 'Amen', but apart from a mumbled 'Yessir' from two of his deputies, he was disappointed. 'On that subject, I've been liaising with Adair County Sheriff's Office – we now have DNA from Billy's mom and dad, so if that poor boy is already in CODIS, we should at least be able to identify his remains.'

No mention of Hicks's role in securing those samples. Fennimore glanced at the deputy; her face was a bland mask, but her jaw tightened and she took a deep breath, letting it go slowly.

'Did you guys go out to the Missouri victims' mobile-home parks, yet?' Hicks asked.

119

'We thought we should talk to you before deciding strategy,' Dunlap said.

Sheriff Launer shifted stance. Perhaps he didn't find the word 'you' inclusive enough, or maybe he didn't like the idea of a detective deferring to an uncertified deputy just one step up from a reserve.

A lean man spoke up. 'CSI Roper,' he said. Roper had slightly protruding eyes, suggesting mild hyperthyroidism. 'The glue residue in the hair – are you having that analysed?'

Launer jumped in. 'It's with the County Lab, as we speak.'

Fennimore said, 'You had a theory about the glue, Deputy Hicks.'

'Yes, Professor.' Hicks looked around the room. 'Professor Fennimore is a forensic-science consultant from Aberdeen, Scotland. He's been advising on the case.' It was a courtesy – introducing him, when Sheriff Launer had chosen not to. 'I noticed that the glue was too high up on the head to bind the mouth – I'm thinking it was more like a blindfold.' The St Louis team were making notes. 'And he cut it off before he dumped the body, taking a hank of hair.' She indicated the position, high up, either side of her own flat cheekbones.

'Could be he was taking the hair as trophies,' someone said.

The FBI psychologist said, 'Could be.'

'The professor thought the killer might be removing forensic evidence,' Hicks said.

'If he did take trophies, it might help us further down the road,' Detmeyer said. 'But if he cut the hair to remove evidence of a blindfold, it could tell us something we could use right now, in our search. It may be that he can't stand to be looked at, which means he could have a physical disability or scar.'

'If it's the same guy, I don't see him showing visible scars,' Hicks said. 'He blends right in.'

'Okay.' Detmeyer paused, taking his time to think it

through. 'If he isn't covering their eyes to hide disfigurement, a blindfold would suggest that he *did* know the victims, and knew them well.'

'What is that?' Ellis asked. 'Guilt?'

Detmeyer shook his head. 'Even sociopaths will cover the eyes, or even the whole face, if it's someone they know.'

Kate Simms introduced herself. 'Laney went missing how long ago?'

'Six months,' Hicks said.

'And she and Billy were living with a man in Adair.' Hicks gave a brief nod, and Simms went on: 'Did you get a description of the man?'

'Their trailer was off the main grid,' Hicks said. 'Added to that, the near neighbours said he was away a lot.'

'Did you get a description or not?' Launer demanded.

Hicks fixed the Sheriff with her bright blue stare. 'I did, sir, I'm just not sure how reliable it is. The only thing they'd agree on was he had a beard and wore his hair long.'

'Well, that narrows it right down,' Launer said.

'Is it possible she hooked up with the killer while her boyfriend was away?' Simms asked.

'She got clean in prison, went to NA meetings after she got out,' Hicks said. 'The ME says so far as she can tell, Laney was off drugs when she died. And in the two months she lived in Adair County, the only male caller was the guy she was living with.'

'Come *on*, Deputy.' Launer smiled, glancing at the rest as though he was embarrassed for her. 'You said it yourself – the neighbours couldn't even agree what he looked like. Did you think maybe that's because it was *different* guys they saw?'

'No, sir.'

The smile seemed to slide around his face as Launer tried to come to terms with being told 'no'. 'Would you care to explain?'

'They didn't agree on the boyfriend, but they were sure

about his car – he drove a small European compact, grey or blue-grey,' Hicks told him. 'That was the *only* car they ever saw. Laney lived quiet. Her brother went to school. Adair Sheriff's Office had twenty-two call-outs to the park in the time she was there, and not one of those was related to Laney.'

Fennimore saw nods of approval: for one person to have completed so much investigative work in such a short space of time was impressive.

'Would now be a good time to go through what we have on the killings in Missouri?' This was Detective Dunlap, the African-American St Louis cop. They already knew some of it from ViCAP, and the similarities between Laney Dawalt and their three victims was striking. Dunlap pulled up a chart listing the similarities between the cases on the projector screen.

'Tulsa PD's dive team recovered grey rope in the pond where Laney was found,' Hicks said. 'I have a picture . . .' She riffled through the papers in front of her. Simultaneously, CSI Roper clicked through evidence photographs on the projector monitor. Hicks slid a glossy colour photo from mid-pile at the same moment he retrieved the image of the rope. She strode to the front and held the print photograph up for comparison.

The image on the screen showed a length of cord, greyish, with red and blue flecks woven into the braid. The rope in Hicks's photograph was stained with red mud, but it was still possible to make out the colours. There was a murmur of approval. The cord was distinctive. Every investigator valued the distinctive. Distinctive was what solved crimes. And the two samples were the same. Lifted from two dump sites of two different victims in two different states, they were the *same*.

They turned to Trey Gaigan's disappearance next. The young detective and Detective Ellis, a big solid tank of a man, gave a detailed account of their visit to Trey's aunt, and the revelation that Trey had sent a postcard after he left.

'You should look at the postcard,' Fennimore said.

'Look at it for what?' Sheriff Launer said. 'They already told you there was nothing on that card but three words and the boy's fingerprints.'

'Did anyone check the stamp?' Fennimore said, doing his best to overlook the Sheriff's alpha-male posturing.

Roper, the St Louis CSI, sat forward. 'Most US stamps are self-adhesive now. I'm sorry they ever replaced the gummed ones – those things were as good as a mouth swab for DNA.'

'He still had to press the stamp in place,' Fennimore said. 'I'm thinking low-template DNA.'

The CSI nodded. 'What we call "Touch DNA",' he explained for the rest. His foot was tapping compulsively under the table, as if he was controlling an urge to get up and sprint round the room. 'It only needs a few cells from the outermost layer of skin to get enough DNA for a match. We've been a bit behind the curve on this in the States, but they used the technique in Boulder, Colorado to clear JonBenet Ramsey's parents of her murder.'

Launer scoffed. 'That postcard must've been handled by a dozen people: postal workers, Trey's aunt, her kids, police, Team Adam.'

'I can't speak for how you do things in these parts, Sheriff,' Fennimore said, not even trying to rein back on the sarcastic tone. 'But I'm pretty sure Team Adam consultants and St Louis PD took care not to contaminate the evidence.'

'What're you implying?'

Simms rolled her eyes and Fennimore realized he'd gone too far. 'What I meant was—'

'I know what you meant,' Launer said. 'And I don't have to take that kind of shit from a chippy Brit who just blew in off the street. You think I'm some Billy-Bob from the Backwoods, scuffing up the crime scene in winkle-picker boots and spitting chewing tobacco on the evidence? Well, you should talk to Abigail Hicks about *that*, Professor.'

'Gentlemen,' Dunlap said.

'No, really – you guys should know what you're dealing with. The reason why you don't have enough evidence for a link to the Creek County murder is *she* screwed up.'

Hicks fixed the Sheriff with her bright blue stare.

'Did you think I wouldn't know?' Launer said, grinning. 'Why d'you think you never got past the six-month probation period?'

Hicks dropped her gaze and stared at the floor, her whole body rigid.

Surely, Fennimore thought, even Launer wouldn't humiliate one of his own team in front of six different agencies?

The two Team Adam consultants were seated near the back of the room, but one of them stood up, a tall man of fifty-plus years with a bald head and a grey goatee. He had the height and physical presence to draw every eye away from Deputy Hicks to him.

'Kent Whitmore,' he said. 'Team Adam.' He spoke in a Midwestern drawl, his voice deep, and it carried easily to the front of the room. 'We really appreciate what you said, earlier, about the work we do, Sheriff.'

Launer was still puffed up, ready for a fight, but he couldn't tell the consultant to shut up and sit down, so he stuttered out a few incoherent words.

'Well, that's very generous of you, Sheriff Launer, sir,' Whitmore said, as though he had been charmed by Launer's eloquence. 'And we're truly honoured to be invited here. Whatever you need, we'll do all we can.' He nodded towards the projector screen. 'If you guys could break down what's needed, we could get straight to work. For instance, if you need to hurry up Mr and Mrs Dawalt's DNA workups from the samples Deputy Hicks tracked down, we can pay for a private lab to get it done. And if you want to circulate information to law enforcement in a wider area, we can get word out to every state you want us to.'

He was telling them what they already knew, while giving Hicks credit for her good work on the case. His mild tone and his self-deprecating words were a reminder of what they were here for, and Fennimore felt ashamed to have allowed himself to be rattled by the Sheriff when Deputy Hicks had risen above his jibes.

Launer wasn't stupid, he knew he'd been outflanked; he could not return to Hicks's 'screw-up' without making himself look petty and foolish, but the alpha male in him still felt the need to assert his authority.

'Mr Fennimore, I'm sure Deputy Hicks appreciates your help, but we got it from here,' he said. 'So, if you don't mind . . ?' He raised a hand inviting Fennimore to use the exit.

Hicks's head came up. 'Sir, you can't just tell Professor Fennimore to leave. He—'

Launer drew a bead on her. 'What did you say, Deputy?'

Fennimore stood. 'It's okay. I'm leaving.'

Dunlap began to protest, but Fennimore insisted. 'Seriously, better that I go. In a multi-agency investigation, you should remember to check your ego at the door. I'm afraid I left mine in my top pocket with the battery fully charged. If you want me, you know where to find me.'

18

Main Street, Westfield, Williams County, Oklahoma

Deputy Hicks found the Professor at Danley's, a bar halfway down an alley off of Main Street. A sign on the door read: 'No firearms – concealed or open carry. No exceptions. That's The Law!' The shopfront window at Danley's was meant to let in light, but a flashing Budweiser sign blocked most of it. Inside, the place was just big enough for five tables and a fifteen-foot-long bar covered in hammered copper.

Abigail Hicks was in uniform, and when she walked in a couple of chairs scraped on the painted wood floor – a reflex reaction – nothing to be alarmed about, but something to keep in mind when she had to decide what part of the bar-room it was safe to turn her back on. She noted that the sound had come from a table in the far-right corner, next to the bar. Three men sat in the dark of a recess under the stairwell, staring out at her like coyotes under a deck. They had dark hair and two of them had full, dark beards, which only seemed to make their eyes gleam all the more bright and dangerous. A ceiling fan turned overhead, not doing much except to stir up the reek of beer, sweat and testosterone.

Fennimore was at the counter with his back to the door and, seeing those characters sitting in the shadows, she felt a shiver of anxiety on his behalf. He was drinking with Bob Ross, the fishing bait guy, which would offer him some protection, but only for as long as Bob-the-Bait stayed sober. Bob was a tough old countryman who believed in old-style hospitality to strangers, but it went without saying that hospitality involved alcohol, and while in his heart Bob was country gracious, in his cups he forgot his love of both friends and brethren and became a mean, moon-cussing, bloodlusting drunk.

The bar owner kept a baseball bat under the counter, Oklahoma State Law making it a felony to take a gun into a bar. He nodded to Hicks, but his eyes kept moving, watching every man in the room, not hurrying, showing no hint of worry, just letting them know he was awake and he was watching.

Hicks slid onto the stool next to Fennimore, side on to the bar so she could keep the three coyotes under the stairwell in her sights.

'Get you anything, Deputy?' Danley asked.

'I'm good, thanks, Dan,' she said.

Fennimore was in murmured conversation with his drinking buddy, but hearing her voice, he looked around.

'Deputy Hicks!' He sounded affable, and only a little drunk, and she was hopeful the same was true of Bob-the-Bait.

'You're a hard man to find,' she said, omitting his name – in Danley's bar, the less people knew about you, the safer you were likely to stay.

'You should've called,' Fennimore said.

'I did. And when you switch your cell back on, you'll see I left a message.'

He grunted, fishing in the side pocket of his pants for his phone. Once found, he switched it on and slipped it into his shirt pocket, missing the first time, and Hicks revised her estimate of Fennimore's level of drunkenness.

'Deputy Hicks,' Fennimore said, 'd'you know Bob Ross?'

Bob leaned forward and raised his glass in greeting.

'We've met,' Hicks said.

'The last time, she woke me up with coffee in the morning,' Bob said with a wicked grin.

'Bob . . .' she warned.

'At the town jail,' he admitted. 'I was sleeping off a drunk.'

She dismissed him with a shake of the head and focused her attention on Fennimore. 'You been here this whole time?'

Fennimore checked his watch. 'About an hour. I mooched in every store in town. I almost bought an antique Shaker rocking chair – buggered if I know why – I sleep most nights in my office, back home.'

'Man after my own heart,' Bob said. He was slurring, but had not yet reached the argumentative stage.

'Bob, here, saved me from a desperate act,' Fennimore said.

There was a paper sack on the bar next to him, and Hicks said, 'I see you did spend *something* – pick yourself up some nice lures at Bob's shop?'

'Lures?' Fennimore said, resting a protective hand on the paper sack. 'Lures! Damnable! They're flies, and dry flies at that.'

The bait man chuckled. 'We already had that conversation, Deputy. This feller's got strong feelings on the subject.'

'Damn right, I have,' Fennimore said. 'Bloody great ugly whizzy things. You might as well dynamite a river for all the finesse in hooking a fish with a lure!'

'You might want to keep it down, sir,' Hicks said, keeping her eye on the biggest of the bearded men. She thought she knew him, and he was trouble.

She stood up and reached for Fennimore's purchases, which put her between the bait guy and the professor. 'You need to come with me.'

'Am I under arrest?' Fennimore said.

'Is that what it'll take to get you out of here?'

Hicks kept her hand on the copper counter, creating a barrier between Fennimore and Bob, knowing she was taking a risk turning her back on the coyotes. She could hear them muttering, and it didn't sound friendly. She lowered her voice and leaned in to the Professor. 'Stay if you want, but there's three guys at a table under the stairwell looking at you like they have already counted the green in your billfold and are wondering how much trouble it would be to relieve you of it.' She was so close she could feel the heat coming off Fennimore's skin.

He swivelled on his bar stool and propped his elbows on the counter behind him. He seemed surprised to see the dark and dusty tables populated.

'Bob,' he said, offering his hand, 'it's been a pleasure.' He took out his wallet, and Hicks edged in front of him to block the view of those hungry faces shimmering in the dark.

They stopped for coffee at the diner on Main Street frequented by the Assistant District Attorneys, court investigators and cops giving evidence at the courthouse, Hicks feeling it would be good for the Professor to be seen around the law while she sobered him up. After his second cup of coffee, she said, 'You were lucky back there.'

'I have the feeling you're not talking about the rather beautiful Adams trout flies I just bought.'

'You need to be careful where you drink, Professor,' she said. 'There are men in these parts would spill your blood for the price of a rock of meth, and some of those men drink in Danley's Bar.'

'Okay.'

'"Okay", you believe me, or "okay", you won't go drinking in back-alley dives again?'

'Both.' He frowned, staring at some sugar crystals on the melamine tabletop. 'You know, I've never been kicked out of a case conference before.'

'You did push pretty hard.' He looked puzzled and she reflected that, for a bright guy, he was awful slow in understanding what makes people tick.

'We need to get one thing straight,' she said. 'Sheriff Launer is my problem – I will handle him.'

He pushed his coffee cup to the centre of the table with the tips of his fingers. 'I shouldn't have interfered.'

She sat back. 'Well, you're just full of surprises, Professor. And your apology is accepted.'

'It wasn't an apology, it was a statement of fact.' He paused. 'He is a nasty piece of work, though, isn't he? Always on the attack. He's got to be hiding something. What's his guilty secret?'

It seemed like today was a day for revising her opinion of Professor Fennimore. She couldn't ignore the question, but she couldn't answer it truthfully, either. *So tell him something that is true and might suffice.*

The waitress appeared from nowhere, and Hicks silenced Fennimore with a warning look. While she filled their coffee cups, Hicks calculated how much she needed to tell the Professor. He was watching her, and she could almost see his nose twitching.

When the waitress vanished back to the kitchen, Hicks told him something of Sheriff Launer's history. 'He was in the military. Served in Afghanistan.'

'A war hero?'

'He was in logistics – not that there's anything wrong with that, an army needs supplies. But he will drop small details into conversations to make people believe he fought gun battles with the Taliban and dodged IEDs to get food and munitions to where they were needed.'

'The reality was more mundane.'

'More harsh words by satellite phone than an exchange of gunfire in the theatre of war.'

'So he came to law enforcement after he left the army?' he said.

130

'When he quit the military, he worked three years at a big hardware store while he studied and got his practice hours in for his realtor's licence.'

'Wait,' Fennimore said, with a grin that told her he wasn't completely sober, yet. 'You're telling me he's an estate agent?'

'If that's what you call selling real estate in England, then I guess so. Made a good living at it, too, selling affordable homes to folks who really couldn't afford to buy. Then in 2006, sub-prime went toxic. His end of the market. And being a resourceful man, he looked around for something else.'

'And law enforcement seemed a natural career change for an ex-military man,' Fennimore said. 'He any good?'

'Oh, those years in logistics made him a natural at stretching his budget. He hired three new deputies, like his campaign publicity says – I'm one of them. But he fired three others who had got to the end of their six months suck-it-and-see contracts. He also reassigned one of his administrators to the county jail as a corrections officer – their hiring rates're lower. She quit.'

'You've researched him thoroughly.'

She shrugged. 'Just trying to understand why he's such a mean sonofabitch.' She watched Fennimore trying to work her out, showing him her blankest, blandest face. After a little while, he gave up with a shrug.

She dropped a ten-dollar bill on the table and stood. 'Let's go,' she said.

'Where to?'

'Up the road a ways,' she said. 'St Louis Task Force's request. They got a few questions they want to ask.'

19

'Let me see her face – her eyes.'

The man in black watches himself on the TV screen, sweating in that damn ski mask as he stripped the duct tape from Laney Dawalt's face, humiliated by his own dumb obedience.

The nitrile gloves he wore were dripping, literally dripping – sweat oozing out from under the cuffs; he was *dying* in the heat and humidity, but he meekly followed orders.

Laney was trussed like a turkey at Thanksgiving, her breasts flattened and pale under tightly stretched food wrap. It's sickening. Disgusting. Fergus is a sick fuck. He keeps thinking up new perversions – 'refinement', *he* calls them. Sick, sick fuck.

He watches himself on-screen, doing as he's told like a loser kid being pushed around on the schoolyard, and his head prickles with the shame of it, because he was that loser kid, and he hates Fergus even more for reminding him.

'Now,' the distorted voice says. 'Do it. Finish it.'

Laney's eyes widened as he approached. He untied the end of the rope and took the strain. He was *dog*-tired that day. She struggled, mewling, bucking against the plastic wrap, her head thrashing from side to side. Her voice was too weak for screaming by then, but she pleaded with him anyway, mouthing the words.

He eased off, paying out the line an inch at a time.

Squeak, squeak, squeak.

She stopped watching him; she looked up at the roof of the kill room, her lips moving like she was praying. He wanted to hear what she was saying and leaned in closer.

Her words sent a pleasant flush through his chest and head and he experienced a tenderness almost like love. She was praying to *him*.

'What the fuck?' Fergus yelled. 'What're you doing?'

The rope slipped. His gloves tore and he felt the burn of the rope. *Squeaksqueaksqueak.* He gripped harder and it held. And all the time Fergus cursed and abused him.

The final moments of the recording, she was quiet: a series of stuttered out-breaths, a tick in her throat as she made the effort to reinflate her lungs. Failed.

The light of terror in her eyes faded and went out, her face slackened; she was still.

'Is she dead?' Fergus's voice sounds deeper than in real life because of the distortion software.

He pinched Laney and nothing happened. 'Okay?' he said.

'Try again.'

His back was turned to the camera when Fergus issued this latest order. On the recording, he sees his shoulders tense, and feels a mix of pity and contempt for himself.

He'd wanted to scream, 'Screw you!' To crash the camera to the floor of the kill room, smash every piece of equipment in the place, then go looking for Fergus, cave his face in, ram his fist down his throat. But he didn't.

On the recording, his screen-self pinches Laney's face and ribs. No response.

'O-*kay*?' he said. 'Satisfied?'

Seconds passed.

'Make sure,' Fergus said. Bastard likes to squeeze every ounce of pleasure from The Kill. 'The Kill', like he hunted them down himself, galloping over a heather moor on a sturdy mount.

'Look.' He scratched his thumbnail down the sole of Laney's foot. 'See? Nothing.' He looked into the camera. 'She's gone, man.'

He pulled the Internet connection.

The man in black takes a cool chug of Coors, his eyes on the blank TV screen, not wanting to miss the instant the recording starts again. When it does, Laney's body is free of the food wrap, but still lying naked on the pallet, her eyes half closed. A small carryall lies open on the floor, next to the pallets – medical kit, tracheal tubes, portable respirator, stethoscope, syringes, a yellow defibrillator pack. A digital camera is set up to the side of the pallet, in view of the second camera, at the foot of Laney's body. The red light is flashing – the camera is recording.

He watches himself perform resuscitation like a pro: epinephrine kick-start, injected directly into the heart. Check pulse. Faint, but regular. Bag and mask for half a minute; move to the head, tilt back to 'sniffing the morning air' position; insert laryngoscope, tilting it up and away to lift the tongue and epiglottis and display the vocal cords. Insert tracheal tube between the vocal cords and into the trachea. Remove the laryngoscope, inflate the cuff with 15 ml of air from a syringe. Attach bag and valve, and ventilate.

He nods to himself. *Like a freaking pro.*

He has no heavy kit – just the bag and tubes – so he needs to watch the rise and fall of her chest closely, taking care not to overinflate her lungs. A minute. A minute and a half. She's not responding. He drags the mask off and wipes sweat from his forehead and face with the sleeve of his T-shirt; his mouth is stretched tight and a high whine escapes his lips.

He checks her pulse again, detects the fatal quiver of ventricular fibrillation.

Jesus, Lord. Frantic, he sets up the defibrillator, slaps pads on Laney's chest, waits for the gauge to show ready, zaps her. No response. He increases the voltage by fifty, then fifty more, weeping, muttering softly, 'Come back, Laney. Please. *Please*, come back.'

One more try. The defib is charged. He tries again. Her body jerks, one hand falls, her arm dangling theatrically over the edge of the bed. She whimpers, her eyes flutter open.

'There you are,' he says softly and rather sweetly. He feels a warmth and generosity that was once a big part of him. He has given her the gift of life.

She keens, her eyes seeking out the laptop monitor, because she knows that the shadowy figure will issue the orders, will decide what happens next. With a spurt of anger, he strides to the laptop and slams it closed.

She whimpers.

'Shhhh,' he soothes. 'It's all right. You don't have to worry about him any more – he's gone.' He brushes a lock of hair from her face. 'It's just you and me now.'

20

Singularity is almost invariably a clue.

A. C. DOYLE, *THE BOSCOMBE VALLEY MYSTERY*

Four days had passed since the big meeting. The St Louis detectives had returned to Missouri, together with Kate Simms, to follow their own lines of inquiry. Detectives were sent to every jurisdiction in Missouri where a body had been found. They worked long hours, talking to police departments and sheriff's offices, photocopying notes: police, autopsy reports, lab reports, witness statements; duplicating audio recordings of interviews; visiting evidence stores to retrieve trunk-loads of boxed paperwork and any physical evidence they could lay their hands on. They had met with Medical Examiners who walked them through their findings, providing digitized copies of autopsy photographs, slides and samples. They had talked to witnesses and potential witnesses, re-interviewed neighbours, friends and acquaintances of the murdered women, as well as schoolteachers and classmates of the missing children. Laney Dawalt had attended Narcotic Anonymous meetings, but they hadn't been able to find a link with the other victims; they kept to themselves, didn't discuss their rehab or recovery with anyone; the very anonymity of the organization made it impossible to find connections.

The British contingent's attitude to witness statements was cheerfully sceptical, but the USA detectives talked enthusiastically about finding someone whose circumstances had changed, making them more inclined to talk.

Each statement – new and pre-existing – had been read and scoured for salient facts; detectives were going through the long and tedious process of logging those details on the FBI's ViCAP database. In the UK, the Serious Crime Analysis Section in Bramshill was working in parallel, entering the same data onto ViCLAS. The two systems had been designed with the same aim: to identify links between violent crimes and catch the criminals, but they weren't designed to talk to each other, so each was put through its paces independent of the other, and the UK and USA contingents took a competitive interest in which system would give them the most useful links and leads.

Meanwhile, in Oklahoma, Abigail Hicks continued her investigation more or less alone. Fennimore had remained in Oklahoma with the dual intention of offering his guidance and keeping out of Simms's way. Launer's position had not softened, so, as it happened, he had to stay out of the Sheriff's way, too. Hicks sent email queries during the day; evenings, they talked about the case, did some fishing – though the trout fishing would have to wait till they had more time, and some daylight to cast the flies. He slept over at her place twice, sharing her bed on the second occasion.

Detective Dunlap was now heading up the St Louis Task Force. He had called Fennimore for advice the previous weekend, putting him on speakerphone so the rest of the team could chip in.

'The hospital lost the images of Rita Gaigan's autopsy,' he'd said. 'The autopsy report said her body was in fairly good shape when she was found. We need those pictures, and Chief Simms says finding things is right up your alley.'

'Oh, he's the patron saint of lost evidence.' Kate Simms.

The sound of her voice had made him smile. 'Okay. The Sheriff's office should have copies.'

'Believe it or not, we actually thought of that, Nick.' Kate again, waspish. 'They're saying that they never received the autopsy pictures.'

'The hospital records department promised to look for them, but their office is understaffed,' Dunlap had added. 'It could take months.'

'Did you try the pathologist?'

'*Nick.*' Simms again, putting all of her exasperation into that one word.

'All right,' he'd said, before she could get any further. 'You spoke to him. But did you specifically mention the missing pictures?'

'Hardly. We spoke to him before we knew they *were* missing.'

'People who deal with the dead can be a bit geeky about their craft,' Fennimore had said. 'And speaking as a fellow geek, I would definitely have taken pictures for my personal archives.'

That was two days ago. The second Task Force meeting was arranged, and Fennimore was invited. The hotel where he was staying had been designated as the Incident Command Post, and Fennimore walked into its function suite to find it filled to capacity.

Detective Dunlap greeted him just inside the door. 'Glad you could spare the time, Professor.'

Sheriff Launer came towards them, smiling through gritted teeth, looking like a pit bull with toothache. 'What the hell?' he demanded.

'He's here at St Louis PD's invitation, Sheriff.'

'You're on my territory, now, Detective.' Launer kept his voice low and the smile plastered on his face, but there was no mistaking he was furious. 'I *told* you I don't want this guy

– we got all the lab rats we need on your team. And two of my deputies are certified CSIs.'

'Did those certificates happen to come with a Ronald McDonald happy sticker on the scroll?' Fennimore said.

'*Professor.*' Dunlap's voice was a dark rumble.

Fennimore shut up.

'The Professor is consultant to the *St Louis* Task Force. You won't hardly see him,' Dunlap said, telling the Sheriff that they might be on his territory but Fennimore was not under his jurisdiction.

They were head to head, the Sheriff's grey eyes dark and flat, but Dunlap held his gaze without rancour, his own brown eyes carrying a look of calm certitude. It couldn't go on for ever – one of them had to concede. In the event, it was Launer; he stalked off with his neck stiff and his hands in fists at his sides.

'I don't think he likes me much,' Fennimore said.

Someone spoke at his shoulder. 'Stop winding him up – you might get on better.'

Kate Simms. He turned to face her, his heart skittering a little. '*He* winds *me* up.'

Dunlap looked at Simms. 'He always like this?'

'It varies.'

'Professor,' Dunlap said, 'stay out of his way.'

Dunlap called the meeting to order. Tables had been set out conference-style, to accommodate forty people; some were already seated, the rest broke from clusters of three and four and moved to join them. Dunlap asked Detective Valance to start them off. The young St Louis detective stood and moved to a laptop that had been set up on the projector table, ready for him. He was fair-haired and boyish, and seemed nervous standing in front of such a large gathering. Fennimore saw Kate Simms give him an encouraging smile.

'The hospital didn't find Rita Gaigan's autopsy pictures,' Valance said. 'But the Professor was right: the pathologist took some of his own, as teaching aids.' He slotted a data stick into the USB port of the laptop.

Rita Gaigan's body was bloated, the flesh mottled brown and green. The fingers, lips, eyes and toes had been predated by turtles and fish, but a spell of severe weather had made the animals sluggish and reluctant to feed, so it was in better condition than might otherwise be expected.

'The Sheriff's report said she was found by a guy ice-fishing,' Valance said. 'This was thirty months ago. You remember that winter.'

He got a murmur of acknowledgement.

'Broke records going back to 1923–4. Twenty-five inches of snowfall and thirty below.'

That would be Fahrenheit, Fennimore thought. Around –35 °C. He remembered BBC news footage at the time: ice storms from New York to South Texas; trees filmed in glassy ice; power lines brought down with the sheer weight of frozen water.

'Guy cut a hole and saw something dark, bumping just below the ice. He reached in, thinking to scoop out a striped bass, held Rita's face in his two hands instead.'

A collective shudder from the fishermen in the room, Fennimore included.

Valance clicked through the images on the laptop. They were sharply focused, good colour contrast. The bruising to her abdomen and chest was clear. And it was similar to the bruises they'd seen in Fallon Kestler and Kyra Pender's post-mortem pictures.

'The pathologist didn't look at these pictures until we asked for them,' Valance explained. 'Just took 'em and forgot 'em.' He clicked to a third image. A smaller, slug-shaped bruise showed on Rita's upper abdomen, towards the right side.

'This bruise isn't in the autopsy report, because it wasn't *there*.' It happened on occasions: a lucky combination of camera angle and flash showed up something that could not be seen under ambient lighting. Fennimore added the interesting bruise to a mind map he was compiling. The next image showed the position of the duct tape residue in Rita's hair. Across her forehead, and at the temples.

Patterns, he thought, adding this to his chart. He did like to see a pattern emerge.

'He used rocks from the locality to weight the bodies,' Dunlap said.

Which was disappointing: brought from elsewhere, they would represent another distinctive feature – they might even take them to a particular location.

'But we did get something on the cords from the institute in Maine.' He nodded to CSI Roper.

'It's a high-strength, low-weight double-braid,' the CSI said, springing to his feet as if he'd suddenly broken free of bonds. 'The same cord at all the dump sites, going all the way back to Fallon Kestler, three and a half years ago. It's designed for marine use – mostly for racing boat rigging. High-quality and specialized – we're checking suppliers now.'

St Louis PD had retrieved the postcard Trey Gaigan sent to his aunt. The St Louis lab was backlogged for weeks and Low-template/touch DNA analysis was delicate and labour-intensive. To speed things along, Team Adam had paid for a private lab to do the workup. They found a tiny quantity of epithelial cells from a fragment of fingerprint-ridge detail on the postage stamp.

'Male DNA,' Dunlap said. 'Not the boy's. Partial profile – only just complete enough for a search, but we do know it's not the boy's. It's running through CODIS now, but don't get too fired up – we could get dozens of hits off it.'

Lab tests and statistical analyses were aspects of any investigation that ran silently in the background. From time to time, they would throw out a useful result, a line of inquiry, even the name of a suspect; sometimes they disappointed – as with the analysis of the glue found on the skin of some of the victims. It was identified as an adhesive used in a duct tape available in every Home Depot and Walmart in the United States.

Deputy Hicks was next. The search for Billy Dawalt in CODIS had come back negative – which at least left some hope of finding him alive. Dawalt senior *was* in the system, however: he'd left blood at the scene of a burglary after he smashed a window to gain entry. The irony was, if he'd consented to the Family Reference Sample in the first place, Dawalt would still be a free man.

As good as his word, Launer had allowed Hicks to go out to Lincoln County, but he'd made it clear to her that he did not want Fennimore hitching a ride. In the event, it didn't matter: wherever Laney Dawalt had met the man she lived with, she had told no one.

'Talking to those folks was like shouting down a well: all you get is darkness and your own voice coming back at you,' she said. Nobody saw Laney with a regular guy, and when she moved back to Adair, she told no one where she was going. The first anyone knew that she was gone was when the park manager knocked on Laney's door and found the place empty.

'I spoke to the manager of the trailer park in Adair again,' Hicks said. 'He remembered something about Laney's boyfriend. Said he was a lot older than her. And he talked funny.'

Detective Dunlap glanced up sharply. 'A few people we interviewed said the same thing.'

'A speech impediment?' Fennimore asked.

'No, sir. Said he sounded like he was from back East.'

'Yeah,' Valance said, his blue eyes lighting up with excitement. 'One of them said he sounded like a "Harvard" type.' He pronounced the word with the elongated 'a' vowels of a New Englander.

They would follow that up as they continued to interview

142

trailer-park residents and former associates of the victims.

The ongoing interviews had discovered another new fact: the man living with the victims wore a maroon Oklahoma Sooners sweatshirt. Launer pointed out that this information was about as distinctive as Hicks's earlier description of the man with long hair and a beard, but the rest disagreed: football affiliations in the States were partisan and it suggested that their mystery man was from Oklahoma, rather than Missouri.

Dunlap's phone buzzed, jittering sideways on the tabletop. He checked the screen. 'The postage stamp gave us three mainland United States hits on CODIS.' This was better than they'd hoped for. Three hits meant just three suspects to track down and eliminate from the inquiry. Dunlap scrolled down the screen. 'One is dead, one in prison and . . . a Henry Connor – ex-con, living in the St Louis area.'

Valance was already checking Connor's details on the system. 'Aggravated burglary, assault of a minor.'

A ripple of excitement ran through the room.

'No current address,' Dunlap said, a hint of disappointment in his voice. 'I'll ask St Louis PD to put a BOLO out on him.' He nodded to Kate Simms to take over while he slipped to the back of the room to make the call.

'The Serious Crime Analysis Section in the UK agree that the killings seem to be on a six-month cycle,' Simms said. 'But the eighteen-month gap between Rita Gaigan and Kyra Pender means there may be victims we haven't found yet. We'll know when we have more data.'

'You want data?' Ellis, the sour-looking detective with a slab of a face and a crew cut, rested his hand on a stack of papers to his right. 'Responders to Team Adam's little infomercial.'

Team Adam had sent out a message detailing the commonalities of the cases to every State Bureau of Investigation in the United States, as well as to County Sheriff's Departments

143

in 473 counties across Oklahoma, Missouri, Illinois, Arkansas and Kansas, the killer seeming to work in a north-east/south-west corridor.

Fennimore eyed the wad of papers. 'How many?'

'Fifty,' Ellis said. 'That's what happens when you go looking for trouble: you find it. Most aren't even listed on ViCAP, because I'm told it's a pain in the ass filling out the forms.' He riffled the offence records with his thumb like they were a deck of cards. 'Fifty murders, in forty states. It'd take months to input all that data.'

Dunlap returned to the table. 'We just don't have the manpower,' he said.

'Well, we can't tell them thanks for the information, but sorry, it's too much work,' Ellis said.

'They could do it themselves,' Fennimore said.

Dr Detmeyer nodded agreement. 'It's how the system is designed to work,' he said. 'If they believe their deaths are connected with ours, it's up to them to find the personnel to get the job done.'

Dunlap said, 'Mr Whitmore, could you help with this?'

'Sure,' the Team Adam consultant said. 'We'll work out a strategy to, uh . . . motivate local PDs to input their own data.'

Dunlap's phone began to buzz again. Heads came up, focused on Dunlap. The detective excused himself, but every pair of eyes remained on him.

'Where?' he said. A pause then, 'We can have someone out there by early evening. He closed the phone and looked at the assembly, a gleam of triumph in his eyes. 'That was St Louis PD,' he said. 'They have Henry Connor in custody.'

21

**Lambert Woods Mobile Home Park,
near Hays, Williams County Oklahoma,
Friday evening**

Red made his way slowly, the trail ahead seeming to bounce from side to side on account of he was weaving just a bit. It was Friday and the start of summer vacation. He had gone to school like Momma wanted, so he reckoned he had earned his quiet beer at the end of a hard day. The beer was stolen, of course – he didn't think the pervert would fall for the same trick twice, but it turned out he was as slow in the head as he was on his feet. The plan was to sit in his den a while, drink his beer, be home by six, like he was supposed to – Momma and the boyfriend had a treat planned, a trip to the Pizza Hut in Hays, on to a movie later. But he'd smoked the last of his weed and fell asleep. Now it was getting dark, so it had to be after eight; time to head home, face the music.

Unsteady on his feet, he tripped a couple times on tree roots and rocks sticking up out of the dirt. The cicadas had been screeching fit to break window glass all day, but as dusk came, they fell silent, one by one, and now he could hear the *peep-peep-peep* of the frogs in the ponds off the track and the softer chirrup of the grasshoppers and crickets. Deep in the woods he heard a birdcall that sounded something like the rattle of two spoons knocking together;

145

close by, a scarlet tanager was whistling itself dizzy trying to claim its territory over the racket. As darkness fell, it gave up.

Red hoisted his backpack on his shoulder and jogged the last hundred yards home. He went around the trailer to the front door and stepped into the living room, blundering through to the kitchen, his head warm and buzzing from the stolen beer. He opened his mouth to call to his mom, but changed his mind: he had the munchies bad, and he would no doubt be sent to his room without his dinner 'cos he was late.

He held his breath, but there was no sound. Maybe they went without him, but he heard the rhythmic creak of the bed in her room. There was a new loaf in the bread box; he took a couple of slices and slathered them with peanut butter, then hooked a cold Sprite from the fridge, intending to take it to his own room and listen to his radio. He clamped the sandwich in his teeth to free up his hands so he could rummage through his schoolbag for his pocket Sony. He stuffed it into his jacket, hid his backpack behind a chair and took a bite out of the sandwich. Dang, that bread was good!

He got as far as the living-room divider, but heard a sound that made his blood freeze. A squeal. Not even human-sounding, more like the tormented scream of a snared rabbit.

His heart thumping, he called, 'Mom?'

No answer.

He left the sandwich and soda on the arm of a chair and tiptoed back to the kitchen, slid a knife from the block on the counter and crept to his momma's bedroom. The door was unlocked. He lifted the handle from the recess and turned it slow and careful, easing the door open as quiet as he could, to take a peek inside.

The room was in darkness and his momma lay on the bed, but he could not make heads or tails of what he saw.

'Mom?'

He took a step inside and she screamed something, but her words didn't come out right and he could not make out what she was saying.

What's wrong with her face?

She tried to get up and for a second he thought she would fly at him, but something held her back. He could not make sense of it.

'Momma?'

To his left something moved – a deeper patch of shadow near the bedroom closet. He swivelled his head and the shadow seemed to grow solid.

His mouth dried and every hair on his neck stood on end; he felt his heart hammering in his throat, beating in time with the words in his head: *Boogeyman, Boogeyman, Boogeyman, Boogeyman!*

22

St Louis, Missouri

Detectives Ellis and Valance got to the Art Deco-style building of the St Louis PD Fourth District just after 8 p.m. Royston, the beat cop who had tracked down Henry Connor, was there to greet them.

'I was on foot patrol when I heard the BOLO,' he said. 'Checked his mugshot first chance I got. Knew him straight away – I rousted this guy sleeping rough under Tucker Boulevard five nights ago, took him to the Housing Resource Centre on North Tucker.' He led them past security, down a corridor. His electronic pass key gave them entry to the interview rooms. 'The centre said they sent him to the New Life Evangelistic Centre on Locust Street. They found him a place at an emergency shelter, but he only stuck around for one night. He could've been anywhere.'

Ellis maintained a bored silence. He wasn't the type to be interested in how Connor was found, only in talking to him now that he *had* been found. Valance could tell by the stiff way his partner held himself that he was on a short fuse. Ellis wanted the patrol cop to take them to Connor and get lost.

'So, where'd you find him?' Valance asked.

'He bounced back to Tucker Boulevard.' Royston opened a

door into a meeting room. A 42-inch monitor was fixed to the wall, a buff folder lay on a chair below it, and a conference phone crouched in the centre of the table like a squashed bug.

'I don't see Connor,' Ellis said, mounting irritation in his voice.

'We have a video link to Interrogation in here,' Royston explained. 'When I said he was sleeping rough under Tucker Boulevard, I mean *right under* – in the sewers. I thought you might want to prepare yourselves.' He picked up a remote-control handset from one of the chairs and pointed it at the monitor.

The man in the interview room wore a trench coat that appeared to have been through trench warfare. His hair was hidden under a greasy cap, but if his beard was anything to go by, it would be long, dirty and matted. The skin of his face was heavily grimed. As they watched, Connor pulled the lapel of the gabardine aside and worked two filthy fingers inside a stained undershirt to scratch his chest hair. You could almost see the fleas jumping.

'This is it?' Ellis jabbed a finger towards the screen. 'This is what I came all this way to see?'

The uniform cop bristled. 'What's with him?'

Valance turned his back on Ellis; there was no talking to him when he was like this.

'He's just cranky.' He grinned. 'He'll be fine when he's had coffee and a doughnut.' Valance held out his hand. 'Thanks, Officer Royston, you went above and beyond. I'll make sure that goes in my report. Sorry it took up so much of your time.'

The cop kept his thumbs hooked in his pockets a moment longer, checking to see he was sincere. Valance held his gaze and finally Royston puffed air between his lips and extended his own hand.

'I pulled Connor's file off the system,' he said, picking up the folder from the chair under the monitor. He handed it to Valance. 'Everything you need is in there.'

Ellis waited until the patrolman was out the door before he said, 'Gee, Valance, that was nice.'

Valance rounded on him. 'What the hell's the matter with you? Connor bounced from shelter to shelter, all over town, but that cop stuck on the trail like a bloodhound. He stayed on duty after hours to meet us, set up an interview room *and* made sure Connor was ready and waiting for us when we got here. I wasn't being *nice*, Ellis, I just wasn't being an asshole.'

Ellis stared hard at him for a long time. He had earned his gold shield before Valance was even born, and the young cop was in awe of him in a lot of ways. But he *was* being an asshole, and Valance was damned if he would back down.

Ellis jerked his chin towards the video link. Connor was picking his nose and wiping his fingers on his pants. 'You see this guy charming Rita Gaigan into his car? Do you think this guy ever even *owned* a car?'

'We asked for Henry Connor, we got him,' Valance said. 'His DNA is on the postcard Trey Gaigan sent to his aunt,' Valance said. 'Come on, Ellis – we won't know if we wasted our time until we speak to the guy.'

'Well, all right.' Ellis stared at the monitor. 'But if I knew I was coming six hundred miles to sit down with a *biological hazard*, I'd've made you come alone.' He headed for the door.

'Were are you going?' Valance asked.

'Didn't you say something about coffee and doughnuts?' Ellis said.

Valance read Connor's file over coffee while Ellis refuelled with a burger and two doughnuts coated with enough sugar icing to induce a diabetic coma.

The Aggravated Assault was at Connor's ex-wife's home: Connor claimed she had unlawfully kept possession of some of his belongings after she kicked him out; she called the cops when he broke the back door window with a golf club to gain entry – she was cut by flying glass, which earned him a year in the county jail. The mugshot from that arrest showed him clean-shaven, his hair cut short; he even wore a shirt and tie. But his eyes were red-rimmed and he looked wild and desperate.

By the time he was arrested for the juvenile assault, Connor had become the man they saw today. He was arrested for swatting a kid who tried to steal his hat, which contained fifteen dollars and forty-six cents – his morning's takings from street sketching down by the Arch on the riverfront. Henry Connor was an art teacher before he lost everything to drink.

When they entered the interview room, Valance took the chair behind the desk and, as they had agreed, Ellis sat in the chair opposite Connor, their knees almost touching.

Connor reeked of old urine and a whole battalion of unwashed feet; this combined with a miasma of last night's liquor oozing out of his pores made short work of the Vick's VapoRub the two men had dabbed under their noses to mask the stink.

Valance placed the file on the desk and tapped it with one finger. Ellis snuffed air through his nose and said, 'You want to tell us about the postcard?'

He stared at them blankly, told them he had no clue what they were talking about. Valance showed him a photocopy of the card, told him the date on the postmark.

'February,' Valance said. 'Two years back. This postcard.' He turned it over to show the image of the Arch, down on the riverfront.

Connor nodded slowly. 'Oh, *I* remember that. I made double what I earned all morning on a five-minute errand. Guy paid me twenty-five dollars cash, and a quart of Jack Daniel's to address the card and go into a post office to put a stamp on it. I told him I would if he gave me his coat as well.' He frowned, remembering. 'That was a terrible winter.'

'Is that the coat?' Valance said, dreading the thought that they might have to seize the darn thing as evidence.

'No, not *this* coat – this is a summer coat.' Connor tugged the lapels of his raincoat, wafting noxious fumes from the folds of his gabardine. 'He gave me a good winter coat. Wouldn't give me his baseball cap, though. Said he needed it.'

'What kind of baseball cap was it?' Valance asked.

'Maroon,' he said. 'With a gold decal.'

Oklahoma Sooners.

'That coat saw me through two winters.'

'Okay, can we get back to the card?' Ellis said.

'Card?'

'The postcard.'

He looked blank, and Valance tapped the photocopy on the table in front of him. 'Which post office?'

Connor scratched his head, then ran one fingernail under the other, dropping scurf onto the greasy fabric of his gabardine.

'Must've been downtown. I would be street sketching down by the Arch.'

'You remember that?'

He shrugged. 'It's what I do.'

Meaning that's what he did every day.

'Where was he while you went into the post office?'

'How would I know?'

'Come on,' Valance said. 'Try. He gave you the cash and the whiskey—'

'No,' Connor said. 'He kept the booze. He waited down the street. Said he wanted to see me put it in the box before he gave me the quart of Jack.' He nodded. 'That's right – he waited down the street – I remember, now.'

Ellis and Valance adjourned to the conference room.

'He sent Connor in to avoid the security cameras,' Valance

said. All US post offices have CCTV in the lobby as well as at side and main entrances. 'The baseball cap was a precaution, in case there was a camera he hadn't noticed.'

'Or Connor's lying,' Ellis said.

Valance raised his eyebrows. 'Changed your mind about him?'

Ellis shrugged. 'The file says he wasn't always a bum,' he admitted. 'And I guess they would've cleaned him up in prison.'

Valance opened the file and they sat side by side to sift through it. 'Okay . . . Until three years ago, Connor was still teaching. We thought the perp chose to take the victims during school vacations so fewer people would notice they were gone, but what if it was because that was when Connor happened to be on vacation?'

Ellis nodded, approving the theory. 'We need to check with his ex-wife what he was doing when the earlier victims disappeared.'

'The Agg-Assault on the ex-wife was two and a half years ago – he'd lost his job by then. It was just before Rita Gaigan disappeared. He was serving a one-year sentence in the county jail. Only did . . . four months.'

It happened, when the jails got jammed up and they needed to make room.

'Was he out when Rita's boy disappeared?'

Valance checked. 'Nope. When Trey Gaigan went missing, Connor was still in jail. And the second arrest, for the assault on the juvenile, was June last year, which rules him out for Kyra Pender. He's not our guy.'

They returned to the interview room and asked Connor to describe the man who had paid him in cash and liquor to put a stamp on a postcard and mail it.

He was average height, Connor told them. Not fat or thin, just average. Mousy hair. Maybe. He had a beard, he remembered that. Then he didn't. Then he thought maybe he did after all. A goatee. Then he swore he wore a Zapata moustache.

'You do remember that bottle of Jack, though, dontcha, Connor?' Ellis said.

'I'm trying my best here,' Connor growled, glaring at Ellis. He had blue eyes, rimmed with a pale waxy deposit you'd normally only see in the very old. The whites of his eyes were yellow, as if his liver had started to leak gall into them.

'What'd he sound like?' Valance said.

'Sound like?'

'How did he talk? Was he from round here, or . . . ?' He let the question hang while the man tried to think through a fog of drink and alcohol-pickled brain cells.

After the longest time, he said, 'Midwest.'

'Okay, that's good,' Valance said. 'So was it a strong accent – real country, maybe?'

'No.' He shook his head, doubtful. 'Not strong, exactly . . . some of the vowel sounds were off.'

'Off, how?' Ellis asked.

'I don't know. Kind of flat, I guess. Asked me if I would do him a "fayvarr", it didn't sit right with the drawl.'

The two detectives exchanged a look.

He mistook it for scepticism and said, 'What can I tell you? I'm more the visual type.'

Valance had a sudden inspiration. 'You think you could maybe sketch the guy?'

'I guess.'

Connor couldn't hold a pencil – the tremor in his hands was too severe. Valance asked for a flip chart and some marker pens.

As soon as he took the pen in his hand, Connor's tremors stopped. He picked the chart up from the table and flung it to the floor, dropping to his knees after it. The two detectives shoved the table back against the wall to give him room.

They watched Connor sketch, beginning with the eyes,

moving to the chin, the hair, sketching in a shirt collar, moving back to the face, adding a line, some shading, thick brows. Three swift lines for the lips. He added a tie, a blur of shadow under the eyes. They held their breath as a face emerged from the broad pen-strokes.

Finally, Connor sat back on his heels, capped the pen and smiled up at them.

Valance gazed from the face of the man in the picture to the ragged figure of the artist.

It was a brilliant portrait. The hunch of the shoulders, the slightly dishevelled appearance. The face had the haunted look of a man on the slide, who sees his own future in the camera lens: Henry Connor on the day he was arrested for Aggravated Assault – the artist had sketched his own mugshot.

23

Red wakes in pitch darkness.

Can't see. Hard to breathe. So hot.

He feels the ground rush beneath him, stones ping against metal. He's in a metal box and he can't remember how he got here. It stinks of piss: his – he knows it's his because he peed his pants back at the trailer.

Then he remembers – he's in the trunk of a car. He feels the rustle of plastic sheeting under him and the hard edges of boxes stacked close together either side of him.

Can't breathe!

He fumbles around him, finds the handle of the kitchen knife and grips it with both hands, thanking God because now he can defend himself.

Got to get some air.

He uses his leg to push the heavy boxes towards the front section of the trunk, giving himself more room. He works his fingers into the lock lever, tries to rock it, but he doesn't have the strength, so he finds a spot under him where the plastic gives a bit and cuts a hole, then drives the knife into the corroded metal beneath, turning it, breaking through the rusted shell of the trunk. The hole is only the size of a quarter, but at least now he can breathe. The car judders and jolts over potholes, and stones rattle against the metal of the trunk. Every once in a while they glide over a smooth surface, which he figures must be a concrete slab at a crossroads – so, a gravel road, must be. He puts his eye to the rust-hole, but it's too dark to tell. He lies next to the hole, his cheek against the cool metal.

His momma was on the bed. It was dark and he couldn't see too good. She was all bandaged up—

He puts a hand to his head, trying to squash the ache out of it. No, she was not bandaged – she was *wrapped*. Made him think of the chrysalids he would sometimes find in the woods. Or a bug all trussed up in an orb weaver's web. Silver on her face – he couldn't see her mouth, her eyes—?

Because they was taped, doofus – with duct tape. Silver duct tape.

Something came at him out of the dark—

Boogeyman, Boogeyman, Boogeyman, Boogeyman!

He whimpers, tears squeezing out the corner of his eyes. But he bites down on his lower lip. *Now you stop it – you gotta think, you want to stay alive, help Momma.*

But as much as he tries, he cannot make sense of it. His head hurts from the heat and the beer and . . . Oh God, Momma screaming behind the tape, trying to warn him, telling him to get out.

He feels sick, and just about has time to get to his hands and knees as he vomits up the beer and taco chips and the bite of peanut-butter sandwich he ate. Then he crawls as far away from the mess as he can get and curls up tight, sobbing till it feels like his heart has been torn out through his chest.

24

Williams County, Oklahoma

The man has arranged cameras and lighting, testing each to be sure they will not fail. He's tense, and takes extra care, knowing that in a sense he has already failed: starting the process in Sharla Jane's mobile home was against protocol, and he had lost the boy because of it. He has to pretend that everything is normal, work out a way to get the boy back later.

His laptop is locked and loaded, ready for action, the Skype icon ready on-screen but dormant for now; he will make the webcam adjustments when he's rigged the table up to mount it on. He'll need the medium height. He chooses it from a stack of three, leaning against the side wall. The tables are beat up and heavy, and require a degree of skill to set up without injury. He decides on the position, lifts the flap with his right hand and slides the bar away from the hinge towards the stays on the underside of the tabletop, opening the scissor-jointed supports with his left.

A sudden burble of noise; his hand jerks, the flap drops an inch, trapping the webbing of his left hand in the metal joint of the table legs. He howls, wrestling with the flap, feels his skin catch and tear on a jagged piece of metal.

'Shit,' he yells. 'Shit!'

He extracts himself from the apparatus and flings the table from him, sends it clattering against the wall and clamps his hand to his mouth, sucking the blood from the wound, tasting salt and copper. He isn't ready yet. He's too damn *early*.

His phone is switched to silent; it buzzes in his hip pocket and he feels it like an electric shock to his balls. He slides the phone out and checks the screen.

A text; one word: 'Skype'.

No. No, no, NO. He takes his hand from his mouth and fresh blood gouts from an ugly tear in the web of skin between his thumb and forefinger. He jams the injured hand to his lips again. *Fuck*, it hurts!

He texts, one-handed: 'Not ready.'

A second later, the phone vibrates in his hand. Another text.

'Don't argue with me, gobshite.'

He flinches, practically hearing the harsh tones.

'NOT READY,' he texts back.

Two sharp buzzes, like a warning, then the message: 'Do as you're told.'

He has a bad feeling; this isn't eagerness for the kill – Fergus always wants everything set up the way he likes it before they make contact – he never rushes things. Fergus is pissed about something, and it's already been a tough night. The man does not feel strong enough to talk face to face, yet, so he texts: 'Email', switches off the phone, then picks up a bag he's left out of camera shot, rummages through the sterile packs, extracts a bandage. It'll take Fergus a moment to log in.

They set up a Gmail account with a nondescript email address: a jumble of numbers and letters. They both have the password, yet neither has ever sent an email from it. A one-word text: 'Email' lets the other know to check the account.

To the service provider it looks like a dormant account, and since no emails are sent, there's no trail for law enforcement to follow back to the service provider.

The man covers the torn flesh with gauze and tapes it in place, wrapping it with a sterile bandage. You can*not* be too careful with cuts.

Feeling calmer, he opens the Gmail account. His accomplice is paranoid about deleting emails before he logs off, so there is only one message in the drafts folder.

The subject line reads, 'Answer the Skype, fuckface.'

Simultaneously, the Skype bubbles and pings, letting him know there's an incoming call. He rejects it, his stomach cramping. The other man is thousands of miles away – it's not like he can *do* anything, but since they've known each other, Fergus has always been able to say, 'Do this' and it's done.

The Skype alert sounds three, four, five times in the space of a couple of minutes. *Fuck it.* He turns on his phone and finds a half-dozen texts, all of them offensive, calling into question his intelligence, his manhood, threatening him.

His hands shaking, he texts, 'I told you, I'm not ready.'

'Don't you dare defy *me*.'

Too angry to be intimidated, he blasts back: 'Defy you? I'm not your goddamn puppet.'

'If you were, I'd cut the strings and walk away right this fucking minute.'

'What is WRONG with you?'

'Ask me why I checked in early.'

This makes him nervous. He hesitates, and a new text message pops up: 'Google Alerts sent me a wee message: you got yourself on the state TV network, you *wanker*.'

He feels a stab of sudden, blank terror.

The text alert sounds again. His hand jerks, and he almost drops the phone.

'They found Laney just outside Hays. And where are you

now? My top-of-the-head guess – very fucking nearby.'

He feels the muscles of his face go lax. *Oh, God. Oh, God . . .*

He looks at the screen, and realizes he flipped out for a second; there's another message:

'Rule No. 1: Do not shit on your own doorstep.'

Like I don't know that. Like I don't fucking know it.

The next message is short. 'They didn't find Billy. So, the sixty-four-thousand-dollar question is: Where *is* Billy?'

He texts back, his hands shaking. 'I took care of him.'

'You put him in a good foster home?' Fergus texts. 'Aw . . . that's sweet.'

Shit. *Shit!* He knows.

A soft whimper from behind him. He tenses.

'Please, be quiet,' he whispers. 'Let me think.'

Three years ago, he was lurking on the forums, reading wannabes blowing off about stuff they had plainly not done. He had just videotaped the light going out in Shayla Reed's eyes; hc had the moment between life and death right there on tape. He thought, *I could show them the real thing, make money.* But Fergus nixed it – said it was 'too risky'. He did as he was told, the videos stayed private and he stayed poor.

Until a thought came, like a whispered secret: *He didn't say anything about the kids.*

There's a special name for prostitutes who work the interstate truck stops – they call them 'lot lizards'. Park in a truck stop on any interstate highway hoping for few hours' sleep, you better have a sign in the cab window; you don't, those girls will pound on your door till you would shoot them just to get some shut-eye. Most of them are so strung out they would do most anything to please you, and if your tastes run to younger flesh, or boys, or the plain weird, you'll find their pimps just yards away, ready and primed to act as your very own personal sex shopper. So, he reached out, exchanged a kid for cash, and then another.

'You sold him, didn't you?'

Jeez, what kind of freaky ESP *was* this? How could he know? But he did, and it was pointless to deny it.

'I have costs,' he texts. 'Overheads.'

The pause before the next message is unbearable, so that when the Skype alert sounds, he's almost relieved. He sets up the table, finds the ski mask in his ready-bag and drags it over his face. It's instantly stifling, and he flicks the switch for the floor fan as he opens the link.

Fergus is sitting in his croft. He can tell by the flicker of firelight on the whitewashed walls. As usual, he has arranged the webcam so his face is in shadow; as usual, his voice is distorted. But they both know that even disguised, even at this great distance, seeing the man, hearing his words if not his voice, still has tremendous power.

'So,' Fergus says. 'You fucked up. Again.'

He stands mute. Every woman he's ever been with said he was a smooth talker, but when he's in a face-off with Fergus, he can never find the words.

In the background, the soft snuffling begins again, and Fergus forgets himself, suddenly leaning forward, eager, his hands on the arms of his chair as though he's ready to leap out of it, forgetting even that he's mad about Laney and Billy. He moves too far forward and his face is lit for an instant by the lamps he arranged so carefully to put him in shadow. Fergus jerks back, but his voice is tense, hungry.

'Is that her? Let me see.'

Behind him, Sharla Jane snuffles and groans and he wishes he'd gagged her, because right now he needs to think.

'I *said* I want to see her.'

'Aren't you the one always talks about delayed gratification?'

Fergus clenches his fists, and he sees a flash of teeth.

'Okay. Let's chat.' He settles back in his armchair. 'Where shall we start? Oh, I know. Did you know that your friendly local sheriff has been talking on his local radio station in

Shit Town, Oklahoma? He said he wanted to find "Li'll Billy Dawalt". Said he'd "found a connection" between Laney's murder and some murders in Missouri. Are you with me so far? You understand the subtext? They're talking about a *series* of murders. The networks love a serial killer, so they pick up the broadcast, take it state-wide. It's all terribly exciting because now it's not just Sheriff Shit Town bumbling about with a clipboard – now, there's an interstate task force investigating: the FBI is involved. They're so fired up, they've even drafted in help from the British police. Which is FAR TOO FUCKING CLOSE TO HOME FOR ME.'

The man in the ski mask lowers his head and grits his teeth like he always does when Fergus is on a rant. His hand is throbbing from the cut and sweat is streaming off him. He wishes he could peel off the mask, but he doesn't have the courage.

'Do you know how many bodies have turned up?' Fergus asks.

He shakes his head, miserable, mute.

'No?' Fergus says. 'Me neither. But for every disposal you fucked to shite, they *will* make a link. Inside of a week, every one-horse town who ever had a female floater will realize there's political capital in this story, and maybe some financial capital too. They'll step forward into the TV spotlight, clutching their post mortem photos, demanding justice for the dead. And some of the dead will be yours.'

They were always 'yours' when there was a problem.

'Billy Dawalt, and all those bairns you used to cover your "overheads" are ticking time bombs, waiting to blow your cover to smithereens. Now I couldn't give a shite about your death wish, but if the cops get to you, they get to me.'

'I don't know where Billy is,' he says. 'He's probably dead now, anyways.'

'You can drop the redneck pretence,' Fergus spits. 'I know you. I know everything about you.'

'Aye?' he says. 'Well, that cuts both ways.'

'Was that a threat, Wee Willie Winkie?' Fergus leans far enough forward for him to see the burning light in his eyes.

He feels his heart pulsing in his throat. That hated name brings back all the misery of his young life.

'Make a threat, you'd better be prepared to back it up.'

'No, no,' he says. 'I'm just saying, we go back a long way.'

Fergus eases back in his chair, chuckling softly, the software distortion giving the sound an eerie quality that makes his balls shrink and his legs turn to mush.

'Here's what will happen next,' Fergus says. 'Law enforcement will revisit dump sites, trace those bitches back to their trailer parks, talk to their neighbours, forensically examine every dusty corner of their little slice of mobile-home heaven. Are you following this? I hope to fuck you are, because your life depends on you paying attention to what I'm about to say. You need to go back and clean Sharla Jane's place down with bleach. You will dispose of the woman *and* the boy as instructed. Do it carefully and quickly.'

He doesn't know that Red got away! Weak with relief, he's suddenly glad of the mask, hoping that what he's thinking doesn't show in his body language; there's still a chance he can make things right.

'I'll be finished here, out of state in forty-eight hours.'

'You FUCKING DIMWIT – can't you understand the urgency?' Fergus is screaming, out of control. He moves in to the monitor again, then dodges quickly back, realizing his mistake, and his face is a smear of red lips and bared teeth, like a tortured soul in a horror flick.

For a few seconds, all the man can hear is Fergus's breath, stuttering, unnaturally deepened by the voice distorter.

'Get rid of the surveillance equipment, the cameras, the table, the apparatus – everything. And get out of there. Right now. And when you've done all that, find a hole to crawl into and lie low until I tell you it's safe to come out.'

Like I'm some kind of cockroach. His impotent fury is replaced by cold, hard anger. He looks over his shoulder to catch a glimpse of Sharla Jane.

'But I got her all wound up, ready to go,' he says with a slight slump of his shoulders to show how disappointed he is.

'Ooo . . . *kay,*' Fergus says, as if he's indulging a small child. 'But you'll need to hurry.'

He grips the monitor in his two hands and brings his face so close to the camera he must be a black blur. He feels a strange calm. 'Let's get one thing straight – I don't *need* to do anything you say.'

He hears a sputter of shock; it sounds something like Sharla Jane's choked breathing, and the comparison gives him strength. Later, he sees this as the moment Fergus lost control and he gained it.

'I'm sick of this circle, jerk. You want to play, get one of your own.' He breaks the connection.

Control. It was always there; he just had to figure out how to take it.

He turns to face the room, and there she is: Sharla Jane Patterson. There is no natural light, but the place is bleached with spot lamps, ready for the cameras to roll. She is tied to a raised pallet. Her eyes are bound with duct tape. Her torso, from her chest to halfway down her thighs, is weighted with a concrete disc. Her throat convulses in the effort to inflate her lungs against 130 pounds of pressure.

25

Red's fingers are sore from working on the trunk lock. He has tried pulling the metal bars and pushing on the levers, but it's hard when he can't see. He wipes the sweat out of his eyes and picks up the kitchen knife, works the blade into the mechanism. It gives a little. He applies more pressure, but the car hits a rock and he's jolted hard, hits his head on the trunk lid; his hand slips and the tip of the knife blade snaps. Cussing, he tries again, but when he works his fingers into the latch he feels a burning pain and screams, dropping the knife. He covers his mouth with his hand to kill the sound of his crying. He has sliced his finger – a fragment of metal must still be caught in the mechanism. He squeezes and squeezes his finger to stop the pain and the bleeding; he knows he should try again, but he is afraid and it hurts so bad.

'You gonna just lay there bawling?' he says out loud. He can hardly understand himself, he's crying so hard. 'Quit crying, you goddamn crybaby – you got to get *outa* here.'

But he can't help it, and for a while he gives way to the pain and the fear. When he is tired of crying, he shucks off his jacket, drags his T-shirt over his head. He wipes the snot and tears off of his face, then wraps the cloth around his hand, ready to try again.

A sudden jolt. He braces himself against the roof of the trunk. The ground is real rough now, and the engine drone sounds different – a higher-pitched whine – and Red hears the whip of branches and underbrush against the car. They must've turned off the road.

After five or so minutes, the car stops.

The boy listens: in the distance he hears another vehicle. It has a low, throaty roar like an SUV, maybe, or a truck. The man gets out of the car and pretty soon the SUV comes up. The engine keeps running, but over the rumble of the engine he hears two voices, both men. Two doors slam, the second vehicle revs up and drives away. He is alone.

He starts on the lock again, but stops straight away. Something just tapped on the trunk of the car. He holds his breath.

Tap, tap-tap, like code.

He gets to his knees, his shoulders hard against the trunk lid. They knew he was there all along – they was just playing with him, pretending to go off in the SUV, but one of them stayed. He grips the broken knife two-handed out in front of him, his hands shaking. The tapping becomes a drumming; he hears a distant rumble of thunder and starts to breathe again: it's rain – just rain. Soon a deluge is hammering on the trunk lid.

26

Incident Command Post, Westfield, Oklahoma
Saturday, 2 a.m.

The rain was a solid grey curtain beyond the wooden walkway. It drummed on the shingle roof and bounced six inches high off the concrete of the car park. Fennimore turned up the hood of his waxed jacket, watching the rainwater sluice down the slope to the road. Abigail Hicks had woken him from a dream in which a girl wearing a sundress walked next to an older man alongside a high wall in a sunny street. A warm breeze riffled her hair, carrying an aroma of river water and flowers. The off-key two-tone of a police siren blasted nearby and, startled, she half turned and took a misstep. *Faux pas*, Fennimore thought, automatically. The man at her side caught her elbow and, as she straightened up, Fennimore strained to catch a glimpse of her face, desperate to find out if it was his daughter, but the man's shoulder obscured his view.

He woke, speaking Suzie's name in his dark hotel room, his mobile phone buzzing on the nightstand next to him, the rain a jet engine's roar outside his window. Hicks didn't say what it was about, just asked if he could be dressed and ready to roll in five minutes.

A lightning flash lit up a Williams County Sheriff's Department SUV as it turned in to the car park; more flashes in close succession, strobing the night sky so that the vehicle seemed to approach in a series of freeze-frames.

Hicks drew alongside the walkway and he swung the door open. Raindrops rattled like peas on the stiff fabric of his hood, and in the two seconds it took to open the door and climb in, he brought a bucketful of water with him; it streamed from his jacket onto the seat, soaking his trousers, and pooled in the foot well.

'Buckle up,' Hicks said. 'We got a body over at Cupke Lake, twelve miles south of here.'

'Billy?' he asked.

'I don't know, Professor. Call came in just after the storm hit. We got a location – a family camping up on the lake, but cell-phone reception's spotty up there even on a sunny day with a tail wind. With all this electrical activity, dispatch lost 'em before they could give much detail – small and naked is all I know. The deputy on night duty headed out just before me – they'll leave a marker at the roadside – that's if they find the place in this storm.'

Hicks drove slowly, ploughing through floodwater and bouncing over potholes, hunched forward at the wheel to try to catch a glimpse of road between sweeps of the wiper blades. A few miles from the lake, she turned on the light bar and the SUV's cabin was washed with alternating blue and red lights.

They would have missed the turning if it weren't for a Jeep Cherokee parked up at the end of the trail to the lake. The headlights flashed frantically as they approached, and Deputy Hicks slowed to a crawl and drew parallel with the driver's door with the storm crashing overhead. She rolled down her window, and the driver followed suit.

'We couldn't stay down there, Deputy,' he apologized,

raising his voice over the roar of the storm. 'The kids were too scared.'

He looked harried himself, Fennimore thought. The entire family were huddled in the Jeep: parents and three kids – a teen and two younger boys who looked like twins.

'That's all right, sir,' Hicks shouted. 'Is the other deputy down there now?'

He shook his head, rainwater dripping from the brim of his baseball cap. 'They drove by ten minutes ago, missed our signal.'

She nodded. 'Could you maybe get in my vehicle, show me where—'

His eyes darted right to his wife in the passenger seat. 'I think I should stay with my family. It's straight down the trail, maybe fifty yards – you'll see our tent where the stream comes in at the edge of the lake.'

'All right.' Hicks thought she understood. 'But, sir?' She lowered her voice and beckoned for him to lean out of the car. 'Are you sure you saw what you think you saw?'

His eyes hardened. 'I was in Iraq. I know a body when I see one.' He glanced back into the Jeep, and then leaned out of the Jeep across the gap between the two vehicles, so his family couldn't hear. 'I think . . .' He hesitated, and it was as if something cracked and broke behind his eyes. 'Deputy, that body is so small . . .' The look on his face said he knew he should go with them, but he just couldn't bear to pull a child out of the water.

'Would you do me a favour, sir?' Hicks yelled. 'Would you stay here, direct the deputy to where I'm at when he comes back along the road?'

He nodded, eager to help, and Fennimore realized she was giving him a way to save face. 'Yes, ma'am. Yes, I will.'

The track was thick with mud, but they didn't have far to travel, and the SUV was built for the terrain, so they pulled up at the lakeside in under a minute. Hicks killed the light bar and switched to a spot, taking in the small spit of land where the family had set up camp between an inlet and what must have been a small stream. Now it was a raging torrent. Their tent was intact, but water was lapping at the door flap.

'I don't see it,' Hicks said. 'Are we too late?'

'Try again,' Fennimore said. 'Take it slowly.'

She swung the beam right to left, tracking across black choppy water, sweeping in to the little inlet ahead of the driving wind; the rain was so heavy you could barely see five yards. There was no sign of a body.

'Damn light is bouncing right back off the rain,' Hicks said, reaching into the seat console for a flashlight. 'I'm going out to take a look.'

As she reached for the door handle, a prolonged series of lightning flashes lit the entire inlet and the light flared off something white tangled up in a broken tree branch.

They were both out of the car and down to the water's edge in a second. Another bolt of lightning, and the white object glowed electric blue in the static flash. It was a body, face down in the water, and the family man was right – it was tiny.

For a moment, Hicks stood, frozen, her flashlight centred on the body, but she made no move.

'Abigail?'

She stared at the body, rising and falling, working free of the branch that held it.

'Deputy Hicks.'

She looked at him, water streaming down her face, her hair plastered to her head, her confidence all but gone. 'What do I do, Professor? I don't want to mess this up all over again.'

Fennimore glanced behind him: the stream had taken down one side of the tent; the polyester flapped and whipped in the wind like a loose sail. In minutes the whole thing would be sucked into the rising waters. He yelled to warn Hicks, but the wind caught his words and hurled them into the storm. He tapped her on the shoulder and pointed towards the tent and she immediately began stripping off her jacket and shoes.

Fennimore yelled, 'You should wait for the deputy.'

She grabbed his jacket lapels and pulled him close, shouting in his ear. '*Cupke* is from the Creek language – means "long". By the time he figures out he missed the turn and heads back, that body will be gone.' She waded into the lake without even a glance backwards.

'Bloody hell, Abigail!' Fennimore splashed into the water behind her and she looked over her shoulder. The gravel shifted under his feet and the torrent tugged at him, and Fennimore nearly lost his balance.

Hicks yelled, 'Stay back.'

Fennimore watched from the water's edge as Hicks seized the lower branch of a cottonwood tree, now part submerged in the encroaching lake. She leaned out and gripped one ankle of the corpse. 'Go fetch a rope from the trunk of the vehicle.'

He ran with the wind at his back, returning more slowly in the face of the punishing gusts. He threw Hicks one end of the rope, and she laced it around her own waist. Fennimore threaded the rope through the crash bars of the SUV, then looped it around his own back.

Hicks lifted the branch to let it float away, but it would not give up its catch, so she broke a smaller branch off with her hands. She was fearless, trusting him to haul her in if she fell. When she had access to the body, she eased her arms under it and gently pulled it to her, cradling it.

She backed up onto the shore with shuffling sidesteps. When she was finally out of the water, Fennimore dropped the rope and rushed forward to help. Hicks lowered the tiny form carefully onto the ground, like a mother setting down a sleeping child. But it was not a child; he could see that now. And she had not been in the water long.

Fennimore experienced a rush of triumph: this woman, small and fragile as she looked in death, might bring their killer down.

27

The simplest explanation is usually correct.

From the general principles of William of Ockham

Incident Command Post, Westfield, Oklahoma

By 4.30 a.m. Dr Quint, Senior Forensic Medical Examiner, had arrived at Williams County Hospital. She declared her intention of taking the body back with her for autopsy. In Oklahoma, all autopsies were conducted by FMEs, and in the eastern half of the state, that meant moving the dead to the Eastern Division Office of the Chief Medical Examiner in Tulsa. Detective Dunlap wanted her input to an early-morning briefing, and Team Adam offered to fly her to Tulsa on their Piper airplane. Dr Quint said she'd be glad of the ride, and could spare thirty minutes.

The dead woman had already been identified from her fingerprints. Sharla Jane Patterson was twenty-seven years old. She had a son, Riley, aged nine, who had spent a year in foster care before being returned to his mother's custody. The Department of Human Services office dealing with his case didn't open till 8.30 a.m., but the emergency team had been alerted and someone would send a copy of Riley's photograph from his file as soon as they got a key holder to open up the office. Sharla Jane's last known address was a trailer park in Osage County, fifty miles north of Tulsa. The County Sheriff was on his way there.

The storm had passed and, at first light, a team of sheriff's deputies and volunteers would return to Cupke Lake to look for the boy.

Another child missing.

The assembled investigators were hollow-eyed from lack of sleep, but wired on strong coffee, adrenaline and the possibility of finding the boy safe.

Detective Dunlap called them to order. 'We need to decide,' he said. 'Release details to the media or not?'

'What harm could it do?' Sheriff Launer asked.

Dr Detmeyer said, 'Most abducted children are dead within three hours of being taken. Sharla Jane Patterson was in the water a few hours; we don't know how long the killer had her before that. Sheriff Launer is right: if Riley Patterson is dead, the publicity can't harm him.'

Launer nodded, a smile of satisfaction on his face.

'But if Riley is one of the twenty-four per cent of children who survive those three hours,' Detmeyer went on, speaking quietly and dispassionately, as if these were mere facts with no real people attached to them, 'then an announcement could put his life in even greater jeopardy.'

'Riley Patterson could still be alive out there,' Launer argued, 'and we are not going to find him sending a couple dozen civilians out in the woods hollering his name. I say we issue a full Amber Alert.' This was a national strategy, using radio and TV networks to mobilize the public.

Ellis said, 'Are you kidding me? Look what happened when Team Adam sent one solitary telex to State Bureaus and Sheriffs' offices.'

'You can't contain TV and radio networks,' Fennimore said. 'Inside of an hour, you'll have every crank, crazed well-wisher and serial confessor jamming the phone lines.'

All eyes turned to him – they knew he was speaking from experience.

The Team Adam consultant spoke up. 'We don't know for

175

sure that Riley *has* been abducted. He could be with a friend, or a neighbour. Could be he's sleeping safe in his own bed.'

'And until we hear from the Osage County Sheriff's Department, we can't know one way or another,' Dunlap said. 'Right now, Riley Patterson doesn't fit the Amber Alert criteria.'

The majority agreed.

'Well, okay.' An irritated frown creased Launer's brow. 'But I got to tell the media *something* – my office has been taking calls about this since four a.m.'

Fennimore wondered how the media had got to know *anything* with an electrical storm raging, and only the interstate Task Force aware of what had happened. He turned towards the meeting-room doors, half expecting to see Launer's tame newspaper editor hovering outside.

'We think this murder and disposal was rushed?' Fennimore got a nod from the FBI behaviourist. 'So maybe he didn't have time to clean up her trailer. And if he left forensic evidence, it could give us his identity.'

'*If* he rushed it, and *if* he didn't clean up,' Launer said. 'And how long's it going to take to process the scene?'

'All right,' Dunlap said. 'Compromise: we withhold information from the media until we search Sharla Jane's home, but issue a state-wide BOLO to law-enforcement agencies for the boy.'

Launer looked sour, but Dunlap had the consensus.

This agreed, they turned to a comparison of Sharla Jane with the other victims. She fitted the victimology: she had served a six-month prison term eighteen months earlier for a DUI offence; she was a former prostitute and an ex-addict. Vulnerable, single women; addicts and ex-addicts – easy targets for paedophiles. Fennimore had heard it said again and again over the past week, but something about it didn't ring true.

'Why have the women been found, but not the children?' he asked.

The question came out of his mouth before he'd had time think it through, and Fennimore did like to have at least a partial answer to questions he posed. But that was just professional vanity; sometimes the best strategy was to ask the niggling questions in the hope that someone – anyone – would come up with an answer.

Deputy Hicks looked uncomfortable. 'You said it yourself, Professor: kids don't float the way adults do.'

'Divers searched Guffey's pond – Billy Dawalt wasn't in there,' Fennimore countered.

'We got twenty per cent of the nation's standing water here in Oklahoma,' Launer said. 'That's a lotta places to dump a body.'

'Yet six women have surfaced, but only one child.'

Ellis shrugged irritably. 'It's obvious – he dumps the women with the trash. It's the *kids* he wants.'

Fennimore blinked away the image of a sombre teenage girl in a sundress, a girl that could be Suzie, stepping lightly beside an older man on a sunny street. 'And after he's . . . finished with them?'

Launer rolled his eyes. 'He murders them, dumps them – like he dumped the mothers.'

'So,' he repeated, 'why have we found only one child's body?'

The Sheriff threw his arms wide. 'I don't know – maybe he buried them, threw 'em down a well, sold 'em on – hell, you had *five years* to think about how a pervert disposes of a kid when he's finished having his fun, why don't *you* tell *us* what he did?'

Dunlap said, 'Hey now, come *on*.'

Deputy Hicks spoke at the same time: 'Sheriff Launer. Sir—'

Launer waved her away. 'I'm not gonna tiptoe around him 'cause of his "personal tragedy".'

Into the shocked silence, Fennimore said, 'He's right. You can't avoid making the arguments, however crudely put, just to spare my feelings.'

Launer eyed him suspiciously, uncertain if he'd won the argument.

'Paedophiles target a "type"?' Fennimore said.

Launer nodded, still wary.

'But if the women they target are a type, then the men who prey on them are too. They fixate on the kids; the mothers are only a means to an end – access to the children. The man who murdered these women had *total* access; he could've abused the children in their own homes, and if he wanted to steal them away, he was in the perfect position. All he had to do is offer the child a lift to school, or to take them for a treat to the video store, or to pick up groceries, and just never go home again. *But he didn't*. He took the mothers along with the children.'

He locked gazes with Simms, and her eyes shone.

Launer raised his shoulders. 'What's your point?'

'Two people are much harder to control than one, especially if one of them is an adult,' Fennimore said. 'He took a huge risk. But a risk worth taking, if it was the *mothers* he wanted, and *not* the children.'

'*What?*' Launer laughed. 'Did you *see* the mugshots?'

Of course they had. Arrest photographs; faces so grey and deeply lined they might have been fifty, rather than twenty-five. The skin of their foreheads and cheeks flecked with red, as if they'd been peppered with buckshot.

'That was before they went through rehab,' Fennimore said.

'I'm with the Sheriff on this,' Ellis said. 'It's not like they're a physical type – you got blonde, dark, tall, short, nineteen years old up to thirty. What they *do* have in common is their kids.'

Fennimore turned to the rest of the gathering. 'How many mother-and-child abductions have you investigated where the *child* was the target?'

Silence.

'Okay, let me put it another way: how many abductions by child predators where the mother was taken as well?' They looked from one to the other, and Fennimore saw raised eyebrows, a couple of head shakes. He sought out Kent Whitmore, the Team Adam consultant who had stood up for Hicks at the first meeting. 'Mr Whitmore?'

The consultant stroked a finger and thumb over his grey goatee. 'I never did investigate a case like that.'

'Of course not. Because child predators lie in wait and snatch the child when they're most vulnerable – which is *when they're on their own.*' It was a massive generalization, and Fennimore hated generalizations, but if he wanted to be heard there was no room for scientific hedging or equivocation.

Around the room, people made eye contact. What he was saying made sense.

Dunlap turned to the FBI psychologist. 'Dr Detmeyer, any thoughts?'

'Professor Fennimore may have something . . .' Detmeyer paused to glance at his notes. 'So far as we can tell, none of the victims was using drugs at the time of death. Rita Gaigan sent her son to her sister's the day before she disappeared, possibly because she feared he was in danger. Laney Dawalt took her brother out of a foster home because she thought she could take better care of him. Sharla Jane Patterson got clean and stayed clean in order to regain custody of her son.'

Detmeyer swept the room with his cool, calm gaze. 'Flawed as they were, damaged as they were, these women *did* care about their children. It *is* possible that the killer chose them for that reason – that he used the children to control their mothers. Threaten a child, and the mother is defenceless.'

'What does that tell us about the man?' Dunlap asked.

'In other circumstances, it would suggest that he might be physically impaired, or that he doesn't feel confident he could overpower his victims,' Detmeyer said. 'But he carried

179

Laney Dawalt a quarter of a mile from the road to a farm pond. Fallon Kestler's body was found ten minutes' walk off a dirt track in swampland – her daughter with her – which means he probably made two journeys from his vehicle to the deposition site over hazardous terrain, probably at night, carrying shifting and unstable weights.' He looked around the room. 'It may be that he enjoys the element of control, that he takes sadistic pleasure in making them fear for their children.'

'Well,' Launer said, 'you're a psychologist, and I guess it's your job to try to understand people. I'm a cop, it's my job to catch this guy, and I don't see how all this talk gets us any closer to getting that done.' He jabbed a finger towards the door. 'There's families out there scared for their kids. There's a boy out in the storm in the hands of a monster. You can call him what you like – paedophile, psychopath – I don't care. But I am not going to sit on my butt. Deputy Hicks, you can stay here. The rest of my guys're coming with me to Cupke Lake, see if we can't find that boy.'

Fennimore knew that this was one of those occasions where he should keep his head down and his mouth shut. But tact had never been one of his strengths.

'I thought you said we wouldn't find the boy with a posse hollering his name out in the woods,' he said.

Launer picked up his hat from the table in front of him. 'Better'n doing nothing.' He made his way to the exit.

'Better, or just more photogenic?'

The Sheriff stopped, already part way through the doors onto the landing. But he seemed to think better of making a fight of it. He jammed his hat onto his head and carried on without looking back, his deputies following close after.

28

The trunk leaks, and Red is so thirsty. An hour into the storm, he licked some rainwater that found its way in through the damaged rubber seals of the trunk, but it made him sick to his stomach and he threw it all back up and now he feels feverish. He tried again and again but he can't get out – he worked the lock of the trunk for hours, his fingers wrapped in bandages stripped from his T-shirt, but it will not open. At last, shivering, he struggles into his jacket and zips it up tight, feels a small hard rectangle against his hip. The Sony is still in his pocket. He takes it out and turns it on low, pillowing his ear on it for comfort.

29

Incident Command Post, Westfield, Oklahoma

By 6.30 a.m., it was 85 °F in the shade and 83 per cent humidity. The hotel's air conditioning took a direct hit in the storm and was out of action, and the conference room was stifling. Kate Simms's shirt clung to her, despite an electric fan blasting a miniature hurricane two feet from her, and when the hotel owner came up with pitchers of iced tea, she succumbed, grimacing at the tooth-rotting sweetness of the drink but grateful for the scoop of ice that came with it.

Dr Quint had left for the county airport ten minutes after the meeting broke up. The Sheriff was directing the search out in the field; Launer had a core of hunters and woodsmen he could call on for help in such circumstances, and so far they had twenty up at Cupke Lake, together with three deputies.

They had drawn a blank on Sharla Jane's last known address, a two-room mobile home rented in her name. Osage County Sheriff's Office reported that she and Riley had moved away three months before. Nobody had seen her with a man in all the time she lived there. She told a neighbour she was moving 'somewhere nice', but did not specify where, or with whom.

'Okay, where else do we look?' Dunlap said.

Kent Whitmore, the Team Adam consultant, spoke up. 'You know, a lot of folks in Ms Patterson's situation will get some type of Department of Human Services assistance – food stamps, aid for dependent children, and so on. DHS can tell you where they're collecting their benefits.'

But Sharla Jane had not picked up her food stamps in three months. And the DHS had her old address.

The conference room had been rearranged, the tables now laid out in pairs; a makeshift office set-up, allowing teams of two to work face to face. The phone company had rigged up additional landlines, though many of the investigators used mobile phones. Four teams began the process of contacting every school in Williams County, but the summer recess was making it difficult to get hold of the right people, and so far they had turned up nothing. Others continued to trawl marine suppliers and haulage contractors, asking about the rope. They now knew it was used in tens of thousands of boat rigs from the Great Lakes to Florida Keys, but for now they were focusing on sailing-equipment stockists in Oklahoma and Missouri.

Detectives Ellis and Valance had hooked up with Williams County administrative staff to call every registered trailer park manager county-wide in the hope of tracing Sharla Jane to her new address. Valance was talking into his mobile phone. He glanced over at Simms; the frozen expression on his face said that something was wrong.

Simms mouthed 'Problem?'

He frowned, gave a quick nod, still listening to the speaker at the other end of the line. Dunlap was talking to the British CSI on the far side of the room. He stopped, touched the man's arm and excused himself, moving towards Valance. Nick Fennimore, seated a few yards away, was on the phone; he finished his call quickly and followed the Detective. At the sight of the three converging on his table, Valance glanced to his left, where the Sheriff's people were at work. They diverted – Simms to the water cooler, Dunlap to the whiteboard nearby, Fennimore stopped at one of the tables and started a conversation with CSI Roper. All of them kept Valance in their line of sight.

He held up a finger, asking them to wait a moment longer while he spoke into the phone. 'Sir, can I ask you to hold for just a second?' He hit the mute button, closed his hand over the phone and stood. He nodded towards the exit and they met in a huddle just outside the swing doors.

'I'm talking to the manager of a trailer park twenty miles from here,' he told them. 'I asked him if he had a Sharla Jane Patterson registered as a resident. He said, "I heard about that." I asked could he be more specific, and he said, "The woman they found in Cupke Lake – her boy's missing, isn't he?"'

His expression grave, Dunlap said, 'Put him on speaker.'

He warned the manager that there were others listening, and introduced himself as the lead detective from the St Louis Major Case Squad.

'Oh,' the manager said. 'She's from Missouri? They said she was from Oklahoma.'

'*Who* said that, sir?' Dunlap asked.

'Was on the radio news,' the manager said. 'Sheriff's deputies got a call from a family camping out at the lake, found the body during the storm. Her son Riley's missing – the Sheriff wanted help with that.'

Dunlap looked at Simms.

'Did you know Ms Patterson, sir?' Dunlap asked. 'Was she registered with you?'

'No, sir,' the manager said, 'she was not. And we got no redhead boys here on the park, just now.'

Dunlap thanked the manager and finished the call. 'Sheriff Launer broadcast a description of the boy,' he said.

'Damn right I did.' Sheriff Launer's voice echoed up the

concrete stairwell. He came up the stairs at a pace, slowing on the landing and turning on his politician's smile.

'We agreed not to announce that we were looking for Riley until we checked their residence,' Dunlap said.

'I remember you *saying* that,' Launer said. 'I don't recall *agreeing*.'

'Fantastic,' Fennimore said.

'Nick,' Simms warned.

He ignored her. 'Have you checked your ratings, yet?'

Launer narrowed his eyes. 'What the hell does that mean?'

'I just hope your campaign promo was worth a boy's life.'

Launer made a move, but Dunlap stepped in his path. He wasn't especially tall, but he was solidly built, and it gave Sheriff Launer pause.

'The cruel statistical truth is that Riley Patterson was probably dead long before Sheriff Launer spoke on the radio.'

Dunlap spoke calmly, and although he was looking at Launer, he was making his case to Fennimore, using his language, asking him to set aside his personal feelings.

The detective was almost certainly right – the boy was probably dead. Simms knew it, and so did Fennimore. He relaxed a little, accepting the truth of it.

'Sharla Jane moved, just like the others,' Dunlap went on. 'The difference is, this time we aren't six months behind the curve. This time, we're right on his ass, and her home will be loaded with forensic evidence. We need to find it and process it.'

A whoop went up in the conference room and, a moment later, Ellis burst onto the landing, a slip of paper in his hand, a fierce grin on his face. 'We got an address,' he said.

30

You look at these scattered houses, and you are impressed
by their beauty. I look at them, and the only thought
which comes to me is a feeling of their isolation and of the
impunity with which crime may be committed there.

A. C. DOYLE, *THE COPPER BEECHES*

Incident Command Post, Westfield, Oklahoma
8.15 a.m.

'Sharla Jane enrolled her son at the elementary school in Hays,
about thirty miles from here,' Ellis said. 'The school principal
turned on the radio news at breakfast. She called the emergency
number, said Riley Patterson was on the school roll.'

The principal had sent a photograph of a small, freckled
child with flame-red hair and a toothy grin.

'Sometimes,' Launer said, with a complacent smile, 'you
got to be ready to *make* things happen.'

Fennimore stared hard at a cobweb high in the rafters
over Sheriff Launer's head and kept his mouth shut.

'Well, let's go round up the posse,' Launer said. 'We got a
scene to process.'

A cavalcade of law-enforcement vehicles drove through
the gates of Lambert Woods Mobile Home Park forty minutes
later. The properties were a mix of standard twelve-foot
mobile homes and double-wides, with a few RVs on the
outer rim.

Sheriff Launer rode point in his marked car. Second in line was a black SUV driven by Detective Dunlap. His passengers were Ellis, Fennimore and Valance. Kate Simms, the two Task Force CSIs, Dr Detmeyer, a number of Missouri cops and the Team Adam consultants followed in four more vehicles. Sheriff Launer had called in two of his deputies, still out at Cupke Lake searching for Riley, but they hadn't yet arrived.

Dunlap pulled up in front of the manager's office beside Launer's car. The air throbbed with the deep-throated sound of a souped-up engine being revved. Radio music blared from a couple of rows down. A woman screamed at two children playing under the window of her trailer. But their arrival, fanning out from the office like a blast wave, prompted the sudden retreat of families and individuals indoors; in under a minute, the place was deserted.

Launer stayed in the driving seat, angling his rear-view mirror to look back down the curve of the road.

Dunlap kept the engine running for the air con, but seemed to be waiting for his cue from Launer. Fennimore looked at Ellis, raising his eyebrows in question, and Ellis's impatience got the better of him.

'What in hell is he waiting for – a gold-plate invitation?'

'His deputies, maybe,' Dunlap said, always the diplomat.

'Best guess?' Fennimore said. 'Cougar 108's radio car. "Sometimes you got to be ready to *make* things happen",' he drawled.

Moments later, a reporter from Cougar 108 showed up in an outside-broadcast van.

The investigators stood in clusters by the side of the road, Simms amongst them, while the Sheriff gave his statement. Simms was talking quietly with Ellis and Valance, exchanging a few words with the CSIs. She seemed relaxed, at ease with them, accepted by them as part of the team, and Fennimore was pleased for her – she'd spent far too many years as an outsider, and that was largely down to her loyalty to him.

He switched his attention to Launer, who gave a few non-committal answers to questions from the radio reporter. This done, he turned to the park manager.

'We're about to process the scene,' he said, loud enough for the reporter to hear. 'But 1 need to check inside the property first. Just to be sure the boy – uh, Little Riley – isn't at the house.'

Fennimore noted the correction: giving the boy a name was better PR.

'Sheriff, I could give you the keys,' the manager said. 'But better if I show you. That trailer is out of the way, five minutes on foot from the main block.'

Launer nodded to the manager and headed towards his cruiser. 'Let's go.'

Fennimore turned to Dunlap: 'Is he *really* proposing a convoy?'

Dunlap said, 'Sheriff Launer, a word?' He edged the Sheriff away from the manager and turned his back on the reporter, lowering his voice. 'We could have tyre tracks out at the property, Sheriff. Maybe we should go in on foot.'

'We?' Launer said, his tone amused. 'This is *my* crime scene, Detective. You want, *you* can tag along.' He glanced at Fennimore. 'But he stays here.'

Launer and Dunlap returned fifteen minutes later, leaving two Missouri cops to stand guard over the property until his deputies got there.

The news was not good.

'There's photographs of Sharla Jane and Riley on the walls,' Launer said. 'But none of the guy she was shacked up with. No clothing, no razor – not even a toothbrush. And no sign of Riley.' He raised an arm, gesturing for someone to come forward. The Sheriff's deputies had finally arrived, one of them lugging a metal scene-kit case.

'Let's blitz that trailer, see what we can find,' Launer said, heading back down the slope towards Sharla Jane's trailer, his deputies in tow.

Fennimore and Dunlap exchanged a look.

'If we ever catch this killer, his defence lawyers will tear Launer's scene work to shreds,' Fennimore said.

Dunlap nodded in agreement. 'We need to stop him.'

'Launer does like to save the county money.' This was from Paul Roper, the St Louis CSI. 'We could process the scene at no cost to the sheriff's office.'

'Perfect.' Fennimore hesitated. 'I'm just not sure I'm the best person to point out the deficiencies of Sheriff Launer's crew.'

'We're not going to find Riley Patterson out at Cupke Lake,' the Team Adam consultant said. 'We should think about moving the search party to those woods.' He nodded in the direction of the wooded hill behind the trailer. 'And now we're sure Riley really is gone, I need to talk to the Shcriff about putting out an Amber Alert.' Whitmore furrowed his brow. 'You want, I could speak to him about the CSIs, too.'

'Mr Whitmore,' Fennimore said, 'you're the soul of tact.'

31

The backwoods, Williams County, Oklahoma
Morning

Red listens. The car has slowed down.

The two men came back early in the morning. One of them got out of the SUV and climbed in the car, backed up the trail all the way to the highway. They motored for a half-hour on a pitted road, vehicle jolting and jarring so badly he had to brace himself like a starfish against the walls of the trunk to save himself from getting his brains bashed in.

Now they are on a dirt track. The driver has slowed up, and the clay is more forgiving than the concrete of the road, so Red has an easier time of it. The swoosh and crackle of the tyres on the unmade surface almost lulls him to sleep, but a sudden buzz has him wide awake. They are crossing a wood bridge. Minutes later, he hears dogs bark; they must be getting close to journey's end. He flexes his legs, getting ready.

The engine cuts out and the car hitches forward a bit, then settles. Red lies on his side, faking unconsciousness; the knife is under him, gripped in both hands. He doesn't know what to do. He feels hot and sick. He is afraid, and wants to cry. He wants his momma. He knows he's never going to see her again. He swears to God he'll never do anything bad ever again if He will only deliver him from this awful place.

He hears voices, a burst of laughter. The trunk opens. He sees a flash of angry eyes – a man, the driver. The man recoils, lifts his arm over his face, cussing at the smell of vomit.

The boy takes his chance – slashing with the knife, he's up, out, running for his life. Behind him a hullabaloo of dogs yapping, howling, straining at their chains, men yelling.

Someone shouts, 'Stop right there, you little fucker!'

The boy risks one terrified glance over his shoulder. The man raises a rifle, and Red's heart stops. He cannot move. A fat woman bumps the shooter's arm, knocks him off target. The shot goes wide and the woman slaps the man round the head.

'Damnit, that's a kid you're taking potshots at, not a goddamn squirrel!' she yells.

For a second nobody does anything.

She looks straight at Red, says, 'C'm 'ere, son.'

Red looks right and left. He's in a wide clearing. Ahead of him, a big house. Another woman stands in the shadow of the front door. Either side of the car, two men: the driver, and someone looks enough alike to be his brother. Two more by a pickup – he recognizes one of them. All of the men are armed.

The woman says, 'There's no place for you to go, son. These entire woods is booby-trapped.' She looks at him like she's waiting for the information to sink in. 'Now c'mon.'

The woman is wearing brown cotton pants and a dazzling white shirt. She stands like a man with her feet turned outwards and her hands making fists. Red watches her, but still does not move. She sighs and takes the rifle away from the man who tried to shoot him. 'Go get him,' she says, her voice tired.

The man takes a step and it breaks the spell. Red spins on his heel. He tears through the woods, running, the hounds after him. But he's on unfamiliar ground and dizzy with the fever – he stumbles and falls. The knife flies off into the underbrush; they are close – real close – he can't go looking for it. He boosts himself up with his hands, staggers a few more steps, hears a crack and the ground gives way under him. He tries to leap out of trouble, but his legs are weak. He falls, spinning, grasping at air, and pictures flash through his mind of bear traps and pitfall traps and the tripwire with the spiked weight at the pot grow in the woods. He blacks out.

32

Aberdeen, Scotland
2 p.m. BST

Josh Brown had found a new toy. He'd read an article on language use in psychopaths and discovered that the university had a word-pattern analysis program called Wmatrix. He thought that he might use it to assess the narrative responses of people who had claimed a miscarriage of justice – a key area of interest to him. Psychopaths' speech is emotionally flat, he'd learned, and displays a high level of instrumentality: 'I wanted this, so I did that.' 'I had to kill her because . . .' They focus on self-preservation and primitive physiological needs – higher-level needs like intellectual and emotional fulfilment do not loom large in a psychopath's narrative. Fennimore had been interviewed three times in the five months between his wife and daughter's disappearance and the discovery of his wife's body, and Josh had been given access to them along with the rest of the Task Force. To amuse himself, he ran the transcribed interviews through Wmatrix. Fennimore, it turned out, was not a psychopath.

Fennimore's case was a cause célèbre on campus – even nationally – and since moving to Scotland to study with Fennimore, it had become a kind of hobby for Josh. He had lurked on forums, occasionally striking up conversations. No leads, so far, but he'd been covering Fennimore's summer-school classes at the university, as well as working with the Joint Task Force, so he only had time for an hour or two a day.

He saved the Wmatrix assessment and opened his photo gallery, finding the image of a man and a girl walking side by side in the sunshine. The man was aged thirty, or thereabouts. He carried a bit too much weight, but wasn't bad-looking. He wore a good suit and had the meaty look of a successful business type. The girl was maybe sixteen; she wore a knee-length dress and held a clutch bag on a thin strap. She was slim, and strode confidently in high heels. This was the girl who might or might not be Professor Fennimore's daughter. Josh had stolen the image from a pen drive that Fennimore had left out on his desk. It wasn't encrypted, which, to Josh's mind, made it fair game.

Fennimore will focus on the girl. Understandable, but it's the wrong approach. Children are anonymous, easily explained, or explained away. They can be moved around, renamed reconstructed so easily. An adult, on the other hand, has a past – a personal history, friends, an education, a career, a reputation, maybe. This is where Josh will start.

He cropped the image and produced a new JPEG of the man's face. He saved it and uploaded it to a free online sketch tool, and with the click of a button he had the image as a sketch. Of all the forums he'd lurked on, he thought that 'Save Suzie!' would yield the best results. But the appearance of an actual photograph online would raise too many questions – it might even get back to Professor Fennimore, and he did not want that. So he saved the sketch and uploaded that to the forum, and waited for the comments to start rolling in.

33

The backwoods, Williams County, Oklahoma
Morning

When Red comes round, he is lying on the earth at the bottom of a pit. Five faces are staring down at him: four men and a woman – not the fat one, a younger one. He doesn't have any holes in him: there are no spikes in this pit. Two dogs are snuffing around the top, sending crumbs of earth and small stones onto him. He flinches, raising an arm to protect his eyes. One of the dogs starts bouncing on its front paws, yowling.

The car driver, the man who tried to shoot him, bats the dog away and leans into the pit, offering his hand. Red sinks his teeth into the fleshy part of the man's thumb. He yells, cussing and swearing, tries to pull back, but the boy hangs on. The others are yelling and laughing but the shooter is roaring like a bull, till someone pokes Red with a stick and he falls on his butt. When he looks up, it's the fat woman.

The men go on laughing, but she looks mad. 'You want to get out of there, boy, you're gonna have to behave like a Christian child.'

Red scowls back at her, digging his fingers into the dirt where he landed.

'Suit yourself.' The woman waves her hand in front of her face like she's chasing flies. 'We can just as easy shoot you.'

Red knows who this woman is. She is Marsha Tulk. The kids in school say she is boss of the Tulk family. And if she says she will shoot you, she is not fooling.

She disappears from the edge of the pit and Red jumps up. 'Wait!' he yells. 'I'll come out!'

She appears again, her face fat and round, her eyes dark and small and hard, but there is a crinkle of fun around the eyes. 'Oh, you will . . . we just got to decide how.'

'I'll be good,' Red says.

She narrows her eyes. 'I want to hear you say it.'

'I'll behave like a Christian child,' he says, his eyes fixed on the damp earth at his feet.

Next second, he's hauled up by two strong arms. The men do not let go, but look towards the big woman with the small, hard eyes.

She stares at him like he's a sorry excuse for a human child, shakes her head and says, 'Bring him up to the house.'

Mrs Tulk sits in a rocker out on the porch. The two men march Red up after her and make him sit on a wood chair.

He wriggles and she says, 'Do I have to tie you down?'

He shakes his head. It's buzzing, or else the cicadas are singing in two-part harmony.

'I can't hear you,' she says.

'No, ma'am, you do not have to tie me down.'

She nods, satisfied, and the men let go of him.

The woman looks at his dirty face, his cut hands and stained clothes. 'Well, little boy, you are a mess.'

The way she says it makes him want to cry, so he frowns hard at the woman's strong right hand, curved loose over the edge of the rocker arm. Her nails are sharp-pointed and the knuckles are big and calloused, yellow, like a bird's claw.

'What were you doing in the trunk of my son's car?' she says.

The four men have gathered round, the man he had bit being tended to by a young woman – the one he saw at the front door of the house – the other three sitting or leaning on the porch rail. The one he recognized is the chunky guy he saw tending the pot grow – the one he hitched a ride off of the first time. None of them is laughing now, nor smiling, neither; they don't look so much mad as mean, and he knows that he needs to be careful what he says next.

'I was escaping.'

'From what?'

'Foster home,' he says.

'Why're you in foster care?'

'My momma died.' He chokes up and cannot speak for a bit, and Mrs Tulk hands him a Kleenex from the pocket of her pants.

'Can I have a glass of water?' He's hot and dizzy, his face all swole up from the heat and the crying. 'Uh, please, ma'am?'

'Let's get this over with first,' the woman says. 'How come you're not living with your daddy?'

He shrugs. 'I don't know who he is.'

The woman shifts her bulk in the chair and makes a *tsk* sound through her back teeth.

'I'm going to ask you a question again, and I want you to answer me truthfully, this time,' she says. 'What are you running from?'

The boy bows his head, his two arms hanging loose between his knees. He can't go home, because he knows his momma isn't ever coming back, and, if he tells her, the police will come and put him in foster care for real.

'I'm running,' he says, taking his time so he can decide on a story she will believe. 'From my foster father.'

'Why?'

''Cos,' the boy says, 'he's a pervert. Wanted me to come see his garter snakes. Said I could "handle the male", like it was something dirty. He made me drink beer—' He widens his eyes and turns them on her, knowing they are blue and innocent as a May morning. 'I didn't want to . . .'

'How old're you?' she says, her face hard.

'Nine years.' Thinking, *She doesn't believe me. I told a lie and she doesn't believe me and now I'm going to die.*

But the woman gazes in wonder at her own boys. 'He's no more'n a baby.'

'Am *not*.'

Her attention snaps back to him and he quails, but her face softens. ''Course you're not. But you're not big enough to deal with that kind of sinfulness on your own, neither. Don't you have *any* family? An aunt, a gramma?'

He shakes his head.

'Where you from, boy?'

'I can't tell you.'

'You will,' she says, leaning forward in her chair, 'or we're going to have a fallin' out.'

He tries to look her in the eye, but can't. 'Ma'am, I swear I don't mean to make you mad, truly I don't, but I can't go back there.'

The terror of what happened to him must show in his face, 'cos she says, 'I'm not going to make you go back, son. I just need to know where you come *from*.'

Now *she's* lying, but he knows better than to say that to a woman like Mrs Tulk. 'But if *you* know, other people will know and *they* might send me back.'

She snuffs a bit and he sees the crinkle of humour around her eyes again. 'Well, you are a smart boy. But that's assuming I would tell anyone, which I won't.'

He looks at the four men around her.

She sees him look and gets mad. 'Gosh almighty, don't you *want* to see that man punished?'

He closes his mouth tight, hearing Rodney Atkins singing 'If You're Going Through Hell' in his head.

Mrs Tulk settles back in her rocker and contemplates him

198

for a while. 'Harlan, where'd this boy get into the trunk of your car?'

The man who tried to shoot him says, 'I don't know, Momma.' He is tall and bearded, dark-haired like the others. He looks strong and powerful, but he seems nervous when he tells her.

'Well, *think*,' she says.

Harlan shakes off the young woman who is fixing up his hand, and she falls to staring at Red instead.

Harlan says, 'I might of left the trunk unlocked over to the . . .' His eyes slide over to the boy then back to the woman. 'The tomato field in the woods.'

'Is that right, boy?' she asks.

Red gives her a someway truthful answer. 'I do recall a powerful smell of tomatoes in the clearing where I climbed in the trunk.' He thinks it would be unwise to mention that the smell of marijuana was just as strong.

She eyes the boy, curious. 'Just how long were you in the trunk of that car?'

'I climbed in just after dark. Mr Harlan drove for a while, then he stopped and drove off with someone else. It was getting light when they got back and we started moving again.'

Her eyes flicker to her son and the boy sees a slight nod. 'How'd you know it was light if you were in the trunk?'

'Ma'am, that old tin can is nothing but rust and air.'

The others laugh and Harlan starts to grumble, but she says, 'You know it's true, son.' Then to Red: 'What's your name, boy?'

'Caleb.' He can see that she knows it's a lie. 'But everyone calls me Red.' Another lie – the kids in school call him all kinds of names, but they do not call him Red.

'I'm trying to help you, son, and you are defying me.'

Red thinks that not many people have ever defied Mrs Tulk.

'I'm sorry, ma'am. But I will not go back.'

'We already had that conversation,' she says, a threat in her tone.

'I'll leave,' he said. 'I want to. Just let me go.' There is a pleading in his voice which makes him feel ashamed, but Mrs Tulk looks like she's giving serious thought to the idea.

The young woman has done cleaning Harlan Tulk's hand. She shoots Mrs Tulk a sly glance while she finishes up wrapping the bandage around his thumb.

'Something on your mind, Haley?' Mrs Tulk says.

'I could keep him,' the younger woman says.

'He might have something to say on that. Like I *said*, he's not a squirrel to be shot at, nor kept like a pet, either.'

'No, ma'am.' She blushes. 'I meant to say I could look after him, just till we find out who he is.'

Red feels a hot flare of alarm, stamps on it – he'll be gone long before they find out who he is.

'Can I, ma'am?' the young woman says. 'Can I keep 'im?'

Mrs Tulk looks at Red. 'Boy, you have put us in a bind. If we keep you here, the authorities might come looking for you and we'd have some explaining to do. If we leave you somewhere – maybe in town – the police will question you and that would bring them here and we'd *still* have some explaining to do.'

'No, ma'am.' Red feels on more solid ground now – they don't want to be troubled by the law any more than he does. 'I would not say one word about you. Set me down on the right road, I can make my own way.' But as he says it, a powerful nausea sweeps over him like a wave. He feels weak and hot and sick, and he doesn't know if he can stand up from this chair.

She sets her rocker to rise and fall, staring at him, weighing him up in her mind. Watching her, the porch starts to sway, he leans forward in his chair and pukes on the deck, splashing the chunky brother's shoes.

There are shouts of dismay and the chunky man says, 'Watch it, you little fucker!'

Fresh tears spring to the boy's eyes and he is humiliated to find he cannot stop them.

Mrs Tulk's right hand shoots out and he flinches from a slap, but her left snakes behind his head, holding him still. She does not slap him, but places her right hand on his forehead; it feels wonderfully cool and soothing.

'This boy is burning up,' she says. 'Did you eat something you should not have while you were out in the woods, child?'

'No, ma'am, I—' He almost said he ate the tacos and a bite of sandwich the night before, but then she might figure his 'foster parents' live close by.

He swallows, wipes his nose with the back of his hand. 'I'm sorry, ma'am,' he says, trying to get the whiny note out of his voice. 'I drunk some water that leaked in the trunk, and I got sick.'

'Harlan.' She raps out the name like it's an order. 'What's in that trunk?'

The tall son shrugs. 'Only a bunch of paper bags and half a sack of blood, fish and bone for the crops.'

'Lord!' she exclaims. 'This boy is poisoned and here we are, keeping him talking.' She looks around her as if everyone but her is to blame for it. 'Haley, take him inside and get him to drink plenty of water.'

The young woman is by Red's side in a second, coaxing him to his feet and cooing soft, foolish words to him.

'If he throws it back up,' Mrs Tulk says, 'give him some more till he can hold it down – and put him in the tub and make sure he washes, too.'

Red allows himself to be led into the cool dark of the house, thinking he does not want to die, but feeling like he's standing outside of himself, watching some other boy walk into a strange house amongst bad people that even bad-asses are scared of.

34

Common sense is the collection of prejudices acquired by age eighteen.

EINSTEIN

Incident Command Post, Westfield, Oklahoma

Afternoon, and the Joint Task Force had gathered at the Incident Command Post for a Skype conference. Dr Quint was to deliver her autopsy findings from Tulsa, while Dr Detmeyer's British counterpart, forensic psychologist Professor Varley, would Skype from the University of Nottingham in the UK. Fennimore had worked with the forensic psychologist on a number of cases.

The CSIs presented their findings at the top of the meeting. They'd found duct-tape residue on the headboard of Sharla Jane's bed, but no prints. There were no signs of the rope the killer had used on the other victims – either in Sharla Jane's trailer, or up at Cupke Lake. Designed for a racing-boat rigging, the rope should float, so it was possible the body hadn't been roped and weighted at all.

Dunlap asked the psychologists for their comments.

'He carefully planned the other killings to reduce the chances of early detection,' Dr Detmeyer said. 'He went to the same trouble on this occasion, but fell down at the last, failing to dispose of Sharla Jane effectively. He may be devolving.'

'Devolving?' Varley said, his voice sharp, impatient. The

team looked towards the screen, which displayed the Skype Conference link. Professor Varley was a pale, lean man, with a long, narrow face and receding hairline. 'Ah, you mean *decompensating*.'

Detmeyer considered the correction in the way that Fennimore might examine a mark at a crime scene: weighing up its usefulness dispassionately but with intense interest. After a few moments, he said, 'I *mean* he could be losing psychological control due to stress; "devolving" is the merely technical term I chose to express that concept.'

Varley raised an eyebrow. 'I see . . . Might we, for the sake of clarity, *avoid* technical terms,' he said, managing to sound both plaintive and bored.

Kate Simms slid Fennimore an amused look from across the table; more than once, Simms herself had needed a layperson's translation of Professor Varley's psychological advice.

'All right,' Detmeyer said. 'We agree that recently he has made mistakes, shown an uncharacteristic lack of control. It's also worth noting that Sharla Jane is the second victim to turn up in Williams County in the space of a month. That could mean he's becoming more impulsive,' he went on. 'Or Williams is familiar territory, perhaps.'

'*Maybe, possibly, could be, perhaps,*' Launer said.

'There are no absolutes in predicting human behaviour, Sheriff,' Detmeyer said.

'Common sense tells you the why of it,' Launer said. 'He meant to dump the body across the county line, like he always does, but he heard on the radio we were onto him. He dumped her fast 'cos he had to, because he never had an interstate task force on his tail before.'

Fennimore had to admit he had a point.

Copies of the photographs were stacked at every place at the conference table. Fennimore shuffled through them: pictures of Sharla Jane on her front porch, smiling and proud of her new home; pictures of her alone; some of her with Riley. Interior shots, mostly, though there was one of Riley standing next to a smoking barbecue under the trees near their house. He was wearing a man-size chef's apron and holding a burger in a set of barbecue tongs.

'Did the pictures yield anything useful?' Fennimore asked.

Roper, the quick, restless CSI, picked up that question. 'They were printed on an inkjet printer – we found it at the house. No fingermarks on the photographs, or the printer, and, before you ask, Professor Fennimore, we checked that barbecue drum inside *and* out. He must've wiped the place down.'

'Sharla Jane had a guy living there for months,' Launer said. 'You must have found him *somewhere* around the place.'

'We got small flecks of blood in the bathroom and kitchen,' the CSI said. 'Nothing to suggest a violent attack. Kitchen, bathroom . . .' He lifted one shoulder as if no further explanation was necessary. 'But with luck, we'll find his DNA in there.'

'So, you got zip,' Launer said, showing his teeth.

'We did find a partial footwear mark on the kitchen vinyl, probably a boot, size twelve,' CSI Roper said.

'The Sheriff's deputies trod dirt all over the place.' Detective Ellis again, looking hot and bad-tempered. 'Could be from any one of them.'

'Who said anything about dirt?' the CSI said.

Fennimore looked up from his scrutiny of the photographs. 'If it wasn't dirt, then . . .' he considered. 'Urine, perhaps?'

CSI Roper nodded. 'We found a dried pool just inside the master-bedroom door. Someone – probably a large male – stepped in it. The first print on the kitchen vinyl was too overloaded to get a clear impression, but we dusted the probable position of his next two steps – got a real nice one.'

'Which is why you should *always* let the CSIs do their stuff first,' Fennimore said to nobody in particular. 'I'd hazard a guess that Williams County deputies have fairly good bladder control. So, I'm thinking terrified nine-year-old.'

Launer scowled at Fennimore and Detective Dunlap intervened, addressing the CSI: 'Anything we can use?'

Roper strode to the front and clicked a memory stick into one of the computer's USB ports. He zipped through images of the trailer's interior, stopping at a footwear mark. 'We got a good impression of the sole pattern – we can trace that back to the manufacturer. This shoe's had more wear on the inner edge – suggests pronation – the wearer's foot rolls inward at the ankle.' He studied the image. 'And here, here and here—' he pointed to nicks and gouges in the pattern '—you can see damage defects.'

Fennimore nodded approval; it was good work. 'Did you—?'

'We took a section of vinyl,' Roper said, anticipating the question. 'And we will try to get it enhanced.'

Launer scratched a mosquito bite on his elbow. 'Those're probably thirty-dollar work boots he bought at Walmart. We got anything to match this boot print to?'

The CSI said, 'Not as yet.'

'Nothing from *any* of the other victims?'

'No, but—'

'So what *good* is it?'

'Wear patterns are unique,' Fennimore said. 'Find this shoe, and we can prove it belonged to this one person and no other.'

'Do I *look* like Prince Charming?' Launer said. 'Find me something I could run through AFIS, I'd be really impressed.'

CSI Roper shrugged. 'Like I said, we dusted everywhere; he wiped down.'

While the discussions went on around him, Fennimore looked again at the family snapshots, propping each one against the monitor of his laptop: Sharla Jane and the boy by the kitchen window, greenish light filtering in through gingham curtains; Sharla Jane framed by the same window on her own, looking pretty and shy; Sharla Jane in a nightgown, with bed-hair, a hand in front of her face to block the shot; the boy sitting at the kitchen counter, his head haloed by gold light, chewing on a burger and mugging, cross-eyed for the camera.

He felt a thud of realization. 'These photographs *are* all taken inside Sharla Jane's trailer in Lambert Woods Park?'

'Sure,' Roper said, blinking from the interruption to his presentational flow. 'What made you think different?'

'The window hangings have been changed.' He held up the image of Sharla Jane in front of the green check curtains, and a second snapshot: her son, seated at the counter with plain gold fabric at the window behind him.

'She changed the drapes,' Launer said. 'So what?'

'When I say the *hangings* have been changed, I mean the style of track.' Fennimore struggled for an American equivalent. 'The *hardware*. Look,' he said. 'The gingham curtains are threaded on a pole, but in this one of Riley . . .' He skimmed the snapshot across to the Sheriff. 'No window pole.'

Heads went down as the team looked at their own copies.

'They switched from rail to rod,' CSI Roper said. 'The gingham drapes are up there, now, and they *are* on a rod.'

'But you said you already dusted for latents,' Launer said.

'We dusted the rod,' the CSI said, a flush of excitement on his face. 'But if our guy switched the rail for a rod, that needs a whole new set of fittings. His prints could be on the *reverse* of the brackets.'

'Not just his prints, and not just on the brackets and rods,' Fennimore said. 'You need one hand for the brackets, one hand for the screwdriver, so where do you hold the screws?' He felt a spark of excitement, watching them think it through. 'You pop them in your mouth. And those nice, sharp, self-tapping threads pick up DNA just like a buccal scrape. Then they get screwed in place, protecting the DNA.'

Roper grinned, already gathering up his scene kit. Launer despatched one of his deputies to accompany him, and when the room settled down, Dr Quint, the FME, began her presentation, joining the Skype conference from her office in Tulsa.

She greeted them all, and got straight to business. 'Sheriff, I'm sending the autopsy pictures through to you.'

While they waited for the images to arrive, she gave a quick summary of the autopsy, reminding them that the body was fresh and animal predation minimal. Sharla Jane was a little underweight, but healthy at time of death. Her eyes were damaged.

'I thought at first it was the turtles,' Quint said. 'You know how those critters love eyeballs.'

The Oklahoman contingent murmured agreement.

'But it wasn't predation.' She looked out at them. 'Sharla Jane's eyes were deliberately sliced open with a sharp object.'

A few murmurs; someone said, 'Yeesh!'

Fennimore picked up a pen and began to doodle, sketching a pair of eyes, glaring out of the page.

'Any ideas on the weapon used?' Dunlap asked.

'My guess would be something real sharp, like a box cutter; it penetrated the cornea and sliced through the iris, damaged the lenses and suspensory ligaments, but didn't cut all the way back to the retina.' There were no comments, and Quint went on: 'She was exceptionally pale. There was faint lividity in her upper back and arms. Externally, there was little else to see – a couple of circular marks on the sternum and left side.' She indicated the places on her own chest and left ribcage.

As she spoke, Fennimore mind-mapped, doodling branches and sub-branches, single words and line drawings, creating something that was half sketch, half summary notes.

'I found a puncture mark on the medial aspect of her left thigh,' the ME said. 'We know that Sharla Jane was a recovering meth addict, but for the Brits around the table, methamphetamine is most often smoked or snorted; it's only very rarely injected. I did find historical evidence of her meth addiction – skin damage and meth mouth – but nothing to say she had relapsed. And no indication of other drug use, except that one mark. I palpated it, found a lump. Now, it'll take a while for the tox to come through—'

'We need to know for sure sooner rather than later, Doctor,' Dunlap said. 'If she was back on the meth, it complicates the whole picture.'

'Patience, Detective,' Quint said. 'When you deal with the dead, often you don't *need* instant results. A full laboratory tox screen *will* take a while, even with the help of our friends at Team Adam. How*ever*, it did seem likely you would want to know fast and, with the right dip strips and a sample of urine, you can get instant results – they use them all the time in rehab units, Federal facilities and the like.'

Sheriff Launer bugged his eyes, spread his hands as if to say, *Can we get to it?*

She shrugged. 'Sharla Jane Patterson was clean. She had not recently used cannabis, cocaine, amphetamine, methamphetamine, benzodiazepines or opiates. But that did not *un*complicate the picture one bit, Detective Dunlap. There was no obvious cause of death – no cuts, blunt force trauma, gunshot wounds, no ligature marks or bruises around the neck to suggest strangulation, no bruising to her chest, or internal organ damage, no bruising to her face around the mouth or nose that would suggest smothering. And yet, she did have petechiae – those are the pinpoint dots which are typical of asphyxiation. Sharla Jane had them on the oral palate, the inner aspects of upper and lower eyelids and behind both ears.' She paused. 'You do not typically get petechiae behind the ears.'

Behind the ears. Fennimore added a cartoon sketch of the back of a head, and punctuated the area behind the ears with dots.

'And there was damage to the back of her throat,' Quint went on. 'Scratches on the soft palate.'

'He choked her – stuck something down her throat?' Valance, the young detective, said.

'Certainly he put something down her throat. But I don't believe he intended to choke her.' She held up a length of clear plastic tubing. 'This is an oropharyngeal airway. You see it a lot in Emergency Rooms.'

'He resuscitated her?'

'Maybe. Med students can be very ham-fisted. I know,' she said, with a rueful smile, 'I *was* one. It doesn't look good if your patients choke on their own blood because a student who couldn't find his ass with both hands and a rear-view mirror rammed a piece of plastic into their vocal cords. So, the manufacturers make these things *real* soft.' She pinched the tube between thumb and forefinger to prove it. 'This guy had to be unusually clumsy, or he tried to insert the wrong size airway.'

'So he *tried* to resuscitate her?' Valance said, confusion writ large on his open face.

'*Maybe*,' she said again. 'If he did chest compressions, you would expect to see broken ribs, or at least some bruising in the chest. But there were no bruises, no breaks.'

'You said she had bruises on her chest and the left side,' Valance reminded her.

'I said *marks*. But we do get those marks a lot on patients who were shocked after cardiac arrest.'

'So,' Valance tried one more time, 'she was bagged and defibbed?'

'*Possibly*,' the ME said.

Launer had heard enough. 'Doctor, we need answers, and all you got is maybes.'

'You got me mixed up with a TV pathologist, Sheriff,' she said. 'I'm paid to work out the "how" of her death – it's up to you to find out the whys and wherefores.'

Offended, Sheriff Launer went on the attack. 'Well, would it be too much trouble to give me a cause and manner of death – I mean, you made a lot of the fact she had no significant injuries, so I assume she suffocated?'

'I don't believe she did suffocate,' Quint said. 'I believe cause of death was exsanguination.'

Launer gave an exasperated snort.

Fennimore focused on his doodle, adding a dotted line between 'asphyxia' and 'exsanguination'. Thinking, *Petechiae behind the ears.*

'She bled out,' Dr Quint went on, 'yet she had no lacerations that might account for it, and no internal bleeding. It *was* a puzzle. And here's another: getting a sample of blood out of a cadaver is never easy, but you *can* find it, if you know where to look. My preference is the femoral vein because it's easy to find and relatively near the surface – why make life hard, right? The right femoral vein was collapsed. Which is not *that* unusual, but generally – and don't tell anyone I admitted to this, because the toxicologists *do not* like it – you can "milk" the blood up the leg till you have enough to stick in a hypodermic and extract a sample. I tried. Didn't work. So I switched to the subclavian vein – that's a big-assed vein, carries blood from your head back to your heart. Runs under your clavicle, about here.' She indicated on her own nicely defined collarbones. 'No blood. Pulmonary artery – zip. I had to insert a hypodermic into the heart to get a volume the lab could work with.'

As the team frowned over the post-mortem photographs, she reminded them of the 'lump' she palpated on the inside of Sharla Jane's left thigh.

'It was a broken-off section of a hypodermic needle in the femoral vein. Sixteen-gauge – that's big – it's the type attached to a shunt for blood donation. So: Sharla Jane was pale, showed negligible signs of lividity, had no blood in the major blood vessels.' She paused, waiting for the facts to sink in. 'I believe he sucked the blood right out of her and watched her die.'

Fennimore looked at his diagram, at the dotted line joining asphyxia and exsanguinations, and when the murmurs died down, he said, 'It doesn't explain the petechiae.'

Quint looked at him like he had rained on her parade.

'Maybe he locked her in the trunk of his car and she suffered oxygen deprivation,' Simms said.

Fennimore shook his head. 'Petechiae behind the ears . . .' He looked at the jug-eared cartoon, dotted with cartoon petechiae. He saw a flash of pale blue Aberdonian light, the seaweed reek of the docks. His mind's eye lit upon a set of plastic tote boxes stacked to the left of his desk in his office at the university. Old reports – reviews of coroners' verdicts.

He had it.

'The petechiae behind her ears suggests traumatic asphyxia,' he said.

'I considered that,' Dr Quint said. 'But there was no significant trauma, no bloating, no discoloration of the face—'

'I reviewed a case, a couple of years back,' he interrupted. 'A lorry driver stopped at a delivery gate, went to open it. The brakes were faulty, and the lorry crept forward, pinning him. He died in minutes. There were no scene photos because the firm's security team found him five minutes after the accident and took him inside. The insurance company contested the widow's claim because there was no internal organ damage, no external signs and very little skin injury. Fortunately, one of the mortuary techs had the foresight to take pictures when the body was first brought in. The driver's face was blue and bloated on arrival, but by the time the post-mortem took place, the signs had vanished.'

The ME nodded, slowly, accepting the possibility. 'You know, this adds a whole new level of sadistic to the resuss attempts.'

Launer broke in on their musings: 'Are you two going to keep on talking in code, or are you going to let us all in on the secret?'

Dr Quint looked at Fennimore. 'Professor?' It was an invitation, professional courtesy: since Fennimore had spotted the significance, he got to deliver his theory to the team.

'It's easy to see petechiae on the eyeballs or under the eyelids,' he said, 'because the skin is thin and well supplied with capillaries. It's much more difficult where the skin is thicker – and petechiae behind the ears takes something exceptional, something like traumatic asphyxia. You call it crush asphyxia. You're even *more* likely to see it where you have repeated trauma, because of the cumulative effect.'

'You mean he did this again and again?' Valance, alone amongst the detectives, looked shocked.

'It's not uncommon,' Dr Detmeyer said.

Varley gave a small nod of agreement. 'The ultimate form of control.'

Fennimore's mind flew to Rachel, his wife; to Suzie, his daughter. Time slipped and, heart pounding, he experienced the rising panic he'd felt those first weeks after they disappeared.

'Which means the killer asphyxiated her, resuscitated her, then bled her to death,' Dr Quint added.

The scientist's need to present the complete picture had saved Fennimore in those early days. It saved him now.

'You missed something,' he said. 'He blinded her, too.'

Everyone turned to him.

'The eyes figure prominently in the presentations of this type of predator,' Detmeyer said. 'Wanting to see and be seen in the final moment.'

'Or see and *not* be seen,' Varely added. 'Blinding a victim goes far beyond functional violence – what he might need to do to acquire and subdue a victim. This level of violence is likely to express an inner narrative – what we term "expressive violence".'

By 'we', they all understood him to mean *we in the UK*.

'What *we* would call his "signature",' Detmeyer said. 'But we were avoiding technical terms, weren't we, Professor?' he added dryly.

The muscles around Varley's eyes flickered and Fennimore thought he looked stung, but after a moment, he inclined his head slightly, accepting Detmeyer's gentle rebuke.

Detmeyer looked around at the assembled team. 'In plain English, the blinding is the outward expression of the offender's fantasy.'

'This guy fantasizes about blinding his victims?' Dunlap asked.

'But he didn't blind the others, he just taped their eyes,' Simms said.

'The "blinding" in those murders was figurative,' Varley said. 'Symbolic.'

Detmeyer nodded. 'With Sharla Jane, he gained the confidence to move his fantasy on to actual blinding.'

Varley agreed, but Simms shook her head.

'Forgive me, gentlemen, but that sounds a bit thin. He's been abducting and murdering women and children for *years*. Now suddenly he starts *blinding* them?'

'Evil men change, just as good men do,' Varley said, dismissive.

Dunlap's mobile phone rang and he excused himself, moving to the refreshments table to take the call.

'You said it yourself, Professor Varley,' Simms said. 'Blinding must always have been part of his fantasy – it isn't just a modus operandi to be adapted to the circumstances.'

'Operand*um*,' Varley corrected.

Simms's cheeks flamed and Fennimore said, 'Why don't you address the psychology, and save the grammar lesson to impress your students?'

A few eyebrows were raised, and Varley bristled visibly.

'You're suggesting something triggered the change in behaviour, Chief Simms?' Detmeyer seemed to be considering the suggestion seriously.

'From one victim to the next he went from taping his victims' eyes to blinding them, and from asphyxiating them to draining them of blood,' Simms said. '*Something* must have happened.'

'You're assuming that Sharla Jane *was* the first victim he bled,' Professor Varley said.

'We don't know that. It could be that the other autopsies simply weren't as thorough as Dr Quint's.'

'Why thank *you*, Professor Varley,' Quint said, hamming up the Midwest cutsie in the tone. 'But we got at least three victims with a normal degree of *livor mortis*. Which, if he drained the bodies, you would *not* get.'

Fennimore raised one shoulder. 'You can't argue with the science. Our man has changed his behaviour. Radically.'

'I agree,' Detmeyer said in his habitually solemn and undramatic tone. 'And he's getting careless. Leaving the shoeprint at the trailer—'

'That's not all he left.' Dunlap had returned to the meeting. 'I just spoke to Roper. They found a partial right index and a good thumbprint in back of a couple of the rail brackets at Sharla Jane's place.'

35

Home. Now he can relax, kick back, watch the recording that changed his life. It's like watching a piece of history being made. He feels a sense of awe, and his finger trembles a little as he hits the playback button on the recorder.

On-screen, he is masked, dressed head to foot in black.

Sharla Jane struggles to breathe under 130 pounds of weight. He remembers thinking should he add another plate, bring it up to 150.

The burn of adrenaline from facing down Fergus had cooled by then, and uncertainty fluttered in the pit of his stomach. The cameras were already set up, the weights in place, so he went through the routine, filming her as he eased the weight off till she was fully conscious, lowering it again, following instructions as he'd always done; the tyrant voice of his accomplice not entirely silenced, at least in his head. Much as he resents it, he's used to being told what to do. Anxious he'd make a mistake, nervous of her dying too soon, he had raised the weights after a bare fifteen seconds, before she was all the way out.

Soon as she gets a lungful of air, she starts coughing and blubbing and begging.

He doesn't respond, and she falls silent. Outside of the kill room is quiet, except for an occasional rumble of noise from a passing truck, and he can almost *hear* her listening, waiting for the squeak of the pulleys to begin again, for the crushing weight on her chest.

But he can't just stand around all night, making up his mind what to do. He curses under his breath, takes the strain of the weight and unwinds the rope from the cleat hook. Straight off she starts to beg, and he rushes it, then flustered, leaves her under too long: when he raises the weight, she doesn't come round, and he has to strip off the plastic wrap, resuscitate her.

When she comes to, he's so relieved he sits back on his haunches and drops his head in his hands so the cameras can't see that he's crying. That was almost the end of it; he felt so adrift right then, he thought, *I don't know how to do this.* In the past he would have begged for forgiveness, but he's a different person, now – different today than he was even yesterday. Stronger. All Fergus ever did was give orders and make him feel like he was in the way.

He watches himself look up at the block-and-tackle system and feels again that sudden hollowing out at his centre. The pulleys. Another of Fergus's 'refinements' – they were just a means to get him out of the way.

He says aloud, 'This is not what I want. It was never what I wanted.'

Sharla Jane sobs with relief. 'No . . . I know that.' The intubation has damaged her voice, and her breath rasps in her throat as she whispers. 'You don't have to hurt anyone—'

'Shut up,' he says. 'No one's talking to you.' He stands with his fingers plucking nervously at the seam of his pants. 'What I meant was, I'll do it my own way.'

He sounds like a kid. Why the hell is he *explaining*? And to her, of all people.

Her eyes are covered, and he needs to get at them, yet he

can't move. He remembers his mouth was suddenly dry as dust and he was too scared to take the tape off, to look in her eyes.

Gradually he becomes aware that she is talking, her voice small and hesitant.

'Please . . . I know I've been a bad person, but Riley – he's just starting out in life. He never hurt nobody.'

'Yeah, well, shit happens. Anyway, he's not the innocent you think he is.'

'He's a *kid.*' She says it with a pity in her voice and he experiences a pang of pity for himself.

'You gave a shit about that boy, you would've never touched meth. You gave a shit about him, you wouldn't've put him through what you put him through.'

'I cared more about crank than I did about him for a little while. But I *never* stopped caring.' Tears seep from under the duct tape, lifting a corner. 'Anyway, the bad things I did aren't Riley's fault,' she says. 'They're mine. Punish *me*, don't punish him.'

'DON'T YOU FUCKING TELL *ME* WHAT TO DO!' He's screaming, out of control, spit flying from his mouth. '*Nobody* tells *me* what to do.'

'No.' She's sobbing and shaking, almost drowning in her own tears and snot. 'No, I know. I'm sorry. I didn't mean for it to sound like that.'

He takes a breath, another, another, another. Sucking in air like it's medicine, backing away from her because what he wanted to do right then was tear her insides out, and losing control terrifies him.

He might edit that part; makes him look bad. But Fergus usually does the editing, and he's not sure he can make a good job of it.

'I'm sorry,' she says again. Her voice is tremulous, but she tries to stop crying. 'Can I make it up to you?'

She's offering him sex, when he can just take it. It's almost funny. He moves in, his mouth close to her ear. 'Time will tell,' he says and she flinches, but the tape holds her.

He could've told her the boy got away, but he can't think of one good reason why he should. Nobody ever comforted him. Nobody ever told him it wasn't his fault. Nor gave him credit, either, for all he did, how hard he tried.

'I'm a glaikit gull,' he murmurs.

He looks down at the woman and a righteous resentment surges like hot acid in his stomach. 'I do *everything* to make it work,' he says. 'I treat you right; I do right by your kids; I bring in money regular, find you a nice place to live. But it's never enough.' He shakes his head. 'Give a woman something, she'll always want more.'

He bends and finds a box cutter in a canvas carryall on the floor behind him, slices through the duct tape over her eyes. She gasps, tries to flinch from the cold steel, and instinct makes him draw back, jarring his injured hand.

'Hey,' he says. '*Hey!*'

She stops, her breath quick and shallow.

'I need you to hold still,' he says, pressing the bandaged web of his thumb to staunch a fresh bleed, grimacing behind his mask. The torn flesh slows him down, but he finally gets the duct tape off her face and hair.

She blinks under the bright spot lamps, her eyes wide and wet with all the crying. He wipes her face with one broad hand and dries it on the seat of his pants, then replaces the tape, wrapping it over and over around her forehead, under the boards of wood, binding her tightly to the pallet.

'That didn't hurt, now, did it?'

She tries to shake her head, says, 'N-nnnn-n.' But she can't move because of the duct tape, and can't speak because she's so scared, and he realizes he's standing over her with the cutter in his hand, just inches from her face.

'I know,' he soothes. 'I know.'

Later, he'll check the recordings on the other cameras, see if the angles make it look closer still.

He retracts the blade, tucks the box cutter in the waistband of his pants and strokes her hair, almost crooning to her. 'That better?'

But removing one threat only makes her focus on another. She stares at the weight above her, and does not look comforted at all.

He smiles. 'Sometimes seeing what's coming isn't a good thing, is it?' She doesn't answer, but she doesn't need to – it's written on her face.

'I'm going to take out the box cutter and cut off the rest of the stretch wrap now. Okay?'

She says, 'Y-huh,' her eyes on the big disc hanging over her.

The blade is razor sharp, and it's the work of a moment. He drops the cutter into the bag at his feet and Sharla-Jane yelps at the sudden noise.

'Shh-sh,' he says. 'Everything's fine.'

He riffles through the contents of the carryall, picks up a sealed bag and tears it open. Bends to find a second and a third; finally hooks a roll of micropore tape with his little finger. He lays them out on her stomach for easy access. Feeling well prepped, he probes the muscles of her thigh, near the groin, using the fingertips of both hands, working in the direction of the knee. She doesn't carry much fat, so it's easy to feel the groove between the two big muscles, find the vein nestled between them on the inner thigh. He keeps the fingers of his left hand in place, so he doesn't lose the vein, picks up the wide-gauge hypodermic; the tube is already attached. No need to sterilize.

'This is going to pinch a bit,' he says.

He inserts the needle and she gives a small 'Yip!' and struggles to raise her head. He clips the tube so he can attach it to a drainage bag without making a mess. He places the bag on the floor and releases the clip. Instantly blood starts to flow.

'What are you doing?' She stares at him, horrified, pleading, and he sees another face, one that has tormented his dreams and coloured his life blood-red since he was eight years old.

'Stop it,' he yells. 'Quit staring at me. I can't stand the way you *look* at me. What am I supposed to do? I CAN'T HELP YOU.'

She closes her eyes and begins to wail, and she's just plain old Sharla Jane again.

He shuts off the flow. Shushes and soothes her until she's calm again: he doesn't want this to happen too fast and, while she's agitated, it'll go real fast.

'Okay?' he says, holding her hand, smoothing the cold sweat off her face. 'Feeling better?'

'Please, don't do this,' she says. '*Please?*'

'You want me to stop?'

She tries to nod, but can't. He turns to the camera.

'Do you want me to stop?'

'Who're you talking to? Please, *please*, why are you doing this?'

'There's *some* out there like to watch. The type of jerk-off who watches pay-per-view porn with a Mastercard in one hand, his pecker in the other. People who like to see the fear and pain in the eyes of a dying woman. Get a kick out of watching the light die in her eyes.' He bends to find something in the canvas bag, then straightens to look into the camera again. 'Well, that isn't me.'

With his finger and thumb, he forces her eyelids open, waits until she is looking at him, then shows her what he has in his hand. The box cutter, its point directly over her right eye.

'Don't.' She's breathing so fast she can barely get the words out. 'Please – don't.'

'Trust me,' he says. 'Sometimes it really is better not to see what's coming.'

She begins to scream.

'That's all right,' he says. 'You go ahead, scream, if it makes you feel better. There's nobody to hear you.'

The man dressed in black stands at the centre of a large, oblong, windowless room. Around him, cameras, tripods, spot lamps, a laptop with a webcam. The signal passes along cables and through steel walls to a satellite dish on the side of a large, rust-red shipping container, shielded from an empty, dusty road on an abandoned and derelict lot.

36

Tulk residence, Williams County, Oklahoma
Afternoon

Marsha Tulk is working on the business accounts. She likes to do numbers work, as she calls it, sitting in the small office that faces on to the front yard, so she can keep an eye on the comings and goings of her family. The yard is quiet, Harlan and Bryce being on a delivery run. Tyler is tending the pot grows in the eastern section and Waylon – well, that boy is probably still in bed. The accounts detail incomes, costs and expenses for the tomatoes, which show a modest profit. She pays her boys out of these profits, to minimize her tax liability, and Federal and state taxes take their share after deductions and expenses. Income from the marijuana is naturally not recorded on this spreadsheet, or anywhere else but her own head. But since the cost of fertilizer, irrigation and fencing is covered by the tomato crops, the only extras in the equation are cost of seed and transport, and the occasional incidental expense to grease the wheels of the gravy train.

She's working through the receipts, spiking those she has entered onto the computer, almost hypnotized by the sedate routine of the work.

The first surprise of the morning is when her door bursts

open and Waylon stumbles in, fully dressed and looking wide awake. 'Momma, you got to come see this.'

The second surprise is he's been watching the news.

On the screen, blue and red flashing lights – a cruiser and an SUV, Sheriff standing in front of them. The next shot is a close-up of a mobile home.

'What am I looking at here, Waylon?' she says, then stops. The camera switches to a shot of the entrance to a trailer park. It's Lambert Woods – Tulk property. 'Drugs arrest?' she asks.

Her youngest son rewinds the TiVo.

'Waylon, I asked you a question.'

'I'm trying to answer, Ma.'

He stops at a picture. It's a school records photograph. And it is without doubt the boy, Red. The caption reads 'Riley Patterson: MISSING'. Well, she never did think his name was Caleb. A crawler on the bottom of the screen gives an emergency contact number to the National Centre for Missing and Exploited Children. The anchorman says this boy attended the last day of school in Hays Elementary and that he lived with his mother over at Lambert Woods Mobile Home Park. This same boy who had sworn to her that his momma was dead and he was running away from a foster home.

Marsha Tulk sits for five minutes listening to the news story so she has it clear in her mind.

She can feel her son getting more and more agitated as he waits.

'Momma, that trailer is the last one before the woods,' he tells her. 'It can't be more'n a mile from one of the pot grows.'

She looks at him, thinking, *That boy* lied *to me*.

'Momma, that boy will bring the cops down on us,' Waylon says, pointing at the TV with the clicker. 'We need to turn him in.'

'Boy, I know the location and grid reference of every grow

we got in these woods,' she says. 'And I decide what "we" need to do.' She pauses, waiting for that to sink in. 'Are we clear?'

He hesitates, then puts the remote down like it's a loaded gun. 'Yes, Momma.'

'Good,' she says. 'You can bring the boy to me.'

Mrs Tulk looks mad.

Waylon wouldn't tell him why he was wanted, but Red could tell it wasn't good. He was beginning to feel better, but now his stomach is doing flip-flops again and his legs are shaking.

Mrs Tulk is waiting on the porch. 'You got some explaining to do,' she says.

'Ma'am, I— '

She raises a finger. 'Before you speak, you should think.'

That's all he's been doing since he got here. When they hauled him out of that pit this morning, he was so scared all he wanted was to get away, but now, after all the thinking he's done, he's scared they'll *send* him away, because everybody in these parts knows you do not mess with the Tulk family, and that means they won't mess with him. The thought that they will make him leave just about strikes him dumb.

'Cat got your tongue?' she says. 'Or are you wondering which lie you got caught in?' She stares at him for a good ten seconds without saying anything, and Red feels like his soul has been ripped out, sliced up, then put back inside him in a place where it does not fit.

He starts to shake and she sighs. 'You'd best come inside, take a look at this.'

His face is on the TV screen with a caption and the CNN news logo next to it.

'Why're the police looking for you, boy?'

He can't tell from looking at the frozen picture on the screen, so he takes a chance she doesn't know the full truth, yet, turns his hands palms up. 'I stole some money when I ran off from the foster—'

She swipes him hard with the yellow knuckles of her right hand, and his head snaps round so fast he hears the bones in his neck crackle.

'Go ahead, tell me another lie,' she says, her face bunched up like a fist. 'See what I'll do if you make me real mad.'

His head clanging from the slap, he tells her everything, right up to how he found his momma tied up, the duct tape on her mouth. He tells her there was a shadow in Momma's room, that it peeled itself off the wall and come at him, and he ran.

'A shadow? You got to do better than that.'

Standing in her hot living room with sweat soaking his back, a cold wind blows through him. 'I couldn't see its face – it didn't have no face.'

Waylon shifts uneasily, but she frowns at her son, tells him to stop fidgeting. 'Make sense now,' she says.

Red sees a shadow face, something shaped out of the dark. A face like a blank slate that you could write whatever horror most scared you on it. But that's kids' stuff, that's fairy tales for dumb kids who don't know that the real scary stuff out there is mostly human.

'Are you telling me he wore a mask?'

A mask. Now he feels stupid.

'Yes, ma'am,' he says. 'It was a mask.'

'So, a man wearing a mask came at you.'

He nods, the picture of him on the TV screen smiling out at him like it's in on the joke.

'Who was it?'

He crinkles his forehead. 'I don't know.' Then he ducks, expecting another slap. She doesn't hit him, but she looks so fierce he knows he can't leave it at that. He has tried hard not to think about what happened that night, and now she's asking him to remember stuff that makes him want to run away and hide.

'Well, what came into your head when that shadow peeled off of the wall and came at you?'

'Boogeyman,' he says, and wishes he had bit off his tongue rather than say it, because Waylon sniggers and makes *woo-ooh* noises.

Mrs Tulk gives him a look and Waylon apologizes, moving to stand a couple steps out of her reach.

'It's understandable,' she says. 'But you do know there's no such thing as the Boogeyman, don't you, child?'

''Course I know it.' Waylon huffs and Red sends him all the hate in his heart with one angry glance, because *knowing* a thing and *believing* it is not the same thing at all. Sure, he *knows* the Boogeyman was a scary story made up to frighten kids, but last night he *believed* the Boogeyman was in that room with him and his momma, and running through the woods he was certain sure the Boogeyman was after his blood.

She stares at him, frowning like she's trying to puzzle something out. 'Run the programme, Waylon,' she says, and he presses 'play' on the TiVo. There are people and police lights, and news cameras. Then a picture of their mobile home comes on the screen. There is crime-scene tape on the front door.

Red looked anxiously up at Mrs Tulk. 'Yes, I know where you're from, child,' she says. 'I know a lot about you. Keep that in mind while you tell the rest.'

'Yes, ma'am.'

'So, you got home. What is the first thing you did?'

'I was hungry, so I grabbed a sandwich and a Coke.'

'Didn't you say your momma expected you home early?'

'Yes, ma'am, but the place was dark, so I figured they was in bed or had gone without me.'

'*They?*' she says.

'Momma and her boyfriend – calls himself Will, but I call him Mullet-head, on account of his hair.'

'Do you?' she says, her eyes half shut.

'Not to his face,' he adds.

'You saying this man with the mullet should've been there with your momma?'

Red nods. He can tell he's said something important, but he can't see what, and before he has time to work it out, she changes the subject.

'Why'd you run into the woods?' she says. 'Why didn't you head down to the manager's office?'

'I tried. But alongside the fence there really *is* a pervert – name of Goodman – keeps asking me to go inside his trailer.' He shoots her a guilty look. 'He's the one I stole the beer off. He tripped me up and I slashed him and got up and run. Next thing I know I'm in the woods.'

'What were you thinking?' she says. 'A bad man's coming after you, you should go where there's people.'

He doesn't know what he was thinking, or if he was thinking at all as he slashed and tore and ran. At one point he had the crazy notion he would lure the faceless man into one of the Tulks' booby traps, then go back and free his mom. But the shaming truth of it was he kept running because he was too scared to stop.

'I just ran.' He hangs his head.

'You didn't just *run*. You climbed into the trunk of a stranger's car. What possessed you?'

'I . . .' He falters. He will have to tell her that he had seen the pot grow before, and he had lied about that too.

'Go ahead, boy. I'll find out soon enough – you might as well tell the truth.'

He takes a breath and lets it go. 'I hitched a ride to Hays in Bryce's pickup one time. So when I saw headlights, I thought I would get in the trunk and when we got to town, I could sneak out, call the Sheriff. I stayed out of sight until Harlan put the tools back in the trunk, and climbed in while he was shutting off the water taps. But he didn't go into town – he just kept on going along the back roads, and I knew we were not going to Hays. I tried to pop the lock but I couldn't get out. And then it stopped and Harlan went off with the other man. They were away all night, and by then it was too late.'

'What the hell do you *mean*, it was too late?' She scowled at him. 'Didn't you think of your momma at all? Why didn't you just ask for help instead of sneaking around the place?'

Red looks away, but the picture is on the TV, watching him, so he looks at her again and decides to be honest. 'I saw what you were growing in that clearing,' he says. 'I did not think you would want me to call the cops.'

Mrs Tulk scratches her chin. 'That much is true. But why'd you lie about why you were on the run? Maybe we could've helped your momma.'

He shakes his head. 'I knew she was dead already.'

'How could you possibly know that, locked in a car trunk all night?' she says.

He shows her his old battered radio. 'I heard it on the news – they found Momma – said her name and everything.'

Finally, she turns and flicks off the TV with the remote clicker, and the room seems suddenly much darker. Riley Patterson takes a breath.

'Mrs Tulk, ma'am,' he says, and he can't stop the quiver in his voice. 'Are you going to turn me in?'

37

Incident Command Post, Westfield, Oklahoma

Detective Chief Inspector Kate Simms sat opposite
Fennimore at one of the pairs of tables in the function-
room-turned-office at the hotel. He was on Skype, talking to
Josh Brown, the PhD student who was covering his summer-
school classes. She'd had dealings with Josh on a major
case she'd investigated the previous winter; Fennimore had
brought him on board, and there was no question that his
psychology training had proved invaluable. Fennimore had
taken the student into his confidence, but Simms preferred
to keep him at a distance. Josh Brown had an uncanny ability to draw others out while he shrouded himself in mystery.
He – a complete stranger, acting incognito – had persuaded
the friends of a victim to give him personal information
about the victim, and although it had helped them to crack
the case, it left Simms with a lingering sense of unease.
She'd done a background check on the student prior to the
prosecutions that came out of their investigation, but he
had no criminal record. So why had he tried to wriggle out
of testifying at the trial? Josh Brown was evasive and shifty
around her, and in return she felt an antipathy bordering on
dislike.

Right now, he and Fennimore were discussing the medical examiner's findings, and the difficulty of tracking down their killer. The doctoral student asked question after question. Odd, she thought, for such a secretive person to be so inquisitive. She moved away, not wanting to be drawn into the conversation.

Deputy Hicks was standing near the window, sipping iced tea, and Simms drifted over to her. The cicadas had been quiet during the morning, but she'd heard the first tentative calls as a series of creaks and buzzes in mid-afternoon and, as the heat and humidity increased, more and more joined the chorus. Within thirty minutes, the racket would be as loud and piercing as the scream of a circular saw.

'Here it comes,' Simms said.

Hicks looked over her shoulder. 'Excuse me?'

Simms lifted her chin towards the window.

'Oh.' Hicks gazed down on the law-enforcement vehicles shimmering in the car park. The harsh light reflecting off them seemed to match the metallic screech of the insects.

Hicks shrugged. 'For me, it's the sound of summer.'

Simms took her words as a rebuff and, with a shrug, reached for a jug of iced water, ready to fill her glass and return to her desk, but the younger woman turned to face her and tilted her head, a small smile playing on her face.

'They have two little drums, right here,' she said, pointing to her abdomen. 'They pop 'em up and down like you'd pop the top of an empty Coke can – only those bugs do it thousands of times a second.'

'Let me guess,' Simms said. 'Encyclopedia Fennimore.'

Hicks grinned, swirling the crushed ice in her glass. 'He is full of facts, isn't he?'

'Which he feels compelled to share,' Simms said, with a smile.

'Can I ask a personal question?' Hicks was watching her, and Simms found her dark-rimmed irises unsettling.

'You can ask . . .'

'Are you and the Professor . . .?'

'Are we what?' Simms said, inserting a chill into her tone.

The younger woman's gaze dropped for a moment, then she fixed her she-wolf eyes on Simms's face. 'Involved,' she said.

'Now, why would you think that?' Simms asked, avoiding the question.

'He seems . . . protective, I guess.'

'Misplaced chivalry,' Simms said, lightly. 'I can take care of myself. And besides, I'm not interested.' She held up her left hand to show her wedding ring.

Hicks said, 'Oh,' but she did not look convinced, and for a moment the two women regarded each other thoughtfully.

A whoop from CSI Roper told them that something good had come in. 'We just hit the jackpot at the DMV.' He connected his laptop to the computer screen so they could all see the driver's details.

'The prints we lifted from the trailer? Thomas Holsten,' he said. 'Commercial drivers' licence.'

Dunlap said, 'Haulage work ties in with his absences from home.'

'Trucker,' Ellis said, sourly. 'I'd put every one of them on CODIS, I had my way.'

Simms studied the man in the picture. He was clean-shaven, his hair cut short – he even wore a shirt and tie. 'He looks more like an office worker,' she said.

'He's a chameleon,' Fennimore said, looking over the top of his computer screen. 'He blends in. A change of clothes and a couple of weeks' beard growth, this could be your redneck suspect.'

'Missouri licence,' Ellis said.

The CSI nodded. 'Registered to a mailing address in Joplin, Missouri. That's just over the Oklahoma state line,' he added, for the Brits' benefit. 'But I wouldn't hold out too much hope on him still being there: this licence is six years old – expiration date, end of July.'

'Only one way to find out,' Dunlap said.

A team of two detectives set off to check on the address in Joplin. Two more teams began canvassing commercial transport firms in Missouri. The licence endorsements told them that their man drove a 'semi' – the equivalent of an articulated lorry in the UK. He was licensed to carry non-hazardous materials only. It was a broad field to winnow, but the team was energized by the news. Two detectives searched land records for properties owned or mortgaged in the name of Holsten. Since the FBI behaviourist thought he might have links with the county, they would begin in Williams County. Holsten might have used his driver's licence to gain a credit card, so another two teams began checking card companies, while the Sheriff's deputies toured local gas stations, convenience stores and fast-food restaurants around Hays with a copy of Holsten's licence photograph.

A call came in from the team in Joplin eighty minutes later.

Dunlap took the call, with every pair of eyes in the room turned to him. 'Yes,' he said, listened for a while, then: 'Yeah. All right, come on in.' He ended the call and looked into their expectant faces.

'The mailing address on the driver's licence is a Chinese restaurant. They say they rented a room over the store to the guy, held mail for him on and off, but he never lived there, and he stopped paying rent a few years back.'

They were further disappointed by the Land Records search. Two Thomas Holstens were registered as property owners in Williams County: an eighty-two-year-old farmer, and an office registered to a licensed professional counsellor whose main residence was in Tulsa. No house or apartment was registered in that name. They were now checking Land Records state-wide.

'He used a false address to get his driver's licence, so the documents he used as proof of ID could also be false – Holsten could be one of several aliases,' Dunlap said. 'We'll just have to hope something turns up on the haulage-company canvass.'

'I've been talking to one of my doctoral students,' Fennimore said. 'It's a long shot, but he thinks we should trawl online forums and emails for key words and phrases relating to what the killer's been doing to his victims.'

Dunlap shook his head regretfully. 'We just don't have the manpower.'

'It wouldn't take much – just some technical know-how. Josh tells me there's a program called a "spider" – it does the searching for you.'

Dunlap turned to Dr Detmeyer. 'Can the FBI help with this?'

'Of course.' Detmeyer hesitated. 'It might take a day or two to get the okay, set it up . . .'

'We don't *have* a couple of days,' Dunlap said. 'We want any chance of saving Riley Patterson, we need to take action *now*.' He sought out the Team Adam consultant, his dark eyes glowing. 'Mr Whitmore?'

Whitmore already had his cell phone in his hand. 'We got techs,' he said. 'I don't see why not.'

38

Tulk residence, Williams County, Oklahoma

Waylon has done as she told him and rounded up his brothers, and Marsha Tulk can tell by the looks on their faces that her boys have had a quiet talk on the way over to the house.

Harlan looks around the big living room. 'Where is he?'

'Haley took the boy down to Elm Creek, see if they can hook a few catfish for supper,' his momma says. 'Which will allow us to talk freely about what's to be done.'

She knows without a word being said that her sons think she should take the boy in to the sheriff's office, but none of them wants to be the first to say it.

She runs through the newsreel, even though Waylon has no doubt told it all, and by the end of it they all look sick.

'All this hoo-ha on our property – why'm I getting to hear about it on the news?' She looks at Tyler: he is the one who collects the weekly takings from the manager's office at Lambert Woods, so he's on the park more than the others.

'I can't be two places at once, Momma – I was out, working on the grows. Sammy tried my cell phone, but you know what reception is like over on the east side.'

Sammy was the park manager.

'Well, why didn't he call *me*?'

'He did, Momma.'

She felt a pang of guilt – she was always leaving the darn thing someplace or other.

'Anyway, they're there, now,' she said.

'They're bound to come up here asking questions,' Bryce says. He is the second youngest and the worrier in the family.

Harlan jerks his head towards the map on the TV screen. 'They found her body forty miles east on I-44,' he says. 'That's got to be where they'll look for the boy.'

For once Marsha thinks Bryce's anxieties are warranted, so she says, 'You think so? Because there seems to be a whole *squad* of police, right on our doorstep, and *not* forty miles down the road, son.'

Harlan *tsk*ed and shook his head. 'I knew we should've sent that boy on his way.'

She narrows her eyes. 'I don't recall you saying that, Harlan. What I *do* recall is Haley saying she wanted to keep him and you not raising any objections. I recall this same child climbed into your car and Bryce's pickup two different times, and neither one of you had the slightest notion he was there.'

'Just proves my point,' Harlan says. 'The boy is slippery.'

'He's doing what he can to survive,' she says.

'Even so, he will bring trouble on us.'

'Already has.' This from Tyler, who will rarely lead a conversation, but will say the *Amens* from the sidelines.

'It wasn't the boy brought the authorities here, it's this mullet-haired man calls himself Will. They're here because he took that boy's momma, and he killed her.' None of them will meet her eye. 'But like Tyler said, trouble is here, one way or another, so what do we do about it?'

'Ain't none of our business,' Waylon says with a shrug.

'None of our business? None of our *business*?' When Marsha Tulk gets mad, she does not get shrill like most women, she roars – strong and loud as any man. 'Pay attention, boy. The news anchor said they're looking into other murders. We rented a trailer to a goddamn *serial killer.*'

'Momma, c'mon,' Tyler says. 'How was we supposed to know?'

She laughs. A hard, cracked sound. 'When they come knocking on our door you're gonna need something stronger than a plea of *stupidity*, boy.'

'I checked with Sammy,' Tyler says. 'He did not sign the rental agreement – Sharla Jane Patterson did.'

'Well, that's something,' she says. 'Did any of you see him?'

The brothers exchange glances and the other three shake their heads, but Tyler says, 'From a distance. He wasn't around much, she paid the rent regular, wasn't no trouble – I didn't have no cause to go over there.'

She nods. 'We tell the police that – the part about him being elusive – not the part about the pot grows, of course.' She allows herself a smile.

'You think that's going to be enough to send them on their way?' Harlan says.

'Why not?'

'Like you said, they didn't find those children with their mommas, and all those agencies camping out on our front yard are not going away until they have searched our woods.'

'No, they are not. But they got no call looking for the boy anywhere but Lambert Hill in back of the trailer park. We got one pot grow in the woods over there. That's maybe seventy plants – which is what? Twelve per cent loss on the entire crop – tops. Wheat farmers lost a darn sight more'n that in the drought last year.'

'We planted those crops and tended them for two months, Momma, and you're telling us to rip 'em out and what – burn 'em?'

'You know I'm not saying that. You boys got plenty of time to lift the crop. Do it right, we might even be able to replant it.'

'They might could've already headed into those woods,'

Bryce says. 'And if we can't get to the grows before the cops find them, we could lose a lot more than twelve per cent – we could go to jail, Momma.'

She flapped one hand, waving away his worrying. 'We'll wrestle that hog when it breaks cover.'

'There's serious investment gone into those grows in seed, equipment and operating costs – not to mention the time and labour every one of us has put in.' This is Harlan, trying to be the businessman. 'We stand to lose – thousands.'

Unreasonable though it is, Marsha Tulk is astonished by her sons' ignorance of their finances. She keeps them in the dark about the monetary side of their businesses, because she thinks if they knew how much they were worth it would turn their heads. Bryce and Waylon are apt to be lazy, and a man is only a man so long as he has meaningful work to do.

Even now she holds back, but can't help showing her irritation. 'Anyone would think you boys did the harvesting and selling with your eyes shut and your minds on something else.'

Harlan stares at her. He is sharper than the others, and she can see him recalculating the value of their crops in his head. 'You're prepared to throw that kind of money away on some trailer-park kid?' he says.

'Well, listen to Mr High-and-Mighty Harlan Tulk – if that boy is trailer-park trash, what are we – The Folks Who Live On the Hill?'

'I never said he was—'

'Did you forget what we grow up in the woods, Harlan? We come from a long line of bushwhackers and bootleggers – so don't tell me that child don't matter because he's *trailer trash*.'

'I'm not, Momma, truly, I'm not. But listen to me: if the cops come looking – and they will – we're going to lose crops.'

'Damnit, Harlan, what turned you into such an old woman?' She sees she has offended him, and, trying to be reasonable, she takes a breath and says, 'If it makes you feel better, you can put up new warning signs. That should slow them down – all we need is enough time to take the grows out before they get to 'em.'

'What the hell?' Waylon throws up his hands. 'Just give 'em the boy, Momma, they won't have cause to send in no search party.'

She rounds on him, fists swinging. 'I have *never* turned *anybody* in to the police my *entire life.*' The rap and crack of her bare knuckles on Waylon's head and back give emphasis to her words.

'Okay, Momma, okay,' Harlan says, getting between them, but not raising his hands to her even in defence, because that is something *he* has never done and never will, not where his momma is concerned.

She squares up to him, her face red and blotched from the heat and her fury.

'I feel sorry for him,' Harlan says. 'Truly, I do. Haley is fond of him and I can see why. But that boy is not kin.'

'That boy has just lost his momma,' she says, 'most likely to the first man in his life that he trusted. Red has stayed alive because he got gone, and we are going to help him stay gone until the man who killed his momma is locked up, or dead.'

When Haley and the boy come home a couple of hours later, she calls him into the living room with all her boys around her to tell him he can stay if he has a mind to. She wants him and them both to understand that she will not have dissent on this.

'But you need to understand,' she says, 'in this household, dog don't hunt, dog don't eat.'

'I can work,' he says, eager. 'I could water the pot grows, mix up the fertilizer.'

'That's quite a lot of work for a boy to do,' she says.

'I don't mind – I could maybe earn some pocket money?' He winces as he says it, but she laughs.

'Son, you are a natural businessman, and I like a boy who is willing to make himself useful.'

Waylon grunts. He is still sulking from the chastisement he received for telling her they should turn the boy in.

She pays him no mind and looks instead at her second son, Bryce. He hates sweat labour, is built too heavy for hot days out in the woods.

'Think you could show the boy how, Bryce?' she said.

Bryce shrugs. 'I could show him, doesn't mean he'd learn.'

'I'm a real quick study,' the boy says.

Bryce shakes his head, doubtful. 'It isn't just the work. Out at the pot grows it's all sweat and skeeters – and if the skeeters don't getcha, the ticks will.'

Marsha nods, sympathizing – her boy just about got ate alive tending their crops.

'I don't mind,' Red says. 'Bugs don't bother me. Momma says I'm too full of bile, makes my blood bitter.'

The way his face creases, Marsha can tell that he realized he had talked about his momma as if she was still around, but she is not about to point that out to him. She just taps his knee, says, 'Well, now. Seems to me the Lord gave you a blessing, and it would be a sinful waste not to make good use of it.'

39

Fergus has received a text. One word: 'Email.'

He hasn't heard from Will since yesterday, when he had the nerve to pull the Internet connection. He feels cut off from a part of his brain. The undifferentiated, lizard part, admittedly; the part that acts on impulse rather than reason. But still . . .

For twenty minutes he resists, but he can't stand it – he needs to know. He snatches his laptop from his briefcase. His programs and files are password-protected, encrypted, safe, but the Atlantic Ocean and half the American continent stands between him and safety right now.

Swiftly, he navigates to their shared webmail account. Clicks to the 'password' box, types in a sequence of numbers, letters and symbols. He hesitates. What if it's a trap? Dread creeps up his spine, raising goose pimples.

He shakes his head. The big numpty wouldn't know a Trojan Horse from a rocking horse. He hits the send key and the inbox opens.

There's a single message in the drafts folder. Subject line: 'Unfinished Business'.

He opens the draft. No message, only a URL and a

password. Just as they did in the early days, live-streaming the kills to the web.

His hands are shaking. He is not used to feeling powerless. He takes a breath, copies and pastes the web address into the search line, enters the password in the dialogue box.

Sharla Jane is taped and wrapped like a parcel. A pink, mewling special delivery. He sits forward in his armchair, feeling sick with dismay but also excited. Because even as he gave the order to shut down, to get rid of her and get out, he had mourned the wasted months they'd spent preparing her. He'd felt cheated that he wouldn't see her at the last.

He watches, irritated, as the mullet-headed cretin gets in the way of camera sight lines and makes a mess of using the weights. His feelings rapidly turn to contempt, watching his accomplice's frantic attempts at resuscitation.

Then Will picks up the hypodermic. *Oh, for pity's sake – is that what this is all about? He wants to play nursey all over again?*

Even so, he doesn't look away for a second; he has to admit, he wants to see how far his protégé will go without the normal checks and balances exerted over his grosser tendencies.

And when Will turns his masked face to the camera and says, 'Do you want me to stop?' Fergus recoils; it's as if the dumb fucker knows what he's thinking. Despite himself, he says, 'No.'

A second later, the kill screams; he sees the blade in Will's hand and he's on his feet yelling, 'No-no-no – *No!*'

This isn't the way it's supposed to go down. It isn't the way it's supposed to end.

One of his throwaway mobiles rings on the coffee table a few feet from him. He launches himself at it. The laptop slips and he tries to catch it, succeeds, but the lid smacks against the sharp edge of the table. Cursing, he shoves it onto the table and sweeps up the phone.

'You ruined her!' he screams. 'You stupid *bastard.*'

'It's hard to see the light die in this one's eyes, huh?'

The response feels like a slap. Destroying Sharla Jane's eyes was an act of defiance – a personal attack on him.

'You forget who you're talking to,' he warns.

'No, I just remembered. You're nothing but a gutless *Jessie* who gets other people to do his dirty work. It's always been about what *you* want. You held me back all these years,' Will continues in that irritating, affected drawl. 'Well, not any more – things have changed.'

'Nothing's changed – you're still the brainless fuck-up you always were. I made all of this possible. *I* laid the ground rules, *I* did the planning.'

'*Planning*? This isn't about planning, it's about *action.* You lived your life through me. You see the world through *my* eyes. You have no idea what it's like to be in the room, to smell the fear, feel the heat coming off them. You think you're some kinda mastermind, but you know what you really are? You're a peeping Tom, watching all those women die through an electronic keyhole.'

He hears the tumbling notes that mean he's been cut off, and stares in disbelief at the mobile phone in his hand.

Moments later, he realizes he has had an actual conversation at his home with a man who's sought by police in two American states, as well as by the FBI. Horrified, he breaks open the phone, strips out the SIM card and bends it backwards and forwards till it breaks. Then he tosses it on the fire and watches the flames turn green for an instant before it is consumed. He picks up his laptop to log off the web page. The monitor is cracked. He paces the room, Will's insults going round and round in his head – *Peeping Tom. Gutless Jessie* – until he feels choked with rage.

He has to get out. He packs a sports bag and slams out

the front door, crunches across the gravel to his SUV and throws the kit onto the passenger seat. Inside, netting; a roll of plastic wrap; nylon rope; duct tape; a hunting knife.

40

*We cannot bear to look away from what
we cannot bear to see.*

ORIGIN UNKNOWN

**Incident Command Post, Westfield,
Williams County, Oklahoma
Sunday morning**

At 5.47 a.m., 'spider' 'bots deployed by Team Adam's techs found a URL that showed a digital video recording on a continuous loop.

The Task Force assembled at six thirty.

'The web address was probably posted first in an Internet relay chat room,' CSI Roper explained; even sitting still, Roper seemed constantly on the move. 'Old technology, but it's still used by hackers, crackers and anyone else who wants to swap illegal information anonymously.

'By six a.m., the link was on three S&M forums,' Roper said. 'By five after, links were popping up all over the web: Twitter, Facebook, newsfeeds – someone even put a section of it on YouTube. It's gone viral.'

The recording showed Sharla Jane, strapped to a pallet. Her eyes were bound with duct tape, and a concrete weight was pressing on her chest. She was struggling to breathe. The weight was attached via a rope to a simple block and tackle. A faceless killer stood over her.

Fennimore's mobile phone rang. Josh Brown. He rejected the call, apologizing to the hushed gathering. Nobody even glanced at him. They were all staring at the scene playing out on the screen.

His phone rang again. Josh again.

'Not *now*, Josh.'

'Don't hang up,' the student urged. 'I found a website. Sharla Jane's on it.'

'We're looking at it now,' Fennimore says. 'How the hell did you—'

'Same way you did – spiders, web crawlers. They don't call it the World Wide Web for nothing.'

'For God's sake, Josh, if he finds out you've been tracking him—'

'He'll think I am just another sad, sick bastard wanting to join his fan club. Anyway, he'd have to be monitoring site traffic, and I doubt he'd do that. He put the link out there because he *wanted* it to be found, Nick.'

'All right.' Fennimore exhaled, trying to control the nervous jitter at the top of his sternum. He glanced at the screen, not wanting to, but knowing that this recording gave them more on the killer than they had gleaned so far in hundreds of hours of investigation. The killer was inserting a laryngoscope into Sharla Jane's throat.

'I have to go,' Fennimore said.

They watched the killing through to the end, though few could keep their eyes on the screen when the man, dressed from head to foot in black, picked up the box cutter a second time.

Detmeyer was the first to break the stunned silence. 'We'll need a recording of this,' he said. 'We should study it.' He sounded pragmatic and emotionless, while Fennimore's arms and face burned like they were being swarmed over by fire ants.

A few minutes later, word came in that the video had been uploaded through a server in Westfield.

'He's here – in town?' Reflexively, Launer touched the gun in his holster.

CSI Roper shook his head. 'The accuracy of a geographic location for an IP address depends on the number of local nodes—'

'Can we get that again, in American?' Sheriff Launer said.

Roper thought about it for a moment. 'Okay, comparable systems . . . Let's say . . . General Post Office – every sizeable town's got one of those, right?'

Launer gave him a hard stare as if he was waiting for a punchline he wouldn't like.

The CSI went on, regardless: 'Mail can be routed through it by the US Postal Service and then out to small communities and individual farms for what – thirty miles?'

'Fifty or more,' the Sheriff said.

'Okay, fifty. So a package comes into Westfield, doesn't mean the person named on the package lives in town, does it?'

'Not necessarily . . .'

'So, the Internet works on the same principle. Stuff gets routed through a server somewhere in Westfield – it acts as a hub where packages of electronic information get sorted and sent on.'

'I can look at a postal package and find an address that would take me to Joe Blow's front yard,' Launer said. 'Can your "IP" address do that?'

'In a big city, maybe. Out here, best we can do is say he's still somewhere in Williams County.' Roper dipped his head, regretful.

They took a break to give everyone a chance to get the phantom smell of blood from their nostrils, the sound of Sharla Jane's screams out of their heads. The smokers escaped outside, not caring about the heat and humidity. Fennimore began making notes. He looked up and saw Abigail Hicks watching him; she looked haunted by what she'd seen. He set down his pen and went over to where she was standing.

'Okay?' he said.

'When he was resuscitating her, I kept willing her to breathe.' She spoke low and fast, as if she was afraid someone might overhear. 'Crazy, huh?'

He shook his head. 'No,' he said. 'Not crazy. Human.'

At that moment, Dunlap appeared at the double doors. 'Ready?'

The majority of the team would go on with what they had been doing before the link came in, while a small group reviewed the recording elsewhere. Since the Task Force had allocated the inn as their command post, the owners had experienced a reversal of their fortunes, and were more than happy to hire out additional accommodation to the investigation.

Fennimore picked up his sheets of notepaper and laptop, and Hicks followed suit.

'Did you see Sheriff Launer?' Dunlap asked Hicks.

'Said he'd seen enough.' Hicks's expression revealed nothing. 'Said he'll talk to you when he gets back.'

Dunlap nodded as if to say, *That figures*. He disappeared onto the landing and Fennimore turned to Hicks.

'Did he say where he was going?'

'Said he was headed out to Lambert Woods to organize the search for Riley.'

'The woods?' Launer had refused to even consider the woods at the back of the trailer park the day before. 'Didn't he tell Kent Whitmore they needed to complete the search of Cupke Lake first?'

'He changed his mind after the news people found out that the skeeters down at the lake were real hungry. Some of those guys already packed up and headed back to the city.'

'Did he speak to Whitmore?' Fennimore asked.

'He took Mr Whitmore with him.'

Fennimore narrowed his eyes. 'What's he up to?'

Her remarkable eyes fixed on his, and he was struck again

by the dark rims that bounded the irises. 'His campaign rival gained two percentage points in two days. He had no choice – he strapped on his six-gun and saddled up for the campaign trail.'

41

Alemoor Loch, Scotland

Gordon checked the dive computer on his wrist; he'd lost count of how many times he had checked it in the last ten minutes. They were at thirty-two metres, and not a glimmer of light from the surface could penetrate to that depth. His integrated compass told him they had reached the deepest section of the loch, which meant another twenty-three metres of dark, cold water beneath them. They would dive for another ten metres, the deepest he'd ever been. He had practised the routine, memorized the dive plan, read the contour maps until he felt he could do the dive blindfold.

Gordon felt a tug on the buddy-line; their divemaster, John, giving the signal to descend. Forty metres. This was the big one; the one Gordon had been building towards for two years. He felt a trickle of anxiety, and stilled it; he was buddied up with John – there was nothing to be anxious about. Together they tilted heads down and began the final descent, allowing gravity and the power of their legs to take them.

At thirty-five metres, his dive light reflected back at him and he slowed. They had prepared for this; it was a rocky outcrop of black shale, and was featured on the dive map he had studied in such minute detail. The overhang went back about three metres, then the cliff continued down. There were jagged rocks here, and they would need to be careful not to snag their gear, but they wouldn't be diving much deeper, so it wasn't a major issue.

Head down, he felt his way along the jagged surface of the rock, using his dive meter and the tracery of bubbles from his mask to reassure him which way was up, because he always got a bit freaked – a bit claustrophobic – when he met hard surfaces in the dark. 'In a bad situation, anxiety quickly turns to panic,' John had told them. 'When panic sets in, all you can fall back on is your training, because panic is a wuss screaming in your ear. It will not listen to reason, and it *will* ruin your day.'

He glanced sideways and saw John's light, four metres away, and told himself everything was fine. They would work their way down another three metres to the edge of the overhang, drop a few more metres to get past the forty-metre mark, then make a controlled ascent. Nothing to it.

Resisting the urge to get closer to the reassuring presence of the divemaster, he checked his dive computer and continued the descent. At thirty-eight metres, his hand plunged into nothingness and he felt a stab of alarm, gasped, stopped, got himself under control.

'Stop-Breathe-Think-Act,' he chanted silently, repeating the club mantra until he was calm.

It would be a bit scary looking into blackness under the overhang, but he challenged himself to do it. He swung to the vertical, gripping the edge of the rock with his fingertips, hanging upside down. *You can do this*, he told himself. He held onto the rock with one hand and, with the torch in the other, he shone the light into the abyss.

'*Jesus!*' He screamed, shoved away from the rock face, bubbles rising frantically from his mask. He kicked wildly, catching his foot against a sharp ridge of rock, felt pain explode in his ankle. He kept kicking. He needed to get up, up and out.

A sharp tug on his wrist sent another shaft of pain radiating through the joints of his arm into the muscles of his shoulder. Still he screamed, sending air boiling from around the regulator in his mouth. He kicked and panted, but couldn't get away, was too panicked to realize he'd reached the limits of the buddy-line.

John hauled him in like a fish, grabbed both arms, shoved him against the rock face and looked into his eyes, holding him fast. He went limp. The divemaster switched his grip, placing his left hand on Gordon's chest to steady him, and signalled with his right. Vertical, palm flat, then two fingers tapped to his temple. *Stop*, it said. *Think*.

Gordon nodded, though tears were misting his mask and his nose was blocked with snot, so he felt he was drowning, and he had to resist the impulse to spit out the regulator. It took a minute, but he got himself under control and John gingerly released his grip. He tapped his own dive computer, held up three fingers, pointed down. Three more metres, he would achieve his goal, surpass it, if he did that extra metre.

He shook his head. *You don't understand.*

John repeated the gesture.

Again, Gordon shook his head. He pointed to his eyes with his first two fingers, used one hand to indicate the rock overhang, then dipped the other under and shook his head again.

John pointed to Gordon's chest and signalled again: *Stop.* Then he pointed to his own chest, then to his eyes. He was going to take a look.

Gordon pinched his thumb and index finger together to make a circle. *Okay.* Though it was far from okay.

The divemaster crab-walked down the steep incline and shone his light under the overhang. Gordon leaned against the rock face. The light began to fade, darkness closed in

251

from the edges of his mask and he gasped, realizing he'd been holding his breath. *Breathe, you fucking idiot.* Hold your breath, and CO_2 builds up in the blood; it's narcotic, and it can kill a diver, fast. He waited with his back to the wall of the cliff and focused on keeping his breathing slow and regular until his CO_2 levels normalized and the torch beam brightened again.

A second later, sharp, frantic arrows of light darted right and left into the dark waters below him. Beams from John's torch. A ball of silver flashed past his face, mushrooming up and out as it rose; air from divemaster's regulator. Gordon had to grip the rock to stop himself tearing after it to the surface. Because when he'd peeped into the darkness under the overhang, he had seen a face staring back at him.

42

The narcissistic person has built an invisible
wall around himself.
He is everything, the world is nothing. Or rather:
He is the world.

ERICH FROMM, *THE ART OF BEING*

Incident Command Post, Westfield, Williams County, Oklahoma

It wasn't any easier watching the recording a second time around, but Fennimore worked to establish a mental distance from what was happening on the screen, focusing on small details: the words the killer used, his movements, his body language, trying to discover context from flashes of the kill room as the clumsily edited recording cut from one camera shot to another.

They were crammed into a tiny meeting room with a single two-foot-square window and a floor fan to make up for the lack of air con, the heat from the data projector cancelling out the meagre cooling it provided. Dunlap, Fennimore, Simms, Hicks and Detmeyer were in the room; Professor Varley was contributing via Skype. They already had a list of physical details from the recording: the bloody bandage around the man's hand; brief glimpses of the walls showing a ribbed surface. Biometrics programs at the FBI had been put to work, estimating the killer's height and build using comparators in the room: the netbook computer on a stand in one of the shots; the defibrillator; cameras and lamps he stood next to; the size of his hands relative to Sharla Jane's face and body. Step length and gait mapped from the recording would be additional identifiers – if they ever got close to the man.

'Dr Quint says the fact he used a block and tackle to raise and lower the weight explains why she didn't find bruising or soft-tissue injuries. The weight was just enough to stop Sharla Jane's lungs inflating.'

Collectively, those present took a deep breath.

Dunlap stopped the recording after the killer resuscitated Sharla Jane. 'What does he mean, "This is not what I want?"' he said. 'Does he feel bad about this?'

'I don't think so,' Fennimore said. 'He says, "I'll do it my own way." As if previously he was acting under instruction, and now he's rejecting that instruction.'

'You think there's a second mind at work here? I'd be fascinated to hear your reasoning.' Professor Varley, sensitive as always to anyone treading – be it ever so softly – on his turf.

Fennimore had set up his own netbook at one of the table placings, so they could all see the forensic psychologist and he could see the digital projector screen. Fennimore borrowed the remote and rewound to the section where the killer lowered the weight onto Sharla Jane's chest, then quickly raised it.

'Look at that – he's fumbling. He hasn't a clue what he's doing – he's used to someone *telling* him what to do.'

Varley looked sceptical.

They watched the killer's frantic attempts at resuscitation.

'He's panicked. Terrified,' Fennimore insisted.

'The death of another human being is traumatic, even for a murderer,' Varley said.

'He's killed five times before; you'd think he'd be better at it,' Fennimore said. Varley opened his mouth to speak, but the killer had started screaming at Sharla Jane, and Fennimore cut across him, pointing at the screen. 'See that? The one time he loses control is when he thinks Sharla Jane is telling him what to do.'

For a few moments, the two men eyed each other, mutually hostile, then Detmeyer, calm and unruffled as always, opened his hand, asking for the remote control. Fennimore handed it over and the psychologist sped through to the last section.

'Do you want me to stop?' the killer said. Then again, gazing directly into the camera lens, 'Do you want me to stop?'

'That repetition,' Detmeyer said. 'He does seem to be talking to someone.'

'Of course he is,' Varley said. 'He uploaded the murder onto the web in a bid for notoriety. He knows he has an audience.'

Detmeyer said, 'Agreed. But he seems to address someone *in particular* in the repetition. And there is a slight stress on the word "you".'

'There is not a *scintilla* of evidence he had an accomplice,' Varley said.

'Okay, the jury's out on that one,' Dunlap said. 'What else do we have?'

'Can you wind back to his self-pitying speech, just before he removes the duct tape?' Simms asked.

Detmeyer obliged and they listened to the killer complain that he did right by the victims, gave them a nice home, but women always wanted more.

'Sounds like he's hankering after a meaningful relationship with the women, but feels doomed to fail,' Dunlap said.

'A man like that doesn't want an equal partnership between two adults, he wants to be worshipped,' Simms said.

For once, Varley deferred to the woman in the room. 'He wants to be seen as a rescuer, a redeemer—'

'A god,' Simms said flatly, and he inclined his head, another tacit agreement.

'Women in Sharla Jane's situation aren't used to being "treated right",' Detmeyer said, paraphrasing the killer. 'His victims just emerged out of the most debased and desperate situations, and he is kind and attentive – at least at first. They must admire him, adore him, even. But as they regain some self-respect, even a little confidence, that relationship will inevitably change. They will see his weaknesses, as well as his strengths. He will sense the downgrading of his status from god to man, and he will *not* like that. They are no longer an extension of him; he feels a loss of control, and he finds that offensive, repellent, even terrifying.'

The recording ran on, and the man screamed at Sharla Jane, 'I can't stand the way you *look* at me.'

'We know he's not disfigured,' Dunlap said. 'Everyone we talked to said he's Joe Average, but he doesn't like to be watched?'

'Disfigurement can be in the mind,' Detmeyer said. 'But he doesn't say, "I can't stand you *looking* at me."' He played back the next section. 'He says, "I can't stand *the way* you look at me." See the expression on her face? She's pleading with him.'

Fennimore nodded. 'Then he screams, "I CAN'T HELP YOU."'

'He's saying he can't give her what she needs,' Detmeyer said.

'A god, failing in his own eyes,' Simms murmured.

Detmeyer nodded slowly, still staring at the screen.

Dunlap spoke up. 'He *cares* that he failed her?'

'Only insofar as it damages his self-image. His little lecture about putting the boy through shit with her addiction shouldn't be mistaken for compassion for the boy. It's self-pity – he's talking about himself,' Detmeyer said. 'He's aware of others only as an extension of himself.'

'But if he identifies with the children,' Simms said, 'there has to be a chance some are still alive?'

She's thinking about Suzie, Fennimore thought and, despite the heat in the room, he felt a chill.

'This is a man entirely without compassion.' Professor Varley had been silent for some minutes, and Fennimore had almost forgotten his presence. 'He exploits the children to gain the mothers' trust, and to exert control over them. That's all.'

Fennimore looked to Detmeyer for confirmation, and he gave a small nod.

'Meanwhile, he's out there, and the kids are still missing,' Dunlap said.

A knock at the door, and Detective Valance entered, bringing a welcome breath of cool air from the corridor. He was holding a sheet of printer paper in one hand and a pen drive in the other.

'Incoming,' he said. 'Team Adam got back on the rib pattern on the walls of the room. They think it's the interior of a shipping container. Ellis put a couple extra teams on the haulage-firm canvass. But that's not the big news.' His gaze shifted excitedly from one investigator to another. 'He just uploaded another recording. A message.'

He clicked a pen drive into a spare USB slot in the netbook and loaded the recording.

The man was dressed in black, as before, masked, with just a slit for the eyes and mouth.

'It was me who put Sharla Jane Patterson on the Internet,' he said, his voice flat and unemotional. 'Laney Dawalt was one of mine, and Rita Gaigan and Shayla Reed – a whole bunch of others, too. But that wasn't me.' He paused, realizing he had contradicted himself, seemed to rethink. 'So we're clear? I *did* it, okay? I *killed* them – but that was me on autopilot. And that is all in the past. I don't follow orders any more. I'm a hands-on kinda guy and, from now on, what I say goes.'

He looked into the camera lens, and behind the ski mask, he smiled. That smile was rammed full of violence and threat and quiet, unfulfilled rage.

'*I* decide when I'm ready to stop,' he says. 'I'm BTK. And I've barely made a start.'

The screen went dark.

'Are we sure this is our man?' Dunlap asked.

'FBI biometrics aren't complete yet,' Valance said. 'But he's the same build, it sounds like him, voice analysis is a good match to the other recording. And here's the kicker: Shayla Reed's name isn't on any list we gave to the media.'

It was their man, all right.

'BTK?' Simms said. 'Sounds familiar.'

'Dennis Rader,' Detmeyer explained. 'Killed at least ten people in Wichita, Kansas between 1974 and 2005. He sent taunting letters to the police. He even named himself – he didn't want the media coming up with something he didn't like. BTK stands for "Bind, Torture, Kill".'

'It's his joke,' Fennimore said. 'Instead of binding, he's *blinding* his victims.'

'So our killer's a copycat?' Dunlap asked.

Detmeyer seemed doubtful. 'Rader stalked his victims, broke into their homes, tied them up and killed them in a variety of ways. He murdered men, women, children – a whole family on one occasion. Ligatures and strangulation played a big part in his fantasies. Our killer gets close to the families, becomes a member of the family, even. We don't know what he did with the kids, but I don't see any real similarities.'

'He aspires to be as notorious as Rader, but he's creating his own legend,' Varley said.

'And, like he said, he just got started,' Hicks added.

There was a moment of sinking dread as they calculated how much worse this was going to get, then something engaged in Fennimore's mind with an almost audible click.

'No. What he *said* was, "I've barely made a start."'

'Well, excuse *me*, Professor Higgins,' Hicks said, with the faintest of smiles.

'It's the difference in construction,' Fennimore said. 'Wouldn't most Americans say, "I just got started", as you did?'

'People do say he talks funny,' Hicks agreed.

'Like he's from back East,' Simms added. 'If we could identify where, exactly . . .'

Dunlap looked to Detmeyer. 'Can the FBI help with that?'

Detmeyer said, 'The Bureau has a forensic linguistics database, but it's designed for threat assessment – and we already know the level of threat this man presents. You need an expert in geographical linguistics.'

Fennimore looked at Varley.

'There's a chap I know at Aston University; he studied linguistics in the United States and retains an interest in the American vernacular,' Varley said. 'I can ask, but I can't guarantee he'll be available at such short notice. And you will need to provide a quality transcription alongside the recording – otherwise you might as well shut your eyes and stick a pin in a map.'

'I'll ask Josh Brown to do the transcription and liaise.'

Simms caught her breath and he thought she might object, but she seemed to think better of it and said instead: 'Our man says he won't follow orders *any more*. Looks like he does have a partner, after all.'

Detmeyer tilted his head. 'It would seem so.'

Varley said nothing.

'He killed all those women because he was *told* to?' Hicks said.

'Oh, I'm sure he wanted to,' Detmeyer said. 'But it seems he wasn't happy with the *manner* of their deaths, until now.' He glanced at Fennimore's computer monitor, from where Professor Varley gazed unsmiling at the gathering. 'I hope the Professor will forgive the jargon, but I think what we have here are "codependency" killers. Individually they might be relatively harmless, but together, it's like mixing potassium and water – the result is explosive. Buono and Bianchi, the Hillside Stranglers, worked together. The average age of a serial killer at the time of their first murder is twenty-eight, yet Buono was forty-three years old when they killed their first victim. Many believe that without the influence of the younger man, Buono would never have escalated to murder.'

Varley nodded. 'Typically, a strong personality dominates the relationship, manipulating a weaker personality. Your killer is the weaker personality, taking orders, effectively acting out the dominant personality's fantasies.'

'Our guy has a horror of being watched by his victims,' Simms said. 'But the dominant partner makes him film himself torturing and killing the women.'

Detmeyer nodded. 'Effectively, he is watched twice – by the victim, *and* by the man on the other side of the camera. Blinding the victims denies the dominant figure his final release, the realization of his fantasy.'

'But more than that,' Varley added, 'symbolically he's "blinding" the other man, who exposes him to scrutiny that he finds painful.'

'So, for our guy it's all about the blinding?' Dunlap asked.

'I think the blinding is only part of it,' Fennimore said, enjoying the stony stare he got from Varley for his impudence. 'He held Sharla Jane's hand as she died. He comforted her as he bled her to death. It's got to be about blood, too. I mean, hasn't it?'

Detmeyer considered and, after a few moments, he nodded in agreement.

Dunlap glanced around the room, waiting for any further contributions. Finally, he fixed Detmeyer with his warm brown eyes. 'So, Doctor, are you ready to write that profile now?'

43

Tulk residence, Williams County, Oklahoma

It's afternoon, and Marsha Tulk has sent the boy to do some weighing in the shed at the edge of the compound.

The boy made himself useful from the get-go. Bryce put him to work on the pot grows on the western side of the highway, out of the way of TV crews and police. He worked all morning from 6 a.m. unsupervised. Did a good job, too. Bryce says he has a green thumb and, as she guessed of him, he is sharp and adaptable. Haley pets him, when he lets her; Harlan ignores him, mostly. Waylon, well, he's a tad jealous and likes to kick the boy in the ass if he gets in the way, but the child is quick and keeps out of reach. Bryce is relieved he won't have to go check on the pot grows as often as he did, and he talks to the boy like he would talk to a grown man about sunlight hours and nitrogen ratios and watering rates.

Before she sent the boy out with Bryce to learn the ropes, she gave him a baseball cap. As he adjusted the clip to fit him, she ruffled his red hair, said, 'You need to keep that hid.'

The boy nodded, tugging the brim low on his forehead. 'We'll call you Caleb or just "Boy" from here on in – that all right with you?'

He said, 'Yes, ma'am,' those pale blue eyes on her.

'Two things you need to remember, boy,' she said. 'Do not get yourself noticed and *never* steal my product.'

She looked at him until he said, 'Yes, ma'am.' But she kept looking like she could see right through his skin to his pot-smoked lungs. She knew he stole from her before – she knew it that first day when he said he had climbed into Harlan's car at the tomato field.

'I know you loved your momma,' she said. 'But drugs is for fools and the weak. Do you understand me?'

He nodded, but she made him say it out loud, and he did – in a clear, solemn tone – though it must've hurt to admit his momma had been weak.

She approaches the shed soft-footed, because she may be sentimental and a sucker for a child in trouble, but she is no fool, and setting the child of an addict to weighing cannabis is taking a big chance, especially if he has developed a taste for it. She lifts the latch and swings the door open fast, but when she looks inside, the boy has his head on his arms at the table, and he's crying.

'What happened?' she says. 'Did someone hurt you?'

'No, ma'am. Nobody hurt me.'

'Then why're you crying, getting the product all wet?'

He wipes his eyes hastily on his T-shirt. 'I was just thinking how Momma woulda loved this place.'

She looks doubtfully at the rough-cut planks and dirt floor of the shed. 'You think so?'

The boy holds up a small bag of dried buds. 'She would've thought she had died and gone to heaven.'

She doesn't know whether to laugh or cry. She feels bad to have made him admit his momma was weak, and goes looking for Tyler, who has been keeping an eye on the trailer park, the police being around and all.

She finds all four of her sons watching the news on TV. They look up when she comes in and she says, 'If this mullet-headed jackass comes looking to find the boy, you can bring him to me.'

Harlan and Tyler look quickly at each other, and Harlan rolls his eyes. Bryce nods, but Waylon asks her why. She gives him a dark look.

'God is forgiving,' she says. 'But I am not.'

44

Lambert Woods Mobile Home Park, near Hays,
Williams County, Oklahoma
Sunday afternoon

When Kate Simms and Deputy Hicks arrived at Lambert Woods, the search was yet to get under way. Sheriff Launer was talking to Kent Whitmore, the tall Team Adam consultant, and Hicks drew them to one side and brought them up to date on the new recording.

'Is there a problem with the search?' Simms asked. 'I thought you'd be started by now.'

'Just waiting for the full contingent to foregather,' the Sheriff said vaguely.

Kate Simms looked around her at the crowd standing about in tree-dappled sunlight at the back of Sharla Jane Patterson's home. Being a Sunday, a lot of the locals had volunteered; women and older teens, as well as the woodsmen and hunters the Sheriff had deployed (his term), in the search at Cupke Lake. There must have been fifty or sixty people, including the Sheriff's deputies; it was hard to imagine who else might be needed.

She looked askance at Whitmore and he nodded towards the access road. The first of a convoy of TV outside-broadcast units was bumping and growling up the track. It seemed the Sheriff had made a few calls, issued some invitations.

'How sure are we about this partnership theory?' Whitmore asked, as Launer preened himself for the cameras.

'It's pure speculation, right now,' she said, and an irritated frown crossed the Sheriff's brow. 'It's all geographical linguistics this and language-pattern analysis that – Professor Fennimore could probably explain,' she added, confident that Launer would not be keen to hand over his carefully engineered TV slot to Fennimore. He sucked his teeth and stared longingly at the TV trucks forming a queue on the access road.

'Well, I'll leave the theorizing to the eggheads,' he said. 'We got a body to find.'

'Boy,' Whitmore said, softly. At Launer's tetchy look, he dipped his head apologetically, but repeated, 'We got a *boy* to find.'

They waited a little longer while the TV cameras set up and the reporters primped, ready for their intros. Finally, Launer moved front and centre, stooped to pull up a bunch of dry grass, held it at chest height, then lightly tossed it into the air, watching as it floated gently away towards Sharla Jane's trailer.

He raised his voice to address the volunteers: 'Wind's coming from the south-west.' He indicated in the direction of the woods. 'Little Riley has not been seen for close to seventy-two hours, so it's likely he's already dead—'

Kent Whitmore cleared his throat. 'You will find cabins out in woods like these,' he said. 'Or maybe Riley hitched a ride. We aren't ready to give up hope yet.'

Launer was momentarily vexed, but he shook it off with a politician's ease. 'There's always room for hope,' he said in a chiding tone, as if someone else had voiced those negative thoughts.

'We'll spread out in a line, work our way south and west

into the woods, and the prevailing wind will—' Whitmore coughed again and Launer frowned, but thankfully he reconsidered the wisdom of telling the mothers and fathers and their teenaged kids to be guided by the stench of death. Instead he looked sad and sincere and murmured, 'Well, you all know . . .'

Simms exchanged a look with Deputy Hicks, glad that Fennimore wasn't around. Launer steepled his hands and made an arrow of them, pointing into the woods beyond the fence but, as people started to form a line, the Team Adam consultant spoke up again.

'Folks?' His bass tones carried effortlessly to the people at the back, and Simms noticed that several of the cameras focused on the big Oklahoman. 'Keep in visual contact with the person either side of you at all times,' he said. 'And if you find anything – anything at all – you should stop and call for assistance, not disturbing what you find.'

Three yards into the woods, at eye height on a young oak, a sign read: 'DO NOT TRESPASS'. Below it, a second board: 'NO HUNTING'.

They walked a few more yards, maintaining the line, and ahead was another sign: 'ARMED PATROLS – ENTER AT YOUR OWN RISK'.

Ten minutes into the search, a new set of boards started appearing on trees at intervals. 'GO NO FURTHER', 'YOU HAVE BEEN WARNED'.

Whitmore asked for a consult.

'Nothing to worry about,' Launer said. 'Just a landowner's empty threats.'

'My advice would be to find out who that landowner is, Sheriff,' Whitmore said.

'We'd lose hours,' Launer said.

A cameraman from one of the TV crews stepped forward, aiming the camera at the two men, and Simms took a step back.

'Sheriff, have you seen any tracks or footpaths in the last

five minutes?' Whitmore said in the same quiet, reasonable tone. 'I don't mean deer trails or rabbit tracks – I mean real, human-trod pathways, like you'd expect to see in wood right next to fifty-plus homes. There's a lot of kids on the trailer park. Kids like the woods, Sheriff, but something is keeping them out of here.'

A few nervous mutterings started up around them, and Sheriff Launer scratched his neck, nodding thoughtfully. 'I understand your concern,' he said. 'But we lose hours, we lose the light. It'll be tomorrow before we can get back in, and that little boy's been missing for three days already. You all can turn back if you want. We'll keep moving.'

Whitmore looked along the line of volunteers and raised his voice again. 'I would advise against anyone going further till we know what we've got here,' he said.

Many of the civilians dropped out, as did Simms and the two camera crews that had followed them in. Prepared for any eventuality, Launer had equipped one of his deputies with a digicam. Launer gave him the nod, and the deputy removed the lens cap and turned the machine on. Launer summoned his deputies with a look and they formed a new line, moving slowly into the underbrush.

Whitmore took out his cell phone as he watched them go. He checked the signal, but after a moment, he shook his head and slipped it back in his pocket. 'You got a signal?' he said.

Simms checked, and shook her head.

He reached into his backpack and took out a satellite phone. Seconds later, he was talking to Detective Dunlap at the Incident Command Post in Westfield; ten minutes after that, he knew that the woods belonged to the Tulk family, and that they had a bad reputation.

He tried the Sheriff's cell. 'Not available,' he said. The calls of the search party were growing faint. 'I think they're still in striking distance.' He stowed the phone and hitched his backpack onto his shoulder. 'I'm going in,' he said.

'All right.' Simms fell in step behind him.

'Ma'am, you should stay.'

'And if you step on a mantrap, who's going to let people know where to find you?'

He hesitated and she shooed him ahead of her. 'It'll be fine. I'll stay a couple of steps behind, let you clear the way.'

He blinked and smiled faintly, and they headed in the direction of the hollering.

Five minutes later, they had almost caught up with the search party. Abruptly, the shouting stopped.

Whitmore yelled, 'Everyone okay?' Launer, sounding tetchy again, hollered for them to stay put. Moments later, he and his crew appeared in single file.

One of the deputies was puffing and blowing anxiously on the lens of the digicam, trying to clear it of dust and leaf debris. Another – the one who had originally been carrying the recorder – was limping slightly and his uniform looked scuffed and dirty. Hicks brought up the rear, resolutely avoiding eye contact with Simms and Whitmore.

'Are you hurt?' Simms asked.

'Only his pride,' Launer said. 'Numbnuts here stepped right into a pitfall trap. I thought you said you weren't coming in?'

Whitworth dipped his head. 'Couldn't get you on your cell phone. Thought you should know this land is owned by Marsha Tulk.'

'Well, I could've used that piece of news five minutes earlier,' Launer said with bad grace.

'You know her?' Whitmore said, and Simms marvelled at his refusal to take offence.

'Her 'n' her brood,' Launer said dryly. 'And I happen to know that the Tulk family residence is eight miles west of here. So, whatever they're protecting in these woods, it isn't house or home, and I'll bet it carries a Federal penalty.'

45

Tulk residence, Williams County, Oklahoma

The Tulk family home stood on a rise in a clear-felled patch of mixed oak, hazel and redbuds, about a half-mile off the back road to Hays. A wooden structure with a cedar shingle roof and wrap-around porch, it seemed to grow out of the clay soil. A mud-spattered Ford pickup and a rusted sedan were parked in front of a barn off to the left. A smaller shed, closer to the house, stood open.

Just two vehicles had made the journey – the Sheriff's cruiser and an unmarked SUV driven by Detective Dunlap, with Detective Ellis and Chief Inspector Simms riding along. The yard was quiet, and the four from out of county remained in their vehicle, the engine running for the air conditioning, waiting for the Sheriff to take the lead.

A man came out of the house. He was big, bearded, built like a wrestler. His beard was jet black and water glistened in it, like he'd just stepped out of the shower. He wore a short-barrelled revolver at his hip. He squinted towards the unmarked vehicle parked at an angle to his front porch, and his gun hand moved to the butt of his weapon.

Simms was firearm trained and she'd never felt so in need of the comforting weight of a Glock 17 at her hip as she did now.

'What is Launer waiting for?' Dunlap said. They waited another ten seconds; still no movement from the Sheriff. Dunlap said, 'The hell with this.' He opened the SUV door and a surge of wet heat swept in.

The bearded man tensed.

'You sure you want to do this, Greg?' Ellis said. 'This is not our jurisdiction.'

Dunlap said, 'He's already freaked out – we sit in our cars eyeballing him for the next ten minutes, he might just use that handgun.'

He stepped down slowly, announcing himself as St Louis Police. The man took a step back, watching both vehicles at the same time.

'St Louis, Missouri? I'd like to see some ID, Detective.'

'I'm going to reach in my back pocket for it,' Dunlap said. 'That okay with you?'

The man nodded, cautious.

Dunlap took his ID wallet out with his left hand, showed him his badge.

At this point, Sheriff Launer slid out of his cruiser, a deputy a step behind him, holding the digicam. Deputy Hicks got out of the back seat a moment later.

'Mr Tulk?' Launer said.

The bearded man looked at the deputy with the camera. 'You can turn that off.'

The deputy threw a nervous look at the Sheriff, but Launer kept his eyes on the man.

'Looking for a "contribution", Sheriff?' the man said.

'What?'

'You should know, I already donated – to the other side.' Tulk smiled for the camera. 'Want to hear why?'

Launer lifted his chin to the deputy and he turned off the camera.

'I'm looking for a little boy,' Launer said. 'Name of Riley Patterson. He might've ended up in Lambert Woods.'

'That's a ways down the road, Sheriff, other side of the highway. You want directions?'

'I know where it is. I need to get in there and look.'

'What's stopping you?'

'One of my deputies got injured.'

'That can happen when you trespass on private property.'

Launer looked down at the holstered weapon on the man's hip. 'You got an open-carry permit, Mr Tulk?'

A movement in one of the front windows, and seconds later a woman appeared on the front stoop.

'He is licensed to carry, Sheriff,' she said. 'Open or concealed. As am I.'

She was big and meaty. She wore a cream blouse loose over a denim skirt, and Simms did not doubt that she wore a gun holster in the waistband.

Launer's eyes shifted from one to the other. 'Like I told your son, I'm looking for a missing boy; he could be on your land up on Lambert Hill, but there are booby traps on that property, and a man has already been hurt. Now, I'm not proposing to *sue* or anything—' a quick flash of white teeth '—but those traps *are* illegal.'

'Well, of course,' Mrs Tulk said, shaking her head at the irresponsibility of others.

'Like I said, nobody's going to sue,' Launer persisted, remaining polite, neighbourly almost, but he was a little red around the eyes and the smile, when it came, had a whiff of shark behind it. 'We just need someone to guide us in there.'

'I wish I could help,' she said, 'but what if one of my boys got hurt?'

Sheriff Launer flushed. 'That's how you want to play it?'

'Play what?' She eyed him placidly.

'You think I don't know what you're protecting up on that hill?'

'I don't know what you mean. But there's a lot of people

out there on the trailer park, any one of 'em could've set those traps.'

'You think because all I got is a few deputies, I don't have the manpower to call your bluff. Well, this here's an interstate task force,' Launer said, acknowledging Dunlap's presence for the first time. 'We got ten officers from St Louis PD just waiting on my word.'

'Uh, Sheriff,' Dunlap warned.

But Launer wasn't listening. 'Team Adam, too,' he said. 'Those guys got serious money, and they will stop at *nothing* to bring a child home. Now, you can cooperate, and we'll walk through those woods, look for the boy, head on out again. Or.' He raised a finger. '*Or* – I can come back with drugs dogs and cadaver dogs and heat-detecting equipment. I'll raise enough volunteers to turn over every leaf and stone. I will tear up every shed, bush and glasshouse up there. If you got so much as a *whiff* of weed on the place, I *will* find it.'

Mrs Tulk remained impassive throughout this speech. When he finished, she said, 'You're looking for pot grows, you should be looking at the Mexicans, 'stead of hassling American citizens.'

'Are you suggesting it's the *Mexicans* up on your hill?'

'Truth is, I don't know what's up there. Haven't been on Lambert Hill in two years. How about you, Harlan?'

'It's been a while,' he said. 'I did find a cleared patch of timber over to Deadman's Ditch a couple of miles north of there when I was out with the dogs, end of May.'

'I don't remember getting a call-out on that,' Launer said, his expression carefully neutral.

'Deadman's Ditch is Tulk land, Sheriff,' Tulk said. 'We protect what's ours.'

'You should follow DEA advice, Mr Tulk,' Launer said. 'See something looks drugs related, you stay the hell away and you call it in.'

'Would you've come running if he did?' Mrs Tulk said.

The Sheriff smiled. 'I'm the boss around here, Mrs Tulk – I delegate.'

'I don't doubt it.' Her mouth twisted like she might spit at his feet.

Launer ignored the woman, keeping his eyes on the son instead. 'You're lucky you didn't get yourself shot.'

'Thing about luck,' Mrs Tulk said, 'it cuts both ways.'

That got his attention.

'You may be boss out there, Sheriff,' Mrs Tulk said. 'But you need to understand: the land hereabouts is Tulk land. And me and mine will stand our ground and protect it, like we always did.' They locked gazes, and Simms could almost smell the ozone as their mutual hatred electrified the air.

Launer stamped back to his car, the deputy with the digicam running to keep up. Mrs Tulk had called his bluff – legally, there was nothing more he could do. Dunlap nodded to Mrs Tulk and he and Ellis turned back to their SUV, but Hicks remained where she was, and Simms lingered, curious.

Mrs Tulk watched Launer's car reverse, spurting gravel from its wheels. She waited until he was on his way back down the dirt track before she finally turned her small, hard eyes on the two women.

Hicks introduced herself, but Mrs Tulk kept her gaze on Simms. 'And who are you?'

'I'm just here to observe,' Simms said.

'Like the *U*-nited Nations.' Mrs Tulk looked Simms up and down. 'I guess you're that British cop they talked about on the news.'

Simms held her gaze. 'Just a mother, trying to help find a lost little boy.'

'Ma'am?' Hicks said, her tone respectful.

Mrs Tulk took her time acknowledging Hicks, but the deputy didn't start talking until she was under the older woman's sharp gaze.

'Riley can maybe identify the man who killed his momma,' she said.

'Yeah. A lot of those news people are saying you got a serial killer, looks like.'

'Yes, ma'am,' Hicks said. 'We think so – and we need to protect Riley.'

'Hm.' Marsha Tulk folded her arms across her wide bosom. 'There was another boy – his momma sent him to live with his aunt just before she was murdered.'

'Trey Gaigan, yes, ma'am.'

'He disappeared a short while after his momma showed up dead. People on the news think maybe your serial killer come back for him.' She shifted her left arm and scratched her elbow with one yellow nail. 'Is that how you "protect" people, Deputy?'

'All respect, ma'am, but Trey wasn't in police custody—'

'Custody! You would lock a boy up to *protect* him?' Mrs Tulk shook her head. 'You got it ass-backwards, Deputy.'

She turned her back on them and returned indoors.

Her son stood with his arms hanging loose and a gleam of satisfaction in his eye. 'You want to search our land, we can't stop you, just take care where you step,' he said.

46

When Harlan went into the house, his momma was punching a piece of dough the size of a man's head at the kitchen table. There was a time when seeing his momma knock and squeeze and shape a dough ball held a kind of excitement; the beery smell of the dough was almost intoxicating, and the promise of the crisp, clean taste of warm bread was a comfort. But that was when he was very young. Now, he saw his momma stretching and twisting and punching that dough, he was just reminded of her strength and the power of her temper.

'Tell me they got those grows on Lambert Hill cleared,' she said.

'They're cleared.' He had been digging and lifting with his brothers all morning. 'Momma—'

'Do *not* say what is in your mind to say, Harlan,' she said, raising one floury hand in defence, and as a warning. 'I don't want to hear it.' She fixed him with her small eyes and the twelve-year-old boy in him quailed, but the man in him got mad. He straightened his back and put some steel in his voice.

'You think if I *don't* say it then it won't happen?'

She growled and fell to pounding the bread some.

'What if Launer follows through on those threats, comes back with a whole bunch of law enforcement and detection dogs and who knows what?'

She snorted. 'You said the place is cleared. Anyway, did you see the way that black cop looked at him? Launer's full of shit.'

'You bet,' he said, nodding. 'But he is not alone; this story made the TV news state-wide. It's on the Internet, Momma, which takes it global. They didn't get the killer yet. They didn't find the boy, but they still need a story – so they'll take whatever they can find, and if that's a bunch of rednecks growing pot out in the woods, they'll take that and call it a scoop.'

'Harlan—'

'They find the pot grows, they'll come looking for more.'

'God*damnit*, Harlan!' She slammed the dough on the board and stood panting.

He planted his fists on the table opposite her and for a long moment they eyeballed each other like two bull stags about to go at it. But, gradually, the tension eased and she sprinkled a dusting of flour on the dough, fell into the rhythm of kneading again.

When he thought she was calm enough, Harlan said quietly, 'Cops are sniffing around 'cos of that boy, and we don't need that. Let one government-funded agency on our land, you might as well send out an open invitation.'

'All right,' she said, though she looked sick when she said it. 'Go fetch him.'

He went out to the weighing shed. The door still hung open, and he thought it was a wonder the cops didn't smell the drying buds, standing out on their front yard. There were no glass windows in the shed, but they kept two large wood shutters tilted open from day till nightfall for ventilation, and they allowed enough light for weighing and checking the harvest. He blinked, coming out of the strong afternoon sunshine. The boy was not at the weighing table.

Hiding. Must've thought the cops might come take a look.

Harlan moved deeper inside. It was a big shed, about thirty feet by twenty-five, and sectioned off with wood screens for different stages in the drying. But Red wasn't behind the first screen, or the second, or the one after that. He checked again, his heart hammering. The boy was gone.

When he went in to break the news, he expected a show of temper, but his momma calmly broke off a piece of dough and dropped it into a loaf tin, a smile playing on her face.

'That boy is slippery as an eel,' she said, and Lord help him, he felt a prick of jealousy at the pride in her eyes.

'Aren't you concerned?'

'Yes, I'm concerned.' she said. 'That his momma's lover will catch up with him; that he'll get cornered by a coyote or a bear.'

'The cops find him, he knows a lot.'

She blew air between her lips. 'He wouldn't tell the cops one word about us,' she said.

Harlan shook his head. 'Momma, he's a nine-year-old *boy*.'

She sighed, irritated to have been set straight. 'Well, you'd better get him back before the cops find him, then, hadn't you?'

'You want me to go *look* for him?'

'Tyler should stay up at the trailer park, keep an eye on things. You can take Bryce and Waylon. Haley, too, if you think she'd be any use to you.'

'So where are we supposed to start?' Harlan said, feeling pissed off and put upon.

'Harlan,' she said. 'He's smart, but he's still a nine-year-old boy – he'll do what any nine-year-old boy would do. He'll head for home.'

47

Incident Command Post, Westfield, Williams County, Oklahoma

Nick Fennimore knew that Josh had the link to the video clip because of his phone call, interrupting the Task Force viewing of it. What he hadn't expected was that Josh was already working on the transcript.

'I read a paper on word use by psychopaths and thought it might be interesting to analyse the dialogue. I mean, how often d'you get the chance to assess a psychopath's word use in a natural setting?'

Kate Simms would no doubt use this little insight into the student's interests as evidence that he should not be trusted, but it didn't seem at all odd to Fennimore: Josh Brown studied psychology for the first three years of his academic career – this was exactly the sort of inquisitiveness and initiative that made him stand out from the crowd.

Fennimore told him their plans to have a geographical linguist analyse the killer's words, and about their suspicions that there might be a second killer – a puppeteer who gave orders from a distance. 'But it looks like our demonic Pinocchio just cut the strings,' Fennimore said.

'And *Seed of Chucky* is born,' Josh said.

'What?'

'Chucky?' Josh said. 'The most iconic doll in horror movies? Never mind. As a matter of fact, I was about to call you when you rang – there's some stuff in here I just can't make sense of.'

'Go ahead,' Fennimore said.

'Sharla Jane asks can she make it up to him, and he moves in close and says, "Time will tell."'

'Yes.' The words were practically burned into Fennimore's auditory nerve.

'Then he mutters something I can't quite catch . . . Maybe "clay pit"?'

'"Clay pit" . . . yes, I suppose it could be,' Fennimore said. 'The farm pond where Laney Dawalt was found was dug out of clay.'

'Then he says . . . "full"?'

'He could be tormenting her, telling her where he dumps the bodies of his victims,' Fennimore said.

'Thing is,' Josh said, sounding doubtful, 'I've played that section over and over, and he doesn't seem to be gloating. What I see is disappointment – bitterness? I don't know.'

'Have you tried altering the bass and treble?' Fennimore suggested.

'No, but I'll give it a go.'

'If that doesn't help, just spell what you think you hear phonetically, and make it clear it's a guess – the linguistics specialists will probably have the technological wizardry to clean up the audio.'

'Okay. Where do I send it when I'm finished?'

'Professor Varley knows someone at Aston University – he'll be in touch as soon as he's cleared it with them.'

'Fine, I'll keep my mobile nearby.'

It was already early evening back in Aberdeen, but Fennimore did not doubt that Josh would work through the night to get the job done. Josh's work obsession and complete lack of a social life was one of the reasons Kate Simms distrusted him. When Fennimore and Kate had worked together all those years ago in the National Crime Faculty, he had relied heavily on her to demystify the subtler nuances of social interaction, but Fennimore had never had any trouble spotting liars and crooks. He knew that Josh was hiding something – on that level he *was* lying – but Fennimore believed that the younger man was sincere, as well as a damn good scientist. In Fennimore's mind, that earned him a fair amount of leeway.

48

Listening by the door inside the weighing shed, Riley
Patterson had heard everything Sheriff Launer said. He knew
Mrs Tulk would not stand by and watch her family and her
business get torn apart – she *had* to turn him in. He crept
out of the shed before they even finished talking. At first he
ran to put distance between him and her boys, but now he's
on the shady side of a wooded ridge he knows will keep him
close to the highway.

Mrs Tulk thinks he has no clue who murdered his momma,
but Red has known since he told her the truth about what
happened Friday. He didn't get it right away, but he woke
up in a sweat that night with it all worked out. Will killed
Momma, and if he wasn't such a baby, he would've known
that without somebody having to tell him. He should've
looked out for Momma, instead of scampering into the woods
like a baby, like a scared little rabbit, like—

Like a goddamn coward.

He feels a pain in his gut like someone punched him hard.
He falls to his knees, and soon he is sobbing, screaming his
anger and hurt.

Locked in the trunk of Harlan Tulk's car the night his

momma died, crying till his chest ached, it felt like he had cried out all the sadness and pain of his life, but this new pain feels like sin. It feels like his wickedness is what brought all this evil down on him and his momma; his cowardice that let it happen.

49

[I]n general it requires an active effort if something unconscious is to become conscious.

ERICH FROMM, *THE ART OF BEING*

Sheriff Launer called off the search of the woods until Monday morning, when two COSAR search-and-rescue dogs were expected to arrive with their handlers. After speaking with Josh, Fennimore spent a few hours in his hotel room, reading emails, replying to student requests for information and guidance and choosing the slides he would use for his presentation at the International Homicide Investigators Association symposium in St Louis. He checked Suzie's Facebook page as a matter of routine, although his stomach clenched every time he opened the link. There were no new postings waiting to be cleared to go on her wall, and he opened the image of the girl in the sundress. The dream he'd had in the early hours of Saturday had disturbed his sleep ever since. In his dream, he saw again the girl in the photograph walking alongside the older man. A warm breeze carried the scent of flowers and a whiff of river water. A police siren wailed – slightly off-key to his British-attuned ear. The girl half turned, startled by the sudden din, stumbled. And he'd thought, *Faux pas* – a false step. What did it mean? He was sure there must be something he'd missed in the picture.

His room phone rang and Fennimore picked up; it was Hicks.

'I'm headed home for the night,' she said.

'Okay . . .'

'I got some takeout food. Want to share?'

'Love to,' he said. 'Why don't you come over?'

After an awkward silence, she said, 'I'm about fifty yards left of the hotel driveway. Why don't you meet me there?'

Minutes later, he was climbing into her beat-up SUV.

'Sorry about the cloak-and-dagger stuff,' she said. 'But the gossip-mongers had a field day when I parked up outside your room last time and . . .' She shrugged.

'So, where are we off to?'

'My place,' she said.

Hicks lived in a rented bungalow down a potholed road on the edge of town. It was tiny: just a sitting room, bedroom, bathroom and kitchen on a large overgrown lot with fruit trees and a tumbledown woodshed. She liked it, she said, because she could sit out on the stoop at night and look at the stars. She must be an optimist at heart, Fennimore thought: the property owed its window on the night sky to the fact that two in every three of the street lights were broken and most of the other houses were abandoned.

They ate fried chicken and drank beer and talked about the case. Hicks was concerned for Billy Dawalt, who seemed to have been forgotten in the scramble to find Riley Patterson.

'Billy's been gone six months,' he said. 'Riley, just three days.'

'I know,' she said. 'Riley's chances are good, compared to the other kids – they'd be better yet, if we could just get the Tulk family to cooperate.'

'Tell me about the Tulks – I gather they're notorious.'

'They are.' Hicks took a bite of chicken and chewed. 'You kept company with Harlan and his brother, Bryce, the day you got drunk in Danley's Bar.' She closed one eye. 'The day I rescued you.'

'I remember being pleasantly pissed,' he said, with what he hoped was lofty disdain. 'I do not recall being rescued.'

'If that's how you need to see it, Professor,' she said, chuckling into the mouth of her beer bottle. 'But those boys were scowling at you from the shadows like wolves in a cave.'

'You make it sound like I was in real danger.'

'The Tulks come from a long and infamous line of outlaws and desperadoes, going way back,' Hicks said. 'Before the railroad came out here – before Oklahoma was even a state – this was frontier land, Indian territory. There was a saying back then: "There is no Sunday west of St Louis, no God west of Fort Smith".'

'And the Tulks still hold to the frontier spirit, is that it?' Fennimore said.

'As a matter of family pride. Only difference is they grow pot in the woods, these days, 'stead of brewing hooch.'

'Which explains the booby traps.'

'And why they're so reluctant to help us search their land.'

Fennimore knew that what he was about to ask would put Deputy Hicks, as a probationary law officer, in a tricky position. 'I understand there was a bit of a spat over at the Tulk place – hints and allegations about pot growing?'

Hicks nodded. 'As I recall, the Sheriff and Harlan did dance around that subject for a bit.'

'Is there is anything in it?'

'Like I said, the Tulks take pride in their family traditions.'

Fennimore knew evasiveness when he heard it. 'I'm more interested in the accusation against the Sheriff.'

She looked at him for some moments. Her she-wolf eyes betrayed nothing more than caution, but Fennimore felt uncomfortable under their glare.

'Abigail, this is just you telling me a campfire tale – a bit of blether,' he said, to break the silence.

She set down her beer. 'All right, but this – what did you call it?'

'Blether.'

She nodded. 'But this "blether" is just between you and me. Okay?'

'Okay,' he said.

Even so, she seemed reluctant to begin. She took a deep pull of beer and set it down again with a sigh, made two abortive attempts to start before launching in.

'Sheriff Launer's campaign flyer says that drug crime is down thirty per cent,' she said.

'I'm guessing the stats don't back his claims?'

'Meth-related visits to the ER at County Hospital are up twenty-three per cent,' she said. 'You're good at math, Professor.' Hard anger flashed from irises. 'Can you explain to me how drug crime could be *down* when drug use is *up*?'

'It is a conundrum, isn't it?' he said mildly. 'How did the Sheriff achieve this mathematical sleight of hand?'

She hesitated, and he thought she might retreat again, taking the safer option of keeping her suspicions to herself, but then she began slowly: 'You can cut drug arrests by half if you push the tweakers to the margins where they won't offend law-abiding citizens. You can "re-categorize" offences, so a meth-influenced psychotic attack becomes a "domestic dispute" – you don't even need to mention drugs. You might arrest a woman for solicitation, but don't write it up in your report that she was so high on meth you had to wait a few hours before you could charge her.'

'Wouldn't it be in Launer's interests to look strong on drugs, especially during an election campaign?' Fennimore asked. 'Surely, more arrests mean he's doing his job?'

She didn't answer directly. 'Politics is all about balancing the needs of your voters against the aspirations of your campaign supporters.'

'I'm not sure I understand,' he said.

'Do you know the single biggest factor in deciding who will win an election?'

'Charm?' Fennimore tried. 'A good manifesto? A winning smile?'

'None of the above – though Launer'd have a head start on the smile thing,' she said. 'No, in politics, it pays to advertise. The Sheriff joined the country club over at Hays, and he works those contacts. He paid for thirty minutes of prime time a week on the radio station for the last six months; you can reach a lot of people on the radio out here. Launer's campaign flyers and posters are designed and printed by Merl and Shona at the *Westfield Examiner.* He buys regular full-page ads with them in behalf of the sheriff's office – and all of that *costs.*'

Realisation dawned. 'You think Launer brokered a deal with the suppliers.'

Hicks frowned at her beer bottle, edging it round with her fingertips on the tabletop, but didn't answer.

'You should talk to the District Attorney,' Fennimore said.

'I told you, the DA's an asshole. Anyway, I got no proof.'

'What about your administrator friend?' Fennimore asked. 'The one he reassigned to the county jail?'

'You mean the one who quit, the day after – moved out of *county*? Last time I called her cell phone, I got an out-of-service message. Professor, all I got is speculation and educated guesses, and I need a *lot* more before I'd poke that bear.'

Abruptly, she scooped up her beer bottle. 'Let's go out back,' she said. 'I need some air.'

They took their beer down the field to the fruit trees. The moon was full and he could see now that the land attached to the property was extensive. The ground sloped away, with row on row of small fruit trees. Peaches and sweet cherries, mostly, already swelling after the recent rains, but also plums and a few pears with teardrop stubs that would produce a good crop, come August. The cicadas had fallen silent, one by one, and now the softer chirp of the crickets and katydids filled the warm, scented night air.

She turned to him, and for once he didn't need to be told what the firefly flashes of emotion in her eyes meant. He could see that she was frustrated and felt powerless to change the situation for the better, because he felt it, too.

Fennimore kissed her, and she kissed him back, her teeth clashing against his, more angry than passionate at first, but gradually the tension left her, and she kissed him deeply while the katydids chirruped and bats whispered low over their heads.

After a time, she eased away from him. 'Still need some air,' she said, laughing softly, leaning her forehead, warm, against his chest.

Fennimore kissed her neck, smoothing his hands over her shoulders, down into the curve of her back. As his fingers explored the waistband of her trousers, she caught his hand.

'We're going to have to take this inside,' she said.

He looked around him. 'Let me guess – Oklahoma law is *real* strict on making love *alfresco*?'

'Worse,' she laughed. 'There's fire ants on the property.'

50

The backwoods, Williams County, Oklahoma
Sunday night

The moon is full, and under clear skies Riley Patterson can see well enough without needing a flashlight – which is a good thing, 'cos he left that behind at the Tulk place. Though he lost an hour with his earlier foolishness, he made up time by not stopping to rest. He does not know where he's headed, except out of here. The fastest route is the highway, but he is too afraid of being seen to head down to it, so he stays on the slight rise, catching glimpses of the road through the trees, gleaming like weathered aluminium in the moonlight.

He has no food or water; just the clothes he's standing up in and his pocket radio, and he's going to need more than that if he wants to survive long enough to make it to . . . wherever he's going. *Just away*, he tells himself – 'cos the little boy in him says if *he* doesn't know where he's headed, how could anyone else?

He follows a deer trail for a bit, trying not to think about the hunger clawing at his belly. Up ahead, he hears a rustle in the underbrush. It comes again, and he stops, shouts, 'Hey, bear!'

He listens a while, but it stays quiet, just the steady

piping call of little peeper frogs and the chirp of the night bugs in the grass either side of the path. He turns a bend in the trail and freezes. Up ahead is a big grey coyote. It stands about twenty-five yards distant and watches him. He waits for it to move off, but it stays on the trail and lifts its snout, testing the air for his scent. The moonlight filtering through the trees looks like scattered silver pennies on its fur. If a coyote don't move, you're suppose to shout, he thinks, so he claps his hand over his head and yells, but the coyote just licks its lips and sits down, curling its tail around its paws.

Riley picks up a stick and waves it. 'Go on, now. Git!'

The coyote lowers its muzzle and its ears flick back, flat to its head. It raises one paw and takes a step forward.

'Get a-*way* from me,' Riley hollers.

It takes another step and shows its teeth, a snarl bubbling in its throat. It moves around to the side, and the boy knows it's trying to get behind him. He drops the stick and runs, the dog rushing after him. He dodges and weaves, hearing it getting closer; any minute he will feel the thud of its paws on his back, its teeth in his neck.

He takes one frightened look over his shoulder and trips. He rolls, feels air whoosh past his face, sees a rock sweep down on the coyote. A trap! He has run into one of the Tulk grows. The dog leaps sideways, but he hasn't bargained for the backswing and the rock catches his right hind leg. It's only a glancing blow and it yelps, but is able to swerve and come at Riley again. The boy is up and running, headed into the woods, because this is where the grow will be, and he knows there will be a fence. If he can get over that, he'll be safe.

Ten yards in, the twigs and leaf litter give way under him and he knows he's hit a pitfall trap. But he's small and light and he's running fast and, by the grace of God, it holds just long enough for him to reach the other side, while the dog, panting at his back, pitches in head first and falls with a dismayed howl into the pit.

Riley gives a fierce roar of triumph. 'I hope you broke your damn neck!' he screams.

There is no sound from the pit, and he edges forward, curiosity getting the better of good sense: one step, another, one more, to peer into the hole.

It leaps at him, snarling and snapping, all white teeth and wild eyes and foaming at the mouth. Red falls on his ass and scrambles backward, kicking with his heels, waiting for its head to appear at the top of the pit.

But the hole is dug deep enough to hold a man, and the dog falls back down.

Riley raises his fist. 'Ha! Get out of *that*, you bastard!' He wipes snot from his nose with the heel of his hand, and realizes he is crying. 'Bastard,' he mutters again.

When his chest stops heaving, he starts off again, taking a wide detour to avoid going anywhere near the pit.

51

Incident Command Post, Westfield,
Williams County, Oklahoma
Monday morning

Detective Chief Inspector Kate Simms left the hotel at five thirty, as the first pale dawn light glimmered in the east. She discovered a path through a small copse behind the hotel and set off at a slow jog. She hadn't had the opportunity to stretch her legs since the Task Force relocated from St Louis. Running was her way to release tension, and since she'd Skyped her family at 1 a.m., she'd been wound like a spring. It was her husband's birthday, and she wanted to catch him before he left for work. It was 7 a.m. back home, and her mother carried Tim, her five-year-old, from his bed still in his Spiderman pyjamas. When she reached forward to touch the screen, he shied away, burying his face in his grandmother's shoulder. No effort of coaxing would persuade him to look at her again, and with a shrug that seemed laden with reproach, her mother whisked Tim off to breakfast. Becky said she was 'too busy' preparing for school to come to the computer at all.

Kieran alone seemed in good spirits. 'Don't worry about them,' he said, relaxed and smiling. 'They're fine.

We all are.' He was going out to celebrate his birthday with some work colleagues that night, he told her. Granny didn't mind watching the kids; in fact, she was taking good care of all of them. Simms had never seen him so content and she reflected, perhaps a little unkindly, that what Kieran had always wanted was a woman who would look after him.

The call left her feeling lonely, depressed and unable to sleep. Running cleared her mind, and the punishing heat left no space to rehash every word and gesture, as she had done in the hours of darkness.

The clump of trees was bounded by the hotel on one side and a gravel road on the other and, as she completed her second circuit, she heard a car approach along the road. She saw a glimpse of a red vehicle; it swept on, but stopped a hundred yards further down the road. She thought no more of it, until a couple of minutes later she saw Fennimore hurrying across the back lot of the hotel, and she remembered that Abigail Hicks drove a red SUV.

Fennimore, you old dog, she thought. She finished her run, showered and changed and headed across the parking lot to the main block for breakfast. The air smelled of hot cedar and melting asphalt. Fennimore came out of his room and waved to her.

'I was coming to find you,' he said.

'I saw you earlier, heading back into the hotel,' she said.

'I needed a walk,' he said.

'Oh?' she said, allowing herself a flicker of a smile. 'Wasn't that Deputy Hicks's car I saw, dropping you off?'

He gave her a blank look.

'Come on, Nick, you don't need to be secretive with me.'

'We all keep secrets, Kate,' he said coolly.

That stung. He meant Tim. She hadn't told Fennimore until recently about her son, born six months after he'd left. He'd never voiced that last forensic detail – even Nick Fennimore wasn't that unsubtle – but the question was there anyway, unspoken but heard. *All right*, she thought. *His relationship with Hicks is off-limits. Change the subject.*

'You said you were coming to find me.'

'I've just had a call,' he said. 'A thirty-two-year-old woman's been found in Scotland. Alemoor Loch in the Borders region. Her child is still missing – a girl aged ten.'

Simms took a breath. 'When did they find her?'

'Sunday.'

'Who called you?' she asked. 'Your FLO?' Fennimore had a police Family Liaison Officer assigned to him during the investigation into Rachel and Suzie's disappearance – standard UK police procedure. Even five years on, they would contact Fennimore if anything remotely like Rachel and Suzie came up, so he wouldn't have to read about it in the papers, or worse, hear it from some hack demanding a quote.

He shook his head. 'Not my FLO – Josh.'

She raised her eyebrows. 'Josh got the news to you *before* Family Liaison?'

'Evidently,' he said, waspish. 'Now, do you think you could climb down off your hobby horse and put in a call to Police Scotland, find out what the hell is going on?'

An hour later, Simms stood in front of the Task Force in the meeting room. Williams County Sheriff's Department were thin on the ground, Launer having recommenced the search of Lambert Woods at first light.

The Scottish victim, like theirs, was a single mother. She disappeared from home sometime during Friday evening or Saturday morning. Post-mortem results determined cause of death as traumatic asphyxia. Her body had been dumped in the loch inside cargo netting weighted with rocks. Backhand hitch knots secured the body inside the net.

'The body was found at three-thirty p.m. GMT on Sunday; she'd been in the water for hours, rather than days,' Simms said. 'No one messed with it at the scene – the divemaster was ex-Navy, knew exactly what to do. A police diving unit was there within the hour. They bagged her and got her to the Borders General Hospital two hours after that.'

'Good possibilities for evidence,' Fennimore said. 'The ropes could retain trapped paint flecks or dirt from his home or car.'

'They're undergoing analysis as we speak,' she said.

'And the daughter?' He avoided her eye.

'Police diving teams have been searching the lake in shifts since the mother was found. There's a rocky overhang in the loch at about forty metres; the mother's body got swept under, and the netting snagged and held. Pure luck. But if the child's body was weighted in the same way, she might have sunk all the way down – and that's fifty-five metres.'

'Which is beyond the permitted diving depths for British police divers,' Fennimore said. 'Clever bastard.'

'The School of Geosciences at Edinburgh University identified the rocks as grey andesitic. You find extensive deposits of it in the Cheviot Hills just north of the border between England and Scotland. The geologists said some of the stones were dressed – chiselled or hammered,' she added, seeing puzzled looks on some of the faces. 'So they could have come from a building, or a wall.'

'Could all these common factors be pure chance?' Dunlap said.

'I could do the Bayesian analysis,' Fennimore said, 'but top-of-the head assessment – bloody unlikely.'

'So, now we got two killers,' Ellis said, 'with a transatlantic connection?'

Detective Valance added, 'And it looks like they took their victims at around the same time.'

'On the bright side,' Fennimore said, 'if these two do know each other, it just got a lot easier to track them down. We're either looking for an American immigrant in the Borders region, or a Scot in Oklahoma.'

52

Riley Patterson is hungry and thirsty, and lost. The land begins to slope downhill and the woods seem to be thinning out. Fearful of losing his cover, he climbs a tree to get his bearings and, seeing the road running north to south with nothing but grass on either side, at last he knows where he is. This is the place where the woods come to an arrowhead and just stop. Half a mile north they start again, blanketing Lambert Hill; he can just make out the curly tops of the trees draped over the hillside like the fur on a bison in summer moult.

He expected to be some way north of here, but the coyote chase must've got him turned around – he has covered just short of eight miles as the crow flies. He could push on, past Lambert Woods Park, another seven miles to Hays, where he might steal a ride; or he could stop and rest. He stares at the road, wanting to sit down and cry. But he has done crying, so he keeps looking, trying to make up his mind.

There's food and water at home, but going home might break the charm: if he knows where he's headed, others can surely guess. If Mrs Tulk told the police he was on the run, it will be on the news, and Lambert Woods will be the first place they'll look.

The news, he thinks, and he feels in his jacket for the little Sony radio; his hand makes contact with nothing but pocket dust. Dismayed, he wiggles his fingers in deeper. It's not there.

He scrambles down the tree to the ground and searches for it, even walking back a short way to see if he dropped it on the last few yards of the hike. It's hopeless: his radio is gone.

In the fields below, the big bluestem grass seems to shimmer in the morning sun, and he yearns to steal down there and cut a handful with his pocket knife so he can suck the juice out of it. But he is afraid, after getting sick drinking the rainwater that leaked into Harlan's car. He needs familiarity – sounds and smells he knows and which make him feel safe; a few hours' sleep in his own bed.

Home, then.

53

Incident Command Post, Westfield,
Williams County, Oklahoma
Monday, late morning

Simms left it to Fennimore to call Josh and ask him to let
their dialect specialist know about the possible Scottish
connection. An hour later, the geographical linguist was
on the line. Detectives Dunlap, Ellis and Valance, together
with Simms, Fennimore and Dr Detmeyer gathered around a
conference phone at the front of the Incident Room. Sheriff
Launer was still searching the woods on Lambert Hill.

Dr Patrick Moran spoke with a Maine accent; he was an
alumnus of Boston University, but gained his PhD from Clare
College, Cambridge.

'Your witnesses were right that your killer is from back
East,' he said. 'He is. Way, *way* east. We're talking this side of
the pond.'

'Our man is from the UK?' Dunlap said.

'Oh, I can do better than that,' Dr Moran said. 'The
pronunciation is overlaid with Midwestern USA, but he
pronounces the letter "r" with the tongue slightly more to
the front of the mouth than you would expect in a true
American. It's typical of Scottish English. The Scots are rhotic

speakers – they pronounce every "r", even in words like "iron", vibrating the tongue against the hard palate.' He paused. 'Let me demonstrate.'

He played a short section of the audio: 'I do *everything* to make it work.'

'Hear that? *Wur-uk*, like there are two syllables in "work".'

Ellis tugged his ear, Valance shrugged, but Simms thought she caught it.

'It's subtle,' Dr Moran said, 'but it's there. Now Josh, who did the transcript, got stuck on something the killer says; he thought your guy said something about a "clay pit" and "full". He *actually* said, "I'm a glaikit gull". It's Scottish dialect meaning someone who's easily fooled. Comes from the Borders – a place called Haweek.'

Fennimore sat bolt upright. 'Can you spell that?'

'H.A.W.I.C.K.'

'Hawick is the nearest town to Alemoor Loch,' Fennimore said.

'Interesting, isn't it?' Dr Moran said. 'Just to be sure, I played that section of the audio to a friend of mine – Douglas Scott. We were at Cambridge together, and he wrote a book on the Hawick dialect. He agreed with me – your guy is from Hawick.'

They thanked Dr Moran for his assistance and got straight to work.

'I'll get on to Police Scotland,' Simms said. 'See if they have anything like this on record.'

Dr Detmeyer said, 'Sadistic killers like these don't suddenly emerge like a moth from a chrysalis – metamorphosing from normal child to predatory killer. Their strange obsessions and cruelty would be evident in childhood – at least, to anyone who paid attention.'

'We're talking about the usual – cruelty to pets, arson, sexual assaults on other children?'

He nodded. 'And a few others – I'll compile a list.'

'Okay,' she said. 'But I'd better tell you upfront, I can ask, but juvenile records are sealed. This could be a non-starter.'

'I'll get Josh to search local news archives for anything that might fit,' Fennimore said.

The search party trailed into the meeting room a half-hour later, looking hot and dirty and despondent.

'No trace of Riley?' Simms asked.

'He was there, all right.' Launer had lost his freshly starched crispness, and Simms felt almost sorry for him. 'Dogs found a kid's den, torn up and kicked about. They lost him for a bit, but picked up a faint trail further in, took us to what looked like a pot grow, but the weed was gone. Dogs went crazy, whining and circling and backtracking. Then one of 'em stopped and dropped on a dirt track next to the clearing.'

'The boy was taken away in a car?' Dunlap asked.

'Looks like.'

'Tyre tracks?' Fennimore said.

He shook his head. 'Someone dragged a landscape rake along the trail.'

'We'll need to process the den,' CSI Roper said.

'You're welcome to it,' Launer said. 'What's left of it.'

'I have the coordinates,' the Team Adam consultant said.

'Take Deputy Hicks with you,' Launer said. 'I'm going home to shower.'

Two hours later, Fennimore took a call. Instantly alerted by the sharpness of his tone, Simms looked up. Ashen-faced, he said a few words, thanked the caller and hung up.

'That was SCAS.'

The Serious Crime Analysis Section had helped the St Louis Task Force with crime-scene analysis on their review cases. They looked at all serious crimes in the UK, providing a statistical breakdown to investigators, as well as descriptive comparisons of behaviours.

'They think there are enough common factors between Rachel and Suzie and the Hawick victim for a closer look.'

'You must have been expecting this, Nick,' Simms said, gently. Rachel was thirty-two when she disappeared. The Hawick victim was aged thirty-two. Her daughter was ten years old, like Suzie. Rachel was found in water, like the Hawick victim.

'Are you okay?'

'Fine,' he said, but it sounded metallic, false.

He stood abruptly, knocking the edge of the table with his knees and sending pens and papers skittering across the melamine.

'Professor?' Dunlap said.

Fennimore started walking, his movements jerky and uncoordinated. Dunlap looked to Simms, but she frowned, shaking her head and, tactfully, he looked away.

'Nick—'

He splayed his fingers, gesturing for her to stay where she was. 'Five minutes,' he said. 'Give me five minutes.'

She watched him cross the room and almost fall through the fire door onto the fire escape. She left it three minutes. He was standing with his hands on the rail, the scream of the cicadas a barrage of sound in the searing heat.

Simms stood next to him and leaned on the rail, her tanned arm next to his. Almost, but not quite, touching.

Gradually, he relaxed a little and looked into her eyes.

'For six years I've wished for something like this, Kate,' he said. 'Thinking it would bring us closer to catching Rachel's killer.'

She squeezed his hand, but he broke free. 'I watched that man put out Sharla Jane Patterson's eyes and bleed her to death . . . I wished that on a woman, on all those women.'

'Nick, this isn't your fault.'

'I know,' he said. 'I know that. But what if this monster did take Rachel and Suzie?'

'By some kind of weird logic, you would have wished it on them? Is that what you mean?' He didn't answer and she said, 'Look, we don't know that there's even a link yet. This is just a routine check.'

'I'm going to go to my room,' he said. 'I need to think.'

He held onto the fire-escape rails all the way down as if it swayed like a rope bridge.

54

That context is crucial is a truism,
but no less true for all that.

NICK FENNIMORE

The Crime Analysis Section was reviewing Rachel and Suzie's disappearance as a matter of routine, Kate had said. But it didn't feel like routine. At the back of Fennimore's mind, like the constant kettle-whistle scream of cicadas, was the fear of what was happening to his daughter.

He pictured the girl in the photograph, walking alongside the older man, and his dream came to him sharp and clear. A warm breeze, the scent of flowers and a whiff of river water. The off-key police siren. The girl turning, stumbling. *Faux pas* – false step. And what was that scent? Roses? No, not roses, foxgloves. Paulownia – the foxglove tree.

Suddenly, he had it. The year they went as a family to Paris, the paulownia trees were in bloom on Île de la Cité. He'd been looking so closely at the girl, he hadn't analysed the context.

Heart hammering, he opened his laptop and pulled up the image. The wall was in deep shadow, but he thought he could just make out regular lines in the structure. The paving on which the man and girl walked was made up of flat stone setts. Was that a slight distortion, or were the cobbles actually curved? He clicked through a few auto-correction options, brightening the picture and altering the contrast; in seconds he was sure – the wall was stonework, and the setts really were curved, in a repeating fan.

He Googled paving: historic road setts; conservation; traditional paving; a few others. In half an hour he'd discovered that the setts were not laid out in a fan pattern, as he thought, but as 'bogens' – a series of stacked and interlocking arcs. He now knew that this type of pattern was typically European.

He zoomed out of the picture and looked again at the entire scene. The green metal dome attached to a swan-necked bracket was a street lamp, as he'd thought; he'd seen that type of bracket on lamps above the riverside walkways beside the Seine. That's what his dreams had been trying to tell him. The picture had been taken in Paris.

It was all about context. And in this new context, the white box van took on a new meaning. He enlarged it. The scribble of black paint might be something more. He increased the contrast and sharpened that section. Yes, those could be symbols or letters scrawled at the top of the roller door. He picked up the laptop and headed out. He needed to talk to Kate Simms.

His mobile phone rang as he picked up his room keys. He answered it, juggling his computer to his left hand.

'You missed your flight.'

He checked the screen. 'Ollie?' Ollie Roskopff was his publisher in the United States. 'What flight? What are you talking about?'

'You were expected on United Airlines flight 6443 arriving into Chicago O'Hare at twelve after midday. You weren't on it.'

Chicago? He struggled to make sense of what Roskopff was saying, but his mind was still on the dream and Paris, and getting to Simms to ask for her help.

'You being on a tight schedule, I asked the area sales director to meet you off the plane.'

A thud of recognition. 'The Chicago gig,' Fennimore said.

'The Chicago gig,' the publisher said, 'yeah. That, and the interview with *That's Entertainment!* Which you missed.'

Bloody hell . . .

'Ollie, I'm sorry, it's this investigation.'

'Well, yes, I could see that you might be a little . . . distracted. It's a big story; it made the networks even here in New York. But when John – that's the rep – called you on your cell, he got bounced straight to voicemail.' The publisher's voice remained even, but the gaps between his words and the tension in his voice told another story.

'I lost track of time,' Fennimore said. 'I thought the Chicago trip wasn't for another few days—'

But Roskopff wasn't finished. 'I walked out of an important commissioning meeting to talk to a very pissed-off journalist at *That's Entertainment!* You know why?' He didn't wait for Fennimore to speculate. 'Because a feature in *That's Entertainment!* can be as good as a hundred thousand of publicity spend. It can boost rankings and generate reviews; it can put you on the must-have list for TV interviews, guest appearances on chat shows. One of our authors got his book on to Oprah's Book Club selection after a feature in *That's Entertainment!* In short: you do *not* piss off *That's Entertainment!*'

'Okay,' Fennimore said. 'We're clear on that.'

'That's just . . . dandy,' Roskopff said, breathing hard. 'You're booked on UA flight 5510. It leaves Tulsa at five fifty-five.' He paused and then repeated: 'Fifty-five ten, at five fifty-five – should be easy to remember, even in your current state of mind.'

'Wait a minute,' Fennimore said. 'I can't *leave.*'

'Sure you can. Your ticket will be at the check-in desk.'

'Ollie, listen, there's been a development,' he said. 'I need to stay close to the case.'

'This is the technological age, Nick,' Roskopff said. 'You can stay in virtual contact a dozen different ways. But your physical presence is required in Chicago in front of a live audience, all of whom have paid fifteen dollars a ticket to see you. That,' he said, 'is where you "need" to be.'

As Fennimore recalled it, the reader event in Chicago was just the beginning; there was a bookstore signing, a seminar at the University of Illinois and a library reading the following day.

'No, Ollie, you don't—'

'Don't tell me I don't get it,' Roskopff said. 'Do you know what a no-show will cost? We hired a theatre. We sold twelve hundred tickets for this event alone. So you'd better haul ass over here or I *will* sue – for lost book sales, for every ticket sold, for disappointment to your readers, for staff hours spent in setting this up, for the fucking *heart attack* you're giving me right now!'

A no-show would put Fennimore in breach of contract. He'd done well from sales of *Crapshoots and Bad Stats*, but he couldn't afford a lawsuit, or the damage it would do to his professional reputation.

'UA flight 5510, Tulsa airport,' he said.

'Arriving into O'Hare at seven forty-five. I laid on a limo, so look out for the driver.' Roskopff reverted to his usual calm and urbane manner, as though the threat of litigation had never been made. 'It's a thirty-minute drive downtown, but you'll just have to be fashionably late. The venue has your technical requirements, all you need is your presentation ready on a USB stick for the techs to plug into the system.'

'Okay,' Fennimore said, already picking, his laptop and checking that the memory stick he needed was in the zip pocket.

'I told the reporter you were hung up on this serial-killer thing, and I was able to negotiate new terms.'

New terms . . . Fennimore waited for the hammer to fall.

'I told him you'd take him somewhere nice for dinner after the event this evening.'

'No problem,' he said, relieved.

'*And* he gets an exclusive on your role in the investigation.'

'That's two conditions – and I can't give *anyone* an exclusive – the investigation is ongoing.'

'Nobody's asking you to give away any secrets – just tell him how you got involved, your contribution to the Task Force. Come on, Professor – I'm asking you to BS him a little; you can do that, can't you?'

'Like a publisher at a book fair,' Fennimore said. He hung up and checked his watch – he had just enough time to email Josh, shower, change and talk to Kate Simms.

He found her in the meeting room. A few heads turned, and he realized that Simms must have passed on the news. She met him at the door.

'All right?' she asked.

He smiled. 'Yes. Thanks.'

Dunlap came over and offered his sympathies. 'We'll be going over the police and autopsy reports, Professor. Of course, if you want to be here, you're in, but you know how brutal it can be, a bunch of cops raking through a cold file.'

Fennimore nodded.

'I'm . . . concerned that folks might hold back with you in the room,' Dunlap said.

'I appreciate your tact, Detective,' Fennimore said. 'And I think I have the perfect solution: I'm heading out to Chicago for a couple of days.' He glanced at Kate Simms. 'Got a minute?'

'Chicago?' she said.

They were seated in a booth in the restaurant. 'Might as

well do something useful while I'm banished to the sidelines.' He preferred to keep his conversation with his publisher to himself. 'I've been thinking about what you said earlier. What if some of the children did survive?'

'Nick,' she said carefully. 'We don't know if Rachel really did fall victim to one of these men.'

'I know,' he said. 'I'm just thinking through possibilities, eliminating lines of inquiry.' He slipped his laptop out of his bag and she shook her head.

'Not the photograph again. Nick, we've been through this—'

'Hear me out,' he said. 'What if Suzie *is* part of this, and the man in the picture is the Scottish connection? Would you really want to dismiss what could be vital evidence?'

'That's low tactics, even for you,' she said.

'I know. But what if this is Suzie, Kate?' Before she could argue, he added, 'And what if I could tell you where it was taken?'

She closed her eyes for a moment and exhaled. 'All right,' she said. 'I'm listening.'

He opened the image and talked her through why he was convinced the picture was taken in Paris, pointing out the green swan-necked lamps, the typically European design in the layout of the setts, knowing and not caring that it was only pity that kept her from leaving.

Then he slid the image so that the white box van was in the centre of the screen, enlarged it and watched her reaction.

She frowned, angling the monitor so that she had a better view. 'Is that graffiti?' she said.

'I think it's a gang tag.'

She nodded, thoughtful. 'Could be.'

'If it is, then it's territorial, and gangs' territories are geographically precise.'

'All true.'

'And I was thinking Paris Police might have a graffiti database.'

'They do,' she said.

'And as part of the Task Force, you would get further with a request for information than I would,' he said.

She was still scrutinizing the picture. 'Email me the JPEG,' she said. 'I'll see what I can do.'

'It might need to be cleaned up and enhanced to get the detail,' he said, and she glanced sharply at him – she knew when she was being manipulated: enhance the image, and the scar/shadow question would be resolved at the same time.

'I said I'll see what I can do,' she repeated.

55

Riley works his way around back of the house through the woods, stepping careful and quiet. By the time he reaches the fence at the boundary of the woods and the trailer park, he is light-headed. He reaches up to grab the top rail and swing over, but can't find the strength to haul himself up. He falls back and just lies there for a minute, staring up at the grasses nodding in a light breeze. He is so dry he can't swallow; it feels like he has glass lodged in his throat, and his tongue feels thick and swollen. His nose twitches, smelling the pungent scent of burning tobacco. Someone is nearby. He rolls into the shade of a bush up near the fence and listens, hears a blast of harsh sound, a squawk of voices.

A police radio? he thinks. *Why're they still here? Why can't they leave me alone?*

He crawls on his belly to the house. There's police tape all around it, and a seal on the door. He carries on down the slope to where the trailer is jacked up, crawls under. It smells of earth and faintly of raccoon scat; he creeps forward, trying not to snuff the smell in his nostrils in case the cop hears. He peeps through the gaps between the front steps. A police cruiser is parked right across the front of the house. A sheriff's deputy leans against his car with his back to the house, smoking a cigarette.

Too tired and weak to go back, Riley lies beneath the trailer with his face pressed to the cool earth.

56

Incident Command Post, Westfield,
Williams County, Oklahoma
Monday afternoon

Web Spiders deployed by the United States techs discovered a forum whose members were discussing the recording of Sharla Jane's murder. A forum member calling himself SouthernKingfish had posted the link earlier in the day. He took issue with those who claimed the murder was faked – a combination of careful editing and CGI effects. One poster said that the 'victim' was in fact a willing participant, an addict, high on meth – which explained the rasp in her voice.

SouthernKingfish wrote that the cops knew different. Sharla Jane, too. He described the resuscitation equipment he'd used. He chose the wrong breathing tube, he explained, and had damaged her throat before changing to a size smaller, and *that* was why her voice was so harsh when she came round.

The damage to Sharla Jane's throat had been kept in-house.

The linguistics specialist confirmed that the style, with its slips into British-English sentence construction, were similar to the video recording of Sharla Jane's murder. Deputy Hicks also pointed out that the southern kingfish was a type of mullet, and their guy had a mullet hairstyle.

The web spider gave them a list of email addresses. From there on in, they needed the Internet Service Provider's cooperation. On behalf of the Task Force, Dunlap asked for and got a warrant to gain access to SouthernKingfish's account, including any messages sent or received.

Within hours, he had a senior technical adviser with the company on speakerphone. Members of the team not out canvassing gathered round.

'No sends, no incoming mail.' The voice at the other end of the line was male, and sounded very young.

'He must have received one email at the very least,' Dunlap said. 'To confirm his account details when he set up the account.'

'Deleted,' the tech adviser said.

'So the account wasn't used?'

'Oh, it got used, just not in the way you'd think.'

'You need to explain,' Dunlap said.

'Okay. So, every time you send or receive an email, it leaves an electronic trail, like pixie dust in the ether.'

'Okay . . .' Dunlap said.

'So, you set up an account, agree a password with . . . whoever, then you draft an email. You don't need to send it, because the other guy can just punch in the password, check the drafts folder for new messages wherever he is. And because it doesn't get sent—'

'No pixie dust,' Dunlap said.

'Right. He deleted everything in the drafts folder.' A collective groan from the team must have been audible at his end, because he added, 'Oh, wait, that doesn't mean they're gone,' the young expert said. 'We keep multiple copies of emails in case the system goes down, or you delete something you didn't mean to.'

'Even if you permanently delete a file?'

314

'It can take a while for us to get around to, uh, emptying the trash can. Deleted files – non-priority, right?'

'So,' Dunlap said, 'what about these particular deleted drafts? Do you have them, or don't you?'

'*Dude*,' the kid said. 'They've been in your inbox like ten minutes already.'

It would take a few hours to work out the chronology and create a discourse from the drafts the technical manager had sent. When they had something near coherent, Dr Detmeyer and Professor Varley would compare notes.

In the meantime, Hicks invited Kate Simms to ride along with her to Lambert Woods trailer park and help with the canvass. She led the way across the car park and stopped at her beat-up Suzuki SUV.

'No department vehicle today, Deputy?' Simms said.

In reply, Hicks handed her a grid, marking out each of the park homes. 'One resident has been hard to pin down,' Hicks said. 'The guy in lot thirty-two isn't home, no matter *what* time of day officers call – his car's outside, but no sign of him. It's the nearest to Sharla Jane's place. If anyone saw something, it'd be him.'

'He's very close to the boundary fence,' Simms commented.

Hicks nodded. 'I'm beginning to think he's sneaking off into the woods to avoid us.' She took her hat off and put it on the back seat. 'Figured we'd go in undercover.' She gave a rare smile; Deputy Hicks had high, flat cheekbones and a naturally guarded expression, but when she smiled, her cheeks dimpled.

The SUV had no air con, so they drove the back roads with the windows down, throwing up a dust cloud behind them.

'Known Professor Fennimore long, Chief?' Hicks asked.

'Ten years,' Simms said. 'But you already know that.' The Task Force had pored over the police files for Rachel and Suzie, so now they knew Simms was with Fennimore the night that his wife and child disappeared, that they'd had dinner, but Simms had gone home to her family instead of sharing the double room Fennimore had booked.

They drove for a few minutes without speaking.

'Is he a good man?' Hicks asked. A flash of those dark-rimmed blue eyes.

Oh, for heaven's sake, Simms thought. *She's fallen for him.* Fennimore would be back from Chicago soon and she wanted to know where she stood.

'*Good* is not a word I'd use,' she said. 'He's . . . odd. He can be rude and insensitive, but he's generous, too. And funny – sometimes. He's clever, though not as clever as he thinks he is.' She stopped, thinking carefully about what she wanted to say next. 'But you should know that he's reckless.'

The deputy relaxed a little. Maybe she grew up around wild boys and reckless men; after all, this was America, founded on the spirit of adventure, a place where the landscape could change from farmland to wilderness in half a mile, and recklessness might be considered a species of courage.

'Reckless, huh?' Hicks slid her a speculative look, and Simms knew that she'd judged right. 'Is that why you avoid him?' Hicks asked.

'That would be none of your damn business,' Simms said evenly.

'I apologize, ma'am,' Hicks said. 'It's just . . .'

'You need to know if you can trust him.'

A hesitation, then Hicks nodded, staring straight ahead.

Simms took a breath, exhaled. 'Listen, Deputy, you're just starting out in your career. I know what a struggle it is to overcome entrenched attitudes in a system that disfavours women.' She saw genuine surprise on the younger woman's face, as if it had never occurred to her that macho attitudes and misogyny could be a part of polite British society.

'Fennimore is a gambler,' she went on. 'And not just with

money. He takes risks because he loves the adrenaline rush; he revels in the thrill of uncertainty – always has done. But after what happened to his family, it got darker, more self-destructive.'

'I guess what happened made him kind of desperate,' Hicks said.

'Yes, it did. And he's just found out that there could be a connection between his wife's murder and the man we're after. He will stop at nothing, do *whatever* it takes, to find out what happened to his daughter.'

'You're telling me not to expect him to stick around.'

Simms thought about it. When she got hauled in front of a disciplinary panel after Rachel's death, Fennimore packed his bags and scooted off to Scotland without a backward glance, and the pain of his abandonment still ached like an old wound. But Fennimore in her life was so much more complicated than Fennimore out of it. Just hours ago, he'd dragged her in to investigate the anonymous photograph without a single scruple, without a hint that he knew or cared that it might make things difficult for her. She sighed.

'Honestly, I'd be more concerned for you if he *did* stick around,' Simms said.

They completed the journey in silence, zipping past flat farmland bordered by wire fences tumbled over with honeysuckle, the grass verges already beginning to brown in the sun, but dotted still with pink and purple flowers. They turned into Lambert Woods Park and drove up to the lot in question. It was rented to a Vincent Goodman. The trailer on the lot was a double-wide with a porch, and looked to Simms like the chalets she and Kieran had rented for holidays on the East Anglian coast. A Ford Taurus was parked outside, and a chaise longue sat under an awning that ran almost the full length of the structure. Deputy Hicks parked at the side of the house, out of sight of the windows. In the distance, they could hear the baying of the tracker dog and the calls of the search party out in the woods.

'I'll go around back,' Hicks said. 'If he comes to the door, keep him talking.'

It was the middle of the day, and hot. The front door slammed shut behind the fly screen as Simms approached. She knocked and waited.

A scuffle of sound at the back of the house, then Hicks appeared, walking alongside a man about her own age and height. His hair was cut short and his beard was trimmed into a neat goatee. He wore a clean white T-shirt and walked with his right hand gripping his left forearm. He looked scared.

'Mr Goodman,' Hicks said. 'Why did you run away?'

'I didn't,' he said. 'I was just going for a walk.'

'You do a lot of walking?' she said. ''Cos we been calling on you for two days, now. You are never home.'

'Might've been asleep.'

She gazed at him in wonder. 'Sir, you must be one heavy sleeper.'

He didn't answer.

'You know what we're here for.'

Simms caught a wild look in his eye that she recognized instantly as the mad scramble of a guilty man.

'Is this about the boy?'

'The boy?' Hicks said.

Simms met Hicks's gaze. They understood each other perfectly.

'I meant the murder. The lady lived over in lot thirty-three.'

'Sharla Jane Patterson. You know her?'

'Not really.'

'But you know the boy,' Simms said.

'Yeah.' He realized what he'd said and she saw a momentary panic in his eyes again. 'No, not like that.'

'Like what?' Hicks asked, acting the perfect foil.

'Like what you're making out.'

The two women looked at each other as though he was a deep mystery to them.

'That boy's a thief,' he said, on the defensive. 'He stole beer right out of my cooler box.'

'You don't say?' Hicks thumbed open her shirt pocket and took out her notebook, frowning and shaking her head like she wondered how standards of common decency had come to this sorry pass.

'Yeah.' He was more confidently indignant now.

'When you say, "the boy" . . .?'

'What'd you come here on the short bus?' he said, instantly losing patience. 'Riley *Patterson*, o' course.'

She tapped her notebook with her pen. 'For the record,' she said, her tone flat, like she was just trying to get the facts straight. 'So, Riley Patterson stole your beer—'

He huffed a sigh. 'Out of my cooler.'

She wrote it down.

'Out of your cooler in your house?' she said, her pen poised over her notebook.

'What?' He looked stupefied for a moment. 'No! He was *never* in my house.'

Sweat broke out on his forehead and covered his arms in a slick sheen, but he kept his right hand in place. 'Is there something wrong with your arm, Mr Goodman?' Simms asked.

'No.'

'May I see?'

'No.' He looked at Hicks as though she might rescue him.

'Tell you what,' Hicks said. 'Show a little cooperation, or we can have this discussion over at the sheriff's office in Westfield.'

His shoulders slumped and he looked like he was about to cry. 'You're gonna take this all wrong,' he said, but he slid his hand away, revealing a healing cut on his left forearm.

The masked killer in the recording of Sharla Jane's murder wore a bandage on his left hand.

'Show me your hands,' Hicks said.

He held them out, trembling, palms down, then palms up. There were no further cuts.

'You need to explain that,' Hicks said.

'The kid come tearing past my trailer the night he disappeared.'

'What time of night?'

'I don't know – it was just after dark, I guess. I was trying to *help* the boy, but the little bastard slashed me with a knife, kept running.'

'Where?'

'Into the woods.' He jerked his head towards the mass of green beyond the post-and-rail fence at the boundary.

'What made you think he needed help?' Simms asked.

'He was crying, running like the hounds a' hell was on his tail. And . . .' He stopped for a second, seemed to weigh up if the next piece of information would get him out of trouble or dig him a deeper hole.

'*And*,' Hicks said, in a tone that said she would poke him with a sharp stick if he didn't get on with it.

'The feller lived with his momma come running right after him.'

This was their first eyewitness confirmation that Sharla Jane's lover was the man they were hunting. Hicks said, 'Uh-huh,' wrote it down like she knew all along.

'And when you saw this fellow running after Riley, what'd *you* do, Mr Goodman?'

'I had *injuries*,' he said. 'Blood *all over* me. I went inside, fixed myself up.'

57

Robert Gordon University, Aberdeen, Scotland
Monday, late evening, BST

Josh Brown sat in the tiny staff kitchen on the third floor of the science building, which had become his unofficial office and occasional crib. The 'Save Suzie!' forum was abuzz. The sketch image he'd uploaded had generated hundreds of responses. Suggestions about the identity of the man in the sketch, direct messages from people asking him to telephone or email them, speculation about who had posted the image. He had replied to all of the messages via the forum or anonymously, using email addresses he created and then deleted, a burner phone for the calls. He'd spoken to people who were earnest, or crazed, or out-and-out con artists, and not one of them had information that he could use.

He closed the forum page and sipped black coffee while he read through a bundle of press clippings from the *Hawick News*. Professor Fennimore had forwarded him a sort of 'Rough Guide to Serial Killers' compiled by the FBI behaviourist. The guide listed the kind of criminal behaviours the Task Force would be interested in for the purposes of identifying their killer. The behaviourist estimated that their man (or men) would be twenty-five to thirty-five years old. Which meant that he (or they) would be teenagers ten or twenty years ago. In the interests of thoroughness, Josh had asked the paper's archivist to send him stories going back twenty years.

There were a lot. Unlike the nationals, local papers thrived on minor details, and would report even the pettiest criminality – which suited Josh's purpose, because if their killer really had been brought up around Hawick, he would have started small.

A two-tone notification on his laptop alerted Josh to incoming email. A fresh crop of stories. He skim-read: teenaged peeping Toms, rabbit slayers and cat tormentors; a couple of fire-starters. The next item didn't seem to fit.

At the top of the page: GIRL HURT IN WALL COLLAPSE. Josh read on: 'Hawick schoolgirl, Isla Bain, was critically injured by a wall collapse in the ruins of a cottage on the edge of Whitlaw Wood. Isla (thirteen) was found under rubble by dog walkers . . .'

He skipped to the next headline: BRAVE TEEN LOSES BATTLE FOR LIFE.

The next, dated a week later: ISLA – POLICE INTERVIEW SCHOOL-FRIENDS.

The final headline: ISLA DEATH WAS MURDER.

'Okay . . .' Josh read the full text. It seemed that a neighbour had seen Isla with a boy, walking in Lynn Wood, a strip of woodland that merged into Whitlaw Wood at its southerly tip. They were some distance away, and the boy, wearing a hooded jacket, was not identified. This was sixteen years ago.

The archivist had added a note: 'The Procurator Fiscal ruled that Isla had been murdered by person or persons unknown. I had a chat with the detective who ran the investigation. Isla's wrists and feet bore ligature marks; she had been sexually assaulted – no usable DNA. She was found on the ground with her hands above her head, as if someone had held them there. The inquiry team was convinced they were looking for at least two attackers – one to hold her still, one to shift the rocks. They'd never thought it was a wall collapse – the nearest damaged section of wall was ten feet away – but they kept it quiet while they interviewed the kids, hoping they would trip themselves up, I suppose.'

Josh dialled the archivist's mobile number. It went straight to voicemail. He typed a fast email, asking for the name and phone number of the archivist's police source. Next, a call to his contact in Police Scotland. They would need to know the names of every boy on the high-school roll that year. That would have to wait until morning, when the school opened, he was told. If Isla's clothing had been kept in evidence, DNA technology had moved on in twenty years: 'usable DNA' had been redefined by low-template DNA. They agreed to be in touch around midday the following day.

Fennimore had called him en route to Chicago – he would be hard to reach until Tuesday evening: DCI Simms would be his first point of contact. He tried Fennimore's phone anyway, but it was switched off. He scrolled through his contacts to Chief Inspector Simms, his thumb hovering over the 'call' icon. Simms didn't trust him, and that made him nervous. It wasn't like he had anything concrete yet. It made sense to get the list of boys on the school roll, talk to the archivist's police contact, liaise with Police Scotland, rather than go in half-cocked.

What difference could a few hours make after fifteen years?

He checked his watch – 9.47 p.m., time enough to head downtown for a drink. The sun had just set. On a fine summer's day, the evening afterglow could take you almost to midnight before dropping fully into darkness, but clouds scudding in on a north-easterly crowded over the Granite City, bringing nightfall two hours early. The wind funnelled down the narrow backstreets, blowing hard, cold rain in across Aberdeen harbour from the North Sea. He turned up his jacket collar and leaned into the wind. It was a ten-minute walk down the back lanes, heading towards Market Street, and as close to the harbour as you could get without diving in. In five minutes he was in the narrow cobbled lane called Back Wynd, a row of trendy shops to his right and the grey granite wall of St Nicholas Kirk churchyard on his left.

The bar was busy, filled out with the night-time crowd: almost exclusively male, young and fit. He wove through the crowd, glad of the warmth, feeling appreciative eyes on him, enjoying the attention, confident of his own good looks. The bar staff knew him, and a nod was all it took to place his order. He peeled off his jacket and pushed his fingers through his hair. The barman handed him a towel with his glass of merlot and he took it, laughing. He rubbed the towel over his head and handed it back to the barman. A movement at the far end of the bar caught his attention. A guy had leaned forward to get a better look; Josh propped one elbow on the bar and met his eye. He was fortyish, fit-looking, dark hair, beard. Josh smiled. Flustered, the man looked away, finished his beer fast and was retreating towards the door before Josh got properly settled on his bar stool.

Pity – he was cute.

Josh ate a burger, chatted up the barman and stayed an hour, drinking one slow pint. He rented an apartment on Charlotte Street for its proximity to the university, and now he headed back to it, taking the same route he had come. There was no break in the clouds, but the rain had stopped, and the wind was at his back. A styrofoam box skittered past him, stumbling and stuttering over the stone setts, the sound echoing from the kirkyard wall like a whispered prayer. After it, a single point of sound, like a stone dropped in a pool. Low in pitch, and solid – a footfall. He slowed his pace, listening intently. It came again, the solid clump of a heel on stone, followed by the slither of shoe leather. The hairs on the back of his neck stood up; he was being shadowed, and not very competently.

He assessed his surroundings: it was eleven thirty at night, and this end of Back Wynd was deserted, the shops shuttered, the gated entrances locked; the kirkyard wall a fifteen-foot barrier on his right. He crossed the road, glancing left, saw the shadow of a man. The shadow made one misstep, then continued on, head down. Josh had already passed the two side streets that might provide an escape route. It was a hundred-yard sprint from here to Schoolhill, and more closed shops. He could turn back, take refuge in O'Neill's pub, but even if he got past his stalker, he'd have to go home sometime and he needed to know what kind of threat this guy was.

Facing a shopfront, Josh feigned interest in the window display. He kept his head low, using his peripheral vision to monitor the man's approach.

The stalker moved closer, his hard leather shoes ringing out on the stone setts, now he wasn't tiptoeing. *Taller than me*, Josh estimated, and heavier. A few more steps and he'd be alongside.

The hands, watch the hands.

As the man passed, he swerved out, giving Josh a wide berth heading up to the crossroads.

His heart hammering, Josh spun right. 'You lost, mate?'

The man danced sideways as if he'd been prodded. 'Sorry, what? Are you talking to me?'

East London. Definitely. Smoothed out, for sure, but it was there.

''Cos you seem to be following me.'

'What? No!' Hands wide, empty.

Josh took a step nearer, recognized the guy from the bar. 'I'll give you some advice for free: you're lost, following someone else is bad strategy. 'Cos where *they* want to go, isn't necessarily where *you* want to be.'

'I don't know what you mean.'

Another step. 'I think you do.'

'This is bollocks.' The man turned to go.

Josh grabbed the guy's left arm, pulling him off balance, shoved his right shoulder. Using his forward momentum, he slammed the guy against the shop window.

The man struggled weakly, but Josh had his wrist in a lock, and he mashed his face against the glass until he stood still.

'Who sent you?' he demanded.

'No one. *Nobody* sent me.'

He tried to turn, but Josh kicked his legs wide. The shoes were fancy Italian jobs with hard leather soles. 'If you're the best they could do, I feel insulted. I mean, who told you it was okay to wear tap shoes on a follow?'

'I *really* don't know what you're talking about,' the man said, his voice high-pitched with fear.

'You do *not* want to fuck with me,' Josh said, increasing the pressure, forcing him into the storefront window till the glass bowed. 'You left the bar an hour ago, and yet here you are on the street, same time as me.'

'I swear, I don't know—' Josh tweaked the wrist-hold and the man cried out. 'All right! Okay . . . I went to O'Neill's.'

'And you just happened to step outside as I passed? I call it a piss-poor cover story.'

His arm was so far up his back by now that the man standing on tiptoe. 'Look, I'm just here on a visit. I heard there were a few gay-friendly bars in town, and . . .'

Josh experienced a moment of uncertainty, relaxed his hold and the man twisted free.

Out of practice, Josh. Out of condition. He moved to the stance, ready for what came next, but the man's hands went up immediately.

'Look,' he said. 'I didn't mean to scare you, but, *Jesus*, you're scaring the shit out of *me*!'

Josh didn't even blink.

'I just . . . I wanted to ask if you fancied a nightcap, but I guess I felt shy . . . I . . . I'm not even "out" yet.'

He was tremulous and vulnerable, and Josh felt suddenly ashamed. 'Look,' he said. 'I'm sorry. Overreaction.'

The man looked at him with tears in his eyes, dug in his pocket for a tissue and wiped his nose, his hand shaking.

Poor little queer, having a hard time coming to terms with his sexuality, plucks up the courage to make an approach and what does he get – Essex Man acting like the Kray twins. They stood three feet apart, Josh uncertain what to do next, until a crowd of people spilled out of O'Neill's and headed up the street.

The guy shrugged. 'I'm shit at this. I should . . .' He turned back down towards the harbour, his shoulders slumped.

Josh called, 'Hey!'

The forlorn look on the guy's face was the decider.

'What about that nightcap?' Josh said.

58

It is discouraging how many people are shocked by honesty and how few by deceit.

NoËL COWARD

Edge of Westfield, Williams County, Oklahoma
Tuesday, 11.30 p.m.

Fennimore had fulfilled his obligations to his publishers, made things right with *That's Entertainment!*, signed books, charmed readers and booksellers in Chicago. He had even won over John, the sales rep he'd kept waiting at the airport, with a case of expensive imported Glenlivet. Now he was back in Oklahoma, sitting at Abigail Hicks's kitchen table. He had planned to stay another night in Chicago and get the first flight on the Wednesday, but when it came to it, he couldn't stand being away from the investigation any longer. He'd managed to catch a direct flight that got him into Tulsa International at 10.15 p.m., hired a car and drove straight over.

As Hicks cooked chilli and rice, she set a cold beer before him and gave him the highlights of the past thirty hours. It was good to hear that the FBI had produced an aged-up the photograph from 'Thomas Holsten's' fake driver's licence, adding a beard and longer hair; that had been distributed to truck companies up and down I-44. He enjoyed listening to Hicks's tale of interviewing Sharla Jane's neighbour with Kate Simms. He wished he'd been there to see it.

'So Goodman saw the boy go into the woods, followed by a man?' Fennimore said.

'He did.'

'Did anyone think to check the fence for DNA?'

She smiled. 'Roper said you'd ask. He found skin cells from an unknown male. Team Adam paid for a private lab to rush the results; it matched the DNA off the rail-rod screws in Sharla Jane's trailer.'

Click. One more piece of the puzzle, Fennimore thought.

'Could Mr Goodman describe the man?'

'Tall, black clothes, ski mask. And he claimed he hardly saw Sharla Jane's boyfriend.'

The Task Force had released a psychological profile of the killer while Fennimore was away, and the boyfriend was named as a Person of Interest.

Abigail Hicks handed Fennimore a plate of chilli rice. 'See anything useful in there?'

Kate Simms had sent him the exchange of emails between an unnamed correspondent and the man calling himself 'SouthernKingfish' – they were sitting in front of him on the red melamine.

'Just two serial killers flinging schoolboy insults at each other.' He flicked to the last page, some way into the name-calling.

'Seriously? You dropped your lassie in *Alemoor Loch*, and *you're* lecturing *me*?' This was from the man wanted by the Task Force.

The reply: 'Do you *want* to be banged up for the rest of your life?'

Their guy: 'Jail, or dead, better than being hooked up with a nurrit-prick too scared to do it for himself.'

'What's a "nurrit-prick"?' Hicks asked, reading over Fennimore's shoulder.

'*Nurrit* is Hawick dialect for a small and insignificant thing,' Fennimore said solemnly.

'They really are at the level of the schoolyard, aren't they?' she said.

'I'll squash you,' the second man had blasted back. 'I'll pin you to a board, you bloodsucker. You fucking *insect* . . .'

'I doubt that, Mr "I'm-too-*English*-to-get-my-hands-dirty",' their guy wrote. 'But you want to come visit, I could give you a few tips.'

Just about everyone on the Task Force had scrutinized the printouts while Fennimore was in Chicago and out of the loop, so his first sight of the full text was at the airport, where he'd downloaded it before boarding the plane. He'd read it many times over since then, but every time he put the emails down, they began preying on his mind.

He scooped up a forkful of rice, set it down without tasting it and began thumbing through the pages again.

'Did Josh dig up anything useful from the *Hawick News* archives?' he asked.

'You didn't hear from him?'

'I told him to liaise with Chief Inspector Simms.'

'She couldn't reach him,' Hicks said.

Fennimore checked his watch; it would be early morning in Aberdeen. This wasn't like Josh. He tried the student's mobile number – it went straight to voicemail. He left a message, sent an email and was wondering whether to Skype, when he realized that Hicks was looking at him, her head cocked to one side.

'Sorry, did you say something?'

'I said, should we be worried?'

'Not sure,' he said, and when he shook his head, the room started to spin slowly clockwise.

'Did you get *any* sleep since you left here?'

He thought about it. 'I dozed on the plane for a bit.'

She took the bundle out of his hands and set it aside. 'Relax, eat something, rest awhile.'

A day and a half of back-to-back events and American

hospitality had left him exhausted and more than a little hungover, he had to admit. Frustrated with himself, he took up his plate of food.

After supper, they went out into the orchard again. She turned her face to the moon, and for some minutes they sipped their beer and watched the bats flit between the trees like cartoon animations.

'Have you ever seen a hunting bat in slow motion?' he asked. 'They use their wings to net an insect – it can be as tiny as a mosquito or a midge – then—' He stopped, and suddenly the sounds around him dimmed. He closed his eyes and saw the faces of people waiting to have their books signed, email messages; words and images swirling in his head until he felt dizzy. Finally, the crickets and the katydids were silenced entirely, and he knew why he'd felt compelled to read the printed pages over and over again. Sweat broke out on his face and neck; he felt cold and sick.

Hicks turned to him, concerned. 'Are you all right, Professor?'

'The man our guy has been communicating with.' Fennimore couldn't seem to get his breathing right, and he had to pause for a gulp of air. 'The Scottish connection – I think he's here, in the United States. I think I spoke to him.'

Hicks stared at him. 'What? *When?*'

'In Chicago. One of the readings—'

Her phone beeped and she cursed, dragged it from her shirt pocket and checked the screen. 'Aw, shit . . .'

'What?' he said, but she was already heading back to the house.

'You can tell me about it on the way into town,' she said. 'He did it again: mother and child disappeared from a truck stop off I-44 twenty miles north-east of Hays.'

59

A midge has a set of mouth parts which are like shearing scissors.

DR ALISON BLACKWELL

It was a short drive over to the Incident Command Post from Hicks's house, so Fennimore kept it brief.

'There was a fan at one of the Chicago events. He was over-friendly,' he explained. 'Acted like he knew me, insisted on shaking my hand, held the grip too long – generally made me uneasy. He sounded English, so I asked him if he was in the States on business. He said a mixture of business and pleasure. He told me he was an entomologist; he'd accepted an invitation from an old friend. But it didn't sound like a friendly visit.'

She shrugged. 'He sounded English, what makes you think he's the Scotch connection?'

'In the emails, the accomplice called our guy an "insect", a "bloodsucker"; threatened to pin him to a board, to which *our* guy wrote, "I doubt that, Mr 'I'm-too-*English*-to-get-my-hands-dirty'." He even offered an invitation, of sorts.'

'When did he do that?'

Fennimore quoted from memory: '"But you want to come visit, I could give you a few tips."'

'I guess . . .' Hicks said. 'But it'd take more than that to convince the Sheriff.'

'Okay . . .' Fennimore dug back in his memory for more details. 'The man at the reading said he was a specialist in *midge* eradication.'

'Midge?'

'What you would call a fly. Scottish midges are notorious bloodsuckers. It's all there, Abigail: the English reference, "insect", bloodsucker, the invitation.'

'And his search-and-destroy mission,' Hicks agreed. 'Well, we better find our guy first, 'cos if the "bug man" gets there ahead of us, we won't stand a chance of finding this woman and her daughter alive.'

The missing woman was Faith Eversley, a twenty-three-year-old single mother; her daughter, Ava, was aged eight. Kate Simms watched Fennimore from across the room. He looked pale and preoccupied, only half listening to Sheriff Launer's report.

'No family,' Launer told them. 'But she's been waitressing in O'Malley's Irish bar in Hays. The bar owner called it in. At six p.m., Faith called from the service area east of Hays. She was due in at seven, said she might be late – her car engine overheated. She said she knew what to do, and she would call back when she was on her way. Now, Faith never missed a day in the four months she's been on the payroll, so when she didn't make that call, the bar owner tried her cell phone. It went to voicemail. She waited some more, called the sheriff's office at eight thirty-five p.m.'

'Do we have a trace on the phone?' Dunlap asked.

Launer shook his head. 'Turned off.'

'Why'd it take till now for us to get to hear about it?' Simms asked. It was well after midnight.

'The truck stop's a hair over the county line,' Launer explained. 'Craig County sheriff called me after he sent a deputy out there, found her car still in the parking lot, hood up, blood on the passenger seat.' He looked around the room. 'Are we agreed this is our guy?'

'Different MO, but the victimology's too similar to be ignored.' Detmeyer, wary, as ever, of overstating the case.

'Well, we don't have time to stand around with our dicks in our hands,' Launer said, instantly tetchy. 'So, you don't mind, I'll take that as a yes. I'm going to send out an Amber Alert for the girl.'

Nods of agreement from everyone, including Detmeyer, who never seemed to take others' rudeness personally.

'The bar owner had a picture of the mother and daughter,' Launer went on. 'The County Sheriff emailed it to me. We need to get that out to the media.'

'And the car should be processed,' Fennimore said. He continued doodling on the back of a document wallet as he spoke, a sure sign he was thinking, rather than distracted.

Launer gave Fennimore a sour look. 'Craig County already processed it.'

'Oh,' Fennimore said. 'You mean Craig County *deputies* processed it?'

Sarcasm, Simms thought. *Great strategy, Nick.* She glanced towards Hicks, but the deputy had preoccupations of her own. She'd perched her netbook on a spare table and was studying the screen.

Simms unfolded her arms and stood up straight, catching Fennimore's eye. He raised his eyebrows as if to say, *What?* She spread her hands – a plea for diplomacy – and he subsided with a frustrated sigh.

Dunlap stepped in: 'If you can smooth the way, Sheriff, we might be able to catch some additional evidence.'

'Craig County *did* invite us in,' Launer said. 'I'll call the Sheriff. Hicks will . . .' He glanced over to where Hicks was still staring at her netbook. 'Deputy *Hicks*.'

She looked up.

'When you're finished playing with your new toy, you can escort these two gentlemen out to the truck stop,' Launer said with a nod to the two CSIs.

'Yes, sir, Sheriff,' she said, not in the least chastened. 'Before I do, I've been looking at the locations. We got victims along four hundred-some miles of I-44, all the way from Bristow to St Louis.'

'I *know that*,' Launer said.

She walked to the two Rand McNally maps of Oklahoma and Missouri taped together on a wall board at the front of the room and pointed to the eastern edge of the map, St Louis being on the Illinois state line. 'Kyra Pender, found in a park in St Louis.' She slid her finger south and west, following the line of I-44 to Williams County. 'Laney Dawalt, her body was dumped in a pond just a few miles east of Westfield. He put 350 miles between those two victims.'

'What's your *point*, Deputy?' Launer demanded.

She pointed to the pin that signified Mr Guffey's pond. 'Laney Dawalt – dumped a few miles east of town.' She moved to the next pin. 'Sharla Jane – Cupke Lake, just twenty miles south of here.' She took a new pin and stuck it in the map to mark the place where the new victim disappeared. 'Faith Eversley – twenty-five miles north of Westfield.'

The three points made an obtuse triangle, with the town of Westfield a few miles west of the longest side. 'He changed his hunting ground,' she said.

Fennimore sat up. 'He's come home.'

'What in the hell makes you think this is home?' Launer demanded.

'Because *that* looks like a cluster,' Fennimore said, jabbing the three points in the air with one finger and joining the dots.

'You got something to say about this?' Launer said, challenging Detmeyer.

'Serial offenders often begin their aberrant behaviour close to home,' Detmeyer said.

'Did I miss something? 'Cos my notes say victim one was dumped in Fort Leonard Wood, Missouri – that's *two hundred* miles from here.'

'We don't know that Fallon Kestler *was* his first victim,' Detmeyer said, quietly, firmly, but without rancour, giving the victim a name.

'Okay, fine. But don't these squirrelly sons-of-bitches usually spiral *out* from home ground, moving *away* from where they live?'

Detmeyer nodded. 'But until now, our unsub was acting under instruction; someone else made those decisions for him – his mentor in Scotland. He broke that bond when he murdered Sharla Jane. He's starting over, going it alone for the first time, feeling under pressure because of press and law-enforcement interest in the murders. Extreme narcissists are often insecure; familiar home ground would offer the reassurance he needs to continue to function.'

'Excuse me, Doctor,' Hicks said. 'Didn't our guy put *himself* under pressure, going public?'

'Yes, he did, but he would feel compelled to do it for the same reason Dennis Rader contacted the police after being inactive for thirteen years: he craves approval, recognition, validation.'

'Didn't he think what would happen when we found out about him?'

'I believe our man *feels* more than he *thinks*, Deputy,' Detmeyer said. 'But remaining below the radar was more perilous to his psyche than exposure could ever be. For what it's worth, I believe he gave himself the name BTK because he wants to be associated with someone who terrorized an entire state for decades, because at heart he feels he's a cipher, a nobody, someone who only ever followed orders.'

'My heart bleeds for him,' Launer said. 'But can we concern ourselves with the two people he has right now? That bitty triangle on the map happens to be the highest-populated area of Williams County. You got forty thousand people in Hays and Westfield alone.'

'We could narrow the search,' Hicks said. 'Canvass haulage companies along a shorter section of I-44.'

The suggestion was approved. Fennimore had dropped out of the discussion and returned to doodling on the sheet of paper. But, as the meeting geared up to a division of tasks, he said, 'Before we break up the meeting, I'm afraid I may have another complicating factor to add to the mix.'

60

Fergus had chosen to drive rather than fly from Chicago, because he was travelling under his own name, on a legitimate passport, and he was sure that when he had finished with his erstwhile collaborator, a check of flight manifests at Tulsa airport would be top of the Task Force's 'to do' list. He stopped to eat and rest in St Louis, the halfway point of his 650-mile journey, reasoning that a British tourist must surely be less conspicuous in a city café than ordering pulled pork and pickles at a rural truck stop. From St Louis, he joined Interstate 44, heading south-west; another five or six hours until he was where he needed to be.

The landscape from St Louis, Missouri to Williams County, Oklahoma was largely featureless. With the exception of a few limestone escarpments, the road rolled across hundreds of miles of flat terrain, with a few small hillocks: a mix of a grassland, fruit farms, cattle ranches and large tracts given over to the cultivation of maize and wheat. Billboards cluttered the edge of the highway, inviting travellers to visit the local museum/shopping mall/historic town, and occasional water towers reared up on spindly legs like Martian invaders from *War of the Worlds*.

To keep from dozing, he listened to country music and read the billboards. The average person would call the drive dull, but for him, the journey was punctuated by moments of intense excitement. He knew this road as if he had travelled it himself – and in a sense, he had, traversing it in the virtual world a thousand times, discovering a new world without ever having set foot in it. His landmarks would seem prosaic to the casual observer: a gloomy stretch of US Highway 68, north of St James, Missouri; a shining patch of water glimpsed from an overpass near a town called Cuba; the whole thrilling tract of forest at Fort Leonard Wood that he would always associate with Fallon Kestler; a zigzag county road west of Marshfield.

Cuba and Marshfield still belonged to him; the police hadn't found those two yet. He would like to stand and look at the actual places, to feel the sun on his skin, to hear the insects and birdsong, to smell the lush, wet grasses, replaying the kills in his head. Perhaps he would make time on the return journey. For him, part of the pleasure was in the deferment of gratification, and knowing where those bodies were – knowing even that they *existed* – was enough for now. He chose not to consider his own recent impulsiveness; the woman in Alemoor Loch was a regrettable aberration. Will had driven him to extremes, but now he was himself again – purposeful, in command. His purpose was clear: Will was dangerously out of control, and the profile the police released of him was uncomfortably close to the reality.

He slipped unnoticed across the Missouri state line into Oklahoma at nightfall as news broke on the radio that another woman and child were missing. He quelled a tremor of rage, knowing who was responsible before the newsreader began to theorize and make comparisons with Laney Dawalt and Sharla Jane Patterson, the age of their children and the degree of concern expressed by the police. They pretended outrage at the thought of one man's private, intensely personal exploration of power over life and death, and called it monstrous. Yet they picked over the dead remains like scavenging birds, speculating on the women's lives and the shocking violence of their deaths, and called it *human interest*. And which of those arbiters of good and evil would refuse if he went to them now and offered to sell his story?

But Fergus has no appetite for notoriety. For him, neither fame, nor infamy, was ever the point: his is a private passion, an extravagance he allows himself at discrete, well-controlled intervals. Will's role had always been to find the kills and execute – yes, 'execute' is the right word – his instructions. Fergus chose the time, means of death, location and method of disposal. Until now. Will had overstepped the mark, and he was about to learn that actions have consequences.

61

Incident Command Post, Westfield,
Williams County, Oklahoma
Wednesday, 2.30 a.m.

'This is him?' Dunlap asked.

'My best recollection of him.' Fennimore circulated, handing out sketches of a clean-shaven man with sandy hair and an unremarkable face. The man who had appeared at one of his events in Chicago, the puppet-master to their killer. Dr Detmeyer had set up a videoconference with a specialist at the FBI's Forensic Imaging Unit, and Fennimore had just finished working with a forensic artist. The Bureau preferred artists to police standard e-fit technologies.

Simms checked her watch; it was late, and the team had already worked a double shift. A few had given up and gone to bed. Launer was long gone – he had a meet-and-greet in Hays at 9 a.m., and recent media coverage promised a good turnout.

'I'll send this to Police Scotland,' she said. 'They should be gearing up for the day about now. Why don't you get a few hours' sleep – I'll call you if they find anything in their databases.'

Fennimore said nothing, but he didn't seem ready to leave

either. The look behind his eyes said he was tormenting himself, thinking he should have read more into the man's words, and she realized that for Fennimore, this meant far more than a random encounter with a killer – this could be the man he had been hunting for five years.

Sensing a change of mood, Dunlap looked up from his copy of the sketch. A quick glance and he had the situation summed up.

'I'll get the sketch out to US Law Enforcement,' he said. Chicago PD had already recovered CCTV recordings from Harold Washington Library, where Fennimore had been approached. 'The security footage will be on the first morning flight into Tulsa. You can review it with my guys, if you want, Professor.'

Fennimore nodded his thanks and Dunlap left them alone.

Simms moved in closer. 'Nick,' she said. 'Don't do this to yourself. You couldn't have known.'

'I shook his hand, Kate, and I felt nothing.'

'Thanks to you, we now have a likeness of him, we might even have him on CCTV. You'll need to be sharp to review those recordings; get some rest,' she said. He began to speak and she added, 'I promise you, if there are any new developments, I'll come and fetch you myself.'

Fennimore gave her a bleak look, but after a moment he walked away. Simms watched him through the door, and tears sprang to her eyes. *Bloody hell.* She turned to face the room. Dunlap was sending an alert out on LEO, the Law Enforcement Online portal, Valance was dozing in his chair; the two deputies on night shift had been told to stay at the Command Post. One sat with a stack of campaign flyers at one elbow and a cup of coffee at the other, and he was painstakingly folding the flyers in half, with Sheriff Launer's face and the word 'VOTE' above the fold; the other, Deputy Hicks, was taking a call at her desk. Suddenly, Hicks sat bolt upright and nodded a couple of times, saying, 'Uh-huh.

342

Yes, sir.' She glanced up, seeking to make eye contact with someone in the room, finally lighting on Simms.

Dunlap was bashing away on his keyboard.

'Greg,' Simms said.

'What?'

Simms raised her chin, indicating the deputy.

'Sir,' Hicks said into the phone. 'I want to put you on speaker, would that be okay?'

In a second, she had everyone's attention.

'I got Jack Tate, from Tate Trucking, on the line,' she said, switching to speakerphone. 'Mr Tate thinks he recognizes the driver's licence photo we sent out.'

'I don't *think*, I *know*.' Mr Tate had a voice that would ring like a bell across a truck yard. 'He changed up a little bit, but that's Bill Weaver, all right.'

Another alias, Simms thought.

Dunlap pointed to Detective Valance, who immediately began a search of the databases.

'Mr Tate's been out of town,' Hicks said. 'His assistant didn't recognize the DMV picture as one of their drivers.'

'I'll have something to say to that dumbass tomorrow,' Tate grumbled. 'I stopped by the office on my way home to see if there was anything urgent, found the picture in my in-tray, called you right away. We got twenty trucks, sixteen drivers and he can't see the likeness? *Jeez.*'

'Do you know where Mr Weaver would be right now, sir?'

'I wish to hell I did – he went AWOL with one of our trucks.'

'He did?' Hicks said. 'Do you have the licence-plate number for that vehicle, sir?' She jotted it down.

'He just completed a delivery to Sullivan, Missouri, picked up an empty container at St James he was *supposed* to drop off at a depot outside of Tulsa, but he never showed.'

'You don't have GPS on the trucks?'

'No, but I could give you his delivery route, and all our

truck tractors got a PikePass.' This was the electronic prepay tag system for Oklahoma's toll roads.

'We'll need the ID for the truck Weaver's driving and an ISO Mark and description for that shipping container, too,' Hicks said.

'I'll wake up my sorry-assed nephew, didn't know one of his own employees, get it to you in under fifteen minutes.'

'Thank you, sir. But before you do that, can you tell me how long Mr Weaver has been on your payroll?'

'Eight months, thereabouts.'

'Has he ever done anything like this before?'

'Matter of fact, he was late delivering an empty container to the depot last fall.'

Hicks made eye contact with Dunlap and Simms.

'Could you be more precise about the date, sir?' Simms had to remind herself that this was an untrained officer on a probationary period; Hicks asked all the right questions and thought like a detective.

'October, early November – something like that.'

The air in the room seemed to contract; Laney and Billy Dawalt went missing in late October.

'We'll need your help to trace that container, as well.'

'Oh, God.' All the strength had gone out of his voice, realizing the significance of her request. Suddenly, he sounded much older. 'I'll get you an exact date, and those serial numbers. Whatever you need, Deputy.'

'There *is* one more thing, Mr Tate,' Hicks said. 'Do you think you could give us a description of Mr Weaver, so we can update that picture?'

'I can do better than that,' he said, some of the earlier vigour returning. 'We take a picture of every new employee – it'll be on his file.'

It took a little longer than fifteen minutes, but by the time the Task Force had reassembled, they had a recent photograph of Weaver, and FBI recognition software confirmed that the facial characteristics matched their previous driver's-licence image. Thomas Holsten was Bill Weaver. They also had the ISO Marks of the two shipping containers that were missing, as well as the licence number and a photograph of the red Peterbilt 387 truck Weaver was driving when he vanished. The address on the driver's licence was another dead end – an empty property on the edge of Joplin, Missouri. It had recently been bulldozed.

'The firm pays for the PikePass,' Hicks explained, 'so statements go to them. We've got everything, from the minute they put him on the payroll.' This would tell them Weaver's favoured routes, and where and when he passed through the tollbooths along I-44 on regular trips.

The new name meant they had to start the canvass over, but at least now they had a photograph that they could rely on.

Launer paired up one deputy with every St Louis detective. They began in Hays and Westfield, radiating outward. By now, it was 3 a.m., so the grocery stores and restaurant outlets would have to wait till later, but gas stations and bars around the towns were worth a try. Hicks was teamed with Valance, but the young detective was taken off the roster last minute, when images started coming in from I-44 tollbooths. Dunlap had requested any truck of the same make, model and year as the one their man had checked out, not realizing how many red Peterbilt 387s were out there. They needed a team to get right on it, and Valance got volunteered.

Fuelled on caffeine and adrenaline, Hicks pulled into QuikTrip gas station and convenience store at the intersection of Main Street and Hays Road. It was dark and hot and she was in serious need of sleep. The canopy lights dazzled, and she squinted up at them. Moths buzzed and circled, butting their heads against the lamps, and she knew how they felt. While she took a few breaths, getting her head back together, a man wearing a dark windbreaker came out of the store. He went to a silver-grey SUV and took his time sliding his billfold into his pocket. She kept her eye on him as she walked inside and let the cool of the air conditioning revive her for a moment. A kid of about nineteen was restocking shelves. He stood up and wiped his hands on the seat of his pants. A door stood open into the stockroom at the back of the store, and country music drifted out.

'Is the manager back there?' she asked.

'Uh, no, ma'am, you just missed him,' the boy said.

'You can call me Deputy,' she said, looking through the window. 'That him?' The SUV was still on the lot.

'Yes, ma'am, uh, Deputy,' the kid said.

She stepped back out and the man with the billfold came forward. He was mid-forties, going a little soft around the middle, and now he was facing her, she could see he wore the company's red uniform polo shirt.

'I help you, Deputy?' he said.

She showed him the picture, explaining that the man she was looking for might drive a semi tractor-trailer or a small European car. He took the picture, like three others had in the last hour, studied it, just like they did, handed it back.

She was ready to turn away, go ask the kid, but he said, 'Yeah, I know him. He's a regular customer, was in yesterday or day before.'

She felt a jolt of energy; a dozen questions flew to her lips, but she held back. *Just shut up and let him talk, Abigail. You do not want to spook him into forgetting something important.* She said, 'Uh-huh,' and nodded slowly like it was no big thing.

'Will . . . something,' he said. 'Never saw a truck. He drives a VW Polo, ice-blue metallic.'

Which was very exact. She raised her eyebrows in question.

'My daughter just passed her driver's test,' he said. 'First time, too. I asked him what he thought of it. He said it was a thrifty car to drive, and he was looking to sell his. I wasn't sure – that car must be eight years old – but he offered to let Amelia try it out on a no-strings test drive . . .'

'He give you a number to call him back?' she asked.

The manager shook his head. 'He said he'd be away a few days, he'd drop by the store when he got back.'

'Did he use a credit card, or cash?'

'Credit card.'

'That's good,' she said. Credit cards left a nice, easy-to-follow electronic payment trail and if they were lucky, a current address. She glanced up at the security cameras. 'They work?'

'Sure,' he said. 'Hard drive stores about three weeks' worth.'

'We're going to need your recordings,' she said.

'Okay.' He looked a little nervous. 'What'd he do?'

She regarded this kindly looking family man, proud of his little girl passing her driver's test first time around, and felt a tremor run through her.

'Sir,' she said. 'You do not want to know.'

62

Incident Command Post, Westfield,
Williams County, Oklahoma
Wednesday, 3.45 a.m.

They got the car's tags from the CCTV recordings at the gas station. The VW Polo was registered to William McIntyre, Junior. William McIntyre Senior died in a car crash eight years before, leaving a widow and a son. The property, a seventies ranch-style house, was inherited by the widow. William Jnr was thirty-five, no criminal record. The McIntyres were immigrants from Scotland, settled in the area for fifteen years; it looked like a bona fide home address. Shona McIntyre, mother to William Jnr, had died two months previously. They had their emotional trigger. They had a genuine name, and now they knew where he lived.

A BOLO was sent out to law enforcement, with the photograph of William McIntyre Jnr. It went out simultaneously on the Crime Alerts section of the FBI website, Fox News and CNN. It was a risky strategy, but their best chance of finding Faith and Ava Eversley alive was to find them soon.

'If McIntyre knows we're onto him, there is less of an imperative to silence them,' Detmeyer said. 'But all of this

348

puts him under greater pressure, and if Faith and Ava *are* in that house, the last thing we want is a hostage situation.'

'And if they're *not* at the house,' Dunlap said, taking up the baton, 'We need him alive.' He looked around the room, then began again, cautiously, still watching them: 'So . . . with this in mind, we've asked for tactical support from the FBI.' He had to raise his voice over groans and grumbles from both contingents. 'A SWAT team is flying in from the FBI field office in Oklahoma City as we speak. It will be *our* collar,' he said. 'They'll do what they need to, and get out.'

'Our job is to lock down the property and surrounding area till they get there.' This was Launer. He was as reluctant as the rest to allow in 'the Feds', as he called them, and as compensation for his forbearance, it was agreed he would take point on the organization of local ops. 'Here's how it will go.' He lifted his chin, and Valance pulled up a Google Earth satellite image on the data projector.

The McIntyre residence was on the outer fringes of Hays in a mix of brick-built houses and single-storey modular homes on a street grid that straggled out into open countryside. A strip of woodland lay between the houses and a railway line, running north to south on the westerly edge of the development. Interstate 44 was five miles to the north, across unfenced, pancake-flat fields.

Another jerk of Launer's chin, and Valance zoomed in closer.

'The older house plots are marked out by fences or hedges,' Launer said. 'But as you can see, the majority got no more'n a patch of grass between the front stoop and the pavement. We *will* be conspicuous, so we need to keep our distance.

'My guys will set up road blocks on US Highway 69, north and south,' he said, indicating strategic points on the map overlay on the satellite image. 'Craig County Sheriff's Office will watch I-44 ramps heading north out of Williams; we'll take the ramps south. Hicks, I want you over by the railway line – you can take Howie. 'You and you—' he pointed to two of his deputies '—sit tight on the dirt roads to the north side of those fields in case he decides to take a short cut, but keep out of sight.'

'There's not much cover out there,' Hicks commented.

'Which is good if he makes a break for it,' Launer said. 'But bad if he hunkers down, 'cos we do not have a clear line of sight to the house.'

Valance switched from aerial to street view; the yard was overgrown with bushes and trees and the windows were shuttered. 'The satellite images could be years out of date, Sheriff,' the young detective advised.

Launer nodded. 'Okay. St Louis Police SUVs are unmarked, so they will move in closer to the house. I want to emphasize, our job is containment,' he said. 'We lock it down until the Feds arrive, and keep the public out of harm's way after they go in.'

He gave the nod to Dunlap; he was finished.

'Right now, we don't know if he's in there or not,' Dunlap said. 'So we watch for McIntyre coming *in* as well as going out.'

They left in convoy, Sheriff's Department cruisers peeling off at the agreed points, no emergency lights, no sirens. The St Louis contingent turned left, off Main Street, driving parallel to the railway line. The cruiser carrying Deputies Hicks and Howard remained at the railway line. Simms and Fennimore were in the second car with Dunlap. Everyone wore tactical vests; no one spoke. The woods stood between them and the houses for the first fifty yards. A right turn brought them to the entrance into the development. The McIntyre residence lay two rows over in NE 1st Street, on the edge of the muddle of houses and modular homes. Most of the houses were in darkness, and Dunlap and the lead vehicle killed their headlights as if by an agreed signal. As yet, they had no clear line of sight to the house. Dunlap radioed through to the lead SUV and they made another right to go around the three sides of the grid and park up at the far end of the street.

An amber glow lit the far side of the rows as they approached.

'We'll stick out like a nun in a whorehouse under those street lights,' Ellis said.

'I don't remember seeing street lights on the satellite images,' Fennimore said.

Dunlap's eyes widened. 'Aw, hell.'

He put his foot down, turning the corner at the same time as the second SUV.

Smoke poured from the house, flames shooting up from a breach in the roof tiles, and a dead pine between the house and the garage was lit up like a torch, its dry branches raining down fire onto the garage roof, while flames licked under the door from inside the garage.

He called the fire department. 'A neighbour already called it in,' he said, unfastening his seat belt. 'They got two trucks on the way.' An elderly couple huddled at the edge of the property opposite the burning house. Seconds later, two fire engines blasted into the street, horns blaring.

Lights came on along the street, and people started to come out onto their porches and driveways to watch.

'We need to get those people back, establish a perimeter and keep this road clear for emergency services to get through,' Dunlap said.

Detective Ellis and a few men from the second SUV began moving the residents to a safe distance. Dunlap's phone rang; it was Launer.

'Sheriff, we'll deal with the situation here,' Dunlap said. It seemed that Launer was eager to move to the centre of the action, but Dunlap stood firm. 'McIntyre could be on his way out,' Dunlap said. 'Your people need to stay focused, intercept him if he makes a break for it.'

An EMT ambulance arrived and the paramedics parked out of the way of the engines and stood watching the spectacle with the rest. For a few minutes, all they could hear was the drone of the pumps and shouted instructions between the firefighters.

A second later, two loud cracks turned heads.

'Gunfire,' Dunlap said. A police siren whooped and was quickly silenced, then a message burst from Dunlap's radio: 'Shots fired – officer down! Unit Four requesting assistance – repeat: Unit Four requesting assistance. Officer down!'

As the paramedics clambered into their ambulance ready for action, a third shot rang out. Fennimore broke through the cordon and was off and running.

'Where the hell d'you think you're going?' Ellis yelled.

He didn't answer. Those shots came from the railway line, and Abigail Hicks was in Unit Four.

Fennimore cut through properties, crossing two roads at a sprint, reaching the scrubby woodland in under a minute. The after-image of the house fire still danced at the back of his eyes and he blinked them away, scanning the roadway for the police cruiser. His breathing ragged, heart hammering, at last he saw something. It was rolled into a shallow trough off the road, partly hidden by brambles and saplings.

He ran to the car. It was empty. Reaching inside, he turned on the light bar and headlights. Ahead, on the roadway, he saw a deputy's hat. He swept it up; Hicks's name was inked along the sweatband. Desperate now, he scouted the length of the ditch, saw a dark form.

'Oh, Jesus . . .'

A police SUV roared towards him, bumping over the uneven road surface, blinding him in its headlights and behind that, the ambulance. Shielding his eyes, Fennimore kept running towards the stricken form. Blood pooled on the asphalt spreading from under the body.

It was Howie, the deputy who had spent his night shift

drinking coffee and folding campaign flyers for the Sheriff. A police cruiser skidded to a halt behind him and he was dimly aware of doors opening.

Fennimore turned to the woods and shouted Hicks's name.

A flashlight bobbed in the dense thicket of trees and underbrush. Someone tackled Fennimore to the ground; simultaneously eight police began yelling a barrage of orders to the figure emerging from the trees.

'It's Hicks.' Fennimore struggled, but Ellis held him.

'You'll get yourself shot, you dumb Brit,' Ellis shouted.

Fennimore yelled, 'Hold your fire – that's Abigail Hicks.'

The deputy stumbled out of the woods moments later with her pistol holstered, flashlight out to the side to show she was hiding nothing. Her chest and left arm were soaked in blood.

63

It's rarely safe to assume.

NICK FENNIMORE

McIntyre residence, near Hays, Williams County, Oklahoma

As the firefighters battled to contain the fire, the sectional door of the garage buckled and fell forwards with a groan of heat-twisted metal. McIntyre's VW Polo was parked inside. Detective Dunlap headed over from a knot of firefighters to where Fennimore was standing with some of the St Louis contingent.

Ellis jerked his chin towards the garage. 'Did you see that? He switched cars.'

'Maybe,' Dunlap said. 'The Fire Chief said they just found a body.'

For a tense microsecond everyone's thoughts flew to Faith Eversley.

'Male,' Dunlap added fast. 'A male body.'

'McIntyre?' Fennimore asked.

Dunlap tilted his head. 'From what the Fire Chief said, I doubt we'll be able to ID him from his physical description.'

CSI Roper did some preliminary work on the body before the ME took it away to Tulsa for autopsy. While Roper scooted back to the Incident Command Post in Westfield to process what he had, Launer went with Deputy Hicks to the County Hospital, but he was back in half an hour.

354

He spoke to his deputies and the fire chief, taking his time, then sauntered over to the St Louis detectives.

'Howie didn't make it,' he said.

'How is Deputy Hicks?' Fennimore asked.

'She'll live.' Launer didn't look at him. 'The house'll be off-limits for a while, yet – you all might want to—'

'Specifically,' Fennimore interrupted, 'what is Deputy Hicks's medical condition?'

Launer ran a slow eye over Fennimore before answering. 'Her *condition* is, she will live. You want me to be more *specific*, she sustained a flesh wound to her upper left arm – a through-and-through – didn't even bleed all that much. Most of what was on her was Howie's.'

'What happened?' Dunlap asked.

'Howie stepped into the woods to answer a call of nature. Hicks heard two shots in rapid succession, radioed for backup and ran to help. She saw Howie stagger up onto the roadway and collapse. When she got to him, she couldn't find a pulse. The medics say the shots blew a hole in the main artery in his right leg; he bled out in under two minutes. The bastard must've snuck up behind him, grabbed his pistol, shot him at close range – probably didn't even take it out the holster. Hicks went in pursuit; the shooter turned and fired. She went down. Didn't see the shooter. Heard a vehicle fire up, didn't get a make on *that* either.' Apparently, Launer thought Hicks should have tried harder with a bullet in her shoulder.

Fennimore and Simms returned to the Command Post at the motel with Dunlap's team. Launer remained at the scene, to 'coordinate operations'; the presence of a growing number of outside-broadcast units for local and state TV might possibly have been a factor in his decision to stick around.

Fennimore rang Josh in Aberdeen – now they had McIntyre's name, it should be easier to search the newspaper archives; it might even be possible to get a fix on their

Scottish connection. But Josh's phone was still going straight to voicemail. Fennimore tried his secretary. It was early, she said, tartly, and he knew Josh kept late hours. But if he *really* thought it was necessary, she could see if he was in the staff tea room downstairs? Fennimore told her no – he would email. This done, he settled in a chair to doze.

The mood of the team was tense but subdued, following the news of Howie's death. Dunlap and Valance started working through Tate Trucking's PikePass records for McIntyre's truck. Drifting in and out of sleep, Fennimore was dimly aware of Kate Simms, tucked away in a corner of the room, having a hushed phone conversation. CSI Roper and the British CSI were in the makeshift lab they had set up in a spare meeting room at the motel, working on prints they had taken from the body.

Simms woke him from a doze. She looked sombre. 'I just had Police Scotland on the phone,' she said. 'They can't reach Josh – have you spoken to him?'

'Recently?' he said.

'I'll take that as a no.' Simms always knew when he was being evasive. 'Nick, what the hell is he up to?'

Fennimore felt he owed it to Josh to give him the benefit of the doubt, even though he really should have been in touch hours ago. But before he could frame a reply, CSI Roper straight-armed through the double doors into the main office. The CSI made for the front of the room; the look on Roper's face said this was important. Dunlap raised Sheriff Launer on his cell, and they gathered around the speakerphone to confer.

'It's McIntyre,' Roper said.

'You're sure?' Launer asked down the line. 'That body was pretty burned up.'

'The firefighters found him face down on the kitchen tiles; the ceiling collapsed on top of him, hand under his body – saved it from the fire,' the CSI said, the fingers of his free hand dancing up and down the seam of his chinos. 'We didn't get a full tenprint, but we got enough to match to Will McIntyre's work locker at Tate Trucking.'

'It's good to confirm his identity,' Fennimore said. 'But that doesn't prove a link to Sharla Jane.'

Roper locked gaze with Fennimore. 'You remember the right thumb and index we got off of the rail bracket at Sharla Jane's place?' he said, excitement crackling off him.

'You got a match to Will McIntyre?'

A quick nod from Roper. '*And* an eight-point match to the partial palm print on the receipt for propane we got from Laney Dawalt's last address.'

Fennimore experienced a surge of fierce joy.

'*And,*' Roper said, as if this wasn't enough, 'the decedent's boots are the right size. The soles are heat damaged, but we got a good class match to the footwear mark we found at Sharla Jane's trailer. Wear pattern looks similar too, but the lab will need to confirm.'

'Score one for the good guys,' Launer said. 'But I don't need to tell you all that McIntyre being dead means we got zero leads on Faith and Ava.'

'We also know that McIntyre is dead, so whoever shot Howie and Deputy Hicks, it *wasn't* McIntyre,' Ellis said. 'Obvious next question: who *are* we looking for?'

'Not our problem,' Dunlap said.

Ellis wasn't listening. 'I mean, are we just *assuming* it was the Professor's pest-control expert?'

'It's rarely safe to assume,' Fennimore said. 'But in this case, the odds do stack up.'

'For, or against?' Well rested, Ellis could be prickly. Add in lack of sleep, caffeine intake, high humidity and poor air con and he was a grizzly bear with a bad case of hives. 'I mean, how do we know he didn't just piss someone off?'

'We don't,' Dunlap said. 'But it's *not our problem*. The Professor's bug-killing Scot *is* a person of interest in the shootings, and if he really is travelling on a UK passport, that makes him a fugitive foreign national, which is FBI territory.'

'The FBI and the Marshals' Service are on it,' Dr Detmeyer said.

'They already checked flight manifests at Tulsa, Oklahoma City and Houston, Texas,' Dunlap went on. 'He didn't fly into Oklahoma. They're looking at car-rental companies in Chicago, in case he came overland. The FBI will keep us in the loop.'

Ellis gave a cynical laugh. 'Come on, Greg, the FBI's a black hole – it just sucks information in and gives back a big fat nothing.'

The atmosphere was hot with embarrassment, but FBI Special Agent Detmeyer eyed Ellis with cool composure.

'I guess we'll just have to hope the Marshals are more effective communicators than the Bureau.' He kept his calm gaze on Ellis, and finally the detective shuffled uncomfortably and glanced away. Everyone seemed to breathe easier.

'But what if McIntyre's killer knows where Faith and Ava are?' Fennimore said into the silence.

'Then we'd better move fast,' Dunlap said. He looked around the room. 'Where do we start?' Ellis opened his mouth to speak, but Dunlap raised a finger. 'Not you,' he said. 'You had your say.'

Ellis ran a hand over his buzz cut. The skin of his scalp looked pink and hot.

'McIntyre came home,' Simms said. 'He was selecting victims from within his comfort zone. Laney Dawalt, Sharla Jane Patterson, Faith Eversley – all within thirty miles of Hays.'

'So . . . we focus our search around his house over in Hays?' Valance suggested.

'Actually, he had at least *two* anchor points,' Detmeyer said. 'His family home in Hays, and wherever he stashed the

358

shipping container – now that *might* be near his home, and it certainly needs to be somewhere he knows well.'

'A shipping container is fairly conspicuous,' Simms said. 'It has to be somewhere it won't arouse interest or suspicion.'

'So . . . what?' Dunlap said. 'Derelict warehouses, empty lots . . .'

'Truck stops,' Valance said. 'He picked Faith up at a truck stop.'

Ellis spoke up: 'He could just as easy be hiding in plain sight at a shipping dock or storage depot.'

Fennimore shook his head. 'He would have to've checked the container in if it was a functioning depot, wouldn't he?'

Dunlap nodded. 'The state-wide alert would've found it by now.'

Fennimore strode to the map on the wall. 'He's working close to home, so we're looking at a stretch of Interstate 44 from, let's say . . . Claremore to Vinita. That's what – forty miles?'

Valance checked it on his computer. 'Close enough.'

'We know that he recorded the last murder inside a freight container. We have the serial number of the two missing freight containers. We know the make, model and licence-plate number of the tractor-trailer he stole. We know he didn't drive the truck home, so he must've used the Polo; we have a description and licence-plate number of his car. We also have PikePass records with times and dates going back eight months. Do we have CCTV for the hours around Faith and Ava's abduction?'

'Yessir.' Valance again.

'I think you have Automatic License Plate Readers at toll-booths?'

'We do in Missouri, but Oklahoma?' The young detective shrugged.

'We have ALPR at tolls, some intersections, too – and all Oklahoma licence tags are licence-plate-reader compatible.'

The observation had come from the back of the room. Deputy Hicks was standing by the doors; she was in a fresh uniform but her left shoulder looked bulked up, and she had hooked the thumb of her left hand into her belt.

Fennimore said, 'Abigail, are you—'

'I'm good,' she said, though she was pale and obviously in pain. 'Go ahead.'

'Okay . . .' Fennimore said, picking up the thread. 'So, we look for McIntyre as he shuttles between home and the truck, and the truck and Sharla Jane Patterson's trailer. We plot as far as we can *forward* to the truck's final stop and also *backward* as he switches vehicles and drives the car back to the trailer park. Any sightings should bring us closer to where the truck is hidden.'

Dunlap looked at Valance. 'I'm on it,' he said.

The St Louis detective turned his attention to Hicks. 'Deputy, you really need to go home and rest.'

'Respectfully, sir,' she said, 'you are not my boss.' She flushed slightly, perhaps shocked at her own rudeness, but pushed on. 'Anyways, don't you want to know why McIntyre is so obsessed with blood?'

'Was,' Fennimore said. 'He's dead.'

'Shoot,' she said. 'That poor mother and child.' Then, 'Who killed him?' Another moment of realization, then, 'Was that his kill-buddy out in the woods, shot Howie and me?'

'We don't know,' Dunlap said, and Ellis snorted.

'You implied that you'd discovered something about McIntyre's past?' Detmeyer said.

'I talked to the ER staff while they were fixing me up,' she said. 'They remembered Will Junior. The McIntyres immigrated to the US from Scotland sixteen years ago; Will was fifteen. Soon as he graduated high school, he took a job as an orderly at County General. He was always mooching around the ER, wanting to know how they did things – intubations, transfusions – said he wanted to train as a paramedic. He had a knack for showing up when they got a real gory accident.'

'A disturbed and disturbing young man,' Detmeyer said.

Hicks shrugged. 'I'd call it darn creepy. One of the ER nurses said she felt sorry for him. He told her he'd got real sick as a kid; had leukaemia, aged nine – this was when they were still in Scotland. His sister donated her bone marrow – she was sixteen, then. Then *she* got sick with . . . uh – wait a minute, I wrote it down.' She dipped into her shirt pocket. 'Haemochromatosis,' she read carefully. 'It's an iron overload in the blood. Their mother blamed the bone-marrow procedure.'

'Rubbish,' Fennimore said. 'It's an inherited condition.'

'I guess Mom wasn't a scientist,' Hicks said, giving him a dusty look. 'Anyway, they treat it by bleeding the patient once a week until the iron levels get back to normal, then every couple of months to keep it under control. Now, his sister had an awful phobia of needles. So, Mom made nine-year-old Will sit with Big Sis and talk to her while she was bled. Told him it was the least he could do, being his fault and all.'

Simms winced, 'I'm guessing this story doesn't have a happy ending.'

'Big Sis kept running off, refusing treatment,' Hicks said. 'She got complications – liver damage, diabetes, heart problems. Died before her seventeenth birthday. And get this: little brother Will was with her when she died. His momma found Will holding his sister's hand and talking to her, long after she was gone.'

64

Driving the back roads, Fergus kept his baseball cap on and his speed down. The gun he'd stolen from the deputy lay under a map on the passenger seat. The news bulletins had named the body at the house as William McIntyre Jnr, a person of interest in the murders of six women and children, so the police must have his fingerprints. Which meant that in his headlong dash for notoriety, that unspeakably moronic *dickhead* had failed to implement protocols: he had left evidence in the trailer.

So, the police knew Will's real identity, but there were still six degrees of separation between Will McIntyre and him; the trick was to keep those lines of connection separate, even as they threatened to converge.

All right. Think.

He hadn't found much in the way of technical gear at the house. Those items must be found and destroyed. There were two places where they might be: the kill room, and Sharla Jane's trailer home. The police already knew about the trailer: it was accessible to any number of people and was therefore most at risk. Decision made, Fergus set the satnav to take him to Lambert Woods trailer park.

65

Lambert Woods Mobile Home Park, Williams County, Oklahoma

The police cruiser lit out of the trailer park around midnight. Riley waits, but he hasn't had more than a few sips of creek water in two days, and finally thirst and hunger drive him out of his hiding place.

He crawls to the back of the house, feverish with thirst. He takes out his pocketknife to cut the police seal, but at first he can't get it open. Whimpering, he tries again, and at last the blade swings back and clicks in place. He cuts the seal and jiggles the door lock till it springs open.

The trailer smells stuffy and old, like it's been empty for years. The blinds are closed and, to his right, the door to his momma's room stands open. It is awful dark in there, and he can't bring himself to look inside Momma's old room. He thinks maybe it was a bad idea to come back. He will just get some provisions and clothes, head into the woods. His backpack is on the lounge chair, the other side of the kitchen counter. Police must've checked it and left it alone, it being empty. He scoots under the counter to fetch it and jams it full of sodas and cheese, a half-loaf he finds in the icebox, staying half turned to the open door of his momma's room.

The light from the fridge blinds him to the dark, and he starts to feel panicky, the skin on the back of his neck rippling. He slams the fridge door, his heart tripping, moves past the bathroom on his left, on to his own room.

One window blind has jammed and a corner of window is exposed, so he stays low, under the level of the sill. Greedily, he cracks the can and guzzles the pop, burps loudly and throws most of it back up. He takes smaller sips until his throat stops hurting. His eye is drawn to his closet door; it's shut, but a corner of cloth has caught between the door and the frame and pokes out like a tongue.

It takes a second to build enough courage, but he boosts himself off the floor and opens the closet. There's nothing in there but his clothes and a pair of sneakers. Not wanting to stick around any longer than he has to, he takes a T-shirt, pants and the sneakers and throws them in his backpack. As he swings the bag onto his shoulder, he notices a pair of shorts and a T-shirt on his bed. Momma must've laid them out, ready for their special summer recess treat. His legs give way and suddenly he's kneeling on the floor, tears pouring down his face.

He curls up, his whole body aching, his head most of all. He takes a hold of the covers and pulls them off the bed, and lies there on the floor, too weak and tired and hurting to go on.

66

I have no special talent. I am only passionately curious.

EINSTEIN

Incident Command Post, Westfield, Oklahoma
Wednesday, sunrise

There were no signs of Faith or Ava at Will McIntyre's house. The CSIs recovered a camera and a quantity of DVDs – the DVDs were unreadable due to heat damage, but some of the labels could be retrievable with enhancement; also personal and business letters – mostly the parents', and mostly destroyed. They would check them anyway; any links back to Hawick could give them McIntyre's accomplice. They also discovered a small shrine to the dead sister in the mother's bedroom. Photographs of a smiling teen, some taken with little brother Will at her side. In every picture, he had sliced out the girl's eyes with a scalpel blade.

Fennimore had still not heard from Josh and, unable to sleep, he sat gloved and Tyvek-suited, tinkering with a digital camera at a workbench in the makeshift lab in the hotel, while he waited for the CCTV footage to come in on the first flight from Chicago into Tulsa.

He positioned a desk magnifier above the camera, which he had placed, per protocol, on a large white sheet of blotting paper. The casing had melted in places and the body had folded in on itself. He held it in his gloved hands and stroked

365

the line of the battery door with a new scalpel, tracing its
outline, as though trying to draw it where it had once been.
Slowly, as carbon dust and plastic shavings accumulated on
the blotting paper, the door revealed itself. He cut down into
the hinge, scraping whisker-fine curls of plastic with each
stroke.

Roper said he was wasting his time, but Fennimore was
curious as to how much of the SD card had survived. The slow,
laborious work kept Fennimore's mind free of oppressive
thoughts, which in itself made the attempt worthwhile.

He replaced the scalpel blade twice, and finally one hinge
yielded with a faint click and he got to work on the other.
In another twenty minutes, he was able to prise the small
oblong of plastic away from the main body of the camera.
The black plastic of the SD card was partially melded with
both the door and the battery, so he had to ease them out as
one. At the business end, the contacts seemed intact.

Gently, using tiny, even strokes of the scalpel blade, he
separated the battery from the card. The copper pins were
discoloured, but intact. The SD card was still melded to the
damaged battery door. He turned it over, examining it closely
under the magnifier; it was slightly warped, but it might
just fit into a card slot. He booted up his netbook, carefully
cleaned the carbon off the contacts using a pencil eraser and
eased the card into the reader slot.

He held his breath. The autoplay dialogue box opened,
presenting him with a list of options. He exhaled slowly, as
if a sudden movement might shatter the image into a million
digital fragments, and clicked to import the files onto his
computer. As the pictures transferred to the folder on his
hard drive, the program flicked through the images like a
card sharp zipping through a pack of playing cards. Some
had been corrupted and all he saw in that short flash was a
generic picture icon and an error warning. But there were
others, too: pictures of the interior of Sharla Jane's trailer,

instantly recognizable; one of what looked like the exterior of a shipping container – *the* shipping container – standing on concrete.

Roper looked over his shoulder. 'You did it,' he said, and Fennimore grinned. But the next image, the last on the card, knocked the air out of him. It was Faith Eversley. She was strapped to a pallet; it looked a lot like the one Sharla Jane had been tied to before she was murdered.

'Fuck,' he said. 'Fuck.'

His phone rang and he checked the screen. 'Josh,' he said. 'Where the hell have you been?'

'It's been a tough couple of days,' the student said, typically evasive. 'The *Hawick News* found something. A thirteen-year-old. They crushed her with rocks, Nick.'

'They?'

'The way the body was found, she had to've been held down, and there was no head injury, so she wasn't knocked unconscious first. Police reckoned there must be at least two of them. I sent you a few press clippings.' Josh went on, 'Police interviewed her schoolfriends – she was seen with an unidentified youth a couple of hours before she was found. I just got a list of all the boys on the school roll from the headmaster – I'm sending it now.'

Fennimore opened the press clippings first; they were dated sixteen years ago. It couldn't be a random coincidence that the McIntyre family emigrated to the United States that same year. He opened the second attachment. Will McIntyre was in the year above Isla, the murdered girl.

He told Josh that they were fairly sure they had their killer, that his name was McIntyre and that they had found him in the burning ruin of his house. 'We think he was murdered by his accomplice,' Fennimore said. 'Now, normally I would say that getting a murdering scumbag off the streets is a good thing,' he went on, 'but this one snatched a mother and child about eleven hours ago. And they're still missing.'

'Shit.'

'Yeah. Look, Josh, the FBI have posted a sketch of the man we're looking for; I'll send you the link. Can you hawk it around your police contacts, the archivist at the newspaper, maybe the school? Sixteen years is going back some, but teachers have long memories – if these two paired up as schoolboys, someone will have noticed.'

'Sure – just send it to the account on the last email I sent you.'

Fennimore hadn't noticed the change of email address. 'Josh, we agreed you would use your academic email for all communications.'

'It's just a precaution. I had a bit of a security issue – no big deal.'

'You're assisting in the hunt for two serial killers, Josh – *any* breach of security is a *very* big deal. Start explaining.'

He heard Josh exhale down the phone. 'My computer's missing.'

'Stolen?' Fennimore said. 'Or lost?'

'Stolen.'

'When?'

'Last night.'

'How? Don't make me drag this out of you, Josh. Just tell me what happened.'

'I brought someone back to my flat. Uh, a man.'

Stupidly, all Fennimore could think was, *He's gay – how the hell did I miss that?*

'I poured us a glass of wine, he must've slipped something into it. I know,' he added before Fennimore could say it, 'I'm an idiot. He was cute – I wasn't exactly thinking with my head at the time.'

'What makes you think you were drugged?'

'We were talking, it was around midnight, Monday, my time. Then . . . nothing, till I woke up middle of the day on Tuesday.'

Fennimore closed his eyes and pinched the bridge of his nose. 'What do the police say?'

Josh didn't answer.

'You haven't reported it? Josh, you have to report this to the police.'

'No,' Josh said.

'If you were drugged, you could have been sexually assaulted—'

'I wasn't. I did the tox analysis, I took . . . swabs. I was drugged, but I *wasn't* raped.'

'Look, if you're embarrassed— '

'Nick,' he interrupted. 'I'm not ashamed of my sexuality, I just – I don't want my DNA on the system.'

'Why?' It was more than a year since they'd first started working together, but Fennimore still hadn't fathomed the student's pathological need for privacy. 'Why don't you want your DNA on the system?'

Josh remained stubbornly silent.

'Okay,' Fennimore said. 'But consider this: as a forensic scientist, you'll have to provide a DNA sample at every crime scene you visit. You need to come to terms with that, or find another line of work.'

It was calculated to shock, but Josh said, 'Elimination DNA samples don't go on the main database.'

Normally, Fennimore enjoyed their combative exchanges. But not today.

'Josh,' he warned.

'I know, I'm sorry. I take your point – I do. But I don't have to deal with it yet, because it wasn't *me* he was after. It wasn't money, it wasn't sex. He didn't take anything – except the computer.'

'What are you working on?' Fennimore asked.

'You know most of it: the transcripts of those recordings. A bit of word-pattern analysis; the UK murders; my thesis.'

'You back up your files?'

369

A slight hesitation. 'Sure.'

'Josh?'

'Of course I do.' He sounded insulted. 'And my computer's encrypted. But I keep trying to tell you, it wasn't *me* he was interested in.'

'Then who?'

Josh remained silent.

'Me?'

'Rachel and Suzie.'

The muscles in Fennimore's neck tightened. 'And what did you tell him, exactly?'

'Come on, Nick.'

Fennimore's mind flew to McIntyre's accomplice. But the man who murdered McIntyre couldn't be in two places at once. So why did this stranger steal Josh's computer?

'This man you picked up – what did he look like?'

'I dunno, beard, short hair. Cute.'

'Jeez—' Fennimore ran a hand over his chin, and took a moment to calm himself, then grabbed the mouse to send the FBI link through to Josh. 'Look at the FBI sketch,' he said. 'Got it?'

A few seconds delay, then: 'Yeah.'

'*Well* – is that him?'

'I don't know, Nick. He looks familiar, but . . .'

'Look, Josh,' Fennimore said, trying to keep a grip on his temper, 'a few days ago, I had an anonymous email. Someone sent me a photograph of a girl – she'd be about Suzie's age.' Josh didn't need to know that he was certain the girl in the picture was Suzie. 'Now *you* tell me you were targeted by a man who's so interested in Rachel and Suzie that he's willing to get in your pants to find out what *you* know.'

Josh began to object, but Fennimore cut him off. 'You should have told me as *soon* as you knew your computer was stolen. Instead of which, I have to prise the information out of you. You've kept material facts from me, Josh.'

'Professor—'

'I don't want to hear it,' Fennimore said. 'Do what I asked you to do, report to me as soon as you know anything. And if you have some kind of flashback and decide you *do* recognize the man in the sketch, I want to know straight away, not two hours down the line when you've had time to concoct a story.'

'Nick, come on. I've been straight with you.'

'Seriously, Josh, I don't think you know how. When this investigation's done, we're finished – I'll assign you another supervisor.'

He cut the connection and glared at the image of Faith Eversley.

'Professor?' Roper said.

Fennimore groaned inwardly. 'I'm sorry you had to hear that.'

'It's okay.' He sounded wary, as if he thought Fennimore might bawl him out. 'But Professor, staring at that photograph isn't doing anyone any good.'

'It's the most recent image we have,' Fennimore said, knowing he sounded fevered, idiotic. 'It's the interior of the container where she probably is *right now*.'

'That's right – it's *inside* – what about the picture of the container? We could maybe get geographic markers off that.' Roper's tone was coaxing, like he was talking a jumper down from a skyscraper ledge.

Maybe I am a bit close to the edge just now, Fennimore thought, clicking through to the penultimate photograph in the file. The container was parked on concrete; a patch of blue sky was visible in the top left corner, and that was it – no locational clues at all. He opened the image of Faith inside the container again, and Roper shook his head and turned away.

Exhaustion and hopelessness and rage were making him crazy, but he couldn't help himself. The Task Force had narrowed their focus using a timeline from McIntyre's movements through tolls and passing through intersections, but it wasn't tight enough. They had times for the truck entering and leaving Interstate 44. They had dates and times for the sightings of the car, but so far they had no intersection between the two. It was all a question of timing; they just needed one more temporal reference—

Suddenly, he had it, and the realization hit him so hard his head rang.

'Roper, could you call Greg Dunlap?'

Roper was by his side in a second, already hitting the speed-dial button as he asked what Fennimore had found.

'Digital photographs are time- and date-stamped. And this,' he said, right-clicking the image of Faith Eversley in the container, 'is the most recent image we have.'

A right-click on the mouse opened a dialogue box. He scrolled to 'Properties' and clicked on the 'Details' tab. Under the heading 'Date taken', was today's date, and a time.

'This picture was taken at eleven minutes past three this morning. That's what – forty minutes before we got to McIntyre's house?'

'About that,' Roper said. 'And the ME's preliminary report says he had extensive injuries – broken bones, fractured skull – the killer worked on him a while.'

'So McIntyre must've parked the container close by – I mean ten, twenty minutes' drive from his house.'

Roper relayed the information to Dunlap and Fennimore scrolled on, wondering at the amount of information that was stored with every digital image: the dimensions and resolution; the f-stop and exposure time; the camera model and make; everything an enthusiastic amateur might want to know. He glanced over the file details and his eye jumped back a line. Below the heading 'Advanced photo' was an extra category – one his own camera did not possess. For a second he froze. Roper saw it the same instant he did.

'Holy *shit*,' Roper said. 'Stand by, Greg, we got an exact location for you.'

The new category, the one that rendered Fennimore mute, read, 'GPS'. They had exact longitude and latitude coordinates for the container.

67

The GPS coordinates of the image took them to a disused gas station fifteen miles out of Hays. The fuel pumps had been removed, but the building was still standing. Seven police vehicles, the local radio station's outside-broadcast unit, Launer's pet newspaper editors and a paramedic ambulance converged on the premises in a matter of minutes. Simms was in no doubt that the state TV networks would follow on.

The front lot was empty, but when they went around the back, there it was, parked on its landing gear: a forty-foot, rust-red shipping container, shimmering in the heat haze. There was no sign of the truck, or the tractor-trailer. It was 85 °F, and the temperature inside the container would be at least ten degrees higher, so with paramedics on standby, twenty officers moved in fast, checking the perimeter before splitting into two teams. Ten stormed the derelict building while the rest tackled the container. Its locking bar was secured with a padlock, quickly dispatched by bolt cutters. Two men swung the doors wide and hot air, sharp with throat-catching ammonia, roiled from the interior. A deputy and a St Louis detective climbed in, weapons drawn, but the deputy returned moments later, his pistol holstered, one hand covering his mouth and nose. He shouted for a medic. Climbing down, he caught Launer's eye and gave a small shake of his head.

'The girl?' Launer said.

'No, sir.'

Seconds later, a paramedic came flying out of the container and landed on the concrete running.

'She's alive,' he yelled over his shoulder. 'We need water – plenty of it – she's burning up.' Police and sheriff's deputies scattered to fetch water bottles from vehicles; two even brought hand-held fans to help with the cooling. The paramedic returned with two bags of saline and for ten minutes they worked on Faith Eversley, dousing her with water, pushing fluids into her, while the search went on for her missing child.

Twenty minutes on, Faith was wheeled on a gurney towards the emergency vehicle, barely conscious. By now several TV outside-broadcast units had arrived; Simms counted two Fox News trucks in amongst them. Launer walked purposefully towards them, but Dunlap intercepted him.

'I think we should wait on the wider search results before making a statement, Sheriff.'

'Well, you're entitled to your opinion, Detective,' he said, smiling and patting him on the shoulder. It would look to the cameras like he was congratulating his co-investigator. Dunlap did not smile.

Fennimore met Simms's eye. 'An eight-year-old girl is still missing and he's electioneering.' He looked ready to do some damage.

'Not our fight, Nick,' she said.

Hicks came from the direction of the derelict service station and they turned to her in anticipation.

She shook her head. 'We turned it inside out – there's nothing but dust and cobwebs back there.'

Simms glanced quickly at Fennimore; he looked grey and strained. 'We have to find the truck,' he said.

'The Sheriff is going to leave a deputy to guard the scene while the CSIs collect evidence,' Hicks said. 'Everyone else is back on the search. He wants me to go with Faith to the hospital, in case she comes round.'

'Where do we start?' Fennimore said.

Hicks looked uncertainly at Simms. 'You should stay close to the St Louis detectives, Professor.'

'To hell with that.' He headed towards his rental SUV.

'I'll go with him,' Simms said. 'Any suggestions?'

'We already know he's close by,' Hicks said. 'But he would have to walk from the truck to the container, and anyone walking on these roads would attract attention, so I'd be looking *real* close.'

Simms waved Fennimore down as he swung towards the exit. Sliding into the passenger seat, she took his netbook from the dashboard. 'Take it slowly,' she said. 'He could be nearby.'

According to the GPS map, there was a cluster of farm buildings about a mile south-west and another two miles north-east of their location. They chose the closest. It was a working farm, and the family was happy to show them their barns, if it meant they would find little Ava a minute sooner – apparently the local cable network was running half-hourly updates.

The barns were stacked with new hay and farm machinery, but there was no truck.

Fennimore opened his netbook and showed the landowner the satellite image of the second farm. 'Do you know who owns this farm?'

The farmer frowned at the cluster of grey-roofed buildings on the satellite image. 'Oh, that isn't a farm,' he told them. 'That was Dawson's Animal Feed warehouse, long time ago. They had a drive-in movie theatre over at Dawson's in the summertime, when I was a kid. But your picture's out of date; storm blew down from the Great Lakes, took the roof right off last month – we been finding sections of it on our land ever since.'

'A feed warehouse might be just the place to hide a truck,' Fennimore said.

'Let's find out,' Simms said.

The main building was down a potholed gravel track, five minutes off the state highway. The roof was gone, just as the farmer said it would be. The aluminium walls, peeled back from the framework, flapped and groaned with the slightest stirring of air. The framework of the film screen survived: a sixty-foot wooden structure with its back to the dirt track. Closely tacked laths, running the length of it, gave it the appearance of a giant open-weave fence. As they drove nearer, Simms could make out a dark hulking shape beyond the screen.

'There,' she said.

Fennimore jammed his foot on the accelerator and seconds later they skidded to a halt ten feet short of a Peterbilt 387. Fennimore reached for the door handle, but she stopped him. 'Stay here. Call Dunlap and give him the coordinates.' She was out and running to the truck before he could argue.

The radiator grille was as tall as she was, and Simms could feel reflected heat coming off it. She swung lightly up to the door. It was locked. Fennimore joined her seconds later. He tried the escape door of the sleeper cab, but it was shut tight. He tried the passenger side. That was locked, too.

Simms shielded her eyes and peered down through the cab window. 'I can't see a thing. Oh, bugger this.' She drew a short, black cylinder from her pocket and flicked it. It extended like a car aerial to about a foot in length.

'How did you get that through airport security?' he said.

She flashed him a small smile. 'I didn't.' She had bought

the baton over the Internet after the field trip out to East St Louis.

She turned her face away from the side window and covered her eyes with one arm, then whacked the window hard with the rounded tip of the weapon. Two, three times more and the window shattered, beads of glass cascading around her.

'But I won't tell if you don't,' she added, reaching in to open the door.

McIntyre had fitted a vinyl-laminated panel with a sliding door between the cab and the sleeper cabin. It was padlocked.

'Ava,' Simms called through the panelling. 'Ava Eversley?' She listened, thought she heard a slight shuffle in the cabin beyond. 'Ava, my name is Kate. I'm with the police – the Sheriff is on his way.'

No sound.

'We've come to bring you home to your mommy,' Simms said.

A tiny choking sound, and a snuffle.

She nodded to Fennimore and relief flooded his face. 'Help is on the way,' he said softly.

'It's stifling in there,' Simms murmured. 'I'm going to try to break the lock into the cabin.' She raised her voice: 'Ava, we're going to get you out of there.' She jammed the steel baton inside the hasp of the lock and levered it. It gave, but only a little. Sweating, she tried again. The screws of the hasp squealed, pulling out of the vinyl by a quarter-inch. Panting, she stopped to get her breath.

'Let me have a go,' Fennimore said.

She handed him the baton and swung out of the cab to give him room. He broke the baton on his first attempt, wiped his face with the sleeve of his shirt and went to work again with the remaining third. The hasp gave at the same instant as the door slider. He fell backwards into the cab, bashing his head against the windscreen.

'Nick!' Simms called.

'I'm okay,' he said, righting himself. 'But I don't see her.' He manoeuvred the panel out from behind the seats and Simms slid it out of the cab door. 'There's a cupboard in here; I'm going to open it.'

Simms climbed back inside as the tiny closet door swung open. Ava was squatting on her haunches, bound and gagged with duct tape. Tears streamed down her face.

Fennimore made soothing noises, but she shied away from him. 'I just want to lift you out, Ava,' he said. 'So you can go and see your momma. This is Kate, and the Sheriff will be here any minute.'

The little girl cowered, squeezing back into the tiny space, trying to talk through the gag.

'All right,' he said. 'Okay, let me just take this away from your mouth so you can tell me what you want. All right?'

She gave a small nod.

'It'll sting, but only for a second.'

She nodded again, her blue eyes wide, and allowed him to ease a corner of the tape away from her mouth.

'I can't come out, the monster'll get me,' she hiccuped and sobbed.

'There is no monster,' he said.

'There *is*,' she wailed. 'I heard it. The man said I should stay real quiet or it would come get me.'

The aluminium siding of the old building moved in a current of air, setting up a moan like all the tormented in hell, and the little girl screamed.

'Aw, that's just the wind,' Fennimore said, approximating a soft Oklahoman drawl. 'Just the wind, flapping the aluminum on that old barn outside.' He pronounced it 'aluminum', the American way. 'Anyway, Chief Simms's got a pistol – right, Chief?' he said.

'First sign of trouble, I'm ready,' Simms said. 'And I'm quick on the draw.'

The little girl thought for a moment, then shuffled forward on her bottom.

Fennimore lifted her out of the closet and held her to him. 'You're all right,' he murmured softly. 'You're safe, now.' She tucked her head under his chin and sobbed as only a child can. Simms heard in it relief that her ordeal was over, sadness that she had been so very afraid, and loneliness and longing for her momma. She held her hands out to take the girl, and for a moment, Fennimore seemed reluctant to give her up, but then he passed her over the top of the driver's seat and Simms carried the little girl, blinking, into the sunlight.

68

Lambert Woods Mobile Home Park,
Williams County, Oklahoma
Wednesday, 8 a.m.

When Riley wakes up, it's daylight. The sick feeling of
loneliness is still there, coiled like a snake in his gut, but he
feels a little bit stronger. He kicks off the quilt, picks up his
jacket, sets his cap on his head and shoulders his backpack.
As he turns, he sees a flash of grey. There's a car parked
under his window.

He squats fast, rising slowly to take a careful peek. It
doesn't look like police, nor one of the Tulks' cars, either.
He holds his breath, listening, but all he hears is his heart
pumping. The front door is no more than five feet from him,
in the lounge; the back door is much further. He edges out
of his room. On his right, the bathroom door is open a crack.
Was it open when he came in? He can't recall.

His legs wobbling, he takes another step. The bathroom
door opens. A man stands looking at him – not Will, somebody
else. The man looks shocked, but only for a second, then he
turns mad – *mean* mad – and he steps forward. The room
feels suddenly small and the man seems to get bigger, like
he is taking up every inch of space and Riley can't see a way

past him. He can't move. The man takes a swipe at him and instinct takes over. He ducks. Off balance, the man stumbles against the kitchen counter and Riley drops, scrambling between his legs, knocking over a kitchen stool. He grabs the front door handle and turns it, leaning on the door with his shoulder. It holds. *The crime-scene tape!*

The man kicks the stool out of his way and lunges forward.

The boy yells, pushing the door again. He hears the tape tear and he's falling. Something stops him before he hits the dirt – the man has a hold of his backpack. He wriggles, trying to get out of the strap, but it is jerked backwards. He kicks out, but the man has him, six inches off the floor, held by the straps of his pack. Riley opens his mouth to scream, but the man pulls him inside the house, slams his head against the door frame. Lights flash behind Riley's eyes, pain shoots through his skull—

69

The basis of optimism is sheer terror.

OSCAR WILDE

Incident Command Post, Westfield,
Williams County, Oklahoma
Wednesday, mid-morning

The Task Force celebrated over a late breakfast at the hotel.
The owners switched the TV to Fox News: Detective Dunlap
and Sheriff Launer were giving a brief statement to the
assembled press and media, Launer solemn and respectful
on the podium, grinning like a shark off it: apparently Faith
and Ava's rescue had taken his ratings ten points clear of
the opposition. Hicks excused herself from the party early;
the doctor who treated her at the hospital had given her
painkillers and she intended to use them.

Fennimore drove her, and she was quiet all the way home.
At her front door, he looked into her face. 'It can be a bit of
an anticlimax, finishing a case like this,' he said.

'That's just it,' she said. 'It isn't – finished, I mean. I know,
we have to prioritize. Faith and Ava had just gone missing
– they were still in the First 48 – our best chance of a good
outcome. But what about Riley Patterson? Nobody even
mentioned him.'

'We'll pick up the search just as soon as people have
rested,' Fennimore said. 'You'll see.'

But driving back to the inn, he admitted to himself that like the rest, he had all but written off their chances of finding Riley Patterson alive. Could he have done more to find the boy? Could there be a clue they'd missed at Sharla Jane's place? He remembered that last cluster of images on the camera they had salvaged from McIntyre's house. Why had McIntyre taken photographs of the trailer's interior? A clock, ornaments, a DVR, a smoke alarm; these weren't family snaps. And following on from these prosaic items, the next two images on the SD card were the shipping container – his kill room – and Faith Eversley.

The party was still going on when he got back, and Fennimore joined a group, chatting over coffee and pancakes. He mentioned the images. Simms was there, CSI Roper and Valance, the young St Louis detective.

'We decided that Sharla Jane's trailer *wasn't* the murder scene,' he said. 'So why would he take pictures of it?'

'Credit-card statements say he only bought the camera six weeks ago,' Valance said. 'Maybe he was familiarizing himself with it before he found his next victim?'

'Possibly,' Fennimore said. 'But if he bought it to take pictures of his victims, wouldn't he practise *inside* the kill room? And why were there no pictures of Sharla Jane on there?'

'We don't know that there weren't,' Simms said. 'A lot of the images were unreadable.'

'But odd, don't you think, that he would choose such banal photographic subjects?'

'Serial killers often *are* banal,' Simms said. 'It's what they *do* that sets them apart.' She stood, and pushed her chair under the table.

'Where are you going?' Fennimore asked.

'To get some sleep. And so should you – you're obsessing, Fennimore. You've got that manic look in your eye.' They both knew what she meant: when Fennimore was like this, he got reckless. He knew, too, that she had seen his desperation as he held eight-year-old Ava. He could still smell the child's cinnamon scent – a scent that reminded him of his own daughter. Which was why he'd found it so hard to give the child up into Simms's capable hands; letting go of that little girl was like letting go of Suzie.

Simms held his gaze, inviting him to leave, but he frowned and looked away, and, after a second or two, she shook her head and walked off.

The others at the table followed a few minutes after, to sleep or rest, but Fennimore couldn't get those images of Sharla Jane's tidy trailer home out of his head.

He went back to his room and lay on his bed, but couldn't sleep. He turned on his netbook and stared at those few images that had survived the fire: a clock, ornaments, a digital video recorder, a smoke alarm. There was nothing special about them. Could they be trophies from other victims? The clock, maybe, he thought, and the ornaments, but the smoke alarm? No. There had to be some other significance to them. Hard to see significance in these bland, utilitarian items: things you might see in any home – things you don't even notice.

Suddenly he thought he knew.

He called Roper's mobile.

'Did you collect the DVR?' he asked.

'What?' The CSI sounded full of sleep.

'The video recorder from Sharla Jane's place – did you bring it in?'

'Well, of course.'

'And there was nothing out of the ordinary about it?'

'Professor, I had two hours' sleep in the last thirty. I'm *real* tired.'

'I understand that,' Fennimore said. 'But those photographs—'

Roper groaned. 'I'm hanging up.'

385

The line went dead.

The room they were using as a laboratory was locked. Hoping to find someone in the restaurant, he went back inside, but the only people there were a waitress and one of the hotel owners, clearing up after the team's late breakfast. He tried to raise Hicks, but it seemed she had followed doctor's orders and taken those painkillers: three times he rang her mobile, and three times it switched to voicemail.

The deputy on duty at the sheriff's office told him to get some sleep; the Sheriff said the Task Force was due to meet again at 4 p.m.

It was the very blandness of the items, so carefully photographed by the killer-that provided the clue. McIntyre quickly grew disgusted with the women and their 'demands' as he saw them, yet he held off killing them. Why? Because his mentor exerted such a powerful influence that even thousands of miles away, he could control McIntyre's impulsive nature. He had persuaded or bullied or cajoled McIntyre into postponing the murders for many months. Again, why?

There was only one plausible answer Fennimore could think of: the other man liked to watch.

Fennimore suspected that these ordinary, unmemorable household items were covert surveillance devices – spy equipment. He knew that such devices could be set up for Wi-Fi access or to record on an SD memory card. The trailer park was way out in the sticks, so Wi-Fi was unlikely. He guessed that McIntyre would send his accomplice recorded footage of his victims living their normal domestic lives.

For McIntyre's partner, it was all about control. And if the two men spoke to each other at Sharla Jane's house – by phone, or Skype – the spy gadgets would have captured it.

Fennimore picked up his keys from the dresser in his room and crossed the car park, just as the first cicadas began to stir. He had his own transport, and he knew the way to Lambert Woods Park.

70

Lambert Woods Mobile Home Park,
Williams County, Oklahoma
Wednesday, 11.30 a.m.

Fergus moved his rental car to the front of the house. It might
be a quiet spot, but there was no sense taking chances. He
opened the boot of the car and returned a few seconds later
with the boy; he was wrapped in a quilt and fitted easily
next to the salvaged electronics. He knew where to look,
because he had told Will exactly where to place them, and
he'd insisted on a full photographic inventory. He got all but
one piece: an edge of dust marked where the digital video
recorder should be. He always said that Will's impulsivity
would get him killed, and it was no consolation to have been
proved right – by association, it put him in jeopardy, too.
He'd Skyped Will to instruct him on where he wanted Sharla
Jane's body dumped. They hadn't used video, but he hadn't
used the voice changer, either, so his true voice would be
recorded on the SD card in the video recorder's embedded
surveillance equipment. He consoled himself that since the
police had Will, and the woman and child were safe, they
might never examine the equipment more closely.

He flipped a corner of the quilt over the child and took

out a makeshift scene kit – gloves and booties, bleach and cloths. He needed to ensure there was no trace of him in the trailer; the struggle with the boy had complicated the clean-up, but Fergus knew how to be thorough. He slammed the boot lid and headed back inside.

Fennimore rolled to a stop on the track to Sharla Jane's trailer. A car was parked outside, the crime-scene seal was broken and the tape had been ripped from around the door frame. The front door stood open. Fennimore listened. The whistling call of a bird came from deep in the woods, and the first of the cicadas had just started their steam-kettle shriek, but there was no sound from inside the trailer. He eased the door open with his fingertips and took a swift peek around the door jamb. There was blood on the frame. He took out his phone and speed-dialled Simms's number. It rang a few times before her voicemail clicked in.

'Kate,' he said softly. 'I'm at Sharla Jane's trailer. There's a grey Toyota Matrix parked outside.' He gave the licence-plate number. 'The seals are broken and there's blood on the door frame. I'm going to take a look.'

He took a breath, swung the door wide and glanced right and left. He had seen the floor plan: master bedroom to the left, bathroom and smaller bedroom – Riley's room – to the right, on the other side of the kitchen counter. All three doors stood open. He could smell bleach, and saw latex gloves and a cleaning cloth on the counter. He was about to back out and wait for police reinforcements when he heard a whimper. The hairs on his neck stood up. At the same instant, he saw a boy's baseball cap under one of the stools at the kitchen counter; it was bloodstained.

His heart stopped. Riley? A low, keening sound from the boy's bedroom made up his mind. Heart pumping hard, he tiptoed across the living room and took a knife from the block on the kitchen counter. He checked the bathroom as he went past: empty. Into the bedroom. He slammed the door open so hard it bounced back off the wall.

A movement to his right. As he turned, a man powered into him, taking him down, knocking the wind out of him, and the knife thudded to the floor and skittered under the bed. Fighting for breath, Fennimore struggled, but the man had him in a bear hug. He snapped his head backwards, catching his attacker full in the mouth. The man grunted in pain and Fennimore twisted free. On his feet in a second, he saw that it was the man who had come to his Chicago reading, the Scot with an interest in midge killing. Fennimore reached down to take hold of the man, but his attacker flicked out with his foot, caught Fennimore on the shin. In a flash of hot pain, Fennimore crashed to his knees. The man lashed out again, connecting with Fennimore's right temple. Fennimore tumbled backwards, cracking his head against the wall. His head boomed with the impact and he felt sick. He tried to get up, but his legs gave under him. Darkness crept in from the edges of his vision . . .

71

Greg Dunlap tore through the gates of the trailer park, dashboard lights flashing and siren blaring. A sheriff's office SUV followed close behind.

'The plate number the Professor gave you is registered to a car-rental company at St Louis airport,' Dunlap said. 'We should have a name momentarily.'

Simms had got to her phone just as it switched to voicemail; if she'd seen it was Fennimore's number, she would have bounced the call, but cop's curiosity had made her check the message. When she heard Fennimore say that the trailer had been broken into and he was about to go in, she didn't hesitate. She woke Dunlap, Launer and Valance – even Ellis got the call to action.

Dunlap swung sharp left at the top of the hill and Simms reached for the overhead grip.

They slewed to a halt twenty yards down the track to avoid Fennimore's SUV, parked behind a grey Toyota Matrix.

Dunlap checked the straps of his body armour. 'Stay well back,' he said. 'If this is our Scottish friend, we know he's armed and will not hesitate to shoot. If you see him, your job is to get out of the way, and stay out of our line of fire.'

'I'm an Authorized Firearms Officer,' Simms said. 'I've enough common sense to know when to keep my head down.'

He seemed surprised at the sharpness of her reply.

'Sorry,' she said. 'I'll keep my head down, I promise. Just get Fennimore out of there safe, okay?'

A third SUV drew up and nine cops – detectives and deputies – including Deputy Hicks, spilled out. All wore body armour; they kept low, using their own vehicles for cover. Dunlap signalled for two to go inside the house and sent another two around the back. The rest split between the grey Matrix and Fennimore's SUV.

The rental-car windscreen and driver's windows were obscured. In the shade under the trees, it looked like the vehicle was fitted with tinted glass. But as they drew closer, they saw that it was misted with blood. Flies had already begun to gather inside.

On Dunlap's nod, Valance went around to the passenger side, weapon in hand. 'Passenger window's open.' He ducked to take a look inside and recoiled immediately. 'Got a body in here.' He cleared his throat. 'Shot to the head.'

Simms's mouth filled with saliva. *Fennimore?*

'It's not Fennimore.'

Not Fennimore. Thank God.

Valance looked over the roof of the car. 'There's a pistol in the passenger well.'

'Leave it there,' Dunlap said. 'The CSIs will take care of it.'

The officers checking the SUV declared it clear.

A shout went up from inside the trailer. 'Got a body in here.'

Simms's heart stopped.

Ellis ducked his head out the door for a second. 'What this asshole *means* is we got walking wounded. We need medical assistance.'

'Jesus, Ellis.' Simms was already running for the trailer. 'You're just as bad. *Who* needs medical assistance – what's their medical need?' Stupidly, superstitiously, it felt as if saying Fennimore's name would make the worst happen. A second later, a figure appeared in the shadows behind Ellis and Fennimore came through the door of the trailer, leaning on the deputy. He was bleeding from a cut to his head.

He took one step down and his legs gave way; he sagged and began to slip through the deputy's hands, but Simms was there in a second, easing Fennimore gently onto the steps.

'Riley?' he said.

'We've just arrived,' Simms said. 'We're still looking.'

'There was a man in the trailer,' he said. 'Did he get away?'

'We've got a body,' she said.

'I want to see it.' He tried to stand, but she held him.

'Just sit a minute and catch your breath.'

Sirens coming on the highway announced the arrival of backup. It would take a while longer to send an ambulance from County Hospital.

'Does anyone have a first-aid kit in their car?' Simms asked, and Valance hurried off to fetch one from his vehicle. She crouched, peering up into Fennimore's face.

'I'm sorry, Kate,' he said.

'I'd slap you round the head if he hadn't got there first,' she said.

He groaned. 'I know,' he said. 'If I admit I'm an arse, will you let me see him?'

'In a minute.'

Valance handed him a sterile pad to hold against the cut, and Simms made him take a sip of water.

CSI Roper was amongst the new arrivals. He got booted and suited and made his way to the grey rental car. A minute later, he straightened up from the vehicle. 'Got an ID.' He held a bundle of documents in his gloved hand, on top of them, a booklet. The maroon cover was instantly recognizable to Simms.

'UK passport,' Roper said. 'Fergus Elliott. Scottish national.'

'I want to see him,' Fennimore insisted.

Simms looked at Dunlap. He nodded and they helped him to the Matrix.

There was a lot of blood and brain matter in the car, and Fennimore had to walk downwind and take a few breaths and another sip of water before he could take a good look.

'That's him,' he said. 'That's the Bug Man. He was hiding in the boy's bedroom. I thought it was Riley.' He straightened up from the car and snuffed air out through his nose. The body was already beginning to ripen. 'Spatter pattern would suggest the bullet entered his skull from the right side, through the open passenger window, most likely.'

Simms glanced at Dunlap. 'I think he's going to be okay.'

The corners of Dunlap's eyes crinkled.

A crowd had begun to gather behind the police cordon. The Sheriff sent Deputy Hicks to control them. She did, and managed not to shrug at the injustice of this petty exile. She recognized a couple of faces – Mr Goodman, Sharla Jane's nearest neighbour, was amongst them. Hicks had checked him out since she and Chief Simms had interviewed him. Goodman had no adult convictions, but did have a juvenile record; that was sealed, so she had not been able to confirm her suspicions. He waved her over.

'Did you find the boy?' The way he said it made her think they should have.

'Not yet. What can you tell me?' she said, falling back on an open question to encourage him to fill the holes in what she knew.

'Saw him up on the fence line early this morning.'

This caused a stir amongst the onlookers.

'When?'

'Around dawn.' Goodman tugged at his little goatee,

enjoying the attention. 'He didn't see me, but I saw him all right, sneaking around back of the house.'

'Well, why in hell didn't you call the helpline? You know that boy's been missing five days.'

He folded his arms, tried on a hard-man look that didn't fit his face. 'What – you think I'm a snitch?'

'No, sir, Mr Goodman. I think you're a nasty little paedophile, bears a grudge against a child won't play your sick games.' She shouldn't have said it, but she was pissed at being put on crowd control on her own case, her shoulder was giving her hell and she couldn't believe she had slept through the chance of bringing Riley in safe.

Goodman stared at her, shocked.

'I don't know what you're talking about,' he said, but from the shuffling of feet and muttering that went on around him, his neighbours were beginning to make connections and understand what had previously only puzzled them about him.

Goodman licked his lips. 'That boy's dangerous,' he yelled, his eyes wild. 'He tells lies, and he steals, and, and he cut me. Look—'

She turned her back on him and walked back to the bunch of officers and deputies over at the house.

'Riley was here?' Dunlap said, when she had finished.

She nodded, the muscles of her neck tight.

'Then he's got to be close by.'

All eyes turned to the Toyota.

Dunlap spoke to CSI Roper. 'Could you please pop the trunk?'

They gathered around the rear of the car with their hands on their holsters. A quilt covered most of what lay inside. Dunlap nodded to Valance and he edged forward, took a corner of the quilt between finger and thumb and gently tugged it clear.

A suitcase was rammed to one side with a laptop computer

case and a collection of electrical goods piled on top of it; Hicks recognized them from the digital images Fennimore had recovered from McIntyre's camera. A small backpack lay next to them, a child's T-shirt spilling out of the top.

'Uh, guys?' Valance said. 'There's blood on the comforter.'

72

They searched the crawl space under Sharla Jane's house and the woods beyond the fence. There was no sign of the boy. The CSIs forensically examined Goodman's trailer and car, but there was no trace of Riley Patterson. Since Deputy Hicks's confrontation with Goodman, several complaints had been made against him by children on the park. A warrant was served to seize his computer and digital camera; the techs found 200 indecent images of children on his computer – enough to charge him with aggravated possession twice over.

News came through from Police Scotland that Fergus Elliott, the dead man in the rental car, had met McIntyre while studying for his Scottish Highers in Hawick. They were two years apart in age, and oceans apart in ability. One of the staff remembered McIntyre as a sad, lost, rather immature child, still struggling to come to terms with the death of his sister years after she passed away. Elliott was his pupil-mentor; they seemed to click, and staff noticed that McIntyre cheered up, became more social, developed a circle of friends under Elliott's guidance. He was particularly popular with the girls.

The bullet that killed Elliott came from Deputy Howard's gun – the one found at the scene. Howie's prints were on it, and so were Elliott's. For Sheriff Launer it was a triumph, although the disappearance of Riley's body remained a mystery and – so he said – a source of great sorrow to him. Launer told the press that he believed Elliott drove Riley's body somewhere, dumped it, then came back to finish the clean-up. He was disturbed when Fennimore went back to the trailer and attacked the Professor. Hearing the sirens as Williams County deputies raced to the scene, he shot himself rather than surrender. The St Louis detectives did not feature in his version of events.

Two days later, Nick Fennimore stopped by Abigail Hicks's place before he left for Tulsa airport. His head was mending, but he was still limping from the knee injury. He was due to lecture at the International Homicide Investigators Association symposium in St Louis on the weekend, and said he thought his work in Williams County was done, anyway. Hicks was still on sick leave, but she planned to attend the first lecture on Saturday. He said they could drive to the airport together, and even offered to pay her air fare, but she declined.

'Something I said?' he asked.

'No, nothing like that.' But she had seen how Chief Simms looked at him when he came out of that trailer with blood on him. Hicks liked to be candid on such matters, so she told him what she had seen, and what she thought it meant. He seemed surprised that Simms had feelings for him, but didn't deny that those feelings went both ways. It was enough.

Hicks thanked him for his offer, but there was something she needed to do before she could attend the symposium with a clear conscience.

Since Goodman said he had seen Riley Patterson on

the fence line the day they found Elliott, she had not been able to sit still for thinking about the boy. But there was that other face she recognized at the edge of the crowd that day. That face kept coming back to her whenever she thought about Riley Patterson. It was Waylon, Marsha Tulk's youngest.

Mrs Tulk came out on the porch as Hicks struggled to open the door of her SUV

'Deputy Sheriff Hicks,' she said, smiling. 'I hope you're healing well.'

'Tolerably, thank you, ma'am.'

'Not in uniform?' she said, taking in the sorry harlequin colours of her Suzuki SUV.

'I'm off duty.' Hicks smiled. 'This is a friendly call.'

'I'll be the judge of that.' After a moment, Mrs Tulk chuckled, taking the harsh edge off of her words. 'Well, come on inside out of the heat.'

She served Hicks iced water and invited her to sit at her kitchen table. The room was clean and homey, the table big enough to seat eight. Mrs Tulk set a plate of cookies between them and sat down opposite, leaning her ham-hock forearms on the scrubbed wood.

'Now. Why are you here, Deputy?'

'I wondered if I might speak to your youngest – Waylon, is it?'

'He's not here right now,' Mrs Tulk said. 'Might I enquire why you want to speak to my son?'

'He was at the Patterson residence when we found the man shot in the car. I wondered why.'

'Lambert Hill is Tulk land,' she said with an incredulous smile. 'He don't need a reason to be walking on family property.'

'I thought maybe he had seen something.'

'Police interviewed him on the day – he would've said.'

'Sometimes it can take a few days for events to make sense – 'specially when it involves a violent death.'

Mrs Tulk's eyes turned stone cold. 'What are you implying?'

'Nothing, ma'am,' Hicks said, but she remembered the burning, half-scared, half-fierce look in Waylon's eyes. 'I'm just saying he looked troubled.'

'It was a troubling incident.' They watched each other and, after a time, Mrs Tulk said, 'A man taking his own life.'

'I should say it was – if that's what happened,' Hicks said. 'But he would have to've brained Professor Fennimore, dragged him inside the house, gathered every item of incriminating evidence, put it in the trunk of his car, then got behind the wheel and shot himself.' She paused. 'Now, that doesn't make sense.'

Mrs Tulk grunted. 'Well, do you believe justice was served that day?'

Hicks sucked her teeth, reluctant to admit it, but eventually she said, 'I do.'

The older woman nodded, approving.

'But I can't sleep worrying about what happened to Riley Patterson.'

'Sheriff thinks Elliott dumped his body—'

'The Sheriff can think what he likes.'

Mrs Tulk watched her like a fox watches a chicken. 'I heard you arrested that pervert, Goodman.'

'He's looking at twenty years in Federal prison.'

'Well, that's got to be a consolation.'

She nodded. 'For the kids he molested.'

Mrs Tulk looked into Hicks's eyes, reading her in a way not many people could. 'But . . . you don't believe Riley was one of them.'

'No, ma'am. And while locking Goodman up will give me a deal of satisfaction, it doesn't bring Riley home, now, does it?'

'What *do* you believe, Deputy?' Mrs Tulk said.

'That someone took Riley out of the trunk of that car.'

'*Riley*, you say, not *the body*. So, this "someone" rescued him?'

'I believe that was their intention.'

'Well, then, they did a Christian kindness to an orphan child.'

'But it would be wrong to keep that child, when he should be under the protection of the State.'

Mrs Tulk smiled. 'You think the State protected that child when he needed it?'

'No, ma'am, I don't, but we already had that conversation. There's people out there need to know he's okay.'

'Who?' Mrs Tulk said. 'Sheriff Launer, so he can muss up that boy's hair in front of the cameras, maybe win a few more votes? Or the Interstate Task Force they been talking about so much on the TV news – that would be a feather in their cap, now, wouldn't it? Or Child Protection Services, 'cos they did *such a good job* when his momma was alive? Hm? You need to understand something, Deputy: all those people watching the news, clucking over their morning coffee and praying for that boy in church – in just a few weeks, they won't even remember his name.'

'You're wrong, ma'am—'

But Mrs Tulk spoke over her: 'Anyway, that kid wouldn'ta had a home to come back to; he would be cooling his heels in foster care right now.' She cocked her head. 'Do you have any notion what foster care is like, Deputy?'

'I was in State foster care five years before I was adopted, ma'am,' Hicks answered sharply. 'I've got a pretty fair idea.'

Mrs Tulk's hard, small eyes reappraised her. 'So, you got a dog in the hunt on this one.' She sniffed. 'Explains a lot. But that being the case, seems you more than most would want to keep a child out of the hands of Child Protection Services.'

Hicks wasn't about to share her feelings about Child Protection Services with Mrs Tulk. She looked the older woman in the eye. 'Maybe you're right. Maybe everyone else will give up. But I promise you, I won't. I *will* keep looking. I *won't* quit.'

'Had a dog like that, once,' Mrs Tulk said pleasantly. 'Would follow a spoor till it dropped. No matter what kind of enticement you offered, or punishment you dealt her, that bitch would *not* come to heel.' She paused. 'Had to shoot the poor thing to put it out of its misery.'

Hicks smiled and tapped the butt of her gun in its holster. 'Guess she couldn't shoot back, huh?'

Mrs Tulk ran her tongue around her teeth and sighed. She moved the plate of cookies to one side, brushed the crumbs from the tabletop and dusted her hands off.

'What would ease your mind, child?' she said, at last.

'Knowing that Riley is safe, well cared for, educated, given a chance in life.'

'And if you were given an assurance to that effect?'

She answered Mrs Tulk with a look that was hard and ungiving. 'I would say there is nothing so reassuring as the evidence of your own eyes.'

Mrs Tulk seemed to consider, lazily scratching one meaty elbow. Then she hauled her sizeable bulk up from the table and went to the back door.

'Caleb!' she yelled, in a voice that tore a hole in the morning quiet and sent the dogs, chained up out of sight somewhere, on a howl.

She stood to one side, watching Hicks's reaction as a black-haired boy came tearing up the steps and slammed open the screen door, bursting into the kitchen like he was about to do battle.

'Whassamatter?' he demanded.

He was nine or ten. He looked longer in the limb, less baby-featured than the pictures they had of Riley. There wasn't a hint of red in his hair, though Hicks noticed that it didn't reflect light the way you would expect naturally black hair to do.

He stopped dead, seeing her, and would have tore back out the way he'd come, but Mrs Tulk barred his way. For a moment, Hicks thought he would try to climb right over that mountain of a woman, but she frowned and bore down on him – just one step, but it was enough and he stood still.

She said, 'Deputy Sheriff Hicks, meet Caleb. He's my sister's daughter's youngest.'

'I didn't see no cruiser out front,' he said, sounding defensive. 'Just a junkyard Frankenstein.'

Hicks stood, folding her arms. 'Did you just insult my vehicle?'

Mrs Tulk said, 'Caleb, here, is sassy and rude, and he is about to apologize.'

He looked quickly from one woman to the other, puzzled at first, then his eyes widened and he seemed to realize he had a role to play in this story. 'Yes, ma'am,' he said. 'I do apologize for making out your car belonged in the junkyard.'

Hicks felt she should be mad for having been insulted twice, but that boy had the bluest, brightest eyes, and he used them to dazzle and charm. 'Well . . . Caleb,' she said, her expression solemn. 'I guess I can forgive you this once.'

'Yes, ma'am.' He shot a look at Mrs Tulk, seemed to read in her face that he needed to say more. 'Uh, thank you, Deputy. Ma'am. Can I go now? I got chores to do.'

'They'll keep,' Mrs Tulk said. 'Deputy Sheriff Hicks was just asking about that redhead kid – Riley Patterson. You knew him, didn't you?'

His face grew still. 'Mighta seen him out in the woods.' He raked his hair across his forehead, and Hicks caught sight of a fading bruise. 'That boy was always out there, making dens and lighting fires.'

'Do you know what might've happened to him, Caleb?' Hicks said, watching him closely. 'I mean, we're pretty sure he was in the trunk of that man's car, and we *know* he was hurt, 'cos his blood was on the comforter inside the trunk.'

'Prob'ly just a nosebleed – something like that.'

'Some people think he's dead.'

'Nu-uh. See, he always carries a pocketknife. I figure he picked the lock of that trunk, run off. He told me he run off a *lot* of times.'

'And where d'you think he would go?'

'Most likely he went all the way to Oklahoma City.'

'Well, now you're just making stuff up,' Mrs Tulk said.

'No, ma'am – uh – Aunt Marsha. He always said that's where he would go when he was a grown-up.'

'Well, he isn't grown up, yet,' Hicks said. 'He's just nine years old.'

'Nine and a half.' He flushed. 'So he said.'

'That's awful young to be out in the big world.'

'Oh, he can take care of himself.' The boy put his head on one side and took a breath, like he'd decided to take her into his confidence. 'Deputy, you shouldn't waste your time on him,' he said. 'That redhead boy is just a pain in the ass. You know he cut that pervert?'

'Is that right?'

'Yes, ma'am.' He nodded, gazing at her with his blue, credulous eyes. 'It was me, I'd just leave him be – there's no telling what a desperate character like that might do.'

'Well . . . Caleb, thank you for the advice,' Hicks said. 'But I can't sleep easy till I know that boy is safe.'

'He *is*. He likes it just fine—' he stumbled over the next few words '—h—wh-where he . . . is.'

'How do you know that?'

His eyes darted from the TV to Mrs Tulk, to the coffee table, finally lighting on the phone hanging on the wall. 'He called me.'

'Right here?' Hicks said, following his gaze like it was a revelation. 'On *that* phone?' She drew her eyebrows down, tapped her chin, letting him know she was thinking it through. 'We could maybe trace the number he called from, get a fix on him.'

'*No-ooo*! He don't want *nobody* to come looking for him.'

Hicks looked the boy over and truly did not know what action to take. He didn't seem hurt or afraid – except of being taken away from here. He was well fed and healthy and bouncing around like a rubber ball, like a nine-year-old boy should be. She could tell someone – Kent Whitmore, maybe – let him make the rough decision. But she recalled the tall, soft-spoken Team Adam consultant at the Mountain Home Conference, last spring, telling her that after Hurricane Katrina, Team Adam reunited every 'lost' child with family, and though nobody expressed regret, they did say some of those kids really didn't want to go back. In amongst all the happy reunions were kids who cried and held onto their foster parents and would not let go. Those Team Adam guys quoted the stats, because a hundred per cent success rate is something you *should* talk about, but she did wonder, if they had the chance over, would they choose to do such a good job? It would not be fair to ask that question, any more than it would be fair to ask Whitmore's advice, and much as she would like to have shared this burden with somebody, she had kept her suspicions to herself, not even talking to Fennimore about it.

The boy looked desperately to Mrs Tulk for help; he was almost in tears now, and Mrs Tulk gave Hicks a stone-cold look. Maybe it was perverse to think it, but Hicks was cheered to know that Marsha Tulk's anger was because the boy was upset.

'Did Riley say what kind of people he was living with now?' Mrs Tulk asked.

'The kind don't take shit from nobody,' the boy said, wiping his nose with the back of his hand.

'Don't you cuss in front o' me,' Mrs Tulk growled.

'Excuse me, ma'am,' he said, instantly contrite. 'I meant

to say they don't take *crap* from nobody.' He concentrated, evidently knowing it was important he got this right. 'He likes the family he is with. It's a big family, but he's got his own room. They got plenty of land, and places to fish, and woods to play in. Food's good.'

Mrs Tulk folded her big hands across her stomach and looked pleased.

'And he gets to grow some of it, which he likes doing and he's good at. He has to do chores – some he likes, some he don't. The older brothers teach him stuff and nobody picks on him, 'cept sometimes the younger one, who's a bit of a snot-nose, but he just keeps out of his way.' He stole a sly glance at Mrs Tulk and her mouth twitched.

For a moment, the two women looked at each other over the boy's head.

'There's food farming, and there's cash-crop farming,' Hicks said, letting Mrs Tulk know that she was fully aware what Marsha Tulk's boys grew out in the woods. 'And then there's cooking. Now, I know cooking can be a lucrative trade, but if I thought that boy was being trained up as a *chef* . . .'

Something dark passed behind the hard, button eyes of the older woman. 'You're new to Williams County, so I guess you don't know,' she said. 'I been a widow coming up sixteen years. My husband was in town with Harlan, my eldest, buying supplies. They heard screams from the alley behind the store and went to see what the commotion was. They found a woman, screaming fit to raise Lazarus. The devil had come in her home and committed an abomination on her kids, she said.

'She was obviously tweaking and he feared for her children, so him and Harlan Junior followed her into a crappy two-room rental off of the alley. What they found there was an abomination all right, but wasn't no devil in the case. She had stabbed her three babies – the oldest of 'em just four years old. The youngest was pinned to the floor with a steak knife.'

405

The boy's eyes widened, and Hicks said, 'Mrs Tulk.'

'Better he hears it than becomes it,' she said. 'That goddamn crankster took out a gun, shot my man six times while he knelt beside her baby.' She didn't tear up, or choke on the words, but she had to stop a moment. 'So, you tell me, Deputy, do you think that I would allow that damn *poison* near me or mine?'

'No, ma'am, I don't believe you would,' Hicks said.

The boy fidgeted. 'Are we done, Aunt Marsha?'

Marsha Tulk cocked an eyebrow at Hicks. 'Are we?'

Hicks tilted her head. 'Not entirely.'

Mrs Tulk rolled her eyes as if she just *knew* it would come to this. 'What will it take?' she said, reaching for her pocketbook.

'He will go to school,' Hicks said.

The older woman looked surprised, but she recovered fast, thrusting the pocketbook back inside her purse and rooting for a Kleenex instead. 'All right.'

The boy looked horrified. 'But, ma'am—'

Mrs Tulk fixed her gaze on him, and he fell silent. 'My boys went to the Elementary up in Westfield.'

He relaxed a little.

'I will drop by, once a month,' Hicks went on. 'Ask how Riley is going on, talk about what he's learning in school. So, Caleb, you'd better keep up with him I will want a full report, and I expect the truth.' Now *she* fixed her eye on the boy and he squirmed. 'If I *don't* get the truth, if I am concerned that Riley is not happy, or properly cared for, or finding it hard to stay out of the way of that snot-nose younger brother, I *will* talk to Child Protection Services.'

She saw fear in the boy's eyes for the first time.

Mrs Tulk put her hand on his black hair. 'Don't you worry about that,' she said. 'That's never going to happen. Because you *will* tell the truth about how Riley is going on.' She looked into Hicks's face. 'And he will be properly cared for.'

Hicks handed him a business card. 'My cell-phone number's on the back,' she said. 'You can call me any time you think Riley needs my help.' He took it, nodded, and she put her finger under his chin and tilted it till they were eye to eye. '*Any time*, night or day. Do we understand each other?'

He nodded again. 'Yes, ma'am, Deputy Hicks.'

EPILOGUE

The only truth is the evidence.

NICK FENNIMORE

Fennimore sat at the desk in his hotel suite in St Louis. He had delivered his lecture, done some networking at the symposium and now he was catching up with the case. He had received notification that Laney Dawalt and Sharla Jane Patterson, the last two victims, were on the spy equipment Elliott had stolen from Sharla Jane's trailer. The spy camera in Sharla Jane's bedroom had recorded an angry exchange between her and McIntyre: Riley was late home and he'd organized an end-of-term treat. McIntyre railed against the child's lack of respect, and grizzled about how unappreciated he was. To appease him, Sharla Jane agreed to take part in a 'sex game'; it was this that the boy had walked in on, the night Sharla Jane was murdered. Riley Patterson, like Billy Dawalt, was still missing.

Meanwhile, in Scotland, police had searched Fergus Elliott's croft and found a computer hidden away in a secret cubbyhole. The drive was encrypted – analysis would be impossible. But they kept looking, and behind a false wall in the basement they discovered videotape and digital recordings dating back sixteen years, all the way to the sexual assault and murder of Isla Bain in Hawick. She was probably

408

their first victim. The 'collection' was meticulously labelled with dates and names: all of the United States victims were catalogued – along with fifteen more.

Their timeline had established that Elliott, a sound engineer, was on tour with a band in Japan and Australia when Rachel and Suzie disappeared, and Josh had confirmed that Elliott was not the man who'd drugged him. Fennimore opened a copy of Fergus Elliott's passport photograph and displayed it beside an e-fit of the man who had drugged and robbed Josh. The student's assailant was handsome, dark-haired, bearded, with full lips and a neat nose. Elliott was narrow-faced and sandy-haired, with a sharp nose and pale, thin lips.

So, the question remained: who did steal Josh's laptop – and why? Josh had hesitated when he'd asked about backing up data. Was there something Josh *hadn't* backed up – something he wouldn't risk to external hard drives or the Cloud? Something, perhaps, that Josh Brown was ashamed of?

He stopped. This wasn't about Josh; it was about Rachel and Suzie. He opened the image his anonymous emailer had sent. The slim girl in an orange dress, stepping out on a Paris street.

He was still staring at his computer an hour later when he heard a knock at his hotel room door. He closed the laptop before answering. It was Kate Simms, and she came bearing gifts. The first was a half of Jack Daniel's, the second was an update from Police Scotland.

As she spoke, she poured an inch of bourbon into a tooth glass and watched him take a swallow. 'There are tiny spots of semen on the dress Isla Bain was wearing at the time she was murdered,' she said. 'Of course, back then, the sample was too small to be tested, but the evidence was in good condition when they retrieved it.'

'They got a usable profile?'

She nodded. 'They'll compare it with DNA samples from Elliott and McIntyre. But I think we already know it's them.'

'It'll help her parents, knowing that those men aren't still walking around,' he said.

She took a sip of bourbon. 'I'm sorry the investigation didn't help you,' she said.

He nodded. 'I was hoping you'd've heard from Interpol about the photograph by now.'

'I have,' she said, though she seemed reluctant to admit it. 'It *was* taken in Paris. But, Nick, it doesn't mean that the girl in the picture is Suzie, or that obsessing over it will help you find her.'

'I know that.' He was lying, because he was sure that the girl *was* Suzie, and just as certain that the picture would lead him to her, but he would lie and lie again, if it gave him one small clue.

'Then tell me you weren't staring at the damn thing on your netbook when I knocked at the door.'

'And if I was?'

'You won't find her by guesswork, Nick. What is it you say? "The only truth is the evidence. It won't lie to you. And unlike witnesses, it won't change its mind."'

'I believe that to be true,' he said. 'But you have to follow the evidence – even if it looks dodgy or unpromising, even if it leads nowhere. And right now that photograph is all the evidence I've got, Kate.'

'It *could* be evidence, or it could be just another snapshot from a sadist who likes to watch you suffer.'

'I'll bear that in mind,' he said, holding out his hand, trying to still the tremor in it.

She took a folded sheet of paper out of her shoulder bag and handed it to him. The upper half was a Paris street map, the lower, an enhanced image of the roller door of the van that was parked a hundred yards from the couple walking along the street.

'You were right,' Simms said. 'It was a gang tag. And it gave them a locality.'

The district meant nothing to Fennimore, but a quick Google search would change that. He opened his laptop, revealing the e-fit of the man who robbed Josh.

'What's this?' she asked.

'Not sure. Does he look familiar to you?'

She leaned in for a closer look and he could smell the liquor warm on her breath. 'I suppose so – in a generic way. But it's an e-fit, Nick,' she said. 'E-fits work from generic characteristics. What's this about?'

'Josh sent it,' he said. He stared at the screen, wondering how best to frame the lie. 'They met in a bar; he was asking questions about Rachel and Suzie.'

'Reporter,' she said, swivelling the laptop so she could see the screen more clearly.

'I don't think so,' he said.

'People asking those sorts of questions – it usually *is* a reporter.'

Fennimore shook his head. The man who drugged and robbed Josh had risked a five-year prison sentence in doing what he did. Surely, even a hack of the lowest order wouldn't chance that. But he couldn't tell Kate that: the theft wasn't linked to their case, the files on the computer were secure. He wanted to ask Josh face to face what could possibly be on the hard drive that would make a man risk drugging and robbing him, and he didn't want to scare the student off.

Simms stared at him for a few moments. 'There's more to this than you're saying, isn't there? Let me guess – Josh's shady past?'

He didn't answer.

'I thought so.' She eyed him solemnly for a few moments. 'All right, have it your way.' She studied the e-fit again. 'But why did you ask *me* if he's familiar – d'you think *we* know him?'

Kate Simms always asked good questions.

'I wish I knew the answer to that.' He picked up the laptop and stared into the computer-generated eyes, wishing he could wrest the truth from them.

'Nick, stop it – it's like that bloody picture all over again.'

His heart missed a beat, then started again, a slow, heavy pulse. That was it. He pulled up the image of the girl in Paris. By her side, an older man. How old? Thirty? Thirty-five?

Kate groaned, seeing the picture on the screen.

'Look,' he said, zooming in on the man's face, resizing the e-fit so that Simms could compare the two. 'Same nose, same mouth. Okay, the hair is different, but that's easily changed.'

She shook her head, began to protest, but he said, 'Please, Kate. One more minute – let me show you.'

He opened Photoshop and imported the Paris photograph. 'If it is the same guy, he's lost some weight . . . The hair is shorter . . . Add a beard . . .' He quickly made the alterations. The likeness was striking.

She frowned, sat next to him. 'It could be,' she said. 'But, Nick, you could be fooling yourself.'

He threw up his hands. Scientific scepticism was usually his role.

'All right,' he said. 'If it makes you feel better, I'll get an expert to do a comparison.'

'And if he agrees with you – what will you do then?' she asked.

'I'll find him,' he said. 'And then I'll find Suzie.'

BELIEVE NO ONE

Also by A. D. Garrett

Everyone Lies